'The *Missing* has a delicious sense of foreboding from the first page, luring us into the heart of a family with terrible secrets and making us wait, with pounding hearts for the final, agonising twist. Loved it.'
Fiona Barton

'*Black Narcissus* for the Facebook generation, a clever exploration of how petty jealousies and misunderstandings can unravel even the tightest of friendships. Claustrophobic, tense and thrilling, a thrill-ride of a novel that keeps you guessing.'
Elizabeth Haynes

'A gripping and disturbing psychological thriller.'
Clare Mackintosh

'As with all her books, C.L. Taylor delivers real pace, and it's a story that keeps calling the reader back – so much so that I read it from cover to cover in one day.'
Rachel Abbott

'A dark and gripping read that engrossed me from start to finish.'
Mel Sherratt

'Kept me guessing till the end.'
Sun

See what bloggers are saying about C.L. Taylor . . .

'An intriguing and stirring tale, overflowing with family drama.'
Lovereading.co.uk

'Astoundingly written, *The Missing* pulls you in from the very first page and doesn't let you go until the final full stop.'
Bibliophile Book Club

'[*The Missing*] inspired such a mixture of emotions in me and made me realise how truly talented you have to be to even attempt a psychological suspense of this calibre.'
My Chestnut Reading Tree

'Tense and gripping with a dark, ominous feeling that seeps through the very clever writing . . . all praise to C.L. Taylor.'
Anne Cater, Random Things Through My Letterbox

'C.L. Taylor has done it again, with another compelling masterpiece.'
Rachel's Random Reads

'In a crowded landscape of so-called domestic noir thrillers, most of which rely on clever twists and big reveals, [*The Missing*] stands out for its

subtle and thoughtful analysis of the fallout from a loss in the family.'
Crime Fiction Lover

'When I had finished, I felt like someone had ripped my heart out and wrung it out like a dish cloth.'
By the Letter Book Reviews

'*The Missing* has such a big, juicy storyline and is a dream read if you like books that will keep you guessing and take on plenty of twists and turns.'
Bookaholic Confessions

'Incredibly thrilling and utterly unpredictable! A must read!'
Aggie's Books

'A gripping story.'
Bibliomaniac

'It's the first time I have cried whilst reading. The last chapter [of *The Missing*] was heart-breaking and uplifting at the same time.'
The Coffee and Kindle

'Another hit from C.L. Taylor . . . so cleverly written and so absorbing that I completely forgot about everything else while reading it. Unmissable.'
Alba in Book Land

C.L. Taylor is the *Sunday Times* bestselling author of four psychological thrillers. Her books have sold over a million copies in the UK and have been translated into twenty-one languages. She lives in Bristol with her partner and son.

By the same author:

The Accident
The Lie
The Missing

C.L. TAYLOR

THE
ESCAPE

avon

This novel is entirely a work of fiction.
The names, characters and incidents portrayed in it are
the work of the author's imagination. Any resemblance to
actual persons, living or dead, events or localities is
entirely coincidental.

AVON

A division of HarperCollins*Publishers*
1 London Bridge Street,
London SE1 9GF

www.harpercollins.co.uk

A Paperback Original 2017

3

Copyright © C.L. Taylor 2017

C.L. Taylor asserts the moral right to be identified as the author of this work

A catalogue record for this book is available from the British Library

ISBN 978-0-00-811807-5

Set in S_____ LT S_d 12/15____ by D_li____ B__k P_o_uc___ Limited,

FSC™ _____ promote
the resp_____ rrying the
FSC lab_____ they come
fro_____ c and
and other controlled sources.

Find out more about HarperCollins and the environment at
www.harpercollins.co.uk/green

For my son, Seth Hall
'Love you forever'

PART ONE

PART ONE

Chapter 1

Someone is walking directly behind me, matching me pace for pace. Her perfume catches in the back of my throat: a strong, heady mix of musk and something floral. Jasmine maybe, or lily. She's so close she'd smack into me if I stopped abruptly. Why doesn't she just overtake? It's a quiet street, tucked round the back of the university, with space for half a dozen cars to park but the pavement is easily wide enough for two people to walk abreast of each other.

I speed up. Elise will be the last child left at nursery, all alone and wondering where I am. I was ready to leave work at 5 p.m. on the dot, but then a student walked into the office and burst into tears. She hadn't got her assignment in on time and she was terrified she was going to get kicked off her course. I couldn't walk away when she was in that state. I had to talk her down. By the time she walked out of the office she was smiling again but sweat was pricking at my armpits. 5.15 p.m. I never leave work that late. Never.

My car is only a hundred metres away. In less than a minute I'll be inside with the door shut, the engine running and the music on. I'll be safe. Everything will be OK.

Fifty metres away.

The woman behind me is breathing heavily. She's sped up too.

Twenty metres away.

I feel a light dragging sensation on the back of my coat; a hand, trying and failing to grab hold of the material.

Ten metres away.

High heels clip-clop behind me as I step into the road and approach the driver's side of my car. I reach into my coat pocket for my keys but all I find is a balled tissue, a small packet of raisins and some sweet wrappers. I reach into my other pocket and my fingers close around the car keys. As I do, a hand clamps down on my shoulder.

My heart lurches in my chest as I twist round, raising my arms in self-defence.

'Woah!' A blonde woman my age jumps away from me, her eyes wide. She's dressed in a thick, padded jacket, skinny jeans and heels. 'I was only going to ask for directions.'

All the fear in my body leaves in one raggedy breath. She just wants directions.

The woman's eyes, heavily ringed with black kohl,

4

don't leave my face. 'Do you know where I can get a bus to Brecknock Road?'

I feel a jolt of surprise. 'Brecknock? That's where I live.'

'Is it?' she says. 'What a coincidence.'

I thought she was in her forties like me but her line-free forehead and arched eyebrows are betrayed by a sagginess to her jaw and a crinkling to her neck that suggest she's at least ten years older.

She glances at my hand, resting on the window of the car. 'I don't suppose you're going there now?'

'I'm sorry?'

'Brecknock Road. Could I have a lift?'

I don't know how to react. I don't want her in my car. Not when I'm feeling like this. I need to calm myself down before I get to the nursery. I don't want Elise to see me in a state.

The blonde's eyes flick towards the pavement as a young bloke in a heavy overcoat strolls past. He's on his phone and doesn't give either of us a second glance.

'My son and daughter are exactly the same. Always got their noses in their phones,' she says convivially as the man disappears around the corner and we are alone again. Either she's completely unaware of how awkward and uncomfortable I feel as a result of her request or she just doesn't care.

'I . . . um . . .' I put my keys in the lock. 'I'm sorry. I'm not going straight home. I need to collect my daughter from nursery and—'

'Elise, isn't it?'

My breath catches in my throat. 'I'm sorry?'

'Lovely name. Quite old-fashioned but that's all the rage these days, isn't it? My daughter-in-law wanted to call my granddaughter Ethel. Ethel, for God's sake.'

'How do you . . .' I study her face again but there's no spark of recognition in the back of my brain. I don't remember ever seeing this woman before. 'I'm sorry, have we met?'

She cackles, a low sound that gurgles in the base of her throat, and holds out a hand. 'I'm sorry. I should have introduced myself. I'm John's mum, Paula. He lives just down the street from you. I've seen you and your little girl getting into your car in the mornings when I take my granddaughter to the park. I look after her sometimes. I'm from Taunton. I don't get into Bristol often.' She glances meaningfully at my car.

'So am I OK for a lift? Now you know I'm not a serial killer?'

I am frozen with indecision. I don't know anyone called John but it's a long street. To say no to a lift would be rude, and I don't want to make an enemy of any of our neighbours, not when it's such a lovely street, but this isn't something I do. This isn't part of my routine.

'Please,' she says, 'I'm babysitting tonight and John will be wondering where I've got to.'

I make a split-second decision. It will be quicker to give her a lift than say no and risk wasting more time with a discussion about it. 'OK. But I'll have to drop you at the nursery. It's not far from Brecknock.'

6

'Cheers, love. Really appreciate it.'

She waits for me to unlock the driver's side door then rounds the car and gets in beside me. I put on my seat belt and put the keys in the ignition. Paula, in the passenger seat, doesn't reach for her seat belt. Instead she runs a hand over the dashboard then squeezes the latch on the glove compartment so it drops open. She rummages around inside, pulling out CDs, receipts and manuals, then reaches down and runs a hand underneath her seat.

I stare at her in disbelief as she twists round in her seat and looks into the footwells in the back seat. 'Can I help you with something?'

She ignores me and clambers into the back seat and feels behind and beneath Elise's car seat, then lifts the parcel shelf and peers into the boot.

'Paula.' I unclip my seat belt. 'Could you stop doing that, please?'

She snaps back round to face me, her lips tight and her eyes narrowed. 'Don't tell me what to do, Jo.'

The transformation is shocking, all trace of her cheerful, friendly demeanour gone. She lied to me. She doesn't have a son called John who lives on our street. She's never strolled down to Perrett's Park with her granddaughter. And I never told her my name.

'I want you to get out of my car,' I say as steadily as I can.

The smallest of smiles creeps onto her lips as she straightens her jacket and settles herself into the back seat. She reaches out her left arm and drapes it over Elise's car seat.

'Pretty girl, your daughter,' she says under her breath but loud enough so I can hear it. 'Isn't she, Jo?'

The malevolence in her eyes makes me catch my breath.

'Get out,' I say again. A man has appeared at the end of the street. If I open the door and shout he'll hear me. Paula sees me looking.

'Now, now. No need to be rude. I've lost something. That's all. And I think your husband might know where it is.'

I stiffen. 'Max? What's this got to do with Max?'

Paula glances over her shoulder again – the man has reached the car behind mine – and pulls on the door catch. 'He'll know what it's about. Just tell him to get in touch. Oh, and, there's something else.'

She digs into her pocket with her free hand.

'You should keep an eye on your daughter's things,' she says as she places a small, soft, multicoloured glove on Elise's car seat.

'And your daughter,' she adds as she gets out.

Chapter 2

Max Blackmore sighs as his mobile phone judders to life, vibrating on the smooth wooden desk that separates him from his editor. He snatches it up and looks at the screen. Jo, again. It's the third time his wife has called him since he left for work at 8 a.m. and he's already had to reassure her that yes, he does think it's OK for Elise to go to nursery with a bit of a cough and yes, he will stop by at the chemist to get more Calpol before he gets home. He's been ignoring his home mobile for the last half an hour and now she's ringing his work mobile instead.

His editor Fiona Spelling leans back in her chair and crosses her arms. She's doing 'the face', the one that signifies that her genial mood is on the cusp of switching to irritable. 'Do you need to get that?'

He tucks the phone into the inside pocket of his jacket. 'It can keep.'

'Are you sure? Because you know she'll ring me if she can't get through to you.'

Max grimaces. He should never have given Jo Fiona's direct line. It was meant to calm her – so she could check he was OK if he couldn't answer his mobile – but she rings the number so often she now has it on speed dial. Literally *speed dial*, programmed into her chunky, ancient Nokia. One for him, two for her mother, three for nursery, four for her boss and five for Fiona. He's begged her to delete Fiona's number but she won't have it.

'It's her agoraphobia,' he says. 'It makes her overly anxious.'

'But she works at the university as a student support officer, doesn't she? How bad can it be if she can hold down a job?'

Max smiles ruefully. He thought the same as Fiona once: that you're basically housebound if you suffer from agoraphobia, but it's not as 'simple' as that – something Jo has explained to him countless times. She isn't afraid of going outside, she's afraid of situations where she can't escape or get help.

'It's bad,' he says. '*Really* bad. Jo works part-time but she won't take Elise to the park or the zoo. She won't even go food shopping any more, not since she had a panic attack in the corner shop because she thought someone was looking at her strangely.'

'Wow.' His boss arches an eyebrow.

Fiona doesn't know the half of it. He and Jo haven't had sex for over a year. They had a dry spell before, when she was so afraid of getting pregnant she

10

wouldn't let him anywhere near her, but then they'd conceived Elise and he'd assumed that everything would go back to normal. It didn't. It got worse.

'Anyway, Max,' Fiona says, gesturing towards her screen. 'Congratulations. I've read your story and it's good. Very good. How does it feel?'

'How does what feel?'

'To get a conviction off the back of your investigation? Five years, he got, didn't he?'

Max smiles for the first time since he sat down. He would have loved to see the look on Ian White's face when the police turned up to arrest him. Evil bastard. He'd set up a national chain of money-lending shops that charged single mums, pensioners and people on benefits ridiculous amounts of interest and then turned up at their home and threatened them with violence when they couldn't pay it back. Coercion, drug-taking and violence were rife. Max had witnessed one of Ian's goons shoving an old man up against the wall of his own home when he said he wouldn't be able to eat for a week if he paid up. He couldn't react. He couldn't stop him. All he could do was pray that the tiny camera in his glasses was getting enough footage to convict the bastards.

'And you weren't worried about your cover slipping? No one at Cash Creditors suspected you?' Fiona asks.

'There were a couple of sticky moments but I talked my way out of them.'

'That doesn't surprise me in the least.' His boss smiles tightly. 'So, are we going to have to start calling you Donal MacIntyre now then?'

11

'Nah.' He waves a dismissive hand. 'He's old hat. Max Blackmore will do fine, although if you want to call me "sir" that would be fine too.'

He stiffens as Fiona's smile slips and she raises an eyebrow. Shit. He always takes a joke one step too far.

Chapter 3

The second the buzzer sounds and the door is unlocked I fly through the nursery, dodging coat stands, a papier-mâché homage to *The Hungry Caterpillar*, and several members of staff.

'Elise?' A bead of sweat trickles down my lower back as I fumble with the catch of the gate at the 'twos room'. Half a dozen pairs of tiny eyes look up at me in interest and alarm as I step into the room. None of them belong to my daughter.

'Everything OK, Jo?' Sharon, a woman with a tight ponytail and an even tighter smile, looks up from her position in front of the children, a picture book in her hands. Another of the nursery staff, a sweet eighteen-year-old called Bethan, looks up from the table she's cleaning. She smiles a hello but there's confusion in her eyes.

'Jo?' Sharon says and I search the faces of the children again, just in case I missed one.

'I can't see Elise. Where is she?'

I don't wait for her reply. Instead I open the door to the garden. It's empty; the sandpit abandoned; an array of brightly coloured plastic tools lying on the sand, illuminated by the security light.

'Jo?' Sharon appears beside me, an irritated expression on her face. 'What's the matter. I'm sure Elise is in—'

'Mummy!'

The plaintive cry from across the room makes me turn. And there she is, my tiny little girl with her dark blonde hair still in the bunches I tied this morning, clutching the hand of Alice, her key worker. I like Alice. She's kind and gentle and she doesn't give me lectures about timekeeping if I'm five minutes late.

'I did a wee wee,' my daughter says proudly as I dash across the room.

'In the toilet,' she adds as I lift her into my arms and press my face into the soft warmth of her neck.

'It was her idea,' Alice says. 'She said she didn't want to wear nappies any more.'

'My God.' I hold my daughter tightly and stroke her hair over and over. 'Oh my God.'

'Jo?' The tone in Alice's voice changes. 'Is everything OK? You look very pale. Is it your stepdad? Did something happen?'

I want to tell her that I have just driven across Bristol at breakneck speed, certain that the woman who tricked her way into my car had somehow harmed my daughter. I rang Max over and over again but he didn't pick up. Neither did Fiona, his boss. I tried to

14

call the police but I couldn't breathe, never mind talk, and I ended the call before it connected. My hands were shaking so much it took me three attempts to get the keys in the ignition and the car started. I want to tell Alice all these things but, more than anything else, I want to get Elise home. We will both be safe there.

'Jo!' Alice shouts as I hurry through the nursery with Elise's legs wrapped around my waist and her small face buried into my neck. 'You haven't signed her out. And you've forgotten her coat!'

I fumble with the door latch. Other parents are waiting to be let in, watching me through the glass panel. Their smiles turn to frustration. I can't get my fingers to work properly, I'm shaking so much. Finally, Sharon appears beside me. She thrusts Elise's bag and coat at me and then opens the door with one swift turn of the latch. I mutter an apology to the other parents as they part to allow me out of the door.

'She looked a bit wired,' a woman says, sotto voce, but loud enough for me to hear, as I step out onto the street.

'Probably a couple too many glasses of wine at lunch,' someone comments and a chorus of laughter follows me out onto the street.

Back home I pause as I reach the living room, Elise's cup of milk in my hand. Outside in the street a woman is laughing – a loud, throaty cackle that makes all the hairs go up on my arms. Paula knows the name of our road. She's seen me take Elise to the park. She's

15

probably watched us leave the house. I've already checked – twice – that all the doors and windows are locked but I dart to the front door anyway and jiggle on the handle to make sure. Still locked.

I hurry back into the living room where my daughter is still on the sofa, staring at the TV, a blanket over her legs, and Effie Elephant, her favourite soft toy, clutched to her chest.

'Milk,' she says as I cross the room, peel back the curtain and peer outside. Two women, both of them dark-haired, saunter down the street. The one on the right cackles again and her friend punches her playfully on the arm. It's not Paula. But that doesn't mean we're safe.

'Here you go, sweetheart.' I force a smile as I hand the cup of milk to my daughter. Her gaze doesn't flicker from the screen. She's entranced by Makka Pakka placing rocks, one by one, into a wheelbarrow. She's relaxed and happy . . . I just wish I felt the same.

'Mummy's just going to pack a few things so we can go and visit Granny and Grandad for a few days. I'll be back in a second. I'm just going upstairs.'

I move quickly, running from room to room, gathering up clothes, nappies, toys, toiletries and medication, freezing whenever I hear a strange sound, shouting down to my daughter to check she's OK. I throw everything into a large wheeled suitcase and then return to Elise's bedroom. I stand in the middle of the room with my hands on my hips as I scan the shelves for anything I may have missed. I can't believe

Max did this to us. He *swore* to me that he would never put our family in danger. He reassured me over and over again that we would be safe, that no one would come after us as a result of his investigation. And I believed him. I don't know who was more naïve, me or him. Our marriage has been on its last legs for a while. I've tried to keep it going, for Elise's sake, but I can't do this any more. I can't spend my life with a man who puts his career before his family's safety.

I return to my bedroom and zip up the suitcase then open it again. Have I got absolutely everything I need for Elise? It doesn't matter if I've forgotten something of mine but we've got a problem if I forget something of hers. I can't ask Mum to leave Andy's side to go to the shops for me. And if I go . . .

I grip hold of the chest of drawers and take a steadying breath. I can do this. I've driven up to Mum's loads of times and nothing has happened. I know the route: M5, A41, all the way up. Approximately three hours. It's nearly 7 p.m. now and Elise will probably sleep the whole way.

'Sweetheart!' I bump the suitcase down the stairs, abandon it in the hall and step back into the living room. 'Mummy needs to put a nappy on you before we go. Just in case you fall asleep and have an accident.'

Elise looks at me and shakes her head.

I hold out a nappy and give her an encouraging smile. 'Let's just pop this on now and then we can go. We're going to see Granny and Grandad.'

'No.' Her bottom lip wobbles. 'No nappy, Mummy.'

'Elise, please.' As I sit down on the sofa I hear the sound of keys being turned in the front door.

A second later my husband flies into the room, his cheeks ashen and his eyes wide. He takes one look at Elise and scoops her up into his arms, pressing a hand against her back as he holds her tightly against his chest. He notices me watching.

'Why didn't you answer your phone?' he says through gritted teeth. 'I thought Elise was . . . I . . . you can't leave a message like that and then NOT ANSWER YOUR PHONE.'

Elise yelps in shock as his shout fills the living room.

'Sorry, sorry, baby.' He strokes her hair, his wide palm cupping the back of her head. 'I didn't mean to scare you.'

'Max,' I say, keeping my voice as steady as I can. 'Can we talk about this in the kitchen, *away* from Elise?'

'I'm sorry!' Max says, the second we step into the kitchen. 'I shouldn't have shouted at you. I was just . . . fucking hell, Jo, you really scared me.' He rubs his hands over his face, peering at me through the gaps in his fingers.

'*You* were scared? Where the hell have you been? I rang you. I called you as soon as it happened.'

'I was in a meeting with Fiona.'

'Seriously?' I can't keep incredulity out of my voice. 'Have you got any idea what I've—'

'I'm sorry. OK. Just tell me what happened.'

He listens, his hands clenching and unclenching at his sides, as I tell him about being followed down the street, about Paula getting into my car, about the threat she made to Elise. I pause when I reach the end, waiting for a reaction, but Max doesn't say anything.

'What?' I say. 'Why are you looking at me like that?'

'I . . .' He runs a hand over his hair. 'I'm shocked I guess. I'm . . . trying to make sense of what happened.'

'Make sense of what? A stranger got into my car, started rooting around for something and then threatened Elise. And she knows you, Max. What is there to make sense of? We need to ring the police.'

'The woman said her name was Paula?'

'Yes.'

'Paula what?'

'She didn't tell me her surname.'

'What did she look like? I worked with someone called Paula about six or seven years ago. She left on maternity leave and didn't come back.'

'Was she blonde, early fifties?'

'No. She was in her twenties, mixed race. And she didn't have a problem with me.'

'You can't think of anyone else called Paula who might know you? Someone you investigated or did a story on?'

'No. I'd remember if I had. And I've only done one investigation, you know that.'

'But you've interviewed loads of people and run hundreds of stories. There has to be at least one Paula that you've pissed off over the years. Maybe we should ring Fiona,' I add before he can object. 'She could search the archives or something. Then we'll have something to take to the police.'

'No.' Max shakes his head. 'Jo, I'm not ringing Fiona. For one she'll be at home by now, and two . . .' He tails off.

'Two, what? Why are you looking at me like that again?'

'Like what?'

'Like you don't believe me.'

'I'm not.'

'Yes, you are. You're giving me the same look you gave me when I told you about my panic attack in the corner shop.'

'Oh God.' Max slumps back against the kitchen unit. The cheap MDF creaks under his weight. Our house isn't the only thing that's falling apart. 'Do we have to talk about that again?'

'Yes, we do. I told you I felt threatened by the way that woman was looking at me and you said—'

'That she was just concerned because Elise was having a tantrum. Jo, it's her shop. If I owned a shop and some kid was screaming their head off I'd stare at the mother too!'

'Today was different! Paula threatened me. She threatened Elise. I can't believe you're not taking this seriously. Look!' I reach into the pocket of my jeans and pull out my daughter's rainbow-coloured glove. 'She gave this to me. There's no way she could have got hold of it unless she'd been near Elise. I put both

20

gloves in her pocket when I took her to nursery this morning.'

My husband runs a hand over the back of his neck and gives me an exasperated look. 'Have you checked Elise's pockets for the other glove?'

I glance towards the front door where I dumped my daughter's things as soon as we came in.

'That's a no then.' Max strides out of the kitchen and into the hallway. He picks up Elise's coat, thrusts his hands into the small pockets and then turns his attention to the bag. He pulls out our daughter's spare clothes one by one. When it's empty he turns his attention to the other clothes, hanging up on hooks by the front door. Scarves, hats, coats, jackets, hoodies and umbrellas fall to the floor as he selects, searches and then discards them.

'She must have taken both gloves,' I say from behind him. 'Max, we need to ring the police.'

But he's off again, sidling past me to the pile of coats hanging on the banister.

'Did you wear this today?' He holds up a soft grey coat from Wallis.

'Yes. Why?'

He thrusts a hand into one pocket, then the other, then holds his palm out towards me. Lying alongside a screwed-up tissue and a packet of raisins is a tiny rainbow-coloured glove.

'Look.' He plucks the other glove from my fingers and places it on his palm, making a pair. 'Two gloves. They were both in your pocket. Did you blow your nose while you were walking to the car?'

21

I automatically touch my nose. My nostrils are red raw from the streaming cold I've had for days. 'Possibly. I can't remember.'

'Well, there you go then. One of the gloves fell out of your pocket when you took out a tissue. And this Paula woman picked it up and gave it back to you.

'You're tired, Jo,' he adds before I can respond. 'You haven't been sleeping well and work has been stressing you out. A stranger got into your car and you freaked out. That's perfectly understandable.'

Irritation bubbles inside me at the patronising tone of his voice and the 'poor little woman' look on his face, and I have to fight to keep my tone level.

'You're right, Max. I *am* tired. And I am stressed. And OK, maybe I got it wrong about the glove, but I didn't misinterpret what Paula said. She definitely threatened me.'

'OK.' He touches a hand to my arm. It's a weary gesture, one that matches the look in his eyes. 'Let's say, for argument's sake, that we do ring the police.'

'OK.'

'Now, imagine that you're a police officer. Someone rings you up to tell you that a stranger handed you something that you dropped and then told you to look after your daughter's things. Does that sound like a crime to you?'

'It does if they also say, "And your daughter" with real menace.'

'Like the woman in the shop looked at you with menace?'

'That was different. I've already told you that!'

22

'OK, fine.' Max crosses the kitchen, lifts the phone from its cradle and hands it to me. 'Here. Ring the police. I'll be in the living room if you need me.'

I watch as he shuffles away down the hallway, hands in his pockets, his shoulders curled forward. As he disappears into the living room Elise squeals with joy and I turn the phone over and over in my hands.

Chapter 4

Weakness. That's what I saw in her eyes. Weakness, fear and indecision. If a stranger had coerced me into letting them into my car I'd have yanked them straight back out again. No, scratch that, I wouldn't have let them in in the first place. But Jo's soft. She's vulnerable. She walks with her head down, eyes fixed on the pavement, fingers twitching against the tired, worn material of her winter coat. She's a natural target. How can you have respect for someone like that? Someone who flinches if you look at her the wrong way? Who doesn't trust her instincts? Someone who is so very, very easy to manipulate . . .

Chapter 5

I didn't ring the police. I thought about it all evening, debating the pros and cons as Max turned on Netflix and settled back on the sofa with a bag of Doritos and a bottle of beer. I could barely look at him. Every crunch, every munch, every slurp made my skin prickle with anger. When we were first married he'd jump to my defence if someone was even inadvertently rude to me on a night out. He'd walk nearest the road on a rainy night to protect me from splashes. He'd jump out of bed and grab his baseball bat if I heard a noise downstairs. I thought he'd be on to the police the second I told him what had happened. Instead he looked at me like I'm some kind of hysterical neurotic. How can I ring the police if my own husband doesn't believe me? All I've got is a first name and a description. What could they possibly do with that? Then there's the fact that I'd have to go into the police station and that's not something I can deal with right now.

At 11 p.m., when Max finally went to bed, I thought about ringing my best friend Helen who lives in Cardiff with her little boy Ben. But it was too late. She'd have been in bed for an hour at least. Instead I sent her a text asking her when would be a good time to have a chat, then I took out my laptop and Googled jobs and places to live in Chester. I've been thinking about moving away from Bristol for a while. What happened last night was the last straw.

Now, my shoulders loosen and my grip on the steering wheel relaxes as I pull into the lane that runs behind Mum and Dad's house on the outskirts of Chester. Elise is asleep in the back of the car, her dark blonde head lolling against her chest, her fingers unfurled and relaxed, Effie Elephant resting on her lap.

Mum appears at the garden gate as I pull on the handbrake and turn off the engine. Her dark, dyed hair looks longer than I remember. It curls over her ears and hangs over her eyebrows. She brushes it out of her face as she approaches the car and taps on the window. I'm shocked by how tired she looks.

'Jo?' she says as I unwind the window. 'What are you doing here? I said to Andy that I could hear a car pulling up.'

Mum's been living in the UK for over thirty years, we both have, but while my Irish accent disappeared within a year of me starting school, hers is as strong as it was the day we left.

'Didn't you get my text?'

'Phone's off. You know I don't like to waste the battery.'

I can't help but smile. 'It might have been urgent, Mum.'

'Wasn't though, was it? You'd have rung the house phone if it was.' She glances into the back of the car as Elise stirs in her sleep. 'Babby all right?'

I want to tell her what happened yesterday. She'd understand why I was so scared for Elise's safety, why I still am. But she's got enough on her plate looking after Dad. I can't put this on her too. Just being here and seeing her face makes me feel like I can breathe again.

'She's fine.' I gesture for Mum to move away from the door so I can open it. 'We just fancied seeing you and Dad. How is he?'

Mum gives me a long look. 'He's not great, love.'

It's the beginning of February but it's so hot in Mum's house that I have to strip both me and Elise down to our T-shirts within minutes of walking through the front door.

'I keep it warm for Dad,' Mum says as I hang our discarded clothes over the back of a chair. 'He really feels the cold now.'

'Can we see him?'

'Let me go and see how he is.'

She disappears through the living-room door and into the hallway. A year ago I'd hear the sound of the stairs creaking as she made her way up to the master bedroom but Dad's been sleeping in the dining room for a while now. He was diagnosed with motor neurone disease three years ago. He'd been unusually clumsy for a few weeks – dropping the coffee jar in the kitchen, spilling tea on himself and tripping over the rug in the living room – and Mum complained to me on the phone that she couldn't get him to see a doctor. When he started having trouble with his speech he finally agreed to see someone. The diagnosis was made scarily quickly and within six months he was walking with a stick. Two years later he was in a wheelchair. Now he's unable to leave his bed.

'What's this?' Elise asks and I dart towards her, intercepting her grabby little hand before she can snatch one of Mum's porcelain figurines from the windowsill.

'It's a ballerina,' I say, guiding her fingers away. 'Isn't she pretty?'

She nods enthusiastically, her gaze still fixed on the statuette. 'Yes.'

I walk my daughter around Mum and Dad's compact living room, pointing out all the other ornaments: the life-sized china robin, the small crystal vase, the little boy reading a book under a windmill, the fairy plates hanging on the wall and a brown and white cow. Every single thing in this room was bought in the UK. Other than Mum's accent, this house is devoid of any trace of our Irish heritage. I gave up trying to talk to her about Ireland years ago. She shuts down whenever anyone questions her about where she's from or why she left. I only know that her best friend was called Mary because Mum got uncharacteristically drunk at my wedding and confided in my friend Helen. She told her that she'd wanted Mary to be her bridesmaid at her own wedding, nearly forty years earlier, but it hadn't been possible. That she missed Mary and hadn't seen her for over thirty years. When Helen suggested that it's never too late to reconnect yourself with someone you love, Mum had replied, 'It is if they hate you.' When Helen probed for more information, Mum disappeared off in search of another glass of champagne.

Mum may have briefly opened up about her old best friend but there's one person she's never talked about – my real dad. He vanished three weeks before my eighth birthday.

She told me that he'd gone away for work but I didn't believe her. I'd seen her friends cross the street when she waved hello. I'd noticed the way voices would drop and our neighbours would stare when I popped into the shop to grab a pint of milk. Kids in the playground started telling me that my dad was a bad man and their parents had told them not to talk to me any more. I didn't understand. I was sad that my dad wasn't at home any more and I knew my mum was upset too. But no one would tell me when he was coming back.

I was excited when I got back from school on the afternoon of my birthday and found Mum waiting at the front door with two packed suitcases. I thought we were going to visit Dad, wherever he was. I thought it was a birthday surprise. I was still excited when, ten minutes later, Uncle Carey turned up in his battered car and drove us to the train station. I didn't want to spoil the surprise but I couldn't stop myself from asking Mum where we were going. She unpursed her thin lips and said, 'Away. That's all you need to know.' Twelve hours later we were in England. And I never saw my dad again.

It was just me and Mum for two years. And then she met Andy. It can't have been easy for him, taking on someone else's child – especially one on the cusp of puberty – but he took it all in his stride. He gave me space when I needed it, he played board games with me when I was fed up and let me walk his cocker spaniel Jessie when we all went out. He told me knock knock jokes that were so rubbish they made me laugh and he tried, and failed, to introduce me to sci-fi. He was kind, funny and awkward and I couldn't help but warm to him. When he asked me if I would mind if he asked my mum to marry him I burst into tears. If he married Mum that would make us a family and he'd be my dad. There wasn't anything I wanted more.

'Dad's asleep,' Mum says now as she steps back into the living room and lowers herself into an armchair. 'I'll need your help turning him in a bit if that's OK. The carer's due this afternoon but I don't want to leave him that long. He'll get bedsores.'

'Of course.'

'CBeebies,' Elise says, pointing at the blank television in the corner of the room.

Mum moves to get up but I tell her that I'll do it. I settle Elise on the other side of the sofa with Effie and, as the *Mr Tumble* theme tune fills the room, I take the seat nearest to Mum.

'How is he?' I ask, keeping my voice low so Elise can't hear. 'How's Dad?'

Mum twists the gold band on the third finger of her left hand. 'He's not good, Joanne. The consultant has him on Riluzole but it's making him very tired. And he's got a mask now, to help with his breathing. There's been talk of a feeding tube but he won't have it.'

Dad hasn't been able to talk for at least a year but he lets you know if he disagrees with something. I saw the look in his eyes and the way his face twisted when Dr Valentine gently suggested that he might want to consider hospice care. Mum was vociferous in her response to the idea, her soft voice unusually loud as though she was literally speaking for both of them. No hospitals and no hospices. Dad wants to die at home. The disease has robbed him of so much – of his freedom, his voice, his body, his dignity – but deciding how and where he dies is his last vestige of control.

'Oh, Mum.' I reach for her hand but she's too far away and my fingers graze the soft wool of her cardigan instead. 'I wish we were closer. I wish there was more I could do. I hate it, being so far away. I feel so guilty.'

'No.' She sits up a little straighter in her seat. 'Don't you be saying things like that. You have your own life, Joanne. A house, a job, a husband and a babby. She needs to be your priority, not us.'

'But what if we moved closer? I hate the idea of you coping all alone. I know you've got the carer but—'

'I've Elaine Fairchild next door. And my friends

from the church. I'm being looked after. Don't you worry.'

But no family. No brothers or sisters or nieces or nephews. I know Mum still keeps in touch with her sisters Sinead and Celeste and her brother Carey – I've seen the Christmas cards on the mantelpiece – but she's too proud to ask for help. She's independent and strong-willed. She had to be, upping and leaving her friends and family and starting a new life with me as a single mum in England, a country she'd never even visited before.

'I'm serious, Mum. I've been looking at jobs. There's one here at the university. I could do it standing on my head. There are loads of good nurseries nearby and I've seen a lovely little bungalow in Malpas. We'd be just down the road.'

She gives me a sideways look. 'And what does Max think of this plan?'

I glance at Elise, sucking her thumb and staring intently at Grandad Tumble. 'I haven't talked to him about it yet.'

'Jo . . .' Mum narrows her eyes. 'What is it that you're not telling me?'

I want to explain how much I've been struggling and how the move could help me as well as her and Dad. I thought that life would get better after Elise was born. I thought that, as soon as I held her warm, wriggling body in my arms, all the hurt and pain of losing Henry in the second trimester of my pregnancy would lessen. I thought my breath would stop catching in my throat, that the panic in my chest every time I left the house would subside. That the terrible, all-encompassing dread that something awful was just about to happen would disappear. But it didn't. It got worse. We had lost Henry and I was terrified that we'd lose Elise too. I couldn't sleep because I was convinced that she'd stop breathing the moment I closed my eyes. I wouldn't let her out of my sight for fear that someone would snatch her. For months I refused to let Max take her out of the house in her pram because I was certain that, if he did, I'd never see either of them again. I had several panic attacks – once after Max went back to work and I tried to go to a local mother-and-baby group in the church hall, another time in the pharmacy when I went to buy Calpol for Elise – but I kept trying, I kept working out in front of the TV, I kept doing my mindfulness exercises. I refused to let it beat me. And then two months ago Mum told me that the consultant had given Dad less than three months to live and the walls began closing in on me again.

When I started thinking about jobs and houses in Cheshire I never truly believed that it could happen. How could I *ever* move to a different part of the country when I couldn't even go to Tesco alone? It was wishful thinking. A pipe dream. But when Paula got into my car yesterday and threatened my daughter, something changed. I didn't turn to jelly. I didn't faint or cry or curl up in a ball. I told her to get out and I went in search of my little girl. Elise's safety and well-being are more important to me than anything else. I know it's not right, the way she's living now, cooped up in the house with me, and I want to change that. I want her life to be an adventure and not a prison.

'I'm not happy, Mum,' I say. 'Max and me . . . it's not been good for a while and it's been getting worse. I want a divorce.'

'A divorce. Are you quite, quite sure? Perhaps couples counselling might help? Or your local priest?'

My heart sinks as she continues to offer suggestions. Elise is totally, blissfully oblivious to what's going on. Her whole world is going to fall apart over the next few weeks and months and it's up to me to protect her as best I can. I can only hope that Max will agree to an amicable separation but, deep down, I know that's not going to happen. Despite his threats to leave in the past, he would never abandon me and Elise. He's an only child and both of his parents are dead – we're all he's got. When I tell him that I want to move to Chester with Elise he's going to be devastated.

Chapter 6

Chester? CHESTER? Max stalks from room to room, his hands balled into fists and tucked under his armpits. Jo's been planning a move to Chester and she didn't think to mention it to him? He'd logged on to her laptop while his was updating and discovered that she'd left three tabs open in Firefox – one for a student-support job at the University of Chester, one for Rightmove and one for a primary school in Malpas. Was that the real reason she'd gone up to Chester? To go to an interview or attend a viewing before she visited her parents? He nearly called her yesterday, when he found the laptop, then changed his mind. This is a conversation they need to have face-to-face. He's been quietly seething for nearly 48 hours.

He glances at his watch as he moves from the master bedroom to Elise's room. 5.17 p.m. Jo texted him earlier to say they'd be home around fiveish.

He squats down to pick up some building blocks and a fluffy bear that have been abandoned in the middle of the room and transfers them to a pink plastic toy bucket beside his daughter's cot. He pulls the curtains closed and straightens Elise's duvet. Then, with nothing else to occupy himself, he sits on the floor beside her cot. He runs a hand over the multi-coloured Peppa Pig duvet cover then reaches for a book from the shelves set into the alcove: *Snug as a Bug*, his daughter's favourite book. He's read it hundreds of times, Jo has too. It's part of Elise's bedtime routine: teeth, pyjamas, milk, book. He's surprised Jo didn't take it with her.

Anxiety twists at his stomach as he gazes around his daughter's bedroom, at the white clouds floating on grey wallpaper on the opposite wall, at the framed picture of a penguin gripping a bouquet of balloons, at the tent-shaped den Elise fills with teddies and rarely enters. It's so quiet without his daughter bouncing around the room, singing gobbledegook songs in her breathy high-pitched voice. So empty. This is what it would be like if Jo took her away. He closes his eyes to block out the thought, but it's not fear he's feeling any more. It's anger. Here he is, tearing himself apart at the thought of losing his daughter when his own father didn't give two shits about him and his brother. You wouldn't have caught Jeff Blackmore moping about in the bedroom, cooing and sighing over a duvet cover and a favourite book. He didn't even know who his kids were half the time.

*　*　*

36

Max holds it together when his family returns just after 6 p.m. He welcomes Jo back into the house with a kiss on the cheek and then scoops Elise up and into his arms and hugs her tightly before setting her back on her feet. She speeds off into the living room, demanding that he play bricks with her. It takes him a couple of seconds to realise that Jo hasn't followed them. She's still standing in the hallway, one hand pressed to her lower back, the other to the wall. She tells him that she put her back out when she helped her mother turn Andy and she's been in the most terrible pain ever since. The three-hour car journey was unbearable, she says, and now she can barely move. He helps her into the living room and takes some of the weight as she lowers herself to the floor so she can lie on her back, then he retrieves the suitcases from the car and carries them up to the bedroom.

Two hours flash by as he feeds Elise, doles out ibuprofen and a glass of water to Jo, and then does the bedtime routine single-handedly as his wife lies on the living-room rug barking out orders. 'Don't forget to brush her teeth.' 'Make sure you plug the Gro-Clock back in'. 'Have you got her milk?' His irritation increases each time he hears her voice.

When he finally returns to the living room, with Elise safely tucked up in her cot, Jo has managed to drag herself into a sitting position, her back pressed up against the base of the sofa. For five minutes they have been sitting in silence, staring at the 'Night, night. See you tomorrow morning at 6 a.m.' image on the television screen. Jo's semi-crippled condition has unnerved him. He knows that now is not the time to have a conversation about what he discovered on the laptop but he can't push it out of his mind. There's no way he can go to work tomorrow with the matter left unresolved. It will eat away at him all day.

'So.' He coughs lightly. 'When were you planning on telling me that you want to move to Chester?'

Jo tenses but she doesn't turn to look at him. 'Sorry?'

'I saw the sites you'd been looking at on your laptop. The house, the job, the school.'

'Can we talk about it tomorrow, please?' Her voice is as stiff as her body.

'No, I want to talk about it now.'

Jo continues to stare at the green glow of the television. 'Please, Max. I'm in pain.'

Max takes a steadying breath in through his nose. If there was nothing to it she'd tell him as much, but her silence is scaring him. What's she playing at? Why won't she just talk to him? 'And you think I'm not?'

'Don't do this, please.' She turns her head slowly to look at him. 'I've had an awful day. Dad's got so much worse and I really don't want to fight with you tonight.'

How can he argue with that? He can't and he shouldn't. But there's always something with Jo. Something that means he has to bite his tongue rather than talk to her about the things that are worrying him. First it was the panic attacks, then the agoraphobia. Now her dad's dying. Andy's been touch-and-go for the last couple of years. They've lived their lives on a knife edge since before Elise was born, exchanging worried glances each time Brigid rings in case it's bad news. And now, on top of everything, Jo has put her back out. Another reason to block him out.

'Is this to do with what happened before you left?' he asks. 'Are you pissed off with me because I didn't call the police?'

Anger flashes on her face. 'Elise was in danger but, instead of supporting me, you patronised me. Poor old Jo, reacting to every tiny little thing. This is our *daughter* we're talking about. I don't care if we're being overcautious, so long as she's safe.'

'Elise was in no more danger than if she'd been crossing the road or playing in the park. Not that she ever gets to do that, when she's so wrapped up in cotton wool that she's suffocating in her own home.'

'DON'T!' Jo snaps. 'Don't you dare go there, Max.'

'I think we should talk about it. I think we should discuss the fact that you're too ill to take our daughter anywhere other than to and from nursery but you're well enough to plan a move up to Chester, are you? To start a new job? To take her to a new nursery? To build a new life for yourself?'

'I'm trying to get well, Max.' Jo's gaze is still steely but her voice sounds choked, as though she's trying not to cry. 'I'm trying to do what's best for everyone: for Elise, for Mum, for Dad, for me.'

'But not for me?' It takes every last bit of control to hide the pain that's tearing at his chest. He's always known that he's last on Jo's list of priorities, but hearing her *say* it hurts like hell.

'Yes, for you!' Jo says. 'I've done nothing but support you for the last twelve years but you never listen when I try and tell you what I want.'

'I listen!' Max jumps up from his seat. 'I do nothing but listen.'

'No, you don't. You don't listen to a word I say. I *told* you not to get into investigative journalism because you were putting us at risk, and you patted me on the head and told me not to worry my silly little self.'

'That's not true.'

'It is. You put yourself first, Max. You've always put yourself first. It's always been about you and your career. I put up with that when it was just you and me but we're a family now.'

'You think I don't know that?'

'Well, you obviously don't care. If you did you would have given a shit when I told you that a stranger had threatened our daughter and—'

'I LOVE ELISE!' Max roars with pain and anger and frustration. His right hand unclenches and he swipes at the framed photos on the mantelpiece, sending them clattering to the ground. Why is she being like this? Why is she attacking him when he's just trying to do the right thing? He's only ever tried to do the right thing. He's vaguely aware of Jo screaming at him to stop as he tornadoes through the room, grabbing, smashing and destroying all the things he paid for, everything he worked so hard for, and then he hears it, he registers the threat that makes his blood go cold.

Chapter 7

I'm watching you, Jo. I've been watching you for a long time. I know where you go, what you do and who you talk to. And I know what your weak spot is. Some women become more powerful when they become mothers. They become more alert to danger, more ready to react, to defend. But you're no tiger mother, Jo. You're prey. And if you try and disappear down a rabbit hole with Elise I'll come after you. I want what's mine and I know exactly how to take it back.

Chapter 8

I should never have threatened Max, but I just wanted him to stop. I'd never seen him that out of control before. I begged him to calm down but it was like he couldn't hear me, or our daughter whimpering upstairs, and so I told him that, if I moved away, he'd be lucky if he ever saw Elise again.

He froze. He stopped still in the middle of the room and he stared. Not at me. Not at the broken picture frames lying on the rug. At nothing. Then he said, 'Elise is crying. I'll go and check she's OK,' and he stalked out of the room before I could object, leaving me in a sea of smashed glass and splintered wood.

As Max's footsteps clump-clump-clumped on the landing above me and the low rumble of his voice drifted down the stairs, I rolled onto my hands and knees, gritting my teeth as I forced myself up and onto my feet. He was halfway down the stairs by the time I got to the living-room door. In his right hand was his black sports bag.

'Max,' I said. 'I'm sorry. Can't we just talk about—'

He walked straight past me, opened the front door and then looked back. His eyes were so filled with pain and hurt it took my breath away.

'Mummy,' Elise says now as I hobble across the kitchen to the cupboard near the sink where we keep our medicine. 'Mummy, back owie?'

'Yes, sweetheart. Mummy's back's still hurting.' I root around the boxes of plasters, Calpol and indigestion tablets but the strongest painkillers we have are a couple of paracetamol.

I swallow them with a glass of water then take Elise's plate from the table and drop it into the sink, then swipe at the jam on the front of her top with a damp dishcloth. I would change her but it's taken me so long to do the simplest thing this morning and we're already running fifteen minutes late.

Somehow I manage to wrestle my daughter into her shoes and coat and out the front door. As I do, the door to number 35 opens and our next-door neighbour Naija appears, walking backwards as she attempts to wrestle her huge double buggy out of the house and onto the path.

'They're doing my head in,' she says, gesturing towards her eighteen-month-old twin boys who are red-faced and screaming. 'I can't wait until we go on holiday next week.'

'I can imagine. I remember when—' I break off mid-sentence.

Someone's watching us. I can sense it, even without turning my head.

And there she is, Paula, standing on the corner of my street staring straight at us.

'Naija, can you keep an eye on Elise for a second?' I reach down and attempt to lift my daughter over the low wall that separates our front gardens but, as I do, my back spasms violently and I wince. I see a flash of amusement on Paula's face and then she's off, walking down the street towards Wells Road.

'It's OK.' Naija reaches for Elise and lifts her over the wall. As soon as she's in her arms I take off, hobbling down the path.

'Paula!' I try to run but I can't stand up straight. Instead I half rock, half gallop along the pavement, gritting my teeth against the pain. It seems to take for ever to reach the corner and, as I turn it, my heart sinks. She'll be long gone. An eighty-year-old could outrun me today.

'Paul—'

I stop sharply. Paula is standing right in front of me, her hands in the pockets of her black padded jacket, her high-heeled feet planted wide. I would have ploughed straight into her if I hadn't stopped so quickly, but she doesn't jolt or step backwards as I draw up next to her. Her kohl-lined eyes flick from the top of my head to the scuffed Clarks shoes on my feet, and then rest on my arm, twisted behind me, my hand on my lower back.

'Hello, Jo.' The top half of her face doesn't move as her lips curl up into a smile.

'What are you doing here?'

Her fixed smile doesn't slip. 'My son lives here. I told you.'

'No, he doesn't.'

'Doesn't he?' She tilts her head to one side. Her mascara-loaded eyelashes unblinking. Her cold, blue eyes fixed on mine. 'That's strange. I could have sworn I just came from his house.'

'What number does he live at?'

She glances up Wells Road towards the small crowd assembled at the bus stop a couple of metres away. A woman with her child glances quickly away, embarrassed at being caught eavesdropping on our conversation, but an elderly woman continues to stare. Paula makes eye contact with her, tilts her head towards me and rolls her eyes. She may as well make twirling circles with her index finger whilst pointing at her temple.

Further down Brecknock Road, Naija is still standing outside her house, one hand on the buggy, the other clutching Elise. When she sees me looking, she lifts a hand from the buggy and holds it out, palm upturned. *What's going on?* Paula shifts position. She's watching them too.

'Leave us alone,' I hiss. 'I don't know who you are or what you want but if you don't stay away from us I'll call the police.'

Paula leans in so close I can smell cigarettes on her breath. 'And tell them what, Jo?'

I react instinctively, pressing my palms against her horrible shiny jacket and shoving her away from me. 'Leave us alone!'

'Oooh.' She looks back towards the bus stop. Now everyone is staring at us, their jaws agape. 'That was assault!' She looks back at me. 'I think the bloke in the black coat is going to call the police. He's got his mobile out, look.'

I don't look. I'm so angry I'm shaking.

'Just leave,' I say through gritted teeth. 'Just leave me alone.'

'I will when your husband returns what he took.'

'He didn't take anything from you. He doesn't even know who you are!'

'Doesn't he?' A slow smile creeps onto her face. 'He would tell you that, wouldn't he?'

'What's that supposed to mean?'

'Just tell him to return my property, Jo,' she says as she turns to leave.

'Why me?' I shout after her as her high heels clip-clop on the pavement. 'Why not talk to Max?'

She turns back and there it is, the same tight-lipped, narrow-eyed look she gave me in my car. 'Because you're more fun, Jo.'

Chapter 9

I fight back tears as I shepherd Elise through the heavy glass door and into nursery. I don't really know what I'm doing here.

I didn't tell Naija what had happened with Paula. Elise was staring up at me with big, worried eyes and I knew that, if I said a word, I'd burst into tears. Besides, I barely know my next-door neighbour. We've made small talk about the children in the front garden and I once emailed her some information about a course she was interested in but we've never been in each other's homes.

'Come on then, sweetheart. Let's get your coat off.'

I feel breathless and sweaty as I pull at the elasticated cuff around my daughter's wrist. If I can just follow the schedule – nursery, work, nursery, home – everything will be OK. Elise will be safe here. I overreacted before. There's no way anyone could take a child out of the nursery without a member of staff knowing. When Elise started I had to provide Sharon with a list of anyone I might send to pick her up, along with a description of them, and then I had to provide a password. They won't release Elise to anyone who doesn't know it.

With Elise free of her coat I lead her towards the twos room, hoping desperately that Sharon isn't in today. She gave me such a strange look the last time I came in, and there's something about her that makes me feel ill at ease. A week doesn't go past when she doesn't take me to one side to tell me off for not labelling Elise's clothes or for forgetting to bring in family photos for a display.

'Jo!' A perplexed-looking woman with a baby in her arms and a shoeless toddler at her feet gestures for me to come to her aid. I'm so stressed I can't remember her name. 'You couldn't hold Mia while I put George's trainers on, could you?'

She thrusts the baby into my arms before I can object. My lower back twinges as I take the weight of the child.

'Dat's George,' Elise says, pointing as the small boy gleefully throws his trainers across the hallway and his mother chases after them.

'Baby,' she adds, pointing at the red-cheeked, drooling bundle in my arms.

'I'm so tired,' the other woman says, crouching down beside her son. She grabs one of his socked feet and wiggles a shoe onto it. 'Mia's still waking me up every three hours for a feed. She's six months old, for goodness' sake. I swear George was sleeping through by now.'

'Looks like she's teething,' I say as I dab away some of the drool on the child's chin with the muslin tucked under her neck.

'Four teeth! She's started biting when I feed her. I don't think my nipples can take much more.' She glances up at me. 'Sorry, too much information.'

'It's fine. I know exactly where you're coming from. The first time Elise did that I was so shocked I shoved her away and she ended up on the floor!'

The other mum laughs but the sound comes to an abrupt halt and she hurriedly looks away. Sharon has appeared beside me with her arms crossed and a disapproving look on her face.

'I don't think potentially injuring a child is a laughing matter, do you?'

Sharon doesn't wait for me to respond. Instead she reaches for my daughter's hand and leads her towards the gate. 'Come on, Elise, let's get you inside.'

I watch open-mouthed as she ushers my daughter inside without giving me a chance to say to goodbye to her.

'Don't worry about Sharon,' the other woman says in a low voice as she helps her son to his feet and reaches for her baby. 'She'll understand when she has kids.'

'OK, Jo,' says the policewoman on the other end of the line. 'I've created a log of everything you've told me and you've got your incident number, haven't you?'

I tap the number written on the pad of paper in front of me, even though she can't see it. 'Yes, I've written it down.'

'An officer will visit you at home tomorrow to take some more details.'

'Do you . . . do you have any idea what time?' I feel awful trying to pin her down, given how accommodating she was when I said I'd struggle to make it to the police station because of my agoraphobia.

'It could be any time, I'm afraid.'

That means I'll have to take a half-day's holiday from work and then pray they don't turn up when I leave to collect Elise from nursery. Or maybe I could keep her home with me?

'OK,' I say, 'that's fine.'

'Great. If anything else happens between now and then, make a note of the date, time and what happened and give us a ring back, quoting your incident number. And if you feel in any immediate danger call 999. OK?'

'OK.' I look up to the ceiling as tears well in my eyes, then take a steadying breath. I didn't expect the police to take me seriously, not after the way Max reacted.

'Is there anything else I can help you with?'

I want to tell her that I'm scared. That I've been home for less than five minutes and every noise, every shadow that's passed the living-room window, has made me jump. I want to tell her that I'm scared that when

50

another police officer comes round to talk to me I'll have to admit that I shoved Paula in the street. There were witnesses – at least half a dozen. If the police track Paula down and she presses charges my career will be over. I'd lose my job at the university and I won't find another. Not here. Not in Chester. Nowhere.

'Wait!' I say before she can put the phone down. 'I've changed my mind. I don't want anyone to come round and see me.'

'Why's that then?' I can hear the frustration in her voice.

'I . . . I . . . it's fine. It'll be fine. I . . . I think I overreacted. Sorry, the line's breaking up. I appreciate your time. Thank you. Bye!'

I jab at the *end call* button, wincing as I sit back against the sofa cushion. I lasted less than half an hour at work. Within ten minutes of sitting down in my chair I was in so much pain from my back I wanted to cry. Then, when I rang my GP to try and arrange an appointment and the receptionist said there was no space for five days, I did cry. Diane, my boss, took one look at me and sent me home. I nearly passed out when I got into the car, and the pain is going nowhere.

I check my phone to see if there's been a reply from Max to the voicemails and texts I sent him at work, apologising for what I said last night and telling him what happened with Paula this morning. When I woke up I picked up my phone, expecting to find a grovelling apology from my husband. He's lost his temper before but he's never smashed things up. Never. That was so out of character it scared me. But there were no new messages and I haven't heard from Max all day – not a call, not a text, nothing. I don't know what I expected. Maybe an 'I'm sorry' or an 'I should have believed you' or even a 'let's talk'. But no, nothing at all. He knows he was out of order last night. The only possible reason for his silence is because he's paying me back for what I said. That's why I apologised. One of us had to break the deadlock.

I hobble into the kitchen, leaning on the walls for support, and rifle through the medicine cupboard again but nothing stronger than paracetamol has miraculously appeared overnight. I've already taken the two ibuprofen that Diane gave me but they haven't touched the edges. I pick up my handbag from where I left it on the kitchen counter when I came in, and upend it. My purse, keys, make-up, tissues, various pieces of paper, an assortment of change and my phone tumble out. And something else – a packet of pills that don't belong to me. I pick them up and turn them over in my hands. They're some of Dad's muscle relaxants. Mum thrust them at me when I mentioned that my back was hurting but I shooed her away, telling her that a couple of paracetamol would sort me out. She must have slipped them into my bag before I left. There's no advice slip in the packet but a quick Google reveals side effects including dizziness, drowsiness, a dry mouth and possible addiction. Nothing overly scary. I make a split-second decision and pop two out of the blister pack and into my mouth. As I swallow them down with a glass of water a wave of exhaustion crashes over me. I barely slept a wink last night: a combination of the pain and the aftermath of the argument with Max. I glance at my watch as I shuffle back down the hallway, check the front door is double-locked, then step into the living room and ease myself down onto the sofa. It is 12.15 p.m. I'll just grab a couple of hours' sleep and, with any luck, I'll feel better when I wake up. I might even be able to do a couple of hours' work on my laptop before I go and pick up Elise.

I wake with a start but my mind is so foggy it takes me a couple of seconds to realise where I am. The living room is dark, the sofa is lumpy and uncomfortable and the house is silent. I turn my head. It's dark outside but the blinds are still open. Unease pricks at my consciousness but sleep still has a grip on me, making me groggy and slow. I twist my wrist up towards my face and squint at the display through the gloom – 6.14 p.m.

Six-fourteen! I shoot up into a sitting position then wince and press a hand to my lower back. Six fourteen! I should have been at the nursery for five-thirty to pick up Elise. Oh my God! A cold chill courses through me as I snatch up my mobile. Five missed calls: three of them from the nursery, two of them from Max.

I ease myself onto my feet and grab my coat from the banister. I hit the voicemail button on my phone and press it to my ear as I stumble out the front door and half hobble, half run down the street.

'Hello, Jo. It's Sharon from nursery. You were due to pick up Elise fifteen minutes ago. I'm sorry to have to remind you about timekeeping again but you really should let us know if you're going to be this late.'

'Hello, Jo. It's Sharon again. Could you give us a ring as soon as you get this?'

'Hello, Jo. It's nearly six o'clock and Elise is really quite distressed that no one has come to collect her. We've rung your husband.'

'Jo, it's Max. Where are you? I just got your message about Paula, and the nursery just rang me to say that you haven't picked up Elise. Where are you? Ring me! Please! As soon as you get this!'

'I'm going to get Elise. Ring me the second you get this.'

My hand shakes as I run a hand over my face, pushing the hair off my damp forehead. The nursery is only a couple of blocks away but it feels miles away. Six hours! I passed out for six hours. My phone rang five times and I didn't hear a thing. Shit. I should never have taken Dad's pills. I should have gone to the chemist. I should have—

I stop short outside the nursery. There are no cars parked up outside and no lights on inside. The entrance hall is empty of buggies. The coat rack, normally heaving with tiny jackets and bags, is bare. I wrap a hand around one of the metal bars on the gate but I don't bother opening it. I'm too late. Elise is gone.

Chapter 10

When his phone rings at 6.35 p.m. Max snatches it up and presses the *call answer* button. For over half an hour he's been pacing the room as call after call all ended in the same way – 'No, I haven't seen Jo all day,' 'No, I haven't heard from her' and 'I hope she's OK. Let me know.'

He gives Elise a reassuring smile as he presses the phone to his ear but she's too busy to notice. She's playing on the double bed with a plastic doll he found in her nursery bag.

'Jo?' He keeps his voice low, so as not to worry his daughter. 'Jo, are you there?'

'Where's Elise? Is she with you?' He can hear the fear in his wife's voice.

'Yes. Where the hell are you?'

His wife sighs with relief then promptly bursts into tears. 'Oh my God,' she cries between sobs. 'Oh my God. Oh my God. Oh my God.'

Max stands up and carries the phone into the bathroom. He can still see Elise through the open door but she's nearly out of earshot now. 'Jo, can you tell me where you are?'

'I'm . . . at home.'

'Are you OK?'

'Yes.' He hears her take a deep breath. It's punctuated by short sharp sobs but she's calming down.

'What happened?'

There is silence apart from a sniff followed by a soft hoo-hoo sound as his wife breathes in through her nose and out through her mouth.

'Jo, what happened?' Max asks again.

'I woke up and it was dark. I overslept. I came back from work earlier because my back was hurting and I fell asleep on the sofa. Oh God. I feel so—'

'You were asleep?' He'd seen her calls flash up on his screen earlier in the day but he'd ignored them. He was in court, covering a domestic battery case, and it wasn't until he was back in the office and the nursery rang that he realised something was wrong. He'd tried to ring Jo and, when she didn't answer her phone, he started to worry. Had something happened at work or was she marooned somewhere, caught in the grip of a panic attack? Then he remembered what she'd told him about Paula.

'You were asleep?' he says again, unable to keep the incredulity out of his voice. 'Jo, we went back to the house but it was locked from the inside. I banged on the door and shouted through the letter box. Didn't you hear me?'

56

'No.' Her voice quavers. 'I didn't hear a thing.'

'I've been ringing all your friends. I was going to call the police.'

'Oh God. I'm sorry. Where are you? Can you bring Elise home? I need to see her.'

'I . . .' Max pauses. He can't dismiss the niggling thought at the back of his brain. 'I made a lot of noise, Jo. I banged and banged. No one could have slept through that.'

'That's because I . . . I took something.'

His grip on the phone tightens. 'What?'

'Some muscle relaxants my mum gave me. They were Dad's. I was in so much pain, Max, and the doctor wouldn't see me.'

'You took prescription drugs meant for a man who's dying from motor neurone disease? Are you mad?'

'I was desperate! I was in pain. You have no idea—'

'No, Jo. *You* have no idea. Did Sharon tell you that Elise wet herself when no one came to pick her up?'

'No. I—'

'Or that she had to put her in another child's knickers because you forgot to take her bag in this morning? And she was *filthy*, Jo. Her top was dirty, her hair hadn't been brushed—'

'Please, Max. Don't make me feel worse than I already do. I could barely move this mornin t I still got Elise ready the best I could. I did to forget her. I didn't do it on purpose!'

Jo continues to try and explain hers

has stopped listening. He's thinking about his dad. He was twelve the first time he found him passed out on the sofa. He'd just got in from school and there was a strange, bittersweet, almost vinegary scent in the air when he opened the front door. He found the tinfoil, sticky with brown liquid, on the bathroom floor.

'Have you done it before?' he asks.

'What?'

'Taken drugs. At home?'

'Are you serious?'

'I wouldn't have asked if I wasn't.'

Over the last couple of months Jo's behaviour has become increasingly erratic. He'd put it down to her agoraphobia and mental health. No, *she'd* put it down to that. Neither of them could pinpoint why she was getting worse instead of better. Unless she was self-medicating . . .

His wife sighs. 'I can't believe you're even asking me that.'

'Sharon said you seemed out of it when you picked up Elise the other day.'

'That was after Paula threatened me! Jesus, Max. Would you listen to yourself? You're being ridiculous. Just bring Elise home.'

'She also said you deliberately dropped Elise when she was a baby.'

'I was breastfeeding and she bit me! I didn't do it on purpose. Jesus, Max. Why are we even having this conversation? Just bring Elise home or I–I'll—'

'Do what? Take her to Chester? Make sure I never

see her again?' Max is shaking with anger. Jo didn't see the state their daughter was in when he turned up to collect her. The nursery staff had done the best they could to keep her occupied but her eyes were red and puffy, her cheeks tear-stained. As if she hadn't been through enough – being kept indoors all the time when other little kids were laughing and playing in the sunshine. He'd done his best to understand what Jo was going through. He'd supported her, he'd listened to her, he'd put his own needs last, telling himself that all Jo needed was a bit of time. But she was turning into someone he didn't recognise.

'Max, don't. I said I was sorry about that. I sent you a text and—'

'Have you got any idea how worried I've been, Jo? I thought that Paula had hurt you. Have you rung the police yet?'

Jo pauses for a beat. 'No.'

There's something about the hesitation in her voice as she says the word 'no' that makes Max frown.

'Why the hell not? Last night you had a go at me because I wasn't taking you seriously and now . . .' he sighs. 'We're going round in circles here. Look, we're in the Holiday Inn and Elise is fine. She can sleep here with me tonight and I'll take her to nursery in the morning. If you pick her up after work we can talk more then. OK?'

'I . . . I don't know. I really want to see her, Max.'

'She's fine. Honestly.' He watches as his daughter clambers off the bed and toddles towards him, arms reaching for a hug, a huge smile on her face. 'I'm sorry for going off the deep end but I was worried, OK, for you and Elise.'

'I'm sorry too. I didn't mean to scare you. Honestly, Max. When I woke up and realised what had happened I . . .' She pauses. 'Can I talk to Elise? Please. I need to hear her voice.'

'Sure.' He places the phone against his daughter's ear. 'Elise, sweetie. It's Mummy. Say hello.'

He listens as his daughter has a garbled conversation with her mother then he wrangles the phone away from her again.

'I need to go. There's a Tesco down the road and I need to grab some overnight things for Elise and some clean clothes for nursery tomorrow.'

'You could come home. There are clothes here,' Jo says, but the fight has gone out of her voice. She's accepted that they won't be coming home tonight.

'Sleep well, sweetheart,' Max says. 'I'll see you tomorrow evening.'

'OK. Bye.'

The line goes dead and Max slumps against the bathroom doorway, completely spent. His daughter, still standing beside him, reaches out her arms to be picked up and he swoops her up. He presses his face into her blonde curls and closes his eyes as her tiny hands wind their way around his neck.

Chapter 11

I saw you, Jo. I watched as you slept, flat on your back, your hands folded on your stomach like a corpse. A nice sleep, was it? Restful? You need to stay awake, Jo. You need to watch what's happening around you because, if you don't, if you close your eyes for one second, you'll lose everything that's ever mattered to you. Oh wait, too late. That's already happening.

Chapter 12

Max leaves the *Bristol News* building through the revolving glass front door, his laptop bag swinging from his shoulder, his mobile phone in his hand. He's running late for his interview with an elderly woman who is the most recent victim of a con by two men masquerading as council drain inspectors. One of them ransacked her house while the other one kept her talking in the living room. He's keen to run a story to warn the public about the scam but, whenever he mentally runs through the questions he needs to ask, he's distracted by other thoughts: a niggling worry about his conversation with Jo the night before.

He'd dropped Elise off at nursery in the morning, as planned, then gone to work. When he went home afterwards, Elise threw herself at him the second he walked through the door but Jo barely reacted. She didn't stand up from the sofa when he walked into the living room, and stiffened when he bent to kiss her hello. He wasn't sure if she felt bad for leaving Elise at nursery the night before or if she was angry with him for the way he'd reacted, but he didn't force a conversation. Instead he waited until they'd put Elise to bed then he reached into his messenger bag and handed Jo a bottle of her favourite wine.

'Peace offering.'

'Thank you.'

He followed his wife into the kitchen and watched as she opened the bottle, poured the wine and handed him a glass.

'I'm sorry,' he said as they settled themselves on the sofa. 'For everything. For losing my shit when I saw you'd been looking for houses in Chester. That was out of order. So was my reaction when you said you'd taken your dad's medication.

'It's the investigation,' he went on. 'It's left me feeling wired and jumpy. And I know that's no excuse but, after spending six months with low-life scum, I assume the worst about people. I overreacted. I'm really sorry, Jo. I shouldn't have taken it out on you.'

Jo maintained eye contact with him throughout his apology but there was a strange, distant look in her eyes. It didn't fade once, not even when he offered to move to Chester with her and Elise. He'd expected her to be excited. He'd imagined her face lighting up. But, instead of throwing her arms around his neck and squealing, she leaned away from him and said, 'I think we both need some space after everything that's happened.'

His instinct was to panic, to tell her that was the last thing they needed. But he didn't. He kept calm and told her he understood. It was fine, he'd stay at the hotel for a couple of nights. Only it wasn't fine, was it? He didn't want to be apart from his family.

'Hello, Martin.'

He is vaguely aware of a woman's voice as he turns right outside the *Bristol News* building and heads towards the multi-storey car park where his car is, but he ignores it.

'Or should that be *Max*?'

He turns sharply. A woman with bleached blonde hair, a black Puffa jacket and plastered-on make-up smiles tightly.

'You look surprised to see me, Max.'

'Do I know you?'

'Nice, I see what you did there.' The woman makes a big show of looking to the left, then the right, as though she's checking who's listening. 'Or was that for your wife's benefit? Is she here? It would be lovely to see her again.'

Max grabs her by the shoulders. 'Stay away from my wife.'

Paula doesn't flinch. She doesn't squeal. Instead she looks him straight in the eyes. 'What did you expect me to do when you've been ignoring my calls?'

'Leave her alone.'

'Take your hands off me. Now,' she adds as a middle-aged couple overtake them on the pavement. The man glances back, a concerned look on his face.

'I'll make this very simple for you,' Paula says in

64

a low voice. 'You give me what you stole and neither of us ever have to see each other again.'

'I don't know what you're talking about.'

'Is that what you told your wife?'

'Are you mentally ill?' Max glances back at the glass doors of the *Bristol News* building. Amy is behind the desk at reception but there's no sign of Scott, the heavily tattooed security guard. He's probably secretly eating pizza in the back office or watching porn on his phone while he takes an extended shit.

'You can play this game all you want,' Paula says softly from behind him. 'Claiming not to know who I am or what I want, but you don't know the first thing about me, Max. You don't even know my last name.'

'But the police will.' He turns to face her. 'Jo's filed a complaint. Go anywhere near her again and you'll be arrested.'

It's a lie, but he's not about to admit that. God knows why Jo didn't call the police. Any sane person would have. But Jo's not well. She starts at shadows. She overreacts. She sees danger where there isn't any.

'The police?' Paula tilts her head to one side and smiles. Beneath her plump red lips are tobacco-stained teeth. Straight, but yellow. 'That was a gutsy move, Max, considering they'll arrest you too once they see the CCTV footage.'

'CCTV footage? Really? Do the characters on *EastEnders* give you messages from God too? Perhaps I should give your carer a call? Or a doctor? See you, Paula.' He raises a hand as he walks away.

She may have scared his wife but she doesn't scare him. Delusional or not, she can't be more than five foot three and nine stone whilst he's six foot two and thirteen stone.

'You'll regret ignoring me,' Paula shouts after him as he steps into the car park. 'I'll get what's mine, even if I have to destroy your family to do it.'

Max takes a sip of his pint and sits back in his chair. The glass judders on the table as he sets it back down. His interview with Mrs Jacobs went well. He got some nice quotes and the photographer who met him at her house snapped some emotive shots of her – vulnerable but brave – but he hasn't been able to stop thinking about his encounter with Paula outside work. Her shouted threat as he walked into the car park has unsettled him. At the time he shrugged it off but it's worked its way into his body and it's sitting under his skin making him feel prickly and uncomfortable.

He takes another swig of his pint then reaches for his phone. He needs to discuss moving back in with Jo – personal space or no personal space.

He calls her number but it's engaged. He waits a couple of seconds then tries again. Still engaged. He could text her instead, but texts can be misconstrued. They need to talk. Max logs into Facebook to while away a couple of minutes while he waits for Jo to finish her phone call. As he scrolls through his news feed, he sees the usual humble bragging, food shots, health updates and political rants but nothing that piques his interest. He scrolls, scrolls, scrolls through his friends' updates then pauses at one of Jo's posts. Elise gazes up at him from the screen. She's sitting at the kitchen table with a plate of scrambled eggs in front of her and ketchup smeared all over her mouth. And she's laughing, really laughing. He checks the time stamp – 7.31 a.m. – and his heart twists with pain. While his wife and daughter were bonding over breakfast he was waking up in a grotty hotel room, alone.

As he continues to stare at the photo an unsettling thought pricks at the front of his brain. It's been nearly 24 hours since he mentioned moving to Chester to Jo and she hasn't said a thing about it. He had a text that morning to say that she'd dropped Elise at nursery on her way to work, but nothing else. What's going on in her head? She should be thrilled that he's suggested moving to Chester. Isn't that what she's wanted all along? Or was it only ever the plan for her and Elise to go? Jo had asked for space and he'd agreed to it – they both need to cool down after everything that's happened – but it's killing him, not knowing how she's feeling.

He logs out of Facebook then logs back in, using Jo's email address and password instead. He'd watched her tap it into her phone well over a year ago, when she was checking Facebook in a restaurant they'd taken Elise to for lunch one weekend. LiLi1108 – his daughter's name and the first four digits of her date of birth. He'd almost told her to change it, that it was too easy to guess, but he'd kept quiet instead.

He holds his breath as he presses the blue *log in* button. She's bound to have changed it.

But no. The screen refreshes and he's in. He exhales loudly as he taps the messages icon and feels a surge of adrenalin as he looks through the messages. He shouldn't be doing this, spying on his wife, but he can't ignore the uneasy feeling in his gut and—

He inhales sharply. She sent a message to her friend Helen at 9.27 that morning. The first five words are in the preview panel.

I'm going to divorce Max.

Chapter 13

'Where's Daddy? Where's Daddy, Mummy?' Elise wanders from room to room, poking her head around the kitchen bar and peering into the downstairs toilet. She's convinced that Max is playing an elaborate game of hide-and-seek. Her face crumples as she completes her second circuit of the kitchen and she plonks herself down on the tiled floor.

'He'll be here soon, sweetheart. I'm sure he just got caught up at work.'

On Tuesday night I asked Max for some space. I was going to talk to him about a separation but he threw me when he mentioned moving to Chester. It broke my heart, the way he was smiling at me and the way that smile slowly faded to confusion. There was a time when his suggestion would have thrilled me but so much has changed over the last few years. We've both changed. I'm a needy basket-case. He's a workaholic. I never would have believed that he'd put us at risk but he has. Whatever he did or didn't do to Paula has to be connected to his work. He's covered so many court cases it's inevitable that there are people out there holding grudges against him. Against us. I spent all of yesterday going back and forth with my decision but when I woke up this morning my head was clear. I knew what I had to do.

Max said he'd be home tonight at the normal time but it's 6.45 and there's still no sign of him. Elise should be bathed and in her pyjamas by now but I held off a bit so she could spend some time with Max first.

My phone pings. It's a text from Helen:

Sorry, sorry, sorry. I'm a shit friend. I thought I'd replied to your text. I just got your Facebook message. What's happened?! I can ring you now if you want?

'Where's Daddy, Mummy?' Elise asks again but this time her question is interrupted by a sharp knocking at the front door. Her face lights up and she picks herself up from the floor, hands on the tiles, bottom in the air, and toddles down the hallway towards the front door.

'Max,' I say as I release the catch. 'I didn't double-lock it. You could have used your—'

But it's not my husband standing outside the house.

'Mrs Joanne Blackmore? My name is DS Merriott from Avon and Somerset Constabulary.' He flashes his badge at me. 'Could I come in, please?'

There are four police officers standing outside my

house: three men and one woman. The man standing closest to me is bald, with thick, black-framed glasses and a dour expression.

'What's this about?' I touch a hand to Elise's shoulders to reassure her and fight to keep my voice steady. There's something about the way DS Merriott is looking at me that makes me feel uncomfortable. 'Is it about Paula? I told the other police officer I'd changed my mind about reporting her.'

'If we could talk inside, please, madam?'

'Yes, yes, of course.'

I usher Elise into the living room and am followed by DS Merriott and the female officer. The two male officers remain in the hall. Elise immediately rushes towards her box of toys by the bay window. I sit down in the armchair. DS Merriott takes the sofa and the female officer squats down by the toy box. She engages Elise in conversation, asking her which is her favourite toy.

'Mrs Blackmore.' DS Merriott inches forward on the sofa and reaches into the inside pocket of his jacket. 'I have a warrant to search your property. We have reason to believe that you may be handling or distributing illegal drugs and this warrant gives us the authority to look in your rooms and outbuildings.'

He hands me an official-looking piece of paper. My name and address are at the top and it's been signed at the bottom by a magistrate.

'Drugs?' The word comes out sharply. When Elise turns to look at me I lower my voice. 'There has to be some kind of mistake. No one in this house does drugs.'

'There's been no mistake, madam.' He gestures towards the hallway where the two male police officers are hovering. 'PC Beare and PC Bagnall will conduct a controlled search now. They'll endeavour not to make a mess.'

'They're going to look through all my things? All my personal things?' The thought makes me feel sick.

'They'll look through everything.'

'There's a wooden box,' I say. 'In the cupboard over there. It's got . . . there are mementos inside, of a baby we lost. Handprints, footprints, a little hat. Please,' – I glance at the two men in the hall – 'please be careful with it.'

They look at DS Merriott who nods.

'We'll get started then, Sarg,' says the younger of the two.

I sit in my seat, rigid with shock, as they head next door into Max's home office. Their boots traipse back and forth on the wooden floorboards as they move around his study. Drawers are opened and closed, papers are riffled through. It's like being burgled whilst you're still in the house. This is my home. This is where I feel safe. I want to run into the office and tell them to get out.

Instead I say, 'Can I ring my husband?'

DS Merriott glances down at the notepad in his hands. 'Max Blackmore,' he says, more to himself than me. 'Journalist at the *Bristol News*. The information we received specifically pertains to you, although, if anything is recovered, we will need to talk to your husband too.'

I feel a pulse of panic. 'Please! I need to tell him what's going on.'

A muscle twitches in his jaw. 'I'm afraid that's not possible.'

The two young police officers move from Max's office to the kitchen. Cupboard doors open and shut, glass tinkles and crockery clatters as they continue their search. There has to have been a mistake, that's the only explanation for what's going on. Max is vehemently anti-drugs and I haven't taken recreational drugs since I was in my twenties. This has to be down to Paula.

'I think I know why this is happening,' I say and DS Merriott give me a sharp look. 'Did someone called Paula tell you I was dealing drugs?'

'I'm not at liberty to reveal details, Mrs Blackmore. All I can say is that a warrant wouldn't have been granted without good reason.'

Exasperation makes my chest tighten but I keep my voice low and controlled as I tell him about Paula. As I speak, DS Merriott watches me intently but he doesn't move. His hands remain in his lap, one on his thigh, the other covering his notebook.

I pause for breath. 'Why aren't you writing this down? It could be important.'

'Possibly. What did your husband say when you told him about these incidents?'

'Well I . . . I only told him about the first time it happened. I didn't tell him about the second time because . . . because . . .' What do I say? I can't tell DS Merriott about me pushing Paula or taking Dad's medication and then forgetting to collect Elise from school. 'Because Max didn't take me seriously when I told him about the first incident. He said he didn't know a Paula. But he's a crime reporter. I imagine lots of people have a grudge against him. Whoever she is she knows him and she's been threatening me and my daughter.'

'And you didn't think to report this?'

'No. Well. I did. I spoke to someone but I . . . I changed my mind. I thought Paula would leave me alone. But she hasn't. She's done this.'

One of the young male police officers appears in the doorway to the living room. He holds out a gloved hand, his fingers almost completely enclosing whatever lies in his palm, but not quite. I can see the corner of a clear plastic bag protruding from beneath his curled little finger.

'Sarg,' he says. 'We've found something.'

Chapter 14

'Please.' I have to fight to control my breathing as DS Merriott leads me towards a black Ford Focus and opens the door. 'I told you. Paula's behind this. I don't do drugs. Neither does my husband.' I look up into the detective's expressionless face. 'Please, if we could just wait until Max gets home he'll back me up.'

'We'll talk at the station.'

DS Merriott puts a hand on the top of my head and lightly pushes me towards the back seat of the car. I twist around and look over my shoulder, searching for a glimpse of my daughter. She's got to come to the station with me because there's no one else to look after her. I was allowed to put her coat and shoes on as one of the male officers took Elise's car seat out of my car then the female officer took over.

'Mummy!' The door on the other side of the car opens and my daughter's curly blonde head appears.

She scrabbles across the seats and parks herself in the car seat in the middle as the female officer gets in beside her.

Elise watches me intently as I strap her in. If I give into the fear that is building inside me she'll become scared too.

DS Merriott, in the driver's seat, glances back at us and I feel myself grow hotter and hotter under his appraising gaze. The metal frame of the car feels like it's closing in and the air feels too thick and cloying to breathe.

'Could you open it?' I gesture at the closed window to my right. 'I need some air.'

'Mummy?' Elise's tiny fingers weave their way through mine. 'Mummy?'

'Are you going to be sick?' DS Merriott asks over the electronic drone of the window being lowered.

I'm too panicky to speak so I incline my head towards the window, take a deep breath of cold February air and count to three in my head as I inhale. I do the same as I exhale. I imagine myself on holiday in Rhodes with two friends, a long time before I met Max. I am lying on my back in the sea, sculling with my hands. My eyes are closed and I can feel the warmth of the sun on my face. I can hear the muffled sound of my friends' laughter. I feel safe, peaceful, relaxed, happy. An intrusive thought pops into my mind, of the two police officers staring at me, judging me, thinking I'm mad, but I push it away. I am not in any danger. Nothing bad is going to happen to me.

It feels like for ever before I am calm enough to

speak. I sit forward in my seat, the back of my shirt clinging damply to my back, and make eye contact with DS Merriott in the rear-view mirror. I'm too ashamed to tell him what just happened.

'I'm OK now.' I reach an arm around my daughter's shoulders and pull her into me. 'Mummy's OK.'

In the last two hours I've been interviewed, photographed and had my fingerprints and DNA taken. I nearly had another panic attack when the female officer said she was taking Elise to a separate room but DS Merriott put a steadying hand on my arm and said, 'The calmer you are the quicker we can do this. You don't want your little girl to get upset, do you?' So I played along; I gave Elise my best 'happy, excited Mummy smile' and told her to have fun with the nice lady while Mummy had a quick chat with the policeman.

I felt like I was in a film, or a nightmare I couldn't wake up from, as the Duty Sergeant told me that I was under arrest on suspicion of the possession of controlled drugs. The questions came thick and fast. Do you want a solicitor? Do you have any illness or injury? Are you suffering from any mental ill health or depression? Are you taking or supposed to be taking any tablets/medication? Have you ever tried to harm yourself?

'No,' I replied to every question. I just wanted it to stop. For them to bring Elise back to me and let us go home. 'Can I ring my husband? Please! I'm allowed a phone call, aren't I? He'll tell you that this was down to Paula. She knows where we live. She's been following and threatening me!'

I was told that they'd ring Max in due course and then my belongings were taken away and placed in a clear plastic bag. I did everything I was told, moving zombie-like as I opened my mouth and held out my hand, but then I began to shake. They'd found drugs in my house. I didn't know how many they'd found, or where. All I knew was what DS Merriott had said to the Duty Sergeant – that they'd found a quantity of class A and class B drugs hidden in my home.

My panic increased as DS Merriott led me through a maze of different corridors. I tried to memorise the route we were taking – a right, then a left, then another left. By the time the detective pushed open the door to a tiny interview room, I was dripping with sweat and struggling to breathe. I took one look at the cramped space, strip-lighting and lack of window and shook my head.

'I can't.'

'Mrs Blackmore, please don't make this difficult.'

'I suffer from agoraphobia and panic attacks. If we go into that room and you shut the door . . .'

DS Merriott looked at me with a kind of weariness that suggested that he'd had the shittiest of shit days and he really didn't want to deal with my neurotic crap. 'You were asked by the Duty Sergeant if you suffered from any kind of mental illness. You replied no.'

'I was scared. I didn't know what would happen if I said yes.'

'We could prop the door open with a chair?' suggested the portly female PC who'd accompanied us to the interview room.

The detective glanced at his watch and sighed again. 'Fine. Let's just get this done.'

I insisted, all the way through my interview, that the drugs weren't mine, that I didn't know how they got into the toilet cistern and that no, I did not take drugs for personal use. After grilling me for several minutes, DS Merriott then asked about Max and whether the drugs could be his. I told him, as calmly as I could, that Max's dad had died from a heroin overdose when Max was a child and there wasn't anyone more anti-drugs than he was. The drugs had been planted in our house by Paula. They had nothing to do with either of us.

He asked me to tell him again what had happened with Paula, and made a few notes on his pad of paper. Then he asked me whether I'd noticed any sign of forced entry when I'd returned home with Elise today. I told him that I hadn't noticed any issues with the front and back doors but I couldn't say whether anyone had tampered with the windows because I hadn't checked them.

At that point we were interrupted by a ginger-haired police officer who stuck his head around the door and announced, 'The husband is here.' I slumped back in my seat. Finally! Max would corroborate everything I'd said and I'd be let go. But DS Merriott wasn't done with me. He dismissed the ginger-haired police officer with a nod, then continued questioning me for another five or ten minutes. Only then did he conclude the interview. I was asked to remain in the room for a couple of seconds while the two officers left. I could hear them talking in low voices in the corridor but couldn't make out what they were saying. The female PC returned to the interview room and sat down opposite me.

'We're just going to sit here for a while,' she said, 'while DS Merriott talks to your husband. Normally we'd return you to a cell but,' – she raised a hand when I gasped – 'given your medical condition I think it's for the best if we remain here. If you feel unwell at any point I will call for the Duty Doctor. OK?'

I feel faint with fear. My husband is on a plastic-backed chair on the other side of the custody suite with our daughter fast asleep in his arms, and I'm back in front of the Duty Sergeant with DS Merriott standing beside me. I have no idea whether I'm about to be charged or not.

'Mrs Joanne Blackmore?' the Duty Sergeant says. He is a tall, thin man with a long nose and a prominent Adam's apple that juts over the collar of his shirt.

'Yes.'

A clear plastic bag containing my purse, mobile phone and jewellery is pushed towards me, along with some kind of iPad and a stylus.

'Sign where indicated, please.'

I pick up the stylus. It quivers across the screen as I write my signature.

'Mrs Joanne Blackmore,' the Duty Sergeant says as he takes it from me, 'I'm going to release you on police bail for the officers to carry out further enquiries. You must return to this police station at 2 p.m. on the first of March unless you are informed in writing that the date or time has been changed or the bail cancelled. If you don't turn up to answer your bail you'll commit a further offence which could result in you being fined, imprisoned or both. Do you understand? If so,' – he hands me the tablet again – 'sign here.'

Chapter 15

'Thank you,' I say. 'For offering to sleep on the sofa tonight.'

Max shrugs. 'I couldn't let you two stay here alone, could I?'

We are sitting side by side on the sofa. The television is off, the curtains are closed and the house is silent, save the occasional crackle from the baby monitor on the windowsill whenever Elise coughs or grunts in her sleep as she turns over. Naija told me she stopped using one for her boys when they turned one but I'm not ready to give up ours yet. I used to think that I'd be a chilled, laid-back parent, but when you've lost one child, that innocence is gone for ever. You can never truly relax. Not when you know how fragile life is, how a strong heartbeat can stop, almost overnight.

My fingers twitch against the rough wool of my work skirt. Work. It feels like a hundred years ago since I was sitting at my desk, answering emails from students, keeping one eye on the clock so I wasn't a second late to collect Elise from nursery. But it was only four hours ago. I still can't process what's happened. I tried to talk to Max about it on the way home but he shushed me, telling me to wait until we'd got Elise home and in bed. I want to get a glass of wine so I can dull the sharp edges of my nerves but I'm worried that Max will judge me if I do.

'You do believe me, don't you? That the drugs weren't mine.'

He crosses his arms over his chest and tips his head back, resting it on the top of the sofa.

'Yes,' he says to the ceiling. 'That's why I came to collect you.'

We both fall silent again. I can tell Max doesn't want to discuss what happened but I have to. It's the only way I can make sense of it.

'I checked all the windows when you were getting Elise ready for bed. They were all locked.'

Max doesn't respond. Instead he continues to stare at the ceiling.

'So if all the doors and windows were locked while I was at work how did Paula get in?'

Max shakes his head wearily. 'I don't know, Jo.'

'Aren't you worried?' I can hear the tight whine in my voice but his lack of reaction is niggling at me. He's an investigative journalist. Why isn't he ringing round all his contacts to find out who Paula is? Why isn't he trying to protect us from anything else happening?

'It's because you don't believe me, isn't it? You think they're my drugs?'

'No, Jo.' He turns to look at me. 'I don't think they're your drugs.'

'But you lost it when I told you about Dad's muscle relaxants. Why aren't you freaking out about this?'

'Because one of us needs to stay rational. We can't both lose our shit.'

'I'm losing my shit? Max, someone broke into our house and planted drugs in our toilet. Possibly the same woman who threatened Elise! Of course I'm losing my shit. I'm scared! What's she going to do next?'

'Jesus!' Max lurches forward and rests his face in his hands and inhales deeply through his nose. His shoulders and upper arms shake as he tries to steady his breathing.

'Look.' He sits back again but his hands remain on his knees as though he is readying himself to jump to his feet at any second. 'The police are dealing with it, OK? I gave them a list of all the cases I've covered recently and all the people who might hold a grudge against me. They're going to look into it.'

'Shouldn't they give us police protection while they do that?'

'Not if they don't think we're in any immediate danger.'

'But we are in danger! Paula knows where we live. She was on the corner of Brecknock the other day.'

'Christ!' His eyes widen with shock. 'Was Elise with you?'

'She was with Naija. I talked to Paula alone but I . . . I did something stupid.'

Max goes very still. 'Go on.'

'I . . .' I rub my palms back and forth on my skirt. 'I pushed her.'

'What?'

'I pushed Paula. She was standing too close to me and I panicked. We were on the corner, next to the bus stop, and there was a small crowd of people waiting. They saw me do it. One of them got their mobile out. I think he was going to ring the police.'

'Jesus Christ, Jo,' Max wipes a hand down the side of his face. 'Why didn't you tell me any of this?'

'I was going to. But then I forgot to collect Elise at nursery and—'

'I came round the next day. You could have told me then.'

'I was going to but . . .'

But why? Because I didn't think he'd take me seriously? Because I thought he'd have a go at me? Because I didn't think he'd care?

'I don't know why I didn't tell you, Max. I should have, I'm sorry.'

He takes a deep breath, rests his head against the top of the sofa again, then exhales slowly.

'You're pissed off with me, aren't you?' I say.

'No.' He closes his eyes. 'I'm . . . fuck . . . this is all so fucked up.' He opens his eyes and turns his head to look at me. 'Paula was waiting for me outside work yesterday.'

'What?' I stare at him in horror. 'What did she say?'

'The same thing she said to you, I imagine. That I had something of hers and she wanted it back.'

'Did you recognise her? Do you know who she is?'

He shakes his head. 'No, but she was convinced she knew me.'

'Are you sure? You're a hundred per cent sure you didn't recognise her?'

'Honestly, if she hadn't called out my name I wouldn't have given her a second glance.'

'If you don't know her why is she doing this?'

'Psychiatric problems? Who knows? Possibly she's become fixated with me because of something I wrote in the paper. I really don't know, Jo.'

'But you believe me? That's she's dangerous?'

Max twists round and shifts one leg onto the sofa so we're looking directly at each other. 'I don't know. I hope not, but she's come after us three times now. Four if you count planting the drugs. I gave DS Merriott a description of her when he interviewed me. He said we need to keep a record of everything – every sighting, everything she says, everything she does. And if we ever feel threatened we're to ring 999 straightaway.'

'Oh my God.' I press a hand to my throat. I was so desperate for Max to believe me but now he does I feel genuinely scared.

'It's going to be OK, Jo.' Max reaches for my hand and presses it between his. 'We can get through this.'

'Can we? What if the police press charges about the drugs? I'll have to go to court.'

'I don't think that's going to happen. The police

only found a small amount. "Personal use", that's what the DS said. I think you'll be let off with a caution whether they find Paula or not.'

'But why did she do it, Max? Why go to all the trouble of breaking in just to plant drugs? Why didn't she ransack the place if she's convinced you have something of hers? It doesn't make sense.'

The TV is still in the alcove to the left of the fireplace, with the DVD player and PlayStation 4 on the shelf beneath it. Elise's iPad is propped up against her box of toys. All the DVDs and games are still on the bookcase. I went through every room in the house when I checked the windows and nothing was missing, nothing was out of place.

'What are you doing?' Max asks, following me as I walk into his study next door. His desk looks the same as it always does – strewn with papers, CDs, coffee-stained mugs and pens. His books are still on the shelves. His records are still in the racks. I open the doors to one of his cupboards and look inside: more documents, more paperwork, more folders.

I turn back to look at him. 'Is anything missing?'

I watch his face as his eyes flick from the desk to the shelves to the racks to the floor. 'No. Not that I can see.'

'Do you swear on Elise's life that you've never taken anything that doesn't belong to you?'

'I swear.' His eyes don't leave mine as he shakes his head. 'I swear on our daughter's life.'

Chapter 16

Why did you do it, Max? Why did you take something that wasn't yours? Because you could? Because you were greedy? Because of Elise? Or all three? You tell yourself you did it for your daughter, but is that the truth – really? If it is, why are you having trouble sleeping at night?

You knew the police were on their way so you acted fast. You grabbed what wasn't yours to take and you ran. You thought you'd got away with it. You thought the police would arrest everyone who knew what you'd taken, but you were wrong. You missed someone. Someone you believed wasn't a threat. You stupid man. You stupid, arrogant man . . .

Chapter 17

Mum is making lunch, bustling around her small kitchen in her worn-down slippers and Cath Kidston apron, filling the table with bowls of salad, bread, crisps and a quiche, fresh from the oven. I told her to let me make dinner but she wouldn't hear of it. So, while Elise 'helped' Mum in the kitchen, I sat with Dad and watched a quiz show with him on the small TV in the corner of his bedroom. He fell asleep partway through and I've been sitting here ever since, listening to the dry wheeze of his breathing and watching the laboured rise and fall of his chest.

We arrived an hour ago. There was no sign of Max when Elise and I got up, just a crumpled blanket on the sofa and a half-empty glass of water on the coffee table. There was no note, nothing. After our conversation about Paula, and Max's apology, I couldn't bring myself to discuss a separation so we spent the rest of the evening silently drinking wine as we watched a sci-fi/horror thing on Film4. I was grateful for his company – there's no way I would have stayed in the house alone – but an apology wasn't magically going to put right everything that was wrong with our relationship. It was too little too late. Or was it? Should I fight harder to save our marriage? It would make Max and Elise happy but what about me? I went to bed early, just to get a bit of time to myself. If Max was upset he didn't complain.

This morning I didn't feel safe, being left alone in the house, and I couldn't face going to work, so I rang Diane and told her my back was playing up again then I texted Max to tell him I was going up to Mum and Dad's for the weekend and I'd speak to him soon. He'll be gutted that he won't get to see Elise for a couple of days and I know I'm running away from talking to him about our marriage but I need to think. I don't want to make a hasty decision I regret.

'Will you come and have your lunch, Joanne?' Mum calls from the kitchen.

Dad doesn't stir. I kiss his rough cheek and creep from the room, gently pulling the door closed behind me. As I do, my phone vibrates in my pocket and a tinny tune fills the air.

I don't recognise the number that flashes up on the screen but it's got a Bristol code. My heart quickens. It must be the police with an update on the drugs investigation. I didn't expect them to get back to me this quickly.

'Hello?' I press my mobile to my ear. 'Jo Blackmore speaking.'

'Hello, Jo,' says a friendly-sounding female voice. 'My name is Lorraine Hooper. I'm a senior social worker in the Child Protection team in South Bristol and I was wondering if I could schedule a visit to—'

'You're a social worker?'

'That's right. I'm a senior social worker in the Child Protection—'

I feel myself sway and have to hold onto the door frame of Dad's room to keep myself upright. 'What's this about?'

'It's nothing to worry about, Jo. I'd just like a little chat. Are you and Elise home this afternoon?'

I try to speak, to frame a coherent question in my mind, but I can't. My brain is anaesthetised by fear. I can hear Mum shouting that the quiche is getting cold but the sound is distant and echoey, as though it's being shouted from the base of a deep well. The police must have informed Social Services about the drugs bust. And now they think I'm an unfit mother.

'There's no need to worry. I'll explain more when we meet,' Lorraine says. 'Is this afternoon any good for you? I have a free appointment at 3 p.m. You're number 37, Brecknock Road. That's right, isn't it?'

'I . . . I'm not there. I'm at my Mum and Dad's house in Chester.'

'With your daughter Elise?'

'Yes.'

'And when were you thinking about coming back?'

'In a couple of days. Sunday. In the afternoon. I haven't decided for sure.'

I don't ever want to go back to our house but I

can't tell Lorraine Hooper that. Or can I? If I tell her what's happened maybe she'll understand. All I've done is protect my child from someone who threatened her. I haven't done anything wrong. None of this is my fault.

'I have an appointment for the same time on Monday,' Lorraine says.

'Do you need my husband to be there too? We're currently separated but I could ask him to come home if he needs to be there.'

'Yes, we do legally have to include both parents.' I hear the sound of paper rustling on the other end of the line.

'OK. I'll tell Max to be there too. He'll have to get time off work but that should be OK.'

'Great, so 3 p.m. on Monday?'

'That's fine.'

'OK, I'll see you then, Jo. Take care.'

The line goes dead. I stare at the phone as it quivers in my palm. I've done nothing wrong. I'm a good mother. So why this feeling of dread?

It's Monday afternoon and my nerves have been building the whole way back to Bristol. Elise distracted me for the first hour, demanding her iPad, a snack or her *Frozen* CD, then insisted that I sing 'The Wheels on the Bus' over and over again until I'd covered windscreen wipers, doors, horn, children, mummies, daddies and the driver on the bus saying, 'Move on back.' Finally she fell asleep. But with the silence came fear. I spent last night Googling different permutations of the words 'drugs', 'drug use', 'drug possession', 'social services', 'children' and 'care'. I found a lot of posts in forums, mostly from women whose partners used drugs and were worried that their children would be taken into care, but I couldn't find anyone who was in the same situation as me. I did find a website that said that if someone had alerted Social Services to potential drug abuse, then a social worker would carry out a basic assessment to decide if there needed to be a more detailed investigation. I barely slept for worrying.

Mum could tell that something was wrong when I joined her and Elise for lunch when I got off the phone, but I distracted her with questions about Dad and his consultant, then I excused myself to the toilet and rang Max. I told him that Elise and I would be coming home today and that Social Services wanted to meet with us. He sounded so alarmed I burst into tears and it took him ten minutes to calm me down. He told me over and over again that no one was going to take Elise from us. They were just following protocol as a result of my drugs arrest and all we had to do was tell the truth and be co-operative and we could get back on with our lives.

I couldn't remember the last time he'd been so gentle and caring. It was like having the old Max back, the one who'd come round to my house in the early days with hot soup and tissues when I had a grotty cold, and sent me flowers at work when he knew I was having a tough day. After Henry was born Max changed. He was supportive initially, in the hospital, on our return home and then at the

93

funeral. Afterwards he closed down. He stopped talking to me. He stopped touching me. He stayed late at work or locked himself away in the study as I sobbed in front of the TV. I made excuses. I told myself that he'd shut down emotionally as a way of dealing with his grief. I waited for him to heal, to come back to me, to open up again, but he got worse. He started snapping at me about small things. Why had I left potato peelings in the sink? Why didn't I answer the door to the postman? Why did I watch so much mindless reality TV? I felt like a burden. A lost cause in day-old pyjamas with dirty hair. He'd lost a son too but he was going to work every day to make sure we had food to eat and a roof over our heads. Why couldn't I pull myself together, like he had – in appearance if nothing else? And then he threatened to leave me if I didn't go and see a doctor. It took every ounce of strength to step out of the front door and get into his car but I did it. I nearly fainted twice in the waiting room. The doctor diagnosed me as suffering from agoraphobia and anxiety and she prescribed an SSRI and a course of CBT. The antidepressant made me feel sick and gave me blurred vision but slowly, slowly, with the help of my counsellor I started to feel better. I was able to leave the house if I knew exactly where I was going and if Max came with me. Eventually I was well enough to go back to work. Max seemed to have respect for me again. Fancied me even. And then Elise was conceived and I became scared and neurotic and my agoraphobia returned with a vengeance.

Guilt gnawed at my heart as Max asked me over the phone if I'd had any time to think about the three of us moving to Chester. He's made mistakes and he's acted selfishly but so have I. And now he wants to put things right. How can I possibly ask him for a divorce when he's trying so hard? Maybe I shouldn't go to Helen's after the meeting. Maybe I should stay in Bristol and talk to Max?

I glance at the digital clock on the dashboard – 2.11 p.m. I've got 49 minutes to turn onto the M32 and get across Bristol. I'd planned on getting home by lunchtime so I could clean the house but Dad had a funny turn this morning and I could tell that Mum wanted me to stay and wait for the doctor with her. I could see the worry in her eyes as she told me that it was OK, that I should go if I was in a hurry.

Shit. The brake lights on the car in front flash red as it slows to a halt. A traffic jam. That's all I need.

Elise is still groggy as I lift her out of the car and onto the pavement. She grizzles as I set her down on her feet; the last thing I want is for her to be crying when Lorraine turns up. I look in desperation toward Naija's window, hoping that I can distract Elise by pointing at the twins, but there's no light on behind the closed curtains. Of course, she told me they were due to go on holiday this afternoon.

'Come on, sweetheart.' I pick her up again and carry her to the front door. No point bringing in our bags. As soon as I've seen Lorraine we'll be right back in the car and on our way to Helen's. I need to talk to her. I've been going round and round in circles in my head, trying to decide what to do about Max, and I haven't been able to reach a decision. Helen's known me for years. She knows Max too – not as well, obviously, but well enough to give me advice. I just hope Max will understand when I tell him that I need a bit more time.

I fit the key into the lock, turn it and push at the door with my shoulder. It opens a few inches but there's resistance, as though something, or someone, is behind it, pushing back. I push harder. I must have knocked a few of Elise's jackets off the peg in my hurry to get out of the house and into the car when we left three days ago. The door opens wide enough for me to fit through, but I don't take more than two steps into the hallway. The smell hits me first – faeces, off food and sour milk – and then I see it, a bin bag crammed behind the front door. It's ripped and torn and there's a trail of dirty nappies, wipes, food scraps, packets, screwed-up envelopes, tissues and tins from the hallway to the kitchen. It looks like someone's attempted to take the rubbish out but the bag split en route.

'Max!' I lift Elise into my arms and step through the rubbish, leaving the front door open behind me. 'Max, are you home?'

I gasp in horror as I glance into the living room. The plant in front of the fireplace has been tipped over and there's soil all over the rug. One of Elise's nappies is on the floor in front of the TV, open and dirty with a Peppa Pig doll face down in the poo.

The coffee table is stacked with dirty plates and mugs and the wine bottle I shared with Max is lying on its side, the dregs staining the cream rug red. This isn't how I left the house. What the hell's happened?

'Max?' I tighten my grip on Elise and back out of the room. My voice rings through the house, but no one answers me.

In the kitchen clothes are spilling out of the washing machine and onto the floor. A tin lies on its side on the work surface, spilling orange beans, and a thick gloop sauce has dripped onto the cupboard below. There are coffee granules, sugar and bread crumbs covering the chopping board. Beyond the food preparation bar, on the kitchen table all the washing I neatly folded and placed into a washing basket has been tipped onto the floor and chairs.

Paula must have come back.

I back out of the kitchen and glance up the stairs. I stand very still, barely breathing. Is she still here, standing silently in my bedroom, waiting for me to make my next move? Where's Max? He said he'd be here. What if he is? What if he was here when she broke in? A cold chill runs through my body and I jolt backwards. My heel catches on something, forcing me off balance, and I tip to the side. Elise screeches as I release one hand to steady myself against the wall. I have to get out of here.

Chapter 18

I barrel out of the house with Elise in my arms, slam the door behind me and smack straight into something – or someone – solid.

'Woah!' An older woman with short, dyed red hair and a wide face lurches away from me.

'Are you OK?' She hitches her handbag and tote back onto her shoulder. 'You look as though you've seen a ghost.'

I want to get as far away from the house as I can but she's blocking the path, effectively trapping me between the bay window and the low wall that separates our house from Naija's. Elise screams in my ear and tightens her grip around my neck, making it hard for me to breathe.

'Please.' I hold up a hand, warning the woman not to get any closer. 'Please just let me go.'

'It's OK.' She takes a step back and raises both hands. 'I'm not going to hurt you.' Her brow furrows.

'You are Jo Blackmore, aren't you? I'm Lorraine Hooper. We spoke on the phone yesterday.'

Relief floods through me as she says her name. I thought she was someone Paula sent round to threaten me. In my haste to get out of the house I completely forgot why I came home in the first place.

'I . . .' I set Elise down on her feet and take her hand. 'I . . .'

'Would you like to sit down for a second,' – Lorraine gestures towards the wall – 'and get your breath back? Then you can tell me what's happened.'

'The house. The house . . .' I fight to control my breathing but the harder I try the more ragged it becomes. My heart's pounding and I feel like I'm about to pass out.

'What's wrong with the house?' She takes a step to her left and approaches the bay window, then stoops to peer inside. The stoic expression on her face morphs into concern.

'It's a little messy,' she says, giving me what I'm sure she thinks is an understanding look. 'But that's OK. We all let the housework go when we've got a lot on our plate. Is your husband at home?'

'I don't . . . I don't . . .'

Frustration rages inside me. Why can't she see what's happened? My house isn't 'a little messy'. It's been ransacked and my husband is in danger. I need to ring the police but I can't speak. I can't fucking speak.

Sweat dribbles down my back and a strange tinny sound fills my ears. I grit my teeth and breathe through my nose. I need to tell her what's happened. I need to find my voice.

'Max . . .' As I force the word out, my legs give way and I feel myself falling backwards.

'Are you feeling any better?' Lorraine asks as I sip from the bright-blue sports bottle she's dug out of her tote bag. The water tastes warm and stale but I sip it gratefully.

We're sitting in my car, me on the driver's side, Lorraine in the passenger seat and Elise in the back. Lorraine lurched forwards as I collapsed, wrapping her arms around me and Elise to stop me from falling, then she gently lowered me onto the low wall. Gradually the black spots disappeared from my eyes but I couldn't stop shaking. Lorraine thought I was cold and tried to persuade me into the house. Then, when I refused, into my car.

'Are you able to talk to your husband, do you think?' she asks softly. I'd expected her to be some kind of dragon but she's more like a kindly aunt. A very strong, sensible aunt.

'Yes.' I reach for her phone. 'Yes, please.'

'Hello?' Max says the second the mobile touches my ear. All the air leaves my lungs in a rush at the sound of his voice. He's OK. He's not hurt. 'I'm sorry I'm late. I'm stuck in traffic. There's been some kind of accident near Temple Meads. I haven't moved in over twenty minutes.'

'Max,' I breathe. 'When was the last time you came home?'

'Um,' – he pauses – 'Thursday, I think. That's when I slept on the sofa, wasn't it? Why?'

'I think we've been burgled. The house has been ransacked. There's a bin bag just behind the front door and it's been ripped open. There's rubbish all the way down the hall and in the living room and kitchen. I was so scared. I thought you might already be home and you'd been attacked.'

'I'm fine, Jo. I'm OK. I've been at work all day.'

'Someone's been in the house again, Max. We need to ring the police.'

'Let's just wait until I get home.'

'Why? Don't you believe me? I'm not overreacting to a bit of mess, Max. Paula's been in our house again. She's trashed it.'

'OK, OK. It's all right, Jo. I believe you.' He pauses. 'Can I have a word with the social worker?'

I glance across at Lorraine who's watching me intently.

'He wants to speak to you.'

She nods pleasantly and reaches for the phone. 'Hello, Max. Lorraine Hooper speaking.'

Now it's my turn to watch and listen but all she says over the next couple of minutes is 'Uh-huh, I see', 'OK', 'thank you' and 'right'.

'Well?' I ask as she tucks her mobile back into her handbag. 'What did he want?'

'Just a chat.'

'About?'

She pauses for a split second and she gazes out of the window, as though she's trying to decide how much to tell me. When she looks back at me she's all smiles again. 'He asked if I'd still be here in half an hour.'

I'm not convinced. 'I didn't hear you respond to that question.'

'Well, unfortunately, I do have to go.' She glances into the back of the car where Elise is slapping her palms against the iPad's screen.

'Not working, Mummy. Beebies not working.'

'Here, sweetheart.' I reach for the iPad but she's unwilling to let go it and screams in frustration. I can feel Lorraine silently watching our interaction.

'Jo,' she says as Elise continues to scream. 'Do you mind if I have another quick peep through your window, and a quick look through the letter box of your house?'

'Yeah, sure.' I'm so focused on the tears running down my daughter's face that I barely register her getting out of the car.

It takes a couple of minutes before I finally get through to Elise that Mummy is not trying to take the iPad, Mummy is trying to fix it and then, finally, she is all smiles and prod-prod, bleep-bleep again. I slump back in my seat and rub my hands over my face. Lorraine is peering through the window of our house, her hands cupped to the side of her head. God knows what the neighbours on the other side of the street are making of all of this.

It's nearly over, I tell myself as Lorraine strolls back down the street towards the car. As soon as she goes I'll call Max to tell him that I'm going to Helen's for the night. We'll call the police if *I think* we should.

Let's see how patronising he is when he gets home and sees the state of the place for himself. I'm not staying here one second longer than I need to.

'Well,' Lorraine says as she hefts herself back into the car, 'I saw the state of the hallway.'

'And?'

'Do you have a cat?'

'Cat!' Elise says from the back seat. 'Tigger cat!'

'My next-door neighbours do,' I say. 'Why?'

'Does it ever come into your house?'

'Sometimes. There's a cat flap in the back door that the previous owners installed. After Tigger came in a couple of times I decided to lock it.' I glance back at my daughter. 'But Elise thinks it's fun to unlock it.'

'Could she have done that before you went away?'

'Possibly.'

'That might explain the torn bin bag and the over-turned plant.' I can hear the smile in Lorraine's voice.

A cat? She seriously thinks a cat was responsible for the state of my house? What about the spilled laundry, the soiled nappy or the dirty cups and plates? Did the cat put them there too? No, of course it didn't. Because Lorraine thinks that was down to me. Does she think I left one of my daughter's toys in a pile of her own shit too? I'm so angry I don't trust myself to reply and for several seconds the only sound in the car is the bleep-bleep-bleep of Elise's game and then I feel a hand on my shoulder.

'You're having a bit of a tough time, aren't you?' Lorraine says softly.

'You have no idea.'

'It must be difficult, looking after your home and your daughter whilst holding down a part-time job, nursing a sick parent and coping with your condition.'

I stiffen and shift away from her touch. How does she know all this?

'We all have different coping mechanisms, Jo, but some are more useful than others.'

'Which coping mechanisms are you referring to? My rabid alcoholism or my out-of-control drug habit?'

She smiles again, a smile that no longer looks warm and supportive but patronising. 'No one's accusing you of anything, Jo.'

'But that's why you're here, isn't it? Because of the police raid. As if I haven't been through enough already!'

'Jo.' She glances towards the back seat, where Elise is still playing her game, completely oblivious. 'You might want to keep your voice down.'

I know I should do as she says. Logically I know I'm not doing myself any favours by reacting like this but I'm fed up. I'm sick of being looked at with suspicion and doubt when I haven't done anything wrong. First Max, then the police, now this woman. I feel like I'm in *The Truman Show*, like strings are being pulled and set pieces arranged just to get a rise out of me. Why can't anyone else see how ridiculous this whole situation is?

'I was *threatened*,' I say. 'Drugs were planted in my home and then it was ransacked. I am the victim here and yet my ability to mother my child is being called into question? Seriously?'

Lorraine shifts in her seat. 'No one's doing that, Jo. We just want to help you.'

'No.' I shake my head. 'No, you don't. This is the same bullshit the health visitor tried to pull on me when I had postnatal depression after Elise was born. Do you know what she told me when I said I was getting less than three hours' sleep a night? Persevere! *Persevere*, how is that helpful? She didn't give two shits about me, she just wanted to make sure that I wasn't about to harm my child.'

'I'm sure that's not true. Mothers with PND often feel paranoid and defensive and—'

'Oh, for God's sake!' I slam my palms against the steering wheel then press my forehead against the back of my palms. I can't deal with this any more.

'Mummy!' Elise wails from the car seat, her little voice shrill and fearful.

'It's OK, Li-Li.' I twist round to look at her. She stares back at me with big, alarmed eyes. 'Mummy's fine. Just a bit cross. But not with you. Never with you.'

Lorraine reaches into the footwell for her bags and pulls them onto her lap. 'I think we should probably leave it there for today, Jo.'

I force myself to meet her gaze but I'm shaking with anger. 'So we're done? You're done?'

'Not quite. We need to reschedule another meeting. I'll be in touch with you and Max to arrange a date.'

'Mummy,' says a little voice from the back of the car. 'Mummy, I did a wee wee. Sorry, mummy.'

Elise pulls up her skirt and, sure enough, the tops

of her tights are stained several shades darker. I completely forgot to put her in a nappy before the journey down from Chester. God knows how long she's been desperate for the toilet.

'Oh, dear,' Lorraine says. 'Do you have any clean clothes for her, Jo?'

It's all I can do not to swing for her.

Chapter 19

Can I have a word? Fiona's request rings in Max's ears as he crosses the office and heads for her door. Five seemingly innocuous words but laden with meaning. He reaches for the door handle and tries to think of other five-word sentences that have struck fear into his heart in the past:

Your dad died last night
I couldn't find a heartbeat
I'm going to divorce Max

He stands up straighter as he enters Fiona's office. Whatever she's about to bollock him about, he can take it. He's been through worse; much, much worse.

'Max.' Fiona nods tightly and makes a sweeping gesture with her left hand. 'Take a seat, please.'

Max does as he's told. His boss gives him an appraising look as he settles himself into the chair. He holds her gaze but doesn't say anything. Let her take the first shot. He's not about to hand her any ammo.

'So.' She leans forward on her elbows. 'It's been well over a week since our last chat and I thought we should catch up. Tell me, how are things in Maxworld?'

Maxworld? He fights not to show his disdain on his face. When did Fiona start using saccharine phrases like that? Has she been reading *Management Techniques for Dummies*? Chapter one: Try and put your employees at ease by talking to them like four-year-olds before you deliver a ruthless bollocking.

He shrugs. 'Not great, to be honest, but I don't think we're here to talk about *Maxworld*, are we, Fi?'

Her smile tightens. 'OK, Max. I'll forgo the pleasantries. I asked you in here because you've been dropping the ball. Over the last week you've been absent multiple times, you've delivered late, you've made beginner's errors in your copy and I've had several complaints from members of the public about your attitude.'

'What kind of complaints?'

'That you were surly. That you seemed distracted and uninterested when you were interviewing them, that you got their names wrong, that you misquoted them. Should I go on?'

Max shakes his head.

'Then,' Fiona continues, 'you decide to go walkabout at half past three today and you don't bother to tell anyone where you're going. It's not acceptable, Max. I don't know if you're resting on your laurels after the success of your loan-shark story or if this is a symptom of some kind of malaise, but it's not gone unnoticed. Not by your colleagues, not by the public and certainly not by me.' She leans back in her chair and folds her arms over her chest. Case closed. Now it's his turn to defend himself.

Max rubs his palms back and forth on his thighs as he organises his thoughts. He'd hoped he'd done enough to fly under Fiona's radar but experience had taught him that was unlikely. Not much gets past her, particularly not slacking. It was only a matter of time before she called him in.

'I'm listening.' Fiona pulls her shoulders back. She's bracing herself for a torrent of bullshit.

'Look.' He holds his hands out wide – open, honest body language to counteract her closed posture. 'I'm sorry. My personal life is going to shit. I try to leave it behind when I come into work every day but it's,' – he pauses and stares down at the rough beige carpet – 'it's difficult.'

'In what way?'

'It's my wife.' He looks up again and meets his boss's steady gaze. 'You know she's not been well for a while.'

'Agoraphobia? Yes, you've mentioned it before.'

'Well, it's getting worse. She's become really unstable. Paranoid. Volatile. And I'm worried that she's self-medicating to cope.'

Fiona listens intently as Max describes how much the altercation with Paula upset his wife, how Jo had shoved someone who was obviously mentally ill and how she'd been arrested for possession of drugs. As he explains why he'd left work early because Social

109

Services had become involved, he catches his boss shaking her head.

He pauses. 'What is it?'

'Why didn't you tell me all this?'

He slumps forward in his seat. 'I was . . . ashamed, I guess. I didn't want anyone knowing how bad things had got. I didn't want to be judged.'

'For supporting your wife?' His boss's hard features soften. 'Who'd judge you for that? Certainly not me.'

'It's humiliating. Social Services, for God's sake.'

Fiona's chair creaks as she leans back. She's uncrossed her arms, Max notices. 'Have you taken her to see anyone? A doctor or a psychiatrist?'

'It's tricky. I'm not . . . um . . . I'm not living at home at the moment. I've been staying in the Holiday Inn. Jo wants a divorce.' He tenses as he makes the admission. Jo confided in Helen about wanting a divorce but still hasn't mentioned it to him. Not when she rang him to ask him to pick her up from the police station, not when she asked him to sleep on the sofa that night and not when she rang him to tell him about the appointment with Lorraine Cooper.

'Oh, dear. I'm very sorry to hear that.'

'I don't know how much of that is down to her mental health issues and how much is down to . . .' He shrugs. 'We . . . we haven't had the easiest of times recently but I thought we'd get through it . . .' He tails off again, suddenly uncomfortable with how much he's sharing with Fiona. It feels good to get all this off his chest, but she's still his boss. She may be sympathetic on the surface but, beneath the understanding veneer, he knows she's weighing up how competent he is to continue doing his job.

'What did the social worker say?'

'She'd gone by the time I arrived at the house. So had Jo and Elise. But I spoke to her on the phone.'

God knows what the social worker had made of the whole situation. He'd asked Jo to give her the phone and then he'd gently explained that his wife had been suffering from terrible anxiety recently and that Lorraine should be aware that there was a possibility that his wife had concocted the story about someone ransacking the house because she was ashamed at how messy she'd left it. He'd certainly noticed how untidy it was when he'd driven Jo back from the police station. Lorraine had listened silently while he explained how worried he was about Jo and her ability to look after Elise. A concern that was shared by at least one member of staff at his daughter's nursery.

'I let myself into the house,' he adds. 'It was an absolute shithole. I get why Jo didn't want to let the social worker in, but nothing had been taken. It certainly wasn't a burglary. Jo's convinced that this Paula woman got in and wrecked the place, but there was no sign of forced entry. All the doors and windows were intact. The only way she could have got in was if she'd walked through a wall.'

'Jesus Christ, Max.' Fiona pushes her hair back from her face. 'I had no idea you were going through all this. Bloody hell. I'd noticed that you were looking a bit more knackered than normal but I'd put that down to a few celebratory nights out.'

He snorts through his nose derisively. 'I wish.'

'What are you going to do?'

Max doesn't answer immediately. He lets his gaze wander to the corner of Fiona's office where an enormous yucca plant stands like a sentry, then he rubs his hands over his face, sighs and lets his hands collapse into his lap.

'What can I do?' he says softly. 'I've tried to support her. I've been there for her when she's needed me to be there. I've given her space when she's asked for it. But she's getting worse, not better. And now I'm really worried about Elise.'

'Of course you are,' Fiona breathes and Max can hear the concern in her voice. Fiona's got children too; one's at university and the other is about to do his A-Levels. She's unashamedly non-maternal but she cooed over Elise's baby photos when he showed them round the office, just like all the other parents. 'Listen, Max, I don't imagine there's anything I can do but, you know, if you need a bit of time off to sort things out then just tell me. And if you're struggling with your workload I can take a look at that too.'

'Thank you.' Normally Max would rather die than be this vulnerable in front of Fiona, but he needs her on side and if that means swallowing his pride then so be it. 'I really appreciate—'

He's interrupted by the shrill ring of his mobile. He fishes it out of the inside pocket, glances at the screen and then looks at Fiona.

'It's Jo,' he mouths. There's no need for him to whisper – he hasn't accepted the call yet – but it feels right. It suits the vulnerable side he's just shown his boss.

'Take it,' Fiona mouths back and Max nods.

'Max!' Jo's voice is loud, so animated that they can both hear it, despite the speakerphone not being on. 'Have you been home yet?'

'I have, yes. Where are you?'

'I'm at Helen's. In Cardiff. I'm staying here tonight with Elise. Did you see the state the house was in?'

'I did, yes.'

'Have you rung the police?'

'I thought you were going to.'

'I'd like you to do it, please, Max.'

'But—'

'I can't ring them. I was arrested for possession of drugs! Please Max, I'm not sure how much more of this I can take . . .'

As Jo continues to rant and rail, Max presses the phone into his chest, muffling the receiver. 'Mind if I take this outside?' he whispers to Fiona.

'Of course,' she says and gives him a look of sympathy and bewilderment. 'Absolutely.'

Chapter 20

I've been into the house twice now. The second time was vile; ferreting around in crap so I could smear it all over the place. But the first time, I was in and out like a flash. Hiding the drugs in the toilet cistern felt like a cheap trick – a cliché – a scene from a million crime shows – but I had to make it easy for the police to do their job.

Getting hold of the drugs was a piece of piss; convincing someone else to report them was more difficult. The police won't take one phone call seriously. They'd be raiding houses all the time if everyone with a grudge rang them up and made an allegation. But I know how to turn people round to my way of thinking, to make them feel sorry for me, to convince them they're putting right a wrong.

Idiots.

People are idiots. They hear and they see what they want to see. If I tell them I'm a victim they see me as a victim. They pity me. They want to help. Helping relieves the awkwardness they feel, those uncomfortable feelings of 'shit, I'm glad that's not me'. Well, let them enjoy that brief moment of superiority, because it's all an illusion. They're the ones who lied to the police. Oh dear. Oh dear. Who's the victim now?

Chapter 21

'Well?' Helen says as I hang up the phone. 'What did Max say?'

'The police haven't been in touch since he rang them yesterday which means we still don't know when someone's going to come round to test for fingerprints. But they're treating it as a burglary, regardless of whether anything was taken.'

'Well, that's good news.' Her anxious expression softens into a smile and she reaches across the kitchen table to tap my hand. 'I told you they'd take it seriously, didn't I?'

I was a silent, shaking wreck when I turned up at her house yesterday evening. For Elise's sake I held myself together all the way from Bristol to Cardiff, but as soon as she and Ben were tucked up in bed I burst into tears. Helen put one hand on my shoulder and guided me towards the kitchen. She sat quietly beside me as I sobbed, then, when I finally quietened, she pushed a glass of red wine towards me and said, 'Talk when you're ready.'

She listened as everything tumbled out, in one big, hopeless, confused mess, then she stood up, walked over and wrapped her arms around me.

'It's going to be OK, Jo,' she said softly. 'You're safe. Nothing bad can happen here.'

That made me start crying again. The relief I felt at being able to talk to someone who wasn't going to criticise me, arrest me or take my child away was overwhelming. I didn't have to be strong, combative or evasive any more. I didn't have to protect Helen from what had happened. I didn't have to worry about hurting her feelings or not adding to her stress. She wanted to help me. And, equally importantly, she believed every word I'd just told her.

'So what happens next?' Helen asks now.

'I don't know. Yesterday the police told Max they'd make enquiries, whatever that means.'

I glance at my mobile, to check I ended the call to my husband before I say any more. He texted me three times after I slammed the phone down on him yesterday. The first one was angry, telling me that he had been in a really important meeting with Fiona when I'd rung up to scream at him. Then, several hours later, a single line – *When are you coming back?* I didn't reply. When I reached for my phone this morning there was another text waiting. *Can you ring me please? I need to know that you and Elise are OK.*

'I don't think he believes me, Helen, about any of

117

the stuff that's happened. He saw the state of the house and he still called me hysterical on the phone. When I finally convinced him to ring the police he asked if I should go back to my GP to get my meds increased.'

She sighs. 'So you're serious, then, about divorcing him?'

'Yes. Our marriage is over. There's nothing left worth saving.' I stand up and peer round the kitchen door and across the hallway into the living room. Elise is sitting on the sofa, one of Effie's ears in her mouth, staring, transfixed, at the television. 'I should take her out. To the park or something.'

There's a small gasp behind me.

'What?' I turn to look at Helen.

'Seriously?'

I stare at her, stumped, and then I understand. She's not the only one who can't remember the last time I suggested taking Elise to the park.

'If you're up to it there's a lovely park five minutes' walk away. I often take Ben there after school.'

I try to imagine walking out of Helen's front door and strolling hand in hand down the street to a park I've never visited before. I picture Elise laughing and squealing as I push her higher and higher on the swings but I'm distracted by my thudding heart and the line of sweat that trickles down my temple. I don't think I can do this.

'Jo.' Helen touches my forearm. 'It's OK. You don't need to. We could bundle Elise up and take her out into the garden. We've still got Ben's old slide and

118

plastic playhouse in the shed. She'll still have a lovely time.'

'But I want her to have a normal life, Helen. I want her to be able to play outside with other children.'

'She does that at nursery.'

'You know what I mean.'

'I do. Of course I do. And suggesting a trip to the park is a good start. One step at a time. OK?'

We have a lovely time playing chase, slides and houses in Helen's back garden, despite the frosty February air. When we finally return to the kitchen our noses and cheeks are pink. We eat lunch, all three of us around the small kitchen table, and Helen and I both laugh at Elise's horrified reaction when Helen dares to put a tomato on her plate. Afterwards I wash up while my best friend produces the remains of a packet of flour, some salt and a jug of water and helps my daughter make play dough. The afternoon passes in a blur of painting, playing and cups of tea. I try my best not to dwell on what's happened, or to worry about what could happen, but I can't ignore the feeling of dread sitting low in my chest. Each time I fall silent Helen notices and cracks a joke or makes a comment, drawing my attention back to her and Elise. I don't know what I did to deserve such an amazing friend, but the gratitude I feel is over-whelming.

'I'll only be gone for twenty minutes tops,' she says now, pulling on her coat. 'You sure you'll be OK?'

'Of course.' I slot another Duplo block into the

castle I'm building with Elise on the living-room carpet. 'We'll be fine.'

Helen does up her zip. 'Help yourself to tea or squash or whatever you need.'

'We'll be fine, honestly. Go and get Ben.'

'OK. Well, I've got my phone.' She taps the pocket of her coat. 'Ring me if . . .' She shakes her head and laughs. 'You're not going to need to ring me! Have a cup of tea. Chill. I'll see you in a bit.'

I hear the sound of her footsteps in the hallway and the click of the front door as she pulls it shut behind her, then there is silence, save Elise's snuffling beside me. Her nose has been running since lunch but I'm not overly concerned. When I first took her to nursery I couldn't believe how many coughs and colds she came home with, but I'm used to the odd sniffle now. Cuddles, Calpol and plenty of sleep, that's normally enough.

'Here.' I pull a tissue out of my pocket and hold it to my daughter's drippy nose. 'Blow.'

Elise presses her face into the tissue and moves her head from side to side, smearing snot over both cheeks.

'Eww!' I dab it away. 'Snot bags!'

My daughter giggles and reaches for the dirty tissue. I hold it above my head and laugh. 'No! It's dirty!'

She stands up and launches herself at me, one hand on my shoulder, the other reaching for the Kleenex.

'Mine! Mine!'

I dig around in the pocket of my jeans for a clean tissue that I can substitute for the dirty one but, as

120

my fingers close over the cellophane packet, my phone rings. Elise wails in protest as I scramble to my feet and cross the hallway into the kitchen where my phone is vibrating on the table.

'Mine!' she shouts, clutching my leg as I press my mobile to my ear.

'Hello?'

'Hello, Jo,' says a voice I recognise. 'It's Lorraine Hooper. Are you free to have a quick word?'

My stomach lurches. 'What about?'

'I'd rather talk to you about it in person if that's possible.'

'I'm in Cardiff,' I say. 'I'm seeing a friend.'

'Right, right.' I can almost imagine her nodding her head. 'Well, it is very important. Were you planning on coming back to Bristol today at all?'

'Not really, no. The last couple of weeks have been really disruptive for me and my daughter and we could do with a couple of days away to relax and—'

'It's your husband,' Lorraine says. 'He's applied to the court for a child arrangement order for Elise.'

'A what?'

'A residence order. Max wants Elise to live with him.'

Chapter 22

'Are you OK, Jo?' Helen whispers as Mr Harrison flicks through paperwork.

I nod mutely but I keep my gaze trained on the closed office door. To get back onto the street I need to turn right, walk down the corridor, take a left, get into the lift, press 'G' and then I'd be out of the glass front doors of Harrison & Partners, family law solicitors. The car is in the NCP car park on Prince Street, floor 3, parked in the corner next to a red Golf GTI. But what if there's a fire? Mr Harrison didn't tell us how to get out safely and I didn't see any stairs when we got out of the lift. I saw some when we came in. They were on the right of the reception desk. The lifts were on the left. So that means if I turn left out of the door and carry on down the corridor and take a—

'Jo.' Helen places her hand over mine and squeezes it. 'He's going to help you. Try not to worry.'

I nod again and focus my attention on the framed

certificate on Richard Harrison's wall, on the gold band on the third finger of his left hand, on his receding hairline, on the dark hairs that protrude from each nostril, on the studious look in his eyes behind his wire-framed glasses. He was almost blasé when I spoke to him on Tuesday afternoon. 'Of course I can help you, Mrs Blackmore. It's natural to panic in a situation like this but you've come to the right place.' Helen was amazing when I told her about the phone call I received from Lorraine Hooper. She got straight onto her laptop and started Googling. Then she got out her phone, rang a number and handed it over to me. The earliest he could see me was today, Thursday. I spent most of Wednesday Googling for information on residency orders and UK family law.

This morning she arranged for Ben's dad to take him to school and pick him up afterwards. We set off for Bristol at quarter past seven, with Helen in her car leading the way and me behind, with Elise strapped in her car seat in the back. We'd considered just taking one car but Helen's got an early meeting tomorrow and she didn't want to end up stranded if she needs to stay with me in Bristol overnight. I didn't want to leave Elise at nursery, not when I'd kept her away for three days in a row, but Helen convinced me it was the right thing to do. Elise would be fine, she said. She'll be surrounded by familiar faces while we talk to Mr Harrison. When we pulled up outside the nursery and I saw my daughter's excited face, any doubts I might have had about dropping her off swiftly disappeared.

'Right.' Mr Harrison looks up from his pile of papers. 'So, as I explained to you on the phone the other day, your husband has applied to the courts for a residence order for Elise, that is to say that he wants the child to reside with him. He has also applied for an interim residence order. This means that the court will decide who Elise will live with while they make their final decision.'

He pauses. 'Do you understand so far?'

I grip the arms of the chair.

'Yes,' I breathe. 'I understand.'

Helen reaches across the gap between our two chairs and touches my hand.

Mr Harrison glances back down at the papers on his desk. He seemed so confident when I walked into his office. He shook my hand firmly, offered us a seat and a coffee, barely reacted when we both said no and then strode back to his seat. But the atmosphere in the room has changed since he's looked through his file. I don't know if it's my trepidation I can sense, or his.

'OK.' He sits back in his chair and runs his hands back and forth over the plastic arms. 'The situation we have is this – your husband thinks that Elise would be safer in his care than yours and, in his court application form, he has listed areas of concern surrounding your mental health and your drug problem.'

'I haven't got one! They were planted.'

'And we'll work together to prove that. We will also have to prove that your mental health issues are being correctly and appropriately dealt with and that they in no way prevent you from being a good mother to your daughter. Your husband mentions your agoraphobia, your anxiety and your irrational behaviour with the nursery staff who care for your daughter. He suggests that you are not fully recovered from the postnatal depression you suffered after your daughter was born, or the second-trimester loss of your son Henry eighteen months earlier.'

I press my hands to my mouth but there's no hiding my horrified gasp. Henry's death was the worst thing to ever happen to either us. It broke us both. I felt as though someone had ripped out my heart. Max did too. I hated God for taking Henry away from us. I hated the world. Why me? Why us? Why Henry? Why punish us by taking our baby away from us before he even got chance to draw breath? The days after Henry's death blurred together. I'd drink myself to sleep only to wake up and feel the pain afresh all over again. Some mornings I cried because opening my eyes meant I was still alive. The pain dragged on and on and on as, somehow, I lived through the most horrible, horrendous, agonising days of my life. I felt as though a hole had been ripped in my chest and it would never, ever close.

And then I got pregnant with Elise. I was so scared. I didn't trust my body any more. I didn't trust God. I'd already lost one baby. What if he took her too? When we had our twenty-week scan I was convinced the sonographer would fall quiet as he searched for a heartbeat. I dug my nails into Max's palm as I waited for those words, those two terrible words. 'I'm sorry.'

But the sonographer didn't say them. Elise was still there, still kicking and punching and moving. Still alive.

I should have felt relieved. We'd passed a milestone but I couldn't relax. There was no way I could relax until she was safely in my arms. But there was no end to my fear. After she was born I barely slept. I kept watch as Elise snuffled in her cot beside me. I was convinced that if I fell asleep she would die. And I wouldn't let that happen, not again. I had lost one child, I wouldn't lose two.

Mr Harrison clears his throat. 'I can see that you're distressed, Mrs Blackmore. You're not alone in finding your husband's allegations shocking and disturbing. I'm afraid most women feel the same way. But that's exactly what they are at this point, allegations. And our job is to disprove them.'

I can't speak – my throat is so tight, I couldn't even if I wanted to. I dig my heels into the thin carpet and tighten my grip on the arms of the chair. *Don't cry. Don't cry.* But I already am.

Why would Max do this? He loves Elise but he would never use what I've been through to strike such a low blow. I know he's found my behaviour irritating and his patience has waned over the last few months, but I'm a good mother and he knows that. I'm the first person Elise sees when she wakes up in the morning and the last person she sees at night. She cries out for me when she has a nightmare. She runs into my arms when she's upset. She loves him but he's never there when she needs him. I am! I've always been there for her. Always.

'Are you OK for me to continue, Mrs Blackmore?'

'Yes.' The word sounds strangled, unintelligible, so I cough to clear my throat. 'But could I . . . could I just see the form? I want to check that it's in my husband's handwriting.'

'Of course.'

Helen frowns as I take the piece of paper with quivering hands.

'What's up?' she whispers, but I can't tear my eyes from the words in front of me. It's definitely Max's handwriting – large and bold with deep biro indentations. And there's his signature at the end, stating that what he's written is a statement of truth.

'Jo?' she says. 'What is it?'

I can't believe that this is really happening. It doesn't feel real. Why would he do this? Why not talk to me? It seems like only last week Max was talking about the three of us moving up to Chester. So why the sudden change of heart? It doesn't make sense. None of this makes sense.

'Thank you.' I hand the court application form back to Mr Harrison then sit back, hard, in my chair. The jolt of pain as the wood hits my shoulder blades is strangely reassuring. This isn't a dream. It's real.

'Am I OK to continue?' my solicitor asks.

'Yes.'

'OK.' He presses his glasses into his nose and reads from the piece of paper I just handed back to him. 'Précising what he's written, your husband says that the nursery have concerns about your lateness and your manner towards their staff. They find you to be abrupt and aloof. They report that you acted unusually when you arrived to collect your daughter on one occasion, that you were sweating and breathless and that you ignored a senior member of staff when she repeatedly asked you why you were disruptive—'

'I was looking for Elise! If I was abrupt and aloof it was because I was terrified that someone had taken—'

'Jo.' Helen gives me a look. 'Just let him . . .' She nods at Mr Harrison to continue.

'Max also says the nursery staff have informed him that Elise has begun to wet herself when she'd previously been toilet-trained. He states that she's turned up to nursery dirty and unkempt on several occasions.'

I shake my head. That was because I had a bad back and Max knows that. And I'm sure I told Alice about it and apologised for the state Elise was in. Or had I just dropped her off and run because I was late for work? I can't remember.

Mr Harrison continues. 'Your husband also states that one member of staff overheard you admitting to another parent that you had deliberately shoved your daughter to the floor whilst breastfeeding her. She also told him that, when Elise started at nursery, you commented that you were glad they provided home-cooked meals because at least then Elise would get four lots of fruit and vegetables a week rather than turkey twizzlers and chips every night.'

'That was a joke!' I look at Helen. 'Max knows I don't feed Elise rubbish.'

'He does,' she says, but I can see the shock in her

128

eyes at the accusations my husband is levelling against me. She's as incredulous as I am.

'Max states that he's spoken to Social Services,' Mr Harrison continues. 'He says they told him that you were obstructive and aggressive during Lorraine Hooper's meeting with you, that you wouldn't let her in because you claimed that someone else was responsible for the dirty and unkempt condition of your home and that she was forced to conduct her interview with you in your car in the street. Max adds that you have a history of mental illness, including postnatal depression, and he thinks that you are struggling to cope with your current condition and the stresses of looking after—'

'Stop!' I hold up my hands. I can't deal with this. It's too much. 'Please, just stop.'

Mr Harrison peers at me over the top of his reading glasses, then slowly lowers the papers in his hands. He clears his throat as Helen gets out of her chair and puts an arm around my shoulders.

'You will get through this,' she whispers in my ear. 'I know it doesn't feel like it now but you will. I promise. I don't know what Max is playing at but—'

'If I could just, er . . .' My solicitor coughs. 'If I could just interrupt.'

Helen reluctantly releases me but she remains by my side, crouched by my chair.

'Go on,' I say.

'What you have here,' – he taps the piece of paper in front of him with his index finger – 'is only one side of the story – Max's story. These are just allegations, serious allegations admittedly, and your husband and his solicitor will have to produce evidence in court to back them up. We, of course, will refute those allegations and build a case to respond. I will need a series of statements from you – about nursery, the drug allegations, your mental health, et cetera – but if you're not up to it today we can schedule another appointment. I know Max's allegations look damning but he hasn't once suggested that you have harmed your child or are likely to do so, and that's important. Are you and Elise currently living in the family home?'

I shake my head. 'I've been staying with Helen for the last few days.'

'Is Mr Blackmore living in the family home?'

'No. He's staying at a hotel. Or at least he was, the last time I spoke to him.'

'Then I suggest that you move back in.'

'I'll stay with you tonight,' Helen says quickly.

I want to tell her that she doesn't need to. That I'm strong enough to go back home alone. But that would be a lie.

'Thank you,' I say gratefully.

'Great,' Mr Harrison says. 'Remaining in the family home will strengthen your case. As will restoring Elise's routine. Not,' he adds quickly, 'that I'm suggesting you keep her at the same nursery. I can see why that would be an issue. But do find her a place somewhere else. Are you employed?'

'Yes, I'm a Student Support Officer at the university, although I haven't been in for a few days.'

'Well, hang on to your job too. We need to convince

the judge that Elise is better off in your care. You say that your husband has been working as an investigative journalist, that he's frequently away from home and you maintain the routine and the stability in your daughter's life. That's what we concentrate on. The rest is circumstantial.'

'So you think you could win?' Helen asks.

He smiles, for the first time since we walked into his office. 'Of course I do.'

'Oh, thank God.' I slump forward and rest my head in my hands. 'Oh, thank God.'

'The court date has been set for four weeks' time. That allows for safeguarding checks to take place with the police and your social worker. I suggest we meet again soon to go over your statement but, in the meantime, you might want to consider visiting your GP to discuss your condition. If we can get him or her onside, to attest to the fact that your condition is being monitored and appropriately treated, that can only serve to help your case.'

'See?' Helen puts an arm around my shoulders. 'It's going to be OK. Everything's going to be OK, Jo.'

I don't reply but, for the first time in a long time, a tiny flame of hope sparks in my heart.

Chapter 23

'Max!' Fiona is standing in the doorway of her office, one hand on her hip, the other on the door frame. She inclines her head, gesturing for him to join her.

Max pushes himself away from his desk, but he does it slowly, torturously, as though it takes all his strength to propel his wheeled chair a couple of inches backwards. In the last half an hour he's received five missed calls from Jo – three to his mobile, two to his office phone. He's set both to go straight to voicemail. It's a cowardly thing to do, but his head is throbbing after a night of heavy drinking and he really can't cope with Jo's histrionics, not when he promised Fiona that he'd get his act together at work.

'Yes, boss.' He approaches his editor with his hands in his pockets and forces a smile.

'Max,' Fiona says curtly, 'I thought I told you to delete my direct number from your wife's phone.'

'Oh God. What's happened?'

132

'I've just spent the last five minutes listening to her rant down the phone. If you'd bothered to answer your own phone you'd know that she's currently in reception, waiting for you to go and speak to her.'

'Shit.' Max holds out his hands, palms out. 'Fiona, I'm so sorry.'

'It's not me you should be apologising to.'

Max shifts his weight from one foot to the other and tries to ignore the feeling of dread that grips his chest. What the hell has Jo told his boss? She was on his side the other day. She overheard how irrational Jo was being on the phone. 'I'm sorry,' he says. 'I'm not sure I understand.'

'Max, I know things haven't been easy recently and I really appreciate you opening up to me about what you've been through, but you can't leave it up to a social worker to tell your wife that you were filing for custody of your daughter and then ignore all her calls. I know you said she's not well but you're only making things worse for yourself by avoiding her. And I really don't appreciate her turning up and causing a scene.'

'I know. I know.' Max lets his gaze drift to his feet. 'I'll talk to her. I will.'

'Excellent. She's waiting for you downstairs in the lobby. You've got fifteen minutes. And if she ever rings me again you'll know about it.'

Max takes the stairs rather than the lift. With each step his anxiety grows. There are two possible scenarios – either Jo's going to be angry and she's

133

going to call him all the words under the sun, or she's going to be tearful and broken-hearted. He'd rather she was angry, he can deal with that. But if she's vulnerable he's going to feel like a shit and second-guess himself. But she's not well. Regardless of how you look at the situation, she's ill and the situation with Paula has escalated her symptoms. He's never seen her so jumpy and scared and her behaviour is becoming increasingly unpredictable. One day she's at home, the next she's at her parents' or at Helen's. Poor Elise is being dragged here, there and everywhere. God only knows what kind of effect Jo's erratic behaviour is having on her. Filing for a residence order was the last resort. He'd tried everything – talking to Jo, reassuring her, offering to move back in. He even offered to relocate to Chester. But she blocked or ignored everything he suggested. Of course she's worried about Paula, why wouldn't she be? But you need a level head to deal with a situation like that. She lashed out at her, for God's sake! Talk about escalating a situation.

If he had custody of Elise he'd make sure she was safe while the Paula situation was sorted. Now his investigation is over he'll be keeping regular office hours and he'll be able to drop Elise at nursery and pick her up. He can take her to the park, to the zoo, to soft play. Jo could take some time out from work and move up to Chester to look after her parents and visit at the weekends. She and Elise could play together in the house while he went out to give them some space. Or perhaps he'd stay with them and join in the fun, that's if Jo ever realises that he's not the bad guy.

Yes, he tells himself as he opens the door to reception and flashes his pass at Scott, the security guard, as he heads through the glass gates. That's what he needs to hang on to – he's not doing this for him, he's doing it for them all.

He can see the anger in his wife's eyes from across the small reception area. She's wearing her blonde hair tied back in a low ponytail and she's dressed in smart black trousers, heeled boots and a grey blouse. In her lap is her grey Wallis coat and her red handbag. Max is confused by her smart appearance, just for a moment, and then he realises – she must have been to see a solicitor.

'Where's Elise?' he asks as he draws closer.

Jo stands up. 'At nursery.'

'You're back then?'

'Yes, we've moved back into the house if that's what you mean,' she says and he suppresses the urge to swear. His solicitor *told* him to move back into the house as soon as possible but he put it off because he thought he had time. Jo sounded so freaked out on the phone the other day he'd assumed there was no way she'd set foot in their house again until the police had arrested Paula. Her solicitor has obviously convinced her otherwise.

As his wife's gaze flicks towards the receptionist and security guard, Max tries to read her body language. Behind the anger in her eyes there's anxiety. He can see it in her white-knuckle grip on her handbag and the way she keeps rubbing her lips together. She's only visited his office once before, when she was pregnant with Henry and arrived to pick him up for their twenty-week scan. Jo was nervous. She said she hadn't felt the baby move for a while, and was sipping orange juice in the hope the sugar rush would get him moving again. The memory of what happened next makes Max's body sag with grief. He feels an overwhelming urge to reach for his wife and hold her close but when she looks back at him with cold, angry eyes the feeling vaporises.

'Why are you doing this?' Jo asks, her voice low and controlled.

Max shakes his head. Thinking about Henry has clouded his mind; his carefully rehearsed lines have gone.

'Why are you doing this?' she asks again.

He looks at his feet, racked with indecision. It's not too late. He could make this stop. He could ring his solicitor and tell him that he's changed his mind. They could all return to the house, all three of them, and try and make things work. But that would never happen, would it? Any hope of reconciliation is a fairy tale. Jo was already planning to move to Chester, long before any of this happened, and she told Helen that she wanted to divorce him. If he cancels the residence order Jo will proceed with the divorce and move up to Chester with Elise. How's his daughter going to have a normal life if that happens? Without him she'll never get to go outside, never get to play with other children in the park. Jo won't take her out and there's no way Brigid or Andy could. Elise needs him. He's her dad and he loves her.

'Because you're not well,' he says, looking his wife in the eye. 'And I think you've been self-medicating to cope. And that's OK. I understand why you'd do that. But this isn't just about you. This is about Elise and what's best for her. I'm not trying to take her away from you. I just want to give her a bit of security while you get yourself well. I never wanted it to come to this, Jo, but what other choice is there? You don't want me in the house. You don't want me to move to Chester with you and you keep disappearing at the drop of a hat. I'm worried about Elise, sweetheart. I just want to make sure she's OK.'

His wife sways back and forth as she stares at him, her eyes wide and disbelieving, her lips pressed together in a thin line.

'I tried to support you,' Max says. 'I did everything I could to—'

He jolts backwards as Jo thumps him on the chest with her balled fists.

'You bastard!' she screams as she hits him again. 'You fucking bastard!'

'Jo.' He grips hold of her wrists as Scott, the security guard, rushes from behind the desk. 'Jo, stop it. I'm trying to help you. Please, don't do this. Please don't make it any harder than it already is.'

'You lied!' she shouts into his face. 'Everything you said on your form is a lie!'

'Miss.' Scott, a thick-set man in his early forties with cropped hair and tattoos snaking from beneath the cuffs of his thick black jacket, appears beside them and puts a hand on Jo's shoulder. 'You need to leave.'

'Get off me!' She twists her wrists out of Max's grip and takes a step backwards. He braces himself for another onslaught but Jo doesn't say a word. Instead she stoops down, picks up her handbag and coat and stalks out of the building.

Max's breath clouds the air as he walks down Redcross Street. He is too busy concentrating on putting one foot in front of the other to feel the cold.

'Sorry,' he mutters as he shoulders a lamp post. He presses a hand to the icy metal and launches himself back towards the centre of the pavement. 'Sorry.'

He continues onwards, autopilot taking over as he heads for his hotel. He only meant to drink enough to numb his emotions but he's had one whisky too many and his vision is as cloudy as his brain. The pavement looms up at him, a grey tombstone littered with fag butts and flattened chewing gum. He reaches out his right hand, touches the cool red brick of an office building and tries to steady himself, but the motion of cars flashing by makes him feel sick. He closes his eyes, blinks several times and looks back at the road but still the cars come, the beam of their headlights so intense he feels like he is on stage. Ladies and gentlemen, boys and girls, please welcome Max Blackmore – shit journalist, crap husband, terrible father.

'Fuck you!' he shouts at the cars, only vaguely aware of a young woman crossing the road to avoid passing him. 'You don't know . . . you don't know what . . .'

He shakes his head and launches himself forward again. Screw them. He's not a bad man. Everything he's done he's done for his child. He thinks fleetingly of his own father, a man who walked out on his family in search of his next hit and died destitute and alone in a dirty squat in East London with a needle in his arm, and he makes a promise to himself. He won't get drunk again. Only a weak man turns to drugs or drink as a crutch to get through life and he's not a weak man. He's a—

He smiles to himself as he spots a familiar sign at the end of the street. It's blurred and illegible but, even in his inebriated state, he recognises it as the name of his hotel. He reaches into the inside pocket of his jacket, in search of his key card, and feels a jolt of panic when his fingers don't close over his wallet. He pats himself frantically then grunts with satisfaction as he finally locates it, along with his phone. He fumbles both out of his pocket, but his grip has gone and they drop to the pavement. He bends to reach for them.

He grasps his phone but, as his fingers graze the leather of his wallet, the air is knocked from his lungs. It is as though a car has mounted the pavement and run straight into him. But it's not a car that bundles him into a side street, hurls him at a skip, then hauls him up by the throat and smacks him in the face.

'Where's the money?'

Max's ears are ringing and he can't open his right eye. He shakes his head in confusion and is rewarded with another punch.

'Where's the money?'

He holds out his right hand, his wallet and phone still, miraculously, in his grasp. 'Here,' he grunts. 'Take it.'

His hand is slapped away and the wallet falls to the ground. 'No, you arsehole. The money. Paula's money.'

'I don't know.' He shakes his head. 'I don't know what you're talking about.'

Pain shoots up his jaw and into his ear as his phone is ripped from his fingers and he's thumped again, then everything goes black.

Chapter 24

It is 11 p.m. Elise is tucked up in bed, still snuffly with cold but fast asleep. I envy her ability to drop off to sleep the moment her eyelids close. I don't think I've had a decent night's sleep in weeks and God knows what time I'll pass out tonight.

I haven't heard from Max since I saw him earlier. It wasn't my husband who traipsed down the stairs of the *Bristol News* building, his eyes trained on his feet until he had no choice but to look me in the eye. He looked like Max. He sounded like Max. But he was so cold, so detached, so utterly lacking in warmth and understanding that I barely recognised him. He wasn't my husband. He wasn't the man I'd fallen in love with, laughed with, slept with and built a life with. He wasn't the Max who held me as I sobbed myself to sleep after we lost Henry. He wasn't the man who held my hand and told me that we weren't going to lose another baby as I pushed Elise into the world.

When I hit him today it was partly through anger and partly to shock him back into himself.

It didn't work.

I managed to hold myself together until I got to the café where I'd agreed to meet Helen and then promptly burst into tears. She ushered me out and back to the car where she sat beside me and held my hand as I cried. When I finally stopped crying and all I could feel was a numb, heavy sensation in my chest, she drove me to the nursery to collect Elise, then took us both home and helped me clear away all the rubbish from the hallway, living room and kitchen.

She went to bed at half past nine but I can't sleep. For the last hour and a half I've been sitting up in bed, with a hardback notepad on my lap, writing a list of all the ways I can offer Elise a stable, happy life, and all the reasons Max can't. The shock I felt when Mr Harrison read out Max's statement has faded. I won't let him take my daughter from me. I will do anything I have to to keep her safe.

Elise cries out – loud, angry, desperate – and I wake with a start. The only light in the bedroom is the red neon glow of the alarm clock beside the bed. 2.57 a.m.

My notebook lies open on the floor beside the bed. I must have fallen asleep as I was writing. But why is the lamp off? I reach out and click the switch. Nothing. Either there's been a power cut or the bulb's gone. My mobile's not on the bedside table. I must have left it downstairs. I swing my legs out of bed, cross the bedroom and reach for the door handle. All the lights are off on the upstairs landing but Elise's door is ajar. Inside, a battery-powered night light casts a dim yellow glow over her bookshelf. I push at the door and slip inside the room. A floorboard creaks under my weight and Elise sits up in her cot, staring blindly in my direction.

'It's OK, darling.' I crouch at the side of her cot and stroke the hair from her face. Her brow is hot and sweaty, her cheeks wet with tears. 'It's just me.'

'Daddy?' she says and my heart twists in my chest. She's got no idea why Max has vanished from our lives. He claims he wants the best for our daughter but how is this good for her? We could have come to a visitation arrangement without involving the courts. I wouldn't have stopped him seeing her. That was only ever an empty threat.

'No, sweetheart,' I say softly. 'It's Mummy. Come on, lie back down. It's still dark.'

'I want Daddy!' she says, but she doesn't protest as I lift her slightly and lay her back down on the mattress so her head's on the pillow.

She closes her eyes as I stroke her hair. 'Ssssh. Ssssh. Go to sleep. Mummy's here.'

As her breathing steadies and slows I step back out of the room, taking care to miss the creaky floorboard at the foot of the cot. When we sleep-trained Elise as a baby, Max and I would take it in turns to shush and pat her to sleep. Crippled by sleep exhaustion, and terrified that she'd wake up again, we'd creep back out of the room, tentatively testing our weight on each floorboard, as though crossing a mine-field.

I exhale softly as I leave the room, then stiffen at a noise from downstairs. It's a high-pitched squeak, like the sound of a trainer stopping abruptly on a tile.

'Helen?' I whisper. 'Is that you?'

I take a tentative step across the landing and reach for the banister.

'Helen?'

I don't want to look over the banister. What if Paula's down there, standing at the foot of the stairs, looking back up at me through the darkness?

It's not a power cut, says a little voice in my head. *She's flipped the switch in the fuse box. And my mobile's downstairs. I can't call for help.*

My heart's beating so hard I feel sick.

You need to look, Jo.

But I can't move. I can't even unfurl my fingers from the banister. All I can do is stare at the pale magnolia wall in front of me and listen.

There are no footsteps, no squeaks, no noise at all coming from downstairs.

The house is silent, save the faint snuffling sound coming from my daughter's bedroom and the *drum-drum-drum* of my own heartbeat in my ears.

Whoever is downstairs is listening too. And they're watching. They can see my fingers, curled over the banister. They know I'm up here. They're waiting to see what I do next.

I snatch my fingers away from the white, glossy rail and sprint across the landing. I don't stop to knock at Helen's bedroom door. Instead I burst straight in.

And there she is. Lying on her back, spreadeagled on the spare bed, the duvet down by her waist, her right hand hanging limply over the edge of the bed.

'Helen!' I tug on his wrist. 'Helen, wake up!'

She groans in response and tries to pull her hand away from me. As she does, I hear another noise – a crashing sound from downstairs.

'Helen!' I yank on her arm again. 'Helen, wake up! There's someone downstairs.'

Her eyes fly open and she stares at me in confusion and shock.

'Jo?' Her voice is thick with sleep.

'I think someone's broken in.'

'Shit!' In a heartbeat she is up and out of the bed, looking frantically around the room. 'I left my phone downstairs. Have you got yours?'

I shake my head. 'No.'

We share a look.

'Fuck,' she says under her breath.

'What do we do?'

'I don't know. Have you got . . .' She scans the room again. 'Have you got a . . . I don't know . . . a cricket bat or something?'

I shake my head. 'No, nothing.' I clutch my friend's arm. It feels clammy under my palm. 'I need to get back to Elise's room. What if Paula . . .'

'Go!' She reaches for the door and shoves me out of the room.

'We've called the police!' she shouts as we sprint

145

across the landing. 'They'll be here soon. You'd better get the fuck out of—'

'Helen, no!' I grab her by the wrist and yank her into Elise's room. 'Help me!' I gesture at Elise's chest of drawers and between us we tug and push it until it's wedged up against the bedroom door. Elise stirs in her sleep, and pushes away the duvet I laid over her just five minutes ago. Miraculously she doesn't wake up.

'What now?' Helen whispers. 'Should we open the window and shout for help? Bang on the walls and try and wake up the neighbours?'

'I don't know.' I'm trying to think clearly but my heart is beating so rapidly in my chest I feel sick. If Paula is alone downstairs we could potentially overpower her. But not if she's armed. Why has she come back? She's had two opportunities now to search for whatever it is she thinks Max took from her. But he didn't take anything – he swore on Elise's life he doesn't know who she is. So either Max is lying or Paula is mentally unhinged. I'm not sure which possibility terrifies me most.

'Jo?' Helen says. 'What do you want to do?'

'There's nothing we can do,' I whisper. 'The window doesn't open. It's been painted shut since we moved in. I've asked Max to sort it a hundred times but—'

'Bang on the wall then?'

I shake my head. 'They've gone on holiday.'

'Fuck.' Helen swears softly.

Chapter 25

I have never been so glad to see the sun rise. For the last four hours I've been lying on the floor beside Elise's cot with one of her teddies propped beneath my head as a pillow and a sheet from her chest of drawers as a blanket. Helen fell asleep beside me about an hour ago. Elise is asleep too, but I haven't slept a wink.

'Helen.' I gently shake her by the shoulder. 'Helen, you need to wake up. It's six thirty. You need to get back to Cardiff to collect Ben.'

She groans softly as she twists from her back onto her side. There's confusion in her eyes as they flicker open and she looks up at me.

'Shit, sorry. I didn't mean to fall asleep.' She sits up abruptly. 'Are you OK? Have you heard anything from downstairs?'

'Nothing since we came in here.'

'Should we go down? Or I can go if you want to stay up here with Elise?'

'I'll go.'

'No, Jo, you can't.'

'It's OK. Honestly. I'll go.'

'Well, I'll stand at the top of the stairs then.'

'All right.'

'Well?' Helen asks as I climb back up the stairs.

I shake my head. 'Nothing's broken. Nothing's missing. The TV, the DVD player, Elise's iPad, they're still in the living room. And both our mobiles.'

'How did she get in?'

'She must have the spare key. It isn't on the hook by the front door any more.'

'When did you last see it?'

'I don't know. I can't remember. I'll have to get the locks changed.'

'What? You can't stay here!'

'Mr Harrison said I have to. He said it would strengthen my case against Max. Anyway, where else can I go? I can't stay at Mum and Dad's, not when he's so poorly.'

'Stay at mine.'

'Are you sure?' She doesn't need to ask me twice.

'Oh my God. Of course.' She glances at her watch. 'Shit. I really need to get changed and go. Can you bundle Elise into the car in her pyjamas?'

'I need to tell Max what happened. And the police.'

'Ring them from my house.'

'What if the police want to come round? I need to be here to let them in and tell them what happened.'

'OK,' she says. 'But I want you to text me every

hour to let me know that you're safe. I'll be back at home from ten o'clock. Turn up whenever you want.'

'I will. And Helen?'

'Yes?'

'Thank you. For everything.'

'This.' Elise reaches into her chest of drawers and pulls out a scratchy blue Elsa dress and throws it on the floor. 'And this.' A pair of rainbow-coloured tights appear next to it.

'How about a nice cardigan?' I suggest.

'No.'

'OK.' I gesture for her to come closer so I can undress her. Now is not the time for an argument about appropriate clothing for the winter. I'll wrestle her into a coat when we leave for the police station. I'm going to ask to speak to DS Merriott. And I won't leave until I do.

'OK then, sweetheart.' I tug down Elise's pyjama bottoms, remove her nappy and put it in the bin in her room, then reach into her chest of drawers for a pair of pants. I put them on then tug the end of one of her pyjama sleeves. 'Let's get this off too.'

She raises her arms obediently and I lift the hem of her pyjama top. I've almost raised it as high as her head when I spot them – dark bruises on both sides of her back, each one the size and shape of a penny. There are four bruises on each side.

I turn her towards me. There are two small bruises on her ribs. They're the size of thumbs.

Chapter 26

The locum couldn't be more different from my normal GP. Old Dr Fullerton always looks exhausted and speeds through my appointments like she can't wait to be rid of me. Dr McGrath, on the other hand, must be in her mid-twenties, and listens intently as I tell her about the marks that have appeared on Elise's back overnight. My eyes fill with tears as I tell her that I think the person who broke into my house did so deliberately to harm my daughter.

The doctor's pale-brown eyes widen with shock as she looks from me to Elise. 'Have you told the police?'

'Not yet. I wanted to get Elise checked over first.'

She looks me up and down. 'And you're OK? You weren't hurt?'

'No. I didn't see them. I woke up in the night and checked on Elise. I thought she was OK but Paula . . . Paula . . .' My throat is so tight I choke on her name. 'She'd already got to her.'

'It's OK.' She pushes a box of tissues to me and then swings side to side on her chair as though she's unsure what to say or do next. I don't imagine this is the sort of situation they're trained for at medical school.

'Um . . .' She clears her throat. 'Any other symptoms? Is Elise on any medication?'

'She's had a cold for a while. I've treated it with Calpol but other than that she's been well.'

'Right, let's have a little look at her, shall we?'

She wheels her chair around her desk so she's almost knee to knee with me. She tilts her head to one side and smiles at my daughter. 'I hear you're not feeling too well.'

Elise, suddenly shy, wraps her arms around my neck and buries her face in my armpit.

'Do you know what this is?' Dr McGrath continues, holding out her stethoscope. 'It's magic. It lets us listen to heartbeats. Would you like to listen to your heartbeat, Elise?'

My daughter shakes her head.

'What about Mummy's heartbeat?'

Elise peers at the doctor from beneath her long curls and she reaches out a hand for the stethoscope. Dr McGrath carefully places the earbuds in my daughter's ear then gives me an enquiring look. I nod and force a smile as the doctor helps my daughter press the cold circular disc to my skin. A confused look appears on Elise's face, swiftly followed by delight.

'I hear your heart, Mummy.'

Dr McGrath lets her play for a few more seconds

then asks Elise if she can listen to her heart. As my daughter happily lifts up her top, Dr McGrath's gaze falls to the penny-shaped bruises on her ribs. 'Could you breathe in and out for me, please, Elise. Big, big breaths in and out.'

My daughter sighs dramatically.

'OK.' The doctor nods at me. 'Could you turn her around so I can listen to her back?'

I feel sick with worry as I manoeuvre Elise into position and Dr McGrath gently lifts her top. Her gaze flicks towards the bruises on either side of my daughter's back but she doesn't comment. Instead she places the stethoscope on Elise's soft skin and asks her to breathe in and out as deeply as she can and then cough. When she's finished she takes Elise's temperature, looks into and behind her ears, at her eyes and inside her mouth. She lifts Elise's hair and looks at her neck. I've brought my daughter to see the GP countless times since she was born but she's never been checked over as thoroughly as this before.

'Are there any other bruises on her body?' Dr McGrath asks as she wheels her chair back a little. 'Anything else of concern that you'd like me to look at?'

There's a look in her eyes that worries me. She's stopped smiling. Her gaze flicks from the top of my head to the scruffy winter boots on my feet as though it's me she's assessing rather than my daughter.

'No,' I say. 'Just the bruising. It looks like someone grabbed her. Like fingerprints.'

'Would you mind removing all of Elise's clothing,

just so I could have a quick look? You can keep her underwear on.'

My hands shake as I help Elise out of her dress, vest and tights. I checked every inch of my daughter's body after I spotted the bruises and I know there are no other marks but I'm still scared, terrified that she might find something awful that I've missed.

Elise hops from foot to foot on the rough surgery carpet. Without clothes she looks tiny, all spindly arms and legs with a little toddler tummy. I might be terrified but she is more than comfortable dancing about in her My Little Pony pants.

Dr McGrath crouches beside her and makes a game out of the examination, asking my child to show her arm, her 'other arm', her foot, her leg. If she notices anything unusual she doesn't mention it. Instead she tells me that I can put Elise's clothes back on.

Once dressed, I carry Elise across the room to a big box of Duplo that's been left out then hurry back to the doctor.

'You didn't answer when I asked about the bruises. Someone grabbed her, didn't they?'

Dr McGrath pauses, her fingers on her keyboard, and looks at me.

'There are ten,' I say, 'two on her front, eight on the back. They're grab marks. That's why I woke up last night. Because Elise cried out. She hasn't mentioned anything today but she rarely remembers when she wakes up in the night.' Dr McGrath's eyes flicker over my face. A small frown appears between her raggedy brows.

'Other than the potential intruder, was Elise roughly handled in any way yesterday? You didn't have to grab her for any reason? To protect her from injuring herself or falling or anything?'

'No, nothing like that. I drove her from my friend's house to her nursery then I met my solicitor, picked her up and took her home.'

'And the nursery staff, they didn't report any accidents or incidents to you when you picked her up?'

'No, nothing. Alice, that's Elise's support worker, she commented on the fact she had a bit of a cold. But I knew that. She's had it for a few days.'

'And you only noticed the bruising today?'

'Yes. I told you. There was nothing last night. I would have noticed when I got her ready for bed.'

'Hmmm.' She presses her lips together. 'Are you OK to play with Elise for a few moments while I make a quick call?'

'To the police?'

'No, to the paediatric unit at the hospital. Nothing to worry about,' she adds quickly. 'I'd just like them to take a quick look at Elise.'

'You agree with me, don't you? You think Paula hurt her?'

'Like I said, we just need to get her checked out.' She gives me a tight smile then swivels round in her chair so her back is to me and reaches for her phone.

Five minutes later she calls me back to her desk. I've been trying to listen in whilst building a fairy castle with Elise but she kept her voice low and I didn't catch a word.

'OK.' She greets me a wide smile. 'I'll just go and get my coat and then I'll drive you to the hospital.'

'There's no need. I've got my car.'

Dr McGrath scratches the back of her neck and clears her throat. 'No, no. I'll take you. It's . . . er . . . protocol.'

'Protocol for what?'

'For referrals to the safeguarding team. It's really nothing to worry about.'

'The safeguarding team?'

'It's just a precautionary measure. The team will look Elise over and answer any questions you've got. Are you OK to hang on here for a second while I just pop out quickly?'

I look from Dr McGrath's empty chair, to her computer screen, to my daughter – my tiny, defenceless, happy daughter, chatting away to herself as she builds a tower then laughing with delight as she smashes it back down. Paula hurt her. She let herself into my house with a stolen key then she climbed the stairs to Elise's room and she watched her sleep. Then she grabbed her so violently that Elise cried out. What happened then? Was she so shocked she dropped her and ran? If I'd just walked in a few moments earlier I could have stopped her. I could have protected Elise.

If the safeguarding team agree that Elise has been hurt then they'll call the police and I'll be taken seriously.

But what if they think *I* hurt her?

I try and mentally shake the thought away but it's

caught in my brain like a fishing hook. Mr Harrison told me that one of the things in my favour was the fact that there's no evidence that I've ever hurt my daughter. There's no sign of a break-in, nothing missing, nothing taken. Will they take fingerprints from the door handles? What if they don't find any? What if the only fingerprints belong to me, Max and Helen? They'll accuse me of hurting her. As soon as Max's solicitor hears about it it's all over. They'll award him the interim residence order and take her away from me.

I glance back at the computer screen. In her haste to get to her car Dr McGrath hasn't logged out and I can see the last thing she looked at. It's a note from Dr Fullerton on my medical record.

Reports increased feelings of anxiety, mistrust and dread. Suffered a panic attack when she thought someone was staring at her. Said she 'feels like she's losing her mind'.

Chapter 27

I rush from room to room, yanking open drawers, rifling through boxes and loading my arms with clothes, toys, toiletries and paperwork. How many times have I done this now? Two, three? But I'm not packing for a weekend away this time. I have no idea when I'll return to this house again. *If* I'll ever return.

I fill the two suitcases on top of the wardrobe, and three overnight bags, and, with nowhere to store Elise's cot linen, I fill a bin bag too. Then I transport them all into the car and cram them into the boot, along with Elise's buggy. Elise is back in front of the TV, distracted by Peppa Pig and a lolly I found in the back of a kitchen cupboard.

I glance at my watch. 10.45 a.m. Half an hour since I fled from the doctor's surgery with Elise in my arms. The receptionist gave me a startled look as I ran past her desk but there was no sign of Dr McGrath. I have no idea what the 'protocol' is for returning to your surgery to find that your patient has absconded with her daughter after you've recommended that they see a safeguarding team but I'm not going to take any chances. There's a cruel irony that the police couldn't be bothered to turn up to my house after someone ransacked it but they may well be on their way here now.

'Max hasn't once suggested that you have harmed your child or are likely to do so, and that's important.' That's what Mr Harrison said. He didn't spell out what it would mean for my case if he had but the implications were clear – you have a chance of winning this as long as you haven't hurt your child.

I need to ring him. But I can't do it here, now, while I'm panicking.

'All right, sweetheart.' I hurry into the living room. 'Mummy's ready to go now. Come on then.'

Elise whines in protest and snuggles into the corner of the sofa, her eyes still fixed on the TV. I turn it off and her whine instantly becomes a howl.

'You can watch Peppa on your iPad in the—' I break off, distracted by a thought. I haven't packed our passports. They're in the cabinet next to the fireplace.

I crouch beside it and pull open the doors. As I do, my heart twists in my chest. There it is – the large wooden box, about the size of a shoebox, with 'Henry William Blackmore' carved into the top and his date of birth beneath it. Inside is a set of hand- and footprints, a photograph, his first scan and the hat and blanket the midwife dressed him in after he was born. While other mothers left the hospital with their babies in a car seat, I left with nothing, nothing apart from those few things. For days, weeks, I wouldn't be parted from them. I held the blanket in my hands during Henry's funeral service and tucked his hat into my bra, close to my heart. Wherever I went, they went too. Then one day, when my grief had slowly cycled through to acceptance, Max suggested that we should buy something special to keep Henry's things in. I went online and bought the most beautiful box I could find and paid to have it engraved. As I put his things inside I felt as though I was burying my son for the second time.

'Peppa!' Elise shouts now, her cheeks flushed and tear-stained. She reaches for the remote control and jabs at the buttons. 'Peppa, Mummy!'

A siren wails in the distance and I snatch at the small pile of passports lying beside Henry's box and shove them into my back pocket. I reach for the box. It feels heavier than I remembered. As I slide it off the shelf Elise slides off the sofa and slaps at the buttons on the side of the 38-inch flat-screen TV, making it wobble precariously.

'Come on, sweetheart.' I tuck the box under my arm and reach for her hand. 'Come on, love. Let's go.'

'I WANT PEPPA!' she screams as I shepherd her out of the living room, down the hallway and out of the front door.

I have to let go of her hand to reach into my pocket for the house key. As I turn it in the lock Elise thumps me on the leg. 'GO WAY! I WANT DADDY!'

I scoop her up with one arm and carry her, kicking

and screaming, to the car and strap her into her seat. I reach into the boot and tuck Henry's box beneath one of the black plastic sacks then retrieve Elise's iPad from under my seat.

'Here.' I press a few buttons and hand it to her. 'Look, Peppa!'

'Don't want it!' She shoves it away.

My phone rings as Elise continues to screech. It says *number withheld* on the screen. It has to be Mr Harrison ringing from his office. He said he'd give me a ring today. I jab the speakerphone button and answer the call.

'Hello,' I say, 'Joanne Blackmore speak—'

I'm cut off by the sound of a woman singing, her deep, rasping voice filling the car. I know who it is. I recognise the voice from the first word, but I'm so shocked I can't speak.

'Ladybird, ladybird, fly away home.'

I jab at the *end call* button but I'm shaking so much my finger slips, missing it. Paula continues to sing, each word staccato and mocking.

'Your husband has left you
And now you're alone.'

'Go away!' I jab at the *end call* button over and over and over again. 'Leave us alone. Please, please just leave us alone.'

'Mummy?' comes a small voice from the back of the car. 'I like that song. Sing it again, Mummy.'

Chapter 28

Max approaches his front door, key in hand. The skin on the back of his hand is swollen and sore from a futile attempt to defend himself. His face is a mess. His right eye is puffy and sealed shut, ringed red, black and brown. He touches the key to the lock then pauses. This is still his house but it is no longer his home. The life he knew two weeks ago – when he'd open the door, shout hello, then poke his head around the living-room door to see what Elise and Jo were up to – is over. Should he have fought harder to make his marriage to Jo work? But he had. He'd done everything he could to support her and make her feel safe and loved. She was the one who'd secretly planned to move to Chester, who'd threatened to never let him see Elise again, who disappeared at the drop of a hat, who'd got off her head in the middle of the day and left their daughter, urine-stained and crying, alone at nursery. Everything he'd done, everything he was doing, had been completely vindicated by the choices Jo had made and the things she'd done.

There was no sign of either of them now. Nine o'clock at night, the house was in darkness and Jo's car wasn't parked in the street. *Where is she? And, more importantly, where is Elise?*

Max's heartbeat quickens as he turns the key in the lock and steps into the dark hallway. He flicks the light switch.

'Hello?'

No answer. Fear pricks at the base of his brain. *Paula wouldn't have attacked Jo and Elise, would she? But she'd sent someone after him.* Last night, when he'd examined his split face in the hotel bathroom last night it wasn't fear he felt, it was anger. Anger with Paula but, more powerfully, anger with himself. *He should have taken Jo more seriously. Paula's more dangerous than either of them thought. He has to protect his family. He has to make this stop.*

This morning, when he woke up in his hotel bed, his face throbbing with pain, his first thought was Elise. He snatched up his phone. 11.07 a.m. He blinked several times with his good eye. 11.07 a.m.? How had he slept so long? He called Jo. Her phone rang and rang and then went to voicemail. He ended the call at the beep. *What should he say?* He was going to tell her that Paula had beaten him up and that he was sorry, he should have taken her threats against Jo more seriously. *Then what?* Ask her to let him have Elise so he could protect her? She would have put the phone down on him.

There was an alternative. Jo and Elise could go up to Chester for a while. They'd be safe up there, while he dealt with Paula. But Jo might refuse to ever come back if that happened. Although she'd have to return for the court case. Once the Paula issue was sorted he'd be able to offer his daughter a safe home and Jo could get the help she needed for her illness. But he couldn't suggest all that on the phone. He needed to see his wife face-to-face. He needed to gauge how she was feeling before he said a word. He had to tread carefully.

'Hello?' Max says again, as he passes the empty living room and heads for the kitchen. He turns back. There was something about the living room that wasn't quite right. Elise's toy box lid is open, so are the doors to the cabinet in the corner of the room. He crouches down beside it and looks inside.

It's gone.

Henry's box is gone.

He runs a hand over the space left behind, as though touching the smooth wood will somehow magically bring it back, and tries not to panic. Jo kept Henry's things on a shelf in Elise's room, then decided that it wasn't the right place and moved it to the cabinet. Maybe she moved it back? Or into their room?

He runs up the stairs, taking them two at a time, and bursts into the master bedroom. The doors to all the wardrobes are open. The chest of drawers too: knickers, tights and T-shirts hanging over the side and lying on a heap on the carpet, along with some of Jo's costume jewellery. Both of her jewellery boxes are open, their contents gone. For a second he thinks they have been burgled but then he notices that the tops of both wardrobes are clear. All the suitcases and bags are gone.

He runs into Elise's bedroom but it's a similar scene – clothes and toys gone, her pillow and duvet missing from her cot.

He walks from room to room to room, his hands in his hair, gripping the roots. Jo hasn't just taken a couple of items of clothing and a few toys for an overnight stay. She's stripped the house of everything that ever held sentimental value for her. Almost everything. On top of the closed kitchen bin are her wedding and engagement rings.

Chapter 29

I thought you were going to fight back, Jo. After you pushed me, the other day, I wondered if, perhaps, you'd finally grown a backbone. But no, instead of staying and fighting you've run away. And you've taken something that belongs to me with you. I can just imagine you now – jumping at every dark shadow, flinching at every strange noise. Are you talking to yourself? Telling yourself that you're overreacting, trying to keep up a pretence for Elise that everything's fine. But everything's not fine, is it, Jo? Deep down you know I'll catch up with you. It's inevitable. One day you'll hear footsteps behind you. Your heart will race and you'll look over your shoulder as you quicken your pace. And then you'll see me.

Chapter 30

'Well?' Helen says as I press the *end call* button on my mobile and place it in my lap. 'What did your solicitor say?'

Elise, playing on the living-room floor with her bricks, looks up and smiles. I tear my gaze away from her. 'That I have to go back.'

'Can you take her to a hospital here instead?'

'No. I have to go back to Bristol. If I don't they'll seize her.'

'Seize her? Jesus. He actually said that?'

Mr Harrison didn't sugarcoat his advice when I just rang him at home on his mobile. He said I'd made a huge mistake leaving Bristol instead of going to the hospital with Dr McGrath. The situation was already extremely serious, he said, and if I didn't take Elise back there was a very real risk that the police would come after us and Social Services would take Elise into their care. Then I wouldn't just be fighting

166

Max for the right to see my daughter, I'd be fighting the state.

'Yes,' I say. 'He did.'

'Did you tell him about the phone call from Paula?'

'I did, yes.'

'He said that I should add it to the harassment diary I'm keeping for the police but, unfortunately, it doesn't actually prove that she was the one who hurt Elise.'

'Oh God.' Helen slumps forward and rests her elbows on her knees. Her face is creased with concern. 'I don't know what to tell you, Jo. I just . . . God knows how you feel.'

'Terrified.'

'Yeah.' She gives me a long look. 'Yeah.'

We lapse into silence, both of us watching Elise as she wraps one of her dolls in a blanket and then puts it to bed on a curtain she's pulled off the sofa. I pull a tissue from the box on the side table by my chair and crouch down beside her to wipe away the stream of snot that's suddenly appeared, then press a hand to her forehead. She feels very warm.

'Is she OK?' Helen asks.

'I'm not sure. Have you got a thermometer?'

'Batteries gone. Sorry. Want me to pop to Boots and get one? I won't be gone long.'

'Would you?' I say and then pause. 'No, actually, I'll get it.'

'But what if you—'

'Have a panic attack? I need to get over it, Helen. I need to prove to the court that my agoraphobia doesn't stop me from looking after Elise. If you weren't here I'd have to get the thermometer myself, wouldn't I?'

In all honesty I'm terrified at the thought of just stepping outside Helen's front door but I have to do it. I'm going to have even scarier situations to deal with when I return to Bristol with Elise – the hospital for one, and then the court. No one else is going to make me better. I have to do it myself.

'OK,' Helen says hesitantly. 'If you're sure.'

I kiss Elise on her hot, clammy forehead and stand up. 'I'm sure.'

My mobile rings, making me jump. For the last ten minutes I've been repeating the phrase 'nothing bad will happen' over and over again in my head as I've walked from Helen's house, down Wesley Lane, left onto Charles Street and right onto Bridge Street, where I stopped to get money out at the cashpoint on the corner. According to the directions Helen gave me, I need to go into the shopping arcade, take the next left after the Pandora store and Boots will be at the end of the mall.

My hand shakes as I reach into my pocket. What if it's Paula again? I should have Googled how to record a conversation on an old Nokia. If that's even possible. Alternatively it could be Max. He's been ringing me on and off all day. I nearly replied several times but Helen talked me out of it.

'What are you going to tell him?' she asked. 'That Paula broke into the house, hurt Elise and then rang you up to taunt you?'

'Yes, of course. It might convince him to take this seriously.'

'What if it doesn't? What if he uses it against you in court? What if he says that you can't protect your child? Or, worse, tries to convince the judge that you were the one that hurt Elise?'

'But you were there. You know what happened.'

'I do. But I don't think you should talk to him about it yet. Talk to your solicitor first.'

But it's not *withheld number* or Max's name flashing on the caller display. It's Mum. How long's it been since I last rang her? A few days? A week? I normally call her every day.

'Hello?' I hold the phone to my ear. 'Mum? Is Dad OK?'

'Sure, he's grand. Well, no. There's been no change, but that's not why I'm calling. Listen to me, Joanne. Max just rang. He asked if you and Elise were up here with me.'

I press a hand to my stomach as a wave of nausea pulses through me. Max knows we're not in Bristol? He must have been to the house to check.

'I told him no, that you weren't here, and he asked where else you might be. He said you weren't answering your phone. What's going on, Joanne?'

'It's . . . it's a long story, Mum. I didn't want to worry you.'

'Well, I'm worried now, so c'mon. What's happened?'

She listens as I give her a condensed version of everything that's happened since we last spoke.

'Oh, Joanne,' she says when I finish. 'Why didn't

169

you tell me any of this before? I can't believe it. Why haven't the police arrested that woman? She can't be allowed on the street, terrorising you like that. And as for Max . . . I can't believe it of him, really I can't. He knows you're a good mammy. Oh, I could kick myself for giving you those tablets . . .'

Now it's my turn to listen as she tries and fails to make sense of what's happened. I feel awful putting this on her. She's got enough to deal with, looking after Dad, but Max has dragged her into this horrible mess too. Will it ever end?

'You need to go back to Bristol, Joanne,' Mum says. 'Running away isn't going to solve anything. You go back there and you need to work with your solicitor to put this right. No one in their right mind is going to believe that you harmed Elise.'

'I know, Mum.'

I turn left after Pandora and walk past Superdry and Castle Fine Art. Boots is practically empty. Two sales assistants, chatting on the tills, don't pause their conversation as I walk by, but one of them, an older woman with short hair and a side-swept fringe, follows me with her eyes. I scurry down an aisle, out of her eyeline, but the feeling of being watched remains.

'Mum, I need to go.' I swap the phone from one hand to the other and wipe my right palm on my jeans. 'I just need to grab something for Elise from the shops then I'll drive back to Bristol.'

'OK, love. Will you go straight to the hospital or to see your solicitor?'

'I don't know. The hospital probably.' I glance over

my shoulder. A man with closely cropped dark hair is examining the toothpaste selection, further down the aisle.

'How was the bruising this morning?' Mum asks.

'Same as yesterday.'

'No new bruises have appeared?'

'No.' Helen suggested we take photos of Elise's bruising last night. We took a couple of her chest and back and some more with my fingers wrapped around her to show that the tips of my fingers barely graze the marks on her back if my thumbs cover the bruises on her back. I don't know if it's enough to prove that I didn't hurt her but Helen thought it was important that we have photographic evidence before the bruises fade.

'Well, that's good news,' Mum says as I switch aisles and pass bottles of shampoo and conditioner and box after box of hair dye.

'And Elise hasn't said anything? She hasn't mentioned seeing a stranger in her room or anything?'

'No, she hasn't said a word.' I swipe the back of my hand over my forehead. I'm too hot in my thick winter coat and my hairline is damp with sweat. I've reached the baby aisle but I can't see any thermometers. Nappies, wipes, creams and earbuds, but no thermometers.

I glance to my left. The man with the close-cropped hair is standing at the end of the aisle. He reaches for something from the top shelf and twists it round in his hands so he can read the back. I can't be sure from this distance but it looks like a packet of disposable breastfeeding pads. He puts them back on the shelf and reaches for something else. It's entirely possible that he's a new dad and his wife has sent him out to buy a few bits and bobs but there's no basket hanging from his arm, no list in his fingers. Something doesn't feel right.

'You need to get the police round,' Mum says. 'They need to fingerprint the door handles because if someone did take your key then . . .'

She continues to talk as I walk to the end of the baby aisle, take a right and head for the make-up display to the right of the shop. Beneath my heavy woollen coat my skin is tingly, my heart is racing in my chest and I am breathing through my nose in short, sharp gasps. As I pass the Rimmel display the tips of my fingers go numb and I feel light-headed and woozy. The air in the shop is too thick, too dense. I can't breathe.

'Mum, I've got to go.'

I end the call before she can object and shove the phone into my pocket. I pause by the Maybelline counter. The ground beneath my feet tilts and sways and I reach out a hand to steady myself. Tubes of foundation fall from the shelf and bounce off the polished floor as a wave of panic crashes over me. I can't let this happen. I need to buy a thermometer. I have to pull myself together. I have to do it for Elise. No one is following me. I'm being paranoid. I'm—

A noise, like trainers squeaking, makes me look up. The man with the close-cropped hair is walking towards me. His hands hang loosely at his sides. He's walking quickly, with purpose, and he's looking straight at me.

'Jo? Jo Blackmore?'

I don't know if it's the look in his heavy-lidded eyes or the set of his thin lips, but I react without thinking. I lurch away from the make-up display, showering the ground with cosmetics. And I run.

Chapter 31

'Are you sure you want to do this?' Helen says through the open car window. The street is empty but she keeps her voice low.

'What other choice have I got?'

'You could go back to Bristol and tell the police everything.'

'And then what? They hand Elise over to Social Services and prosecute me for harming her? They already think I'm a drug addict.'

'That's not true. They let you out on bail.'

'But they didn't do anything when Paula threatened me, did they? And they didn't turn up when I rang to say someone had ransacked my house. As long as Paula is out there Elise is in danger. No one believes me, Helen. Not the police, not Social Services and certainly not Max.'

Helen's face creases with concern. 'I believe you. So does Mr Harrison. Your mum does too. Oh God,

174

Jo. I wish there was something I could do. Can't you stay with me another night and see how you feel in the morning?'

I glance into the back of the car where Elise is resting her head against her car seat, her eyelids flickering open and then closing again as she fights the urge to fall asleep. Her cheeks are flushed pink and her forehead is clammy, despite the teaspoon of Calpol I gave her five minutes ago. I know it's just a cold or a viral infection but she should be tucked up in her cot, not shifted from place to place. How is she ever going to get better if she hasn't got time to rest?

'No.' I shake my head. 'I can't risk going back to Bristol. If the police arrest me they'll give Elise to Max. Paula knows where he works and where we live. I wouldn't be surprised if she knows where Elise goes to nursery too. She could still get to her. The only way to keep her safe is to leave.'

'If you're sure.'

'I am. Thank you. For everything. For letting me use your car and for these.' I tap the envelope on the passenger seat. 'You could get into a lot of trouble if the police realise you gave them to me.'

'I'll tell them you stole them.' She laughs lightly. 'Are you sure you don't want my mobile too?'

My phone had just enough battery life left to ring Helen from my hiding place – a skip on Mill Lane Road – before the screen went black. I don't know when I'll get to charge it again but I know Mum's phone number off by heart and Helen's written hers on the envelope she gave me. And if I need to ring

Mr Harrison I'll call one of those 118 numbers from a phone box. Really I should get myself a new phone, something pay-as-you-go that can't be traced, but there's no way I'm about to risk going back into the centre of Cardiff.

'No,' I say. 'I might need to get in touch with you. But thank you.'

'It's the least I could do,' she says. 'Where do you think you'll go now?'

I shrug. I ran through all my options while I was waiting for Helen to show up with the car and Elise. I could go up to Chester but the police will know about my mum. Mr Harrison told me this morning that the police would come after me if I don't take Elise to the hospital and I've watched enough missing persons programmes to know that they've got access to cash withdrawals, motorway CCTV, mobile phone signals and social media to track anyone in the UK. My only option is to leave the country. And there's only one place in the world where I've ever felt truly safe.

'Ireland,' I say. 'I'm going back to Clogherhead.'

Chapter 32

Elise runs from one end of the caravan to the other, then scrambles onto the sofa and slams both palms against the net curtains covering the window, making me jump.

'Dark!' she says, yanking the net curtain up and pointing outside. 'Dark, Mummy!'

'Yes, it is, isn't it?'

We arrived at the caravan park four hours ago, after the woman in the Fishguard ferry office told me that the next sailing was at 2.30 a.m. Eleven hours' time. I took one look at Elise, her eyes ringed with dark circles, her nostrils crusted with snot, and booked the sailing for 2.30 p.m. tomorrow instead.

Spending another night in the UK feels risky. Someone managed to track me to Cardiff but I avoided the motorway on the way here and haven't used my dead mobile or a cashpoint since I left. I considered booking us both into a hotel or B&B in

Fishguard then I spotted a policeman walking through the town and swiftly changed my mind.

The woman at reception wasn't keen on giving me a static caravan just for one night but she finally relented. It was February, she said, and business was quiet. What harm would it do? I paid quickly, in cash, and ignored her question about our plans for tomorrow.

I nearly drove straight back out of the park when I saw where the caravan was situated, right on the edge of a cliff – only a low metal fence separating us from a near-vertical drop down to the black, swirling sea. I didn't feel any better after we went inside. It was like walking into a rectangular, corrugated fish bowl, with two windows on each side and only one door. I locked the door behind us then checked that all the windows were locked and closed the curtains. Then I did the circuit again, double-checking. The television didn't work so I wedged myself into the corner of the sofa and pulled Elise onto my knee. From that angle I could see three of the windows and the door. That left one window directly behind me. I tried to relax and read *Snug as a Bug* but I could barely speak, my breathing was so shallow. The words danced on the page as shadows moved in my peripheral vision and I couldn't shake the feeling that, at any moment, someone was going to slam through the window and grab us. That's how we ended up playing dolls in the bedroom, wedged between the side of the bed and the windowless wall until the tight knot in my stomach had loosened and my breathing had slowed.

'Li-li,' I say now as I walk out of the tiny bathroom. 'Do you want to play a game?'

She turns away from the window and looks at me excitedly. 'Yes.'

I feel sick to my stomach but I keep my tone light and playful. 'It's a dress-up game.'

'Princesses!' Elise bounces off the sofa and runs up to me. She pulls at the hem of my jumper. 'Elsa dress. Elsa dress, Mummy!'

'Actually, darling,' – I touch a hand to the towel on my head as I crouch down next to her – 'I thought we could play a different kind of dress-up game. Mummy will dress up as Helen and you can dress up as Ben.'

Elise shakes her head. 'No, Mummy. Princess game.'

'We can play that tomorrow, when we get to Ireland. But I thought it would be fun to pretend to be Helen and Ben first.' I touch the plastic bag that's leaning up against the door. 'Helen gave me some of the clothes Ben wore when he was two, like you. Shall we put them on? See if they fit?'

Elise shakes her head, more resolutely this time, and her bottom lip protrudes. 'No.'

'Look!' I pull the towel from my head and shake my hair loose. My daughter's jaw drops, her eyes widen and then fill with tears. She backs away, shaking her head.

'Don't like it. Don't like it, Mummy.'

I lift a strand of my damp, newly red hair and twirl it around my finger. 'When I dry and curl it and put glasses on I'll look just like Helen. It's a funny game, isn't it?'

Elise doesn't look convinced.

Monday morning and it's all I can do not to burst into tears each time I look at my daughter. Her red patent shoes, white tights, grey dress and scarlet cardigan are gone, shoved into the tiny bin in the cupboard beneath the sink, along with a pair of Ben's Spiderman underpants. I couldn't bring myself to throw away Elise's pink and white spotty knickers. I let her wear them under the jeans – the only part of her identity that I hadn't disposed of.

Now, tear-stained and puffy-eyed, she plucks at the worn green Ben 10 sweatshirt I wrestled her into this morning and scuffs one trainered foot against the other as she arranges her dolls on the tiny caravan table. But it's not Elise's outfit that's making my heart break. It's her hair. I knew there was no way she'd willingly let me cut her blonde curls so, as she munched on a piece of toast this morning, dropping crumbs onto the sofa as she gazed out of a window, I sat behind her with a pair of nail scissors. I lifted up curl after curl and snipped them away. Silent tears rolled down my face as I added them to the pile of blonde hair in my lap. I was worried that I'd have to dye Elise's hair as well as my own and was flooded with relief when I opened Ben's passport. He was only two when his photo was taken. His hair was lighter than it is now, still sun-bleached from a holiday to Spain – the last one Helen and Jake took before

180

they split up. But it was short, much shorter than Elise's wild mop. Her hair's not long any more. I can see her forehead, her ears and the nape of her neck. I have snipped away her softness. I have shorn her of her identity. She looks, to all intents and purposes, like a small boy.

She wailed when she realised what I had done. In my haste to finish I touched the cold metal of the scissors to the back of her neck. I didn't hurt or nick her but her right hand flew to the nape of her neck and she twisted round so suddenly that the hair in my lap flew up. Elise stared at me with wide, horrified eyes as it drifted back down, settling on me, her, the sofa and the rough, worn caravan carpet.

'My hair.' She touched the crown of her hair, her ears, her cheeks. 'My hair, Mummy!'

She looked so shocked, so uncomprehending, so betrayed that all the soothing words I'd prepared to console her with instantly dried up on my tongue and I burst into tears. For weeks I've been telling anyone who will listen that I'm not a bad mother but, in that single moment, I felt like the worst mother in the world. My daughter had sat between my legs, at peace, safe and secure, and I had abused her trust. I hadn't just cut her hair against her will, I'd scared her. For the first time since I'd left Bristol I doubted my decision to run. I should have taken her to the hospital, let the doctors look her over and let Max win. She'd still have her hair, her clothes, her home, her identity. She wouldn't have to endure stifling car journeys or claustrophobic caravans. She wouldn't be able to run into my room for a good-morning hug or press her lips against mine before she fell asleep at night. If I could prove I hadn't hurt her she'd see me maybe once during the week and every other weekend. I'd justified my escape because I didn't want that for her. I thought she'd suffer without me. But had I made that decision for her, or for me?

Now, as she reaches for a baby bottle and presses it to her doll's lips, I step into the narrow bathroom and force myself to look into the mirror. I touch a hand to my own hair. The vivid red has drained the colour from my face and I look pallid and tired, but when I hook Helen's glasses over my ears I look more like her than I did twelve hours ago. My nose is longer and wider than hers and my chin is narrower but our eyes are the same murky green, our lips generous and full. If the customs officer gives the passport photo more than a cursory glance there's no chance we'll make it onto the ferry. If he asks Li-Li her name there's no way she'll say Ben. It's a risk, but so is staying in the UK. I pull on a tonged curl, then release it. It pings back into place. Time to go.

Chapter 33

I warned you, Jo. I told you not to sleep. I said something awful would happen if you slept, didn't I? Only you didn't listen, did you? I could have taken your daughter from you as you slept alone in your bed, completely oblivious to the fact that I was in the house. I could have swept Elise up in my arms and spirited her away and you'd never have seen her again. Only your daughter isn't as stupid as you, Jo. She woke up when I let myself in. She stared at me from between the bars of her cot – her eyes wide and startled – as I stood at the entrance to her bedroom. As I crossed the room she tried to climb out of her cot, to escape, but she lost her footing and tumbled towards the ground. I caught her. I saved her from harm. And I would have taken her if she hadn't cried out.

PART TWO

Chapter 34

The iron hisses, releasing a cloud of steam as Mary lifts it from the crisp cotton sheet and places it in its holder on the right of the ironing board. She grips the edges of the sheet and, in a practised move, slides it off the board. She agitates the cotton with her thumbs so the edges of the sheet align near her feet, then she folds the sheet in two. She folds it again and again, until it becomes a tight, neat square. She runs the iron over it once more, then, with one eye on the clock above the fireplace, carefully places it on the pile to her left.

It's 3.12 p.m. There is no time for a cup of tea today but she still has a few minutes to spare before the children come out of school so she darts into the hallway and stands still, listening. There are five rooms in Seamount House B&B but business is quiet in February and only one room is occupied. She hasn't seen Mr Hogan since breakfast at 8 a.m. He told her he'd be driving to Drogheda for business and would return in the early afternoon but she hasn't seen him yet. No matter. She leaves the hall and enters the kitchen. Her slippers make a soft swooshing sound on the granite tiles as she crosses the floor. Once in the utility room at the back of the house she removes the apron she's been wearing all day and drops it into a laundry basket. She selects a clean apron from a pile on the shelf, pulls it over her head and ties it behind her back, then reaches for the plastic basket of window-cleaning products.

She glances at her watch. 3.14 p.m. She pauses at the mirror in the hallway. She fingers the pearls at her neck, a gift from Patrick many years ago, then touches a hand to her hair and smooths down a short blonde strand that's standing to attention on the crown of her head. She sweeps her fringe across her forehead and pats it into place then tilts her head forward to examine her roots. She grimaces. Only 67 and pretty much 100 per cent grey, just like her mother at the same age. She'll have to ring Siobhán and bring her appointment forward by a week. She won't have the other ladies gossiping about how she's letting herself go. She can't abide being talked about. She had enough of that 32 years ago when she couldn't walk down the street without hearing, 'Oh, poor Mrs Byrne,' 'God bless her soul' or 'It's a terrible thing that happened.'

She looks at the clock again – 3.16 p.m.

She darts into the dining room and carefully removes the ornaments from the sill then shifts the net curtain along its wire so it hangs at the side of the window. There are three panels of glass – two side panels that can be opened and a larger central panel that can't. Mary opens one of the side windows and a gust of cold February air blasts into the room. It's expensive to heat such a large house and it will take at least an hour for the dining room to warm up again once she's closed the window, but Mary doesn't mind. It's a small price to pay for the excited chatter of the children as they skip and run down the road.

Mary reaches into the basket, pulls out the glass cleaner and, holding it about half a foot from the window, squeezes the trigger. The glass mists instantly. She squeezes again. The sound of a child's laughter drifts through the open window. Mary squeezes the trigger again. Is there a more beautiful sound?

As shouts, cries, giggles and mumbles join the laughter, Mary reaches for her yellow polishing cloth and swipes at the mist covering the window. A child's face appears. It's little Aoife Flannigan from three streets down. She looks so smart in her royal-blue sweatshirt with the little yellow crest near her collarbone.

'Hello, Mrs Byrne!' She jumps and waves. Her mother, Sinead, appears behind her. She's six months pregnant and her grey woollen coat is straining at the seams.

'How're ye, Mary?'

'Grand. And yourself?'

'Fat. And getting fatter.' She pats her bump and laughs.

Aoife and Sinead continue on down the hill, hand in hand. The little girl looks up at her mother and says something but it's carried away by the wind and Mary can only watch and speculate as Sinead's face lights up. But then little Aiden O'Connor and his twin brother Declan appear and Mary nods and smiles and asks them how they're doing even though her heart is twisting in her chest. And then there's Margaret Ryan with her three grandchildren. She's waggling her finger at the eldest, Fionnán, and the other two are laughing at him behind her back, jumping around and pulling faces. Margaret doesn't stop to say hello to Mary but she does raise a hand and nod as she walks past. She looks tired and at the end of her tether but she doesn't know how lucky she is. Mary would give anything to walk a gaggle of grandchildren home from school and then sit them around her kitchen table, listening to their silly stories as they fill their bellies with the contents of her fridge.

But the smile doesn't slip from her face as she squirts and wipes, buffs and polishes. By the time the last little straggler strolls past the B&B Mary's front windows are gleaming. But then they always are. There isn't much chance for them to get dirty when they're cleaned five times a week.

As the street falls silent Mary reaches for the window catch and pulls it closed. She returns the basket of cleaning products to the shelf in the utility room and fills the kettle in the kitchen, then she climbs the stairs to the room at the top of the house. Niamh is waiting for her, as she always is, in the silver-framed photograph on the dressing table – always smiling, eyes filled with love. Mary presses her fingers to her lips then touches the photograph. Time to go and see her daughter.

Mary pulls her hat down over her ears and tugs at the zipper of her thick winter coat, but it's already up around her neck. A thermal vest, a dress, thick tights, two cardigans, her warmest winter boots and a scarf and she still feels as though the wind and rain are biting into her bones.

The streets are deserted, the schoolchildren long gone. Everyone else is at work or else sheltering in the warmth of their living rooms. The wind is strong, the sea an angry grey mouth that roars at her from the bottom of Main Road. There are always people on the beach – all through the year – walking their dogs, driving their cars or taking in the sea air, but even the gulls have abandoned it today.

Mary Byrne feels like the last woman left on earth as she gets into her car but there was no way she could have remained in her house today. Even if she was laid up with flu like poor Mr Carey, she'd still find a way out of the house. It's the 21st of February. Nothing and no one could keep her inside.

Mary bows her head and crosses herself as she pushes at the heavy iron gate and enters the churchyard. The wind has whipped up the fallen leaves and the ground is littered with their crisp brown skeletons. They crunch underfoot as she makes her way through the graveyard. She pauses beside a grave and crosses herself again.

Sacred to the memory of
Conor Michael Healy
21 September 1925 – 4 November 1995
*'Whosoever shall confess me before men, I will
also confess him before my Father who is in
Heaven.'*
And also of his wife
Ciara
5 July 1928 – 31 December 1995

Seven weeks. That's how long Mary's mother had managed to hold onto life after her husband died. Everyone said it was of a broken heart and it was – figuratively and literally. The doctor said she'd had a heart attack in her sleep. Mary had been the one to find her the next morning, lying on her side, one hand reaching across the empty side of the bed as though reaching for her lost husband.

Mary says a short prayer and continues onwards, clutching the ornamental rose bush she bought the previous day to her chest. She put it in two plastic bags before she left the house, to protect it from the wind. She prefers bringing plants to the graves. Flowers die so quickly and it's always so heart-breaking to remove them from their vases, their stems dry, their heads bowed and faded.

She hurries onwards, past the grave of old Mrs McDonagh who died four weeks earlier, still a mound rather than flat, and heads towards the back of the church. She slows her pace as she draws closer to the grave she is looking for. It happens every time she visits it, as though grief weighs down her boots.

In loving memory of
Niamh Maria Byrne
Beloved daughter of Mary and Patrick
2 January 1981 – 21 February 1983
And also of
Patrick Byrne
Beloved husband of Mary, father of Niamh
25 August 1947 – 12 April 1988

Mary's knees creak as she crouches down beside the grave. She crosses herself, says a prayer, then touches her fingers to her lips. She presses the kiss against her husband's name then presses her fingers to her lips again and kisses her daughter. Thirty-two years to the day since she lost Niamh. They say time heals all wounds, but some wounds are too deep, too violently inflicted to ever recover from. Mary has half a heart. It was smitten in two the day Niamh died, then cauterised the day she found out who was responsible. She cannot remember Patrick leading the Garda into the dining room as she sat at the window staring, unseeingly, into the street. She cannot remember the words the Garda used. But she can remember the pain that sliced her in two. She can remember the scream.

Chapter 35

'Boat!' Elise calls from the back of the car as we inch closer to the ferry. 'Boat, Mummy!'

'Yes!' I glance at the rear-view mirror. There's a line of cars behind us, stretching all the way back to Fishguard harbour. I can't see any police cars but that doesn't reassure me. They could be in an unmarked car or already on board, waiting.

The car in front of me pulls forward and enters the mouth of the ferry. As it does, a man in a high-visibility jacket appears and waves his arms at me. For one terrifying moment, I'm convinced he's a policeman, but then he points across the gloomy bowels of the ferry, directing me to park up at the end of a short queue of cars. My heart is in my mouth as I turn off the engine and it takes me several attempts to undo my seat belt.

'Mummy,' Elise says as I click the buckle open and lift her out of her car seat, 'bad smell.'

She's right. The car port stinks of petrol fumes. It catches in the back of my throat as I weave through the parked cars and head for the stairs with my daughter in my arms and the ferry vibrating beneath my feet. With my bright-red curly hair and Helen's spare black-rimmed glasses I feel horribly conspicuous, but there's no time to go back to the car for a hat. I need to find a place to hide as soon as possible. Elise squirms and arches her back, desperate to be put down, as I duck into the stairwell. I climb the steps at a jog, my weight on the balls of my feet. My breathing is laboured and my heart is pounding in my chest even before I reach the top of the first flight but a clanging sound from below spurs me on. Someone else is coming up the stairs. I can hear their footsteps on the metal steps and the muffled voices – male and female.

'Mummy!' Elise squeals as I speed past deck 8. Her voice seems to bounce off the walls and it's all I can do not to press a hand over her mouth. Instead I whisper for her to shh and increase my pace. The muscles in my thighs are burning now and I'm sucking in air in noisy gasps but I have to keep going. I studied the map of the ferry this morning and I know exactly where we need to hide.

Just when I think I can't take another step I reach deck 9. The narrow doorway opens up into a vast space, with signs pointing to the canteen, cinema, children's play area and the shop. Everywhere I look there are people. Families, couples, pensioners and children – queuing for food, peering out the windows, shovelling food into their faces, playing cards at tables and feeding coins into slot machines. The cacophony of voices, bleeps, bangs, clanks and clunks overwhelms me and I feel a sharp stab of fear. How do I escape if something goes wrong? From studying the map I know where the lifeboats are but there are so many people on board. We'd be crushed in the stampede if something went wrong.

'Excuse me.' A hand on my shoulder makes me jump and I spin round, expecting to see Paula or a policeman standing behind me. Instead an elderly man in a tweed jacket gives me a yellow-toothed smile. 'Could we get past, please?' Beside him is an equally elderly woman, her hand in his.

'Yes, sorry, of course.'

I step to the side and, as I do, I spot the sign for the toilets.

Fifteen minutes. That's how long we've been hiding in a toilet cubicle. Every minute has felt like an hour. Elise demanded we leave the moment she finished her wee, yanking at the lock with Ben's jeans still pooled around her feet. I distracted her by launching into a whispered rendition of 'The Wheels on the Bus'. When her attention waned, I slid all the silver bracelets off my wrist and gave them to her to play with, repeatedly shushing her whenever her babble grew unbearably loud.

'Elise,' I say now, then tense as the main door creaks open.

'Sssh.' I press a finger to my lips and hold two

fingers of my other hand above my head like ears. 'Quiet mice.'

My heartbeat thumps in my ears, almost blocking out the soft squeak of shoes on the tiles beyond the door, then the cubicle door beside us slams open, shaking the dividing wall. Seconds later I hear the sound of the lock being drawn. Logically I know it could be any one of a hundred different passengers on the ferry but fear has too tight a grip on me for me to be able to think clearly. The main door creaks open again and a new sound fills the small toilet, a slow clip-clopping, and I keep my eyes trained on the gap under the toilet door. What kind of shoe is going to appear behind it – a shiny policeman's shoe, a man's boot or a woman's high-heeled shoe?

'I know you're in here!' says a woman's voice.

I press my fingers to Elise's lips and widen my eyes, urging her to remain quiet. Normally she'd yank at my hand and laugh. Not now. Now she goes very, very still as she stares at me with large, frightened eyes, my bracelets dangling from her fingers. She's picked up on my fear and is as scared as I am.

'I know you're hiding,' the woman says.

A pair of high heels appears beneath the toilet door then BAM! The door rattles on its hinges. Elise jumps so violently my hand falls from her mouth. The bracelets tumble to the floor and her startled cry fills the air.

'Shit! Sorry, sorry! I was just . . .' The boots disappear from beneath the door and the wall of the cubicle next door vibrates at exactly the same time that two small voices explode with laughter.

'We're in here, Mummy!'

'Josh, Isaac, out! Game's over.'

I hear the sound of a lock being pulled back and the scuffle of trainers on tiles as the two boys are yanked out of the cubicle.

'You didn't find us!' one of them cries jubilantly.

'Out!' Elise wriggles off my lap with tears in her eyes and slams both palms against the door. 'Out!'

'I'm so sorry,' the woman says, over my daughter's shouts. 'I didn't mean to startle you. I didn't think anyone else was in here.'

'It's OK. I . . . um . . .' I stand up and straighten my clothes. 'Is the ferry on the move? Have we left the dock?'

'I think so, yes.'

I pick up my bracelets, slide the lock away from the catch and open the door. Elise barrels past me and almost smacks straight into one of the small boys.

'Sorry!' I usher her out of the way and through the door, without making eye contact with the other mother, and down a corridor. I almost cry with relief as I catch a glimpse of the view through the window. We are out at sea.

'Sea!' Elise kneels on her seat and slaps her palms against the window as I wrestle my mobile phone charger into the power point beneath the table. 'Birds! Clouds! Look, Mummy. Look!'

'Shh. Yes, I know.'

The woman at the table next to us has glanced round three times since we sat down. She's older than me, early fifties maybe, and her two children have headphones on and are staring intently at the tablets on the table in front of them. Her husband is reading the paper and has thwarted every attempt she's made at conversion with a grunt or a shrug of the shoulders.

Elise notices the woman watching her and stops bouncing on her seat. She smiles shyly then bangs on the window with the palm of her hand. 'Sea!'

'Yes.' The woman catches my eye and smiles. 'It's very grey, isn't it?'

'Fish!' Elise says, pointing. 'Fish in the sea.'

'Yes, lots of fish.' The woman's eyes travel the length of my daughter's body, taking in her scuffed trainers, overly long jeans and worn sweatshirt. They linger on her hacked hair. She senses me watching and meets my gaze. 'I remember when Robbie was that age.' She nudges the teenager beside her. He rubs at his arm and inches away from her, without looking up from his iPad. 'He was forever chattering away. Can't get a word out of him these days though. What is he?' She looks back at Elise. 'Two? Three?'

'Two and a half.' I try not to show my nerves in my voice but, underneath the table, I'm digging my fingernails into my knees.

'What's your name, little one?' The woman waves her hand to get Elise's attention.

I hold my breath as my daughter studies the woman's face. She steadfastly refused to say that her name was Ben when we played 'let's pretend' before we left the caravan a few hours ago. How do I explain her appearance if she tells the woman her real name?

'Li-Li,' my daughter says under her breath then turns back to the view.

'Lee,' the woman repeats. 'Nice to meet you, Lee. I'm Mel. And Mum?' She looks back at me.

'Helen,' I say softly.

'Lovely name. George has got a sister called Helen. Haven't you, darling?' She reaches across the table and taps the top of her husband's newspaper. He shakes it lightly and grunts irritably.

'We're taking the kids to Galway,' Mel says. 'To see some of George's relatives. Lovely place. Have you been?'

'No.' I shift in my seat. I should have bought a newspaper like George but I haven't got so much as a book to hide behind and Mel's obviously in a chatty mood. The last thing I need is to be grilled about where we're going and why. I glance at my mobile. Only 4 per cent charged. We're three hours into our journey and only an hour from Ireland. Turning it on is a risk but I haven't spoken to Mum since yesterday and I need to check whether dad's OK. I don't know whether the police will be able to trace me if I quickly text her then turn the phone off again. Even if they could there's no way they could get to Rosslare in the next hour. Or could they? They might ring the Gardaí and tell them to meet me when the ferry docks.

'Do I know you?' Mel tilts her head to one side and narrows her eyes. 'The more I look at you the more familiar you seem.' She taps the top of her husband's newspaper again. 'Do we know Helen?'

'I . . . I don't think so. I just have one of those

200

faces.' I stand up abruptly and reach for Elise's hand. 'Do you want a wee?'

My daughter shakes her head.

'We could go to the play area afterwards. They might have a slide.'

Her face lights up and she scrambles across the plastic chairs towards me. Mel watches her, a frown creasing her forehead. I lower my daughter to the ground then reach for her hand.

'Come on then, darling. Lovely to meet you,' I say to Mel. Her husband twists in his chair and nods at me then folds his newspaper and lays it on the Formica table in front of him.

'Anyone want another coffee?' He waves a hand in front of the faces of his teenaged children and mouths the word 'drink'. As he does, my gaze falls to the black and white photograph on his folded newspaper. It's a photo of me and Elise, crouched in front of the tree last Christmas. Above it is the headline:

Bristol mum on the run with her two-year-old daughter.

Chapter 36

'Brigid, hello, so lovely to see you.' Max opens his arms wide and steps forward for a hug. His mother-in-law steps backwards, into the safety of her kitchen. She was openly shocked when she opened the door to him but in a single step she's reined in her emotions. Now she's giving him a cold hard look.

'I'm sorry, I know I should have called.' He thrusts the bouquet of service-station lilies at her. 'But I didn't think you'd agree to see me.'

'You'd have thought right.'

It's like staring at a lined, grey-haired version of his wife, but unlike Jo, who wears her heart on her sleeve, Brigid is a closed book. Eleven years he's known her and yet he's never had a conversation that didn't go beyond the superficial or mundane. Whenever he'd tried to delve deeper, to enquire about Brigid's life back in Ireland, she'd change the subject or make an excuse to do something in another room. Jo had warned him, told him that her mother would refuse to discuss anything before 1983 when they'd moved to England, but he was a journalist, for God's sake. He'd got information out of local councillors whose job it was to deflect awkward questions. But Brigid was impenetrable. He was pretty sure that even if she was waterboarded, she'd still hang onto her secrets. But even the most closed of people had their Achilles heels and hers was Jo. If he could just work out which buttons to press he was pretty sure she'd let something slip eventually.

'Please, Brigid.' He puts a hand on the door frame but doesn't step inside the house. 'I can imagine what Jo's told you and how you probably feel about me but you've only heard one side of the story. There's a lot you don't know.'

'I've heard enough.' Brigid reaches for the door handle and takes a step forward. She's going to close it in his face, he has to think fast.

'She hurt Elise.'

Brigid freezes at the mention of her granddaughter's name.

'She was covered in bruises.' Max's voice cracks as he remembers the conversation with the social worker. Lorraine Hooper had called him shortly after he'd returned to his hotel, asking if he knew where his wife and daughter were. She told him that Jo had taken Elise to the doctor because she'd discovered some suspect bruising. But she'd run off rather than accompany the doctor to the hospital.

Elise, covered in bruises. He feels sick just thinking about it.

'Please, Brigid, I wouldn't have driven all this way if I wasn't worried sick. You have to help me.'

His mother-in-law tightens her grip on the door and, for a second, he thinks that it's over. His attempt to get her onside has failed, but then the door swings all the way open.

'You'd better come inside,' she says. 'But you can't stay long. Andy's nurse will be here shortly.'

'I don't know how much Jo has told you,' Max says. He is sitting across the kitchen table from Brigid, gripping the mug of tea she silently made and then passed to him. 'But she's really not well. Mentally, I mean.'

'Mmm huh.' His mother-in-law continues to gaze at him, her blue eyes bright but unreadable behind her tortoiseshell glasses. She hasn't said a word since she invited him into the kitchen.

Max isn't perturbed. Brigid's eyes might be steely but he can tell by her body language that she's absorbing every word he's saying. She continues to listen as he tells her about Jo's mood swings, her anxiety, her fearfulness and her secretive behaviour.

'I know she was planning on moving up here,' he says. 'And that she wants a divorce. Did she mention either of those things to you?' Brigid glances away, just for a split second, but it's enough to confirm his suspicions. Of course she knew. And she knows where Jo is too.

He decides not to talk to Brigid about Jo's drug

problem, particularly as she was the one who gave her the pain medication. Nor does he mention Paula, or Jo's erratic behaviour at the nursery. What he needs to stress is the fact that his wife is vulnerable and unwell and she needs help.

'That's why it's so important that we find her,' he says, stressing the word 'we'. 'The police rang me earlier to tell me that someone spotted her on the ferry to Ireland. Do you know where she's gone?'

Brigid shakes her head. 'I don't know.'

'I think you do. Brigid, I know she's your daughter and you're trying to protect her but keeping quiet is only going to make things worse for her. By running away, not only is Jo risking Elise's safety but there's a very real possibility that she might end up in jail.' He pauses and waits for his words to sink in.

'Jail,' his mother-in-law repeats. An emotion he can't read passes over her face like a cloud.

'Jo is in very, very serious trouble, Brigid. The court has issued a search and find order. Which means that, when she's found, she'll be arrested.'

He can sense that he's found her weak spot. Her hands resting on the cotton tablecloth are shaking, and the skin at the base of her neck is flushed red. The rash appeared almost as soon as he said the word 'arrested'.

'Do you . . .' He pauses. This question will either break her or she'll shut down. It's a risk but it's one he has to take. He's already asked her several times where she used to live in Ireland and she answered him with silence. 'Do you know anyone in jail, Brigid?'

His mother-in-law jolts back in her seat and stares at him, her eyes wide and her lips parted. He's cracked her. She's about to tell him where Jo's gone.

'Will you have another cup of tea?'

It takes all of his self-control not to swear. Instead he forces a tight smile and nods, not trusting himself to speak.

Chapter 37

When I think of Ireland I don't think of cramped B&B rooms with fuzzy televisions fixed high on the wall, bathroom fans that sound like jumbo jets taking off, and windows that don't open. I think of cold, windswept beaches. I think of picnics in brown paper bags. Of oranges, red lemonade, Tayto crisps and ham sandwiches – or Heinz sandwich spread for a treat. I think of Mum, laying out a tartan blanket, then sipping from a flask of hot tea. I think of baby oil being rubbed into my skin 'to put a bit of colour in those cheeks'. Of treat days when we wouldn't bother with picnics and we'd warm our hands on brown paper bags filled with chips instead, the scent of vinegar mingling with the salty sea air.

Dad never came to the beach with us. If he wasn't at work he was at the horses, the pub or the Gaelic Athletic Association clubhouse. Sometimes he'd take me to the horses with him on a Sunday, to give Mum a break. I'd sit in the car with a bottle of fizzy drink, a book and a packet of crisps whilst he spent hours by the track. I'd grow bored with my book finished and no one to talk to and I'd go in search of him.

'I'll be wit' ya in a minute.'

I don't remember much about my dad but I remember him saying that. It was his Sunday-afternoon mantra, washed down with six pints of beer and a couple of whisky chasers.

I'd lose track of the number of times I'd climb in and out of the car and how many 'minutes' it would take before we finally set off for home with Dad swinging round the lanes and me gripping the door handle in the passenger seat. Neither of us wore seat belts. Dad said there was no need. He was a good driver, he said. He'd been driving those same lanes since he was seventeen. He could get us home blindfolded if he needed to.

I had no reason to disbelieve him. He was my big, strong da. Not tall, and certainly not the broadest of men, but there was a solidity to him that made me feel safe. He wasn't affectionate, but sometimes he'd bring me a quarter of sweets when he came back from a week on a building site somewhere or other, or he'd ruffle my hair when he got back from the match and he'd tell me what a good girl I was. And it was enough. He was enough.

And then, all of a sudden, he was gone.

I swing my legs over the edge of the bed and stand up, taking care not to disturb Elise who's curled up on the duvet with Effie Elephant in her arms. She fell asleep in the car. She didn't even stir as I carried her up the stairs of the B&B and laid her down on the double bed. Before we even left the ferry I'd decided against spending the night in Rosslare. There were too many Brits everywhere and, with our photo splashed across every newspaper I saw, I wanted to get as far away from the port as I could, so I headed for Wexford instead. It was 7 p.m. by the time I spotted a B&B with a vacancy sign in the window. The landlady, a small, thin woman with dyed black hair, glasses and hollows under her cheekbones, was polite but cool as she answered the door. Yes, she had a room. Yes, we could stay one night but she'd need paying in advance. I silently thanked God for the money exchange on the ferry and counted out €50 into her outstretched palm.

I pull the curtains closed. In the morning I'll take Elise for a walk to find a payphone. I need to let Mum know that we're OK. Helen too, if there's time. I've watched enough police dramas to know that they often tap phones to try and trace missing people or serial killers. If the call is kept short they don't have enough time to locate the caller but I don't know how true that is. It might be safer to ring in the morning, before we set off up the coast.

I step into the bathroom and use the toilet. As I stand back up again, black spots dance in front of my eyes and I have to grip the sink to steady myself. I've barely slept in God knows how many days. I didn't sleep at all in the caravan. Every time my eyes would close there'd be a clunk or a clang from outside and they'd fly open again. But I feel less exposed up here in the eaves of the B&B. There's only one escape route, straight down the stairs, but there's a flat roof about twenty feet below our window. If there was a fire or an emergency I'd lower Elise down in a sheet and then find my own way down. But I can't think about that now. I need to sleep.

I sit up with a start, hands flailing in the darkness. My right hand hits the wall. As I snatch my fingers to my chest the blackness fades to grey and objects loom out of the shadows – a wardrobe, a small table, a closed door, a lamp lying on its side. Elise is curled up beside me on the bed, snuffling in her sleep. She stirs as I touch her shoulder but she doesn't wake. I glance at my watch to see what time it is but it's too dark to make out.

I shuffle off the bed and open the bedroom door, just enough that a slim stream of light enters the room and illuminates the face of my watch. 9.12 p.m. I reach for the door handle to close it again, then pause. The sound of voices drifts up the stairs towards me: the low rumble of a man's voice and the higher pitch of a woman's. I step onto the narrow landing and hold my breath as I listen. Logically I know it's the landlady talking to her husband or another guest, but logic is overruled by fear. The voices are still too muffled for me to be able to hear what they're saying so I take a step down the stairs. It creaks under my weight. I freeze, and listen again. The conversation below continues unabated. I glance back at the door to our room. Beyond it my daughter is still asleep. She's safe. But she could wake up at any second. I take another step down the stairs, slotting my foot into the gap between the carpet and wall. This time it doesn't creak. I step again and again, pressing myself up against the wall. I'm on the first floor now. There are four bedrooms here. All the doors are shut. As I inch my way around them and approach the top of the flight of stairs that leads down to the ground floor I catch something the landlady says, 'That's just terrible. I'll keep an eye out. Thank you for letting me know.'

But I still can't make out what the man she's talking to says in reply. His voice is too deep, his Irish accent too thick. I take slow, shallow breaths as I reach for the banister. I'm so close now that the slightest noise would attract their attention. A glimpse, that's all I want. My fingers fold around the white glossed wood. Slowly, slowly, inch by inch, I bend at the waist and lean over the banister.

Peaked hat. Labels. Pale-blue shirt. Navy stab vest.

A split-second view, but it was all I needed to confirm my worst fears. A member of the Gardaí – the Irish police – is standing in the hallway with his arms folded across his chest. My first instinct is to run, to pound back up the stairs as fast as I can, but he'll be after me like a shot. What then? What do I do? My skin prickles with fear. The landlady can't have recognised me from the Garda's description. Why else would she say she'd keep an eye out? But what if she'd pretended she hadn't seen me because she knew I was standing at the top of the stairs? What if she'd signalled to the Garda with her eyes – *she's actually up there* – in the hope they'd catch me unawares?

I press a hand to my face, muffling the short, sharp breaths I'm taking in through my nose, and sidestep to my left. I take another step. Then I climb the stairs, back to the wall, moving sideways. Quiet. I must be quiet. It takes for ever to get to the attic but then I'm back in the room. I push the door too, as silently as I can, and the key trembles in the lock as I turn it. Elise, still curled up on the bed, mumbles in her sleep and rolls over. She's so small, so helpless. She'll be terrified if she's separated from me. This place, these people, they're utterly foreign to her. If she's taken from me, I need to make sure that she's cared for by someone she loves. I need to ring Mum.

I lift my handbag from beside the bed and carry it into the bathroom. I sit on the edge of the toilet, my heart thumping in my ears as I rummage around inside it. Where's my phone?

Finally my fingers close over the faux leather case. I jab at the button on the side.

'C'mon, c'mon, c'mon.' It takes for ever for the phone to come to life and the photo of Elise to appear.

I wrap my phone in the folds of my jumper as it flashes to life and plays a loud, twinkling tune. I tense, and listen for Elise's confused cry, but the only sound in the room is the muted call of the phone.

It falls silent and I look at the screen. Only got 2 per cent battery life left. I need to be quick. Fifteen missed calls, multiple voicemails and twenty text messages. I scroll through the missed calls first – Max, Max, Max, Mr Harrison, Mr Harrison, Lorraine Hooper, Mum, Mum, Helen, Diane – the list goes on and on. I feel sick each time Max's name appears. He'll jump on the first plane to Dublin when he finds out that I've been caught. I've got no hope of getting Mum over here first. Even if she could leave Dad. And Helen won't be able to leave Ben.

The phone hangs limply in my hands as all the adrenalin that surged through me as I ran up the stairs drains away. Whatever I do, whatever I say, it's over. When the Garda comes upstairs I need to stay as calm as possible for Elise's sake. If I'm scared, she'll be scared too. I'll wake her gently, give her one last cuddle and reassure her that everything is going to be OK. I'll tell her that I'll never stop loving her, no matter what.

I cross the room and open the curtains. Elise grunts as the plastic curtain rings slide across the tracks. Outside, the street lights flicker and glow, their amber light cutting through the dusky gloom of the street. The narrow residential road is flanked with parked cars. My car is two cars down, the back seat and boot crammed with the remnants of my life in Bristol. I didn't bring any of the suitcases inside. I couldn't, with Elise in my arms. The Garda's car – white with a blue and yellow stripe – is parked directly outside the B&B.

'Mummy,' Elise mumbles from the bed.

'Go back to sleep.' I half turn but, as I do, a figure appears in the street below. Even in the half-light I can make out what he's wearing – a peaked cap, short-sleeved blue shirt and a stab vest. I press a hand to my chest as he approaches his car, unlocks the driver's side door and steps inside. And then . . . nothing. I can't see him any more. I have no idea if he's radioing for backup or informing the station that he's going to arrest me.

'Mummy,' Elise says again. 'Milk. Milk, please, Mummy.'

In the street below, the car's indicator light flashes. A moment later the car pulls into the road, crawls to the end of the street, turns right and disappears. I press my forehead against the cool glass of the window and all the air rushes from my lungs in one long, slow breath. He's gone. I was so certain . . . so sure that –

Knock. Knock.

I spin round, my skin prickling with fear. Elise stares at the bedroom door, her sleepy eyes suddenly alert.

Knock. Knock. Knock.

The sound is louder this time, more urgent. Were there two policemen downstairs? I glance towards the window on the other side of the room. I could still try and escape. But the door looks old and cheaply made. It reverberates with every knock. One shoulder barge and it would swing open.

Knock. Knock. Knock.

I want to ignore it. I want to dive under the duvet, put my fingers in my ears and hum as loudly as I can to block out the incessant knocking but I'm not a child any more. I no longer believe that closing my eyes will make me disappear.

'OK, OK.' My fingers fumble at the lock and Elise wails for milk as I open the door.

I can do this. I can be calm. I can hold myself together.

'Sorry to disturb you so late.' The landlady tucks a strand of black hair behind her ear. 'But I thought you should know that the guards have just been. Three cars were broken into on this street earlier today and if you've got anything valuable in your car you might want to bring it up to your room.'

I saw her lips moving. The words 'guards', 'car' and 'valuable' are buzzing around my brain but they may as well be in a foreign language for all the sense they make. I was so relieved to see my landlady, and not a second policeman, at my door that I didn't process a word she said.

She stares at me over the thick, black rim of her spectacles. 'Will you be getting your things from your car?'

'Yes . . . yes . . . sorry. Yes, I'll . . .' I glance back at Elise, who's slid off the bed and is opening and closing the door to the wardrobe. Slam. Slam. Slam.

The landlady grimaces. 'I'll stay with the little one if you'd like. If you're quick.'

'Yes, of course. Thank you. Thank you so much.'

I can still feel her puzzled stare boring into my back as I pull on my coat, jam my feet into my shoes and hurry down the stairs, taking them two at a time.

Chapter 38

We are speeding up the M1. There are no leaves on the trees but the fields on either side of the motorway are green and the verges are thick with gorse. We've passed Dublin and still nothing looks familiar but I am relieved to have left Wexford and be back on the road, heading north. There were grey skies when we left but there are hints of blue between the dark clouds. It feels like an omen, a sign that I'm doing the right thing.

We left the B&B after breakfast. Elise turned her nose up at the white and black pudding but wolfed down the sausage, bacon, beans and half a slice of toast. I picked at my own breakfast, too tired to eat.

I leave the motorway and take the R152 towards Drogheda. I'm about half a mile down the road and overtaking a tractor when the engine of the car makes a strange stuttering sound as I press on the accelerator.

'Shit,' I swear under my breath as the engine

warning light flashes on the dashboard. I tap on the accelerator again. This time the car doesn't respond. I glance in the rear-view mirror. Elise is asleep in her car seat. I could carry on and hope the car holds out until we arrive – I'm only about half an hour away from Clogherhead – but it's too much of a risk. I have no idea whether it's a minor issue or not. I've got no choice but to pull over.

I dig through the suitcase in the back of the boot, shifting jumpers, socks and underwear to one side as I search for my mobile. The road is quiet now, the tractor long gone. A couple of cars slowed as they passed us, parked up on the verge, but I've waved them all on. Help means questions and I still have no idea whether Elise and I are in the Irish press. There must be a mechanic nearby who could turn up and tow us to his garage. I've still got nearly €150 in notes and if it costs more than that to fix the car . . . actually I don't know. I don't know how I'm going to pay for accommodation in Clogherhead either. I should have got some more cash out in Wexford. Even if the police could trace the withdrawal they'd have no idea where I went next.

'Damn it.' I shove the jumpers, socks and underwear back to the other side of the suitcase. 'Where is it?'

'Aha!' I snatch up the phone and press the button on the side. Nothing happens; the screen remains black. I press it again, holding the button for longer this time. Still nothing.

I prise open the back of the phone with my finger-nails and rub the battery between my hands but I know it's futile, even as I slot it back into place and press the button again. I threw the phone into the suitcase last night, when I thought the police were about to arrest me. After I brought the suitcases upstairs Elise demanded something to eat and I forgot all about it.

'Oh God.' I run my hands over my face and take a deep breath. What now? What the hell do I do now?

I hear the car before I see it; the purr of the engine as it slows and the crunch of tyres as it pulls into the verge behind me. It's a black Mercedes – large, sleek and powerful. Sunlight glints on the windscreen, making it impossible for me to see who is inside.

Someone's come to help. Oh, thank God.

No.

Wait.

A spark of fear courses through me as I remember that I'm not some random woman who's broken down by the side of the road. I'm on the run. My face is plastered all over the newspapers. People are looking for me.

If the Mercedes had stopped to help me, the driver would have flashed their lights or beeped the horn as they pulled onto the verge. They wouldn't have slid quietly up behind me and turned off the engine.

I take a step away from the open boot and towards Elise's door, my eyes still trained on the black car less than twenty metres away.

Have they been trailing me the whole way from Wexford? I didn't spot them in my rear-view mirror. Were they deliberately hanging back, hiding behind other cars as they followed my every move? Did the landlady realise who I was this morning and ring the Gardaí? Or is it Paula? Is she sitting beside the man who chased me through Boots? Who's behind the windscreen, watching me and waiting?

There's an almost silent *clunk* as the catch on the driver's side door releases. They're getting out.

'Elise!' I yank open her door and pull at the catch on her car seat. Effie Elephant drops from her grasp as she stirs in her sleep, and falls into the footwell. 'Elise, wake up! Come on, sweetheart! Elise, we need to go!'

Chapter 39

Max swigs from his bottle of beer. He'd really like a cigarette too but he can't bring himself to spark one up. Elise might be miles away but this is still her home and he doesn't want her to come back to a house stinking of fags. It's important that everything stays exactly as it was when she left. She'll be traumatised, after the ordeal Jo's putting her through, and she'll need stability and predictability when she returns.

Not that he's any closer to finding her. There was a brief moment at Brigid's when he thought he was going to get a break. Andy's carer turned up while Brigid was making a second cup of tea, and she led him into the bedroom, giving Max the run of the house. He headed straight into the living room, hoping to find a photo or letter that would reveal where Jo had gone. He pulled open the top drawer of a chest of drawers in the corner of the room: knitting stuff. He tried the second drawer: coasters, placemats and linen. When he yanked at the third drawer Brigid walked in. He didn't bother to try and defend himself. Instead he turned and walked straight out of the house without saying a word.

He takes another sip of beer then places it on the coaster to the right of his laptop. Going to Brigid's was a waste of time but when he returned home he found Jo's birth certificate in a folder in the bottom drawer of her chest of drawers, along with Elise's birth certificate, the mortgage agreement and a couple of old bills and credit-card statements.

He unfolds it and scans the information at the top:

Child's full name: Joanne Mary Gallagher
Date of birth: 05 July 1975
Mother: Brigid Gallagher
Father: Unknown

Unknown? He raises an eyebrow. So Brigid gave birth to Jo before she got married? In 1975. No wonder his mother-in-law gets prickly whenever she's asked about Ireland. It must have caused quite a scandal at the time.

Place of Birth: Cork

Max narrows his eyes as he examines the map of Ireland on the screen in front of him then rests an elbow on the desk and scratches his head. Cork's on the south-west coast. He could have sworn that Jo told him she grew up on the east coast of Ireland.

She'd definitely mentioned the sea and beaches several times when they'd talked about their childhoods.

'Gah!' He thumps the desk with his fist. Why didn't he listen when she told him where she grew up? Now he's stuck. With no father listed on the birth certificate and no idea what his name was, his only clue to Jo's whereabouts is her mother's name.

Brigid Gallagher.

He types the name into Google and presses *enter*. 290,000 results.

Shit.

Brigid was definitely married to Jo's father at some point. He can remember her telling him about a photo she found of her mum and dad's wedding day. Brigid had hidden it away somewhere and Jo took it. He opens a website – one where you can search for Irish marriage records – but they don't carry records post-1950 so he tries a genealogy site instead.

BINGO!

There's a record of a Brigid Gallagher marrying a Liam O'Brien at the church of the Sacred Heart, in the parish of Laytown, diocese of Meath, on 5 August 1975, four weeks after Jo was born.

He flicks over to Google Maps and looks up Laytown. It's on the east coast of Ireland. That has to be it.

He tabs back to the genealogy site and scrolls down, looking for more information. What the fuck? There's another Brigid Gallagher listed, only this one was married to Joseph Kearney – same church but four months later.

Shit.

He clicks on both entries, looking for Brigid's home address on the marriage banns, but it's not listed online. The only way to get hold of it is to pay for a copy of the marriage certificate but that would take up to two weeks. Screw that.

He types the address of the Sacred Heart church into Google. No phone number. Damn.

He sits back in his chair and rubs his hands over his face. When the police rang him at 9 a.m., to tell him about the sighting of Jo and Elise on the ferry yesterday, they said they didn't have any more information. And yet he's found a lead in less than half an hour. What the fuck are they doing?

He could hand this information over to them and hope they act on it, but it's killing him, being so passive, letting them take control. The more time passes the more frantic his imagination is becoming. What if Jo's already moved on from Ireland? What if she's taken a flight to Barbados or Dubai or some other country that isn't part of the Hague Convention? He'll have lost Elise for ever.

No. He sits forward in his seat and drums his fingers on the desk. He can't trust that the police will act quickly enough, not when there's so much at stake. He needs to go to Ireland himself. If he flies to Dublin, he can rent a car and drive to the church. If they let him view the marriage banns he'll have two addresses, two potential Brigid Gallaghers, and a rough idea where Jo has gone.

He opens the top drawer of his desk and rummages

through the pens, Post-it notes, USB sticks and receipts. No passport. He opens the second drawer and does the same. And the third drawer, and the fourth drawer. He stands up, glances around his office and heads for the living room. He must have left it in the cupboard in the corner of the room. As he yanks the door open and sees the space left behind by Henry's memory box his stomach tightens. He ignores the sensation and rifles through the books and board games left behind, carefully at first, then more desperately.

'Where the fuck is it?' he shouts as he scoops everything off the shelves and onto the floor. 'Where's my fucking passport?'

Chapter 40

'Come on, Elise. Come on.' I pull my slumbering daughter out of the car and hurry towards the front of the car without looking back. I can hear the crunch of shoes on gravel. The driver of the Mercedes has got out of the car and is crossing the small stretch of verge. They're coming. They're getting closer. Where . . . where . . . where do I go? Where do I hide? There are hedges on both sides but they're too dense and prickly to let us get through to the field. My breath is coming in fast, raggedy gasps and I feel light-headed with fear. Where do I go? The road is my only other option. I'll flag down a car, but there aren't any. Why are there no other cars?

I risk a glance back as I round the bumper. A man with shiny black shoes, a dark suit and close-cropped hair meets my gaze. He doesn't look away. Instead he takes another step towards me, his hands clenching and unclenching at his sides.

I take a step closer to the road. It's still deserted. Where are the cars? Where are the people? If I scream no one will hear me. No one apart from the crow wheeling overhead, cawing loudly. My only choice is to run, but there's no way I can outrun him, not with Elise in my arms. Plead then? He might have children of his own. He might take pity on me. But not if he's a policeman. If he's a policeman he'll force me into that car and he'll take me back to England. I'll never see my daughter again.

'Please!' I shout as I reach the edge of the road. 'Please, don't.'

The man pauses. He's reached the boot of my car. He glances inside and then at me. A frown wrinkles his brow. Is he with Paula? Is that why he just looked in the boot? He thinks I've got whatever it is she stole from Max. I have to convince him that I don't have anything of hers, that there's no point hurting us, that I'll give him everything I have if he'll just let us go.

A deep, bassy rumble fills the air and the ground beneath my feet vibrates. Something large and heavy is travelling down the road towards us: a truck or a tractor. I can't see anything from where I'm standing. It must be behind me. I need to step into the road and flag it down. I take a step to my left. As I do, the man jolts back to life and hurries towards me.

'Wait!' he cries as I step into the road. 'Watch—'

A horn sounds, a rush of air hits me full in the face and Elise screams in my ear. And then I'm yanked backwards, forcefully, by my shoulders.

'Jesus!' the man breathes as an articulated lorry rumbles past, just centimetres from where I was standing. 'You could have had yourself killed.'

'I'm sorry, I'm sorry, I'm sorry.' I brush Elise's shorn hair away from her face as her nails bite into my neck and she stares up at me with wide, uncomprehending eyes. I could have killed her. I could have killed us both.

'You're shaking,' the man says. 'You need to sit down.'

I don't resist as he guides me towards a patch of grass at the edge of the verge. I don't twist away as he grabs my elbow the moment my legs give way beneath me, and carefully lowers me into a sitting position.

I continue to shake for several minutes, then, as the man sits beside me, I burst into tears.

'Just do it,' I say as I bury my face in Elise's hair and tears roll down my cheeks. 'Just do whatever you're going to do.'

'You what?' He leans away, observing me with a confused expression on his face as he rubs a hand back and forth over his hair. 'I . . . er . . . I'm not sure I understand.'

Irish. He has a rich, deep Irish accent. I lift my face from Elise's hair. Up close I can see that his nose is narrower, his chin wider and his pale-blue eyes are more deeply set than the man who chased me through Boots. He's younger too, early thirties maybe.

'I stopped because I thought you were having trouble with your car,' he says. 'I'm sorry if I scared you. I was just about to introduce myself when you ran into the road and . . . well . . .' He tails off and gazes longingly in the direction of his car.

'I'm sorry. I'm . . . I'm . . . just a bit jumpy.'

'English, are you?'

'Irish,' I say. 'But I've been away for a while.'

'Quite a while, I'd say!' Fine lines appear around his eyes as he smiles. His face looks less threatening but I'm still wary. 'Where are you heading?'

'Why do you need to know that?'

'Oh, OK, OK.' He holds out both palms. 'I was just going to offer you a lift somewhere if you needed one, that's all.'

Do I trust him? Just because he's Irish doesn't mean he's not a threat. He could still be an undercover policeman.

'Do you know anything about cars?' I ask. 'The warning light came on. I think there might be something wrong with the engine.'

'No, engines are beyond me, I'm afraid. I thought you might need a tyre changing or have battery trouble. I've jump leads in the boot.'

'No, I'm pretty sure it's the engine. Is there a garage round here? I was going to call one but . . .' I pause. I don't want to tell him that the battery has gone in my mobile. I feel vulnerable enough as it is, without him knowing that.

'There are plenty in Drogheda,' he says. 'I'm on my way back to Clogherhead. I could drop you off en route if you want.'

It's the second time he's offered me a lift. Either

he's genuinely friendly or he really wants to get us into his car.

'No.' I shake my head. 'That's OK, thank you. I'll . . . um . . . I'll ring.'

'OK, well,' – he gets to his feet, brushing grass from his backside and legs – 'I won't bother you any longer. You have a good day, OK.'

I say nothing but, as he walks back to his car, Elise wriggles in my arms and demands that I let her go. I've only got one carton of apple juice and a couple of bananas in the car. Once they're gone I'll only be able to keep her occupied for as long as the iPad battery lasts. I could ask if I can use the stranger's phone to ring a mechanic but we could be here for some time before one turns up. If they turn up at all. I need to trust my instincts and my gut is telling me that we'll be safer if we go than if we stay.

'Wait!' I shout.

The man pauses beside his open car door and looks back at me. 'Yes?'

'You're going to Clogherhead?'

'That's right.'

I shift Elise off my lap, take her hand and get to my feet. 'I'm really sorry. I'm very tired and we've had a long journey. I'm not normally so rude when a stranger offers me help.'

'Right.' Now he looks wary.

I walk towards him holding out my hand. 'Helen Carr. And this' – I gesture towards Elise – 'is my son Ben.'

He takes my hand and squeezes it. 'Sean Hogan. Pleased to meet you, Helen.'

Sean hasn't stopped talking since we got into his car. He's told me about his landlady (widowed, no children), his job, his parents and his plans to buy a house in Clogherhead. He's from Dublin originally, he tells me, but he's grown tired of the bustle of the city and he wants to live somewhere quieter and settle down, get married and have kids. He meets my gaze as he says this and the base of his neck flushes red, as though he's just admitted something embarrassing. I didn't have him down as a nervous man but his breathless monologue and damp brow betray him. As he talks I watch his face. He's older than I initially thought. The laughter lines around his eyes don't disappear when he stops smiling and there are a few greys speckling the dark hair at his temple. He's probably late thirties, early forties tops. I wasn't wrong about his eyes though. They're the palest blue I've ever seen, made paler by his dark eyelashes and thick eyebrows.

'So, are you married then, Helen?'

Sean's gaze leaves the road and flicks towards my hands, gathered in my lap.

'Widowed,' I say softly. Separated or divorced would be closer to the truth but both answers would invite more questions than I'm willing to answer.

'I'm sorry,' he says. 'That must be tough on the little one, and you, obviously.'

I twist round in my seat to look at Elise but she's staring out of the window, looking for the sea.

'Yes,' I say.

We lapse into silence as the road becomes more winding as we leave Drogheda behind. There's a low wooden fence to the left with a stream beyond it, and a long stone wall to the right. The fields are dotted with trees and little white houses with grey roofs. Above us the clouds have gathered into thick white knots, blocking out the sky. I want to break the silence, to let Sean know that he didn't say anything inappropriate, but how? If I tell him that I'm fine, that I'm over my husband's supposed death, he'll find that strange. If I tell him that 'Ben' is missing his dad I'll further lower the mood. I decide on small talk instead.

'Do you have brothers and sisters?' I ask, at exactly the same time that Sean says, 'Do you still have relatives here?'

We both laugh and the awkwardness lifts.

'Three sisters,' Sean says. 'I'm the youngest.'

I smile. 'That must have been interesting.'

'Particularly when they dressed me up like a dolly when I was,' – he pauses – 'sixteen.'

We both laugh again.

'The sea!' Elise shouts from the back of the car, arm waving. 'The sea!'

I look beyond Sean and there it is, beyond the grass verge and a cluster of holiday cottages, stretching across the landscape like a faded blue blanket. The sea. So pale it almost blends into the sky. It's been 33 years since I last saw it but my stomach still flips and a feeling of utter joy floods my body. I wind down the window and inhale the air, sucking it deep

231

into my lungs. I can't smell the sea. I can't smell anything at all, but the exhilaration makes me throw back my head and laugh. I've dreamed of this place since I was eight years old; dreams that became so blurry over time it was almost as though I'd imagined it. It's nothing like I remembered, but it's real. It's here. My daughter is squealing with excitement and I'm smiling so much my cheeks are aching. I'm home.

As Elise quietens and I press my head against the seat rest and take a deep, contented breath, Sean glances at me and smiles. 'I wish I'd recorded that. I could have sold it to the tourist board for a ton of euros. Want to do it again? I might get enough for a deposit for a house!'

Chapter 41

Mary hurries from the kitchen at the sound of the car pulling up outside the house and steps into the hallway. She scurries back to retrieve a yellow duster and a can of polish from the cupboard under the sink, then busies herself spraying and buffing the small hall table. She knows she's being ridiculous, feigning a reason to bump into Mr Hogan, but he's such a lovely young man, a proper breath of fresh air, and she really enjoys their chats. So nice to be able to talk about something other than ailments, soap operas and gossip for a change. Not that she doesn't appreciate the ladies in the church group, they're lovely women – on the whole. And they got her through a terrible time when she lost Niamh and Patrick within five years of each other. But they're not close. Not like she was with Brigid. She could have told her anything.

'Will you look what I've got here for you!' Sean opens the door with a flourish and ushers into the hallway a tired-looking woman with wild red hair holding a scruffy-haired boy in her arms. 'New guests!'

The woman looks at her with startled eyes. She reminds Mary of her next-door neighbour's cat. It gives her the same kind of suspicious look from the wall when she steps into the garden, then quickly scurries away.

'I'm sorry we didn't ring ahead,' the woman says, 'but my phone ran out of battery and when the car died too,' – she glances behind her, towards Mr Hogan, who's closing the front door – 'Sean kindly stopped and offered us a lift. He said you might have a room free.' She pauses then, when Mary doesn't immediately reply, and adds, 'If not we could hire a cottage. If Sean wouldn't mind giving us another lift.'

'Oh, shut up.' He slaps a friendly hand onto her shoulder, making her jump. 'I'm sure Mrs Byrne can sort you out with a room. Can't you, Mary?'

Mary stiffens at the casual use of her first name but Sean softens it with a wink. He's playing with her – being all jovial and flirtatious. It's a little game they play, where Sean pretends she's not 67 and she pretends he's not young enough to be her son. It's ridiculous, a woman of her age playing along like she does, but it's harmless, make-believe, like the soaps her friend Cathleen Quinn likes so much. But she can't play along now, not with new guests. It wouldn't be appropriate. So she doesn't return his smile.

'If you'd have thought to ring me, Mr Hogan, I could have prepared a room,' she says, knowing full well that all of her rooms are spotless and the linen was freshly laundered yesterday, despite not being used.

'It's OK, honestly,' the red-haired woman says, setting the child on its feet. 'I don't want to put you to any trouble.'

'It's no bother,' Mary says. There's something about the woman that isn't sitting right with her and not just the fact that she's English. They get a lot of tourists in Clogherhead, of all different nationalities, but there's something odd about this one. Whenever she speaks there's a breathy tone to her voice as though she's attempting to suck the words back in even as she says them. And she seems to wilt under Mary's gaze, stooping as though she's trying to hide without actually leaving the room.

'If you're sure,' the English woman says. 'Oh, Lee, be careful with that!' She snatches up the statue of the Virgin Mary from the hall table before her boy's reaching fingers can grab it. She places it back on the table and looks at Mary. 'I'm so sorry.'

'No bother.' Mary bends at the waist and peers at the child. 'You didn't want to break it, did you? You just wanted a look?'

The child takes a step back, towards its mother, but its eyes are still on the statue.

'Here.' Mary crouches down with the statue in her hands and holds it towards the child. 'You can touch it if you like, but only gently, just with a finger.'

The child takes a step forward hesitantly.

'It's OK,' his mother says.

The boy reaches out a finger and presses it against the face of the statue.

'Lovely, isn't she?' Mary says. She studies the child's face. He has very soft, fine features for a boy. Lovely dark, feathery eyelashes framing the most brilliant big blue eyes. Niamh had green eyes. 'As green as a meadow,' Patrick used to say. She was a curious child too, always getting into everything. Mary couldn't turn her back on her in the kitchen without her opening a cupboard and rifling through the pots and pans.

'She's pretty,' the child says, in the same soft English tone as his mother and the image of Niamh sinks back into the depths of Mary's mind like a stone dropped into the sea.

She stands back up and puts the statue back on the table. 'Lee, did you say his name was?'

'Ben,' Mr Hogan says.

Mary looks at the mother. The expression on her face has changed from fraught to fearful. 'I thought I heard you call him Lee.'

'My Lee Lee,' the child says, pointing to his chest.

'Yes,' the mother says. 'I do call him Lee, too. His name's Ben but Lee's his middle name. He prefers it.'

'I see,' Mary says, but she doesn't. There's something about the mother's response that doesn't quite ring true. Why would you let a child choose its own name when you'd chosen a perfectly good one? And then introduce that child by the name they didn't like? 'Well, I'm Mary Byrne. And you are?'

'Helen.'

'Will you be staying long, Helen?'

'In Clogherhead?'

'No. Here.' Strange or not, she can't let them go to the holiday cottages – not with the damp that would settle on the boy's chest and the electricity meters that have a tendency to turn themselves off at all times of the day and night. And anyway, she has rooms to fill. 'Will you be staying long here, at Seamount?'

'I don't know. Maybe a week. Maybe longer. I . . . I'm not sure of my plans just yet, but at least a week.'

'I don't have a cot for the little one.'

'That's OK. He can share a double bed with me.'

'No bother. Let's call it a week. You can settle up with me next Tuesday and let me know if you'll be staying for longer. Does that sound OK to you?'

The woman smiles for the first time since she stepped through the door. 'That sounds wonderful. Thank you. Thank you so much.'

'You can thank me when you leave. You'll find a list of house rules in your room but make sure you abide by this one.' She crosses the hallway and taps the small plaque affixed to the front door.

Make sure the door is properly shut when you enter and leave.

Chapter 42

Enjoying your time in Ireland, are you, Jo? Have you taken Elise to the Wicklow Mountains? Or to Powerscourt Gardens? Or perhaps to the beach? Oh, wait, you won't have done that because you're hiding. You're sweating it out in run-down B&Bs, jumping at every sound and starting at every shadow. You're driving for miles, checking in the rear-view mirror to see who's following you. Do you see my face looking back at you? Do you dream about me at night? I imagine you're in quite a state by now. Dark circles under your eyes because you can't sleep. Trouble breathing? Feeling trapped. That's because the net is closing in around you, Jo. I look forward to seeing how much you squirm when you finally realise that you've been caught.

Chapter 43

The stairs creak as I walk down them, hand in hand with Elise. I feel like an intruder, creeping around in this huge, empty house, and, as we walk into the breakfast room, I immediately look for Sean. But there's no sign of him. Or anyone else for that matter. After Mary showed me to my room last night Sean told me that we were the only guests. Low season, he said, and business was quiet. Not that it bothered him. He's been staying with Mary on and off for two years – whenever his firm sends him up to Drogheda for a client meeting. He could have stayed in a hotel in town but he'd chosen Clogherhead instead because he wanted to be by the sea. Mary's B&B was the only one with a free room.

'Mary's lonely,' he said. 'She won't admit it but it's there, you know? Like a dark cloud hanging over her.'

I was surprised by how insightful he was, how much he seemed to care about our landlady. Not that I could sense any vulnerability in her. She'd been brusque and cold as she'd talked me through how to operate the shower and the TV, and there were laminated signs all over the house, telling guests what they could and couldn't do.

'Will you be wanting the Irish breakfast then?' Mary suddenly appears behind me, making me jump. It's eight o'clock in the morning and she hasn't got a hair out of place. Her blonde fringe is neatly combed across her forehead, showing off the small pearl earrings in her earlobes. They match the string of pearls around her neck, oddly incongruous against her blue and white striped apron. It's only her slippers, grey and faded with the backs trodden down, that aren't perfectly polished or neatly pressed.

'Yes, yes, please.'

'And the little one?' Mary's gaze falls to Elise who's making a grab for the condiments basket on the nearest table.

'He'll have the same. But no black or white pudding, please.'

'Take a seat then.' She gestures at the table nearest the window. 'Will you be wanting tea or coffee?'

'Coffee, please.' I pull out a chair and settle my daughter onto it. 'And a cup of milk for El . . . Lee . . . if that's not too much trouble.'

A strange expression crosses Mary's face. It's only there for a split second but long enough for me to worry. I must never slip and call Elise by her full name. If anyone suspects that she's not a boy questions will be asked and we'll have to leave. Not that

240

we can stay long. It won't be long before Paula or the police realise my connection with Clogherhead and turn up looking for me. I need to find Mum's sisters and brother, maybe even some of my cousins. I'm hoping they'll be able to point me towards another part of Ireland where I really can disappear. I'll need to borrow some money too, enough to tide me over for a few weeks. After that, I don't know. At some point I need to ring Mr Harrison to ask if he's heard from the police. The best outcome would be him telling me that Paula's been arrested and I'm safe to return to the UK. And the worst? I don't want to think about the worst. I don't want to spend the rest of my life looking over my shoulder.

Last night, after Mary finished her guided tour of my room, Sean tapped on the door and asked me if I wanted any help finding a mechanic to fetch my car. When I told him I'd use the iPad to look one up he laughed. Mary didn't have Wi-Fi, he said, but he could sort one for me if I wanted. I could have hugged him. Instead I gave him a warm smile and said that if there was anything I could do for him in return just to ask.

'No, you're all right, I—' He broke off, gazing past me to the window where Elise was playing. My stomach lurched. She'd dug one of her dolls – a baby in a pink hat, dress and booties – out of one of the plastic bags and was pressing her face to the glass, telling her to look outside. Shit. We'd cut our hair, we were wearing borrowed clothes and using Helen and Ben's passports (I'd hidden our originals in a side pocket of the suitcases, along with Max's that I'd accidentally snatched up when we left), but it hadn't occurred to me to ask Helen to lend me some of Ben's toys. I'd automatically snatched up Elise's favourites when I'd packed up the house. I hadn't considered that someone might see her playing with them.

'It's . . . he . . .'

Sean smiled. 'C'mon now, Jo. We're a bit more open-minded over here than you might remember. Well, some of us anyway. If a little boy wants to play with dolls it's no skin off my nose. All good preparation for being a da.'

Sean took my silence as a sign that it was time for him to leave and then gave me a nod.

'I'll leave you alone. You must be tired after all the day you've had. Don't worry about the car. I'll sort it.'

I didn't see him for the rest of the day but when I woke up this morning there was a note pushed under the door:

Mechanic has got your car. They said they're a bit backed up with work but they'll look at it as soon as they can. If you need to rent one while you're waiting give me a shout and I'll give you a lift to Drogheda – there's a few hire places there. Sean.

When Sean originally said he'd give us a lift I was so relieved to get off the verge I didn't give the car a second thought. But last night I barely slept for worrying about it. It was Helen's car, not mine. What if someone vandalised it or got it started and drove it off? What if someone reported it to the police and they knew I'd been driving it?

'There's milk over there,' Mary says now. She points

242

at a sideboard on the other side of the room. 'And juice and cereal if you want it. I'll be back shortly with your coffee and breakfast.'

She leaves the room before I can thank her. A couple of minutes later she returns with a coffee which she places wordlessly in front of me. Ten minutes after that she enters the room with two plates in her hands.

'Two breakfasts.' She places them in front of me and Elise.

'Thank you.'

'No bother.'

I expect her to leave the room again but she doesn't. She goes over to the sideboard and opens the cupboard. She takes out a packet of cornflakes and fills the plastic cereal dispenser. Then she does the same with the rice crispies.

'First visit to Ireland?' she asks as I cut up Elise's sausage and bacon into small bits.

'No.' I shake my head. 'But it's been a long time since I was last here.'

'You're on holiday then?'

'Yes.'

Mary says nothing and the silence hangs heavily in the room. She isn't done asking questions.

'Will your husband be joining you?' she asks, keeping her tone light. 'I only ask because I do have a room with a double bed and a single but I'd need time to prepare it.'

'No. It's just me and Lee. I'm widowed.'

Mary stops wiping down the sideboard and grips the edge, as though steadying herself.

'You could travel the world and you couldn't escape grief,' she says softly. 'You'd have to cut out your own heart to be free of it.'

There's a ring on the third finger of her left hand but I know she's widowed, Sean told me as much in the car. I can see the pain in Mary's eyes. Pain I caused by lying to her. Why didn't I just tell the truth?

'I'm sorry.' I stand up and cross the dining room. 'I've upset you.'

'No, no.' She stands up straighter and backs away. 'I'm grand. You go back and finish your breakfast. You don't want it getting cold.'

'But . . .'

She shoos me away. 'Do you have any plans for today? It's not due to rain until later, if you're wanting to take the little one to the beach.'

I have distant memories of playing on the beach with my cousins, of the three of us searching for shells and peering into rock pools. But it's not my fond memories that draw me out of Mary's B&B and down the road towards the shore. And it's not about whether Mary thinks I'm strange for driving all this way and then holing myself away in my room for half a day. This is about Elise. She deserves a normal childhood, or as normal as I can make it given the circumstances. She needs to feel the wind on her face and the sand under her feet. She needs to run and play and squeal. I'm her mother and it's my responsibility to show her the world and explore it with her until she's old enough to do so herself.

I've barely been out of the car since we left Cardiff, other than to walk around the ferry, enter a B&B, or when the car broke down. After years of telling myself that something awful would happen if I left the house, three utterly terrifying things happened, one after another. Paula threatened me, twice, and a strange man chased me through a shop. But I didn't hyperventilate or have a panic attack. I shouted and I shoved. I ran and I hid. It was real danger that I was responding to, not imagined. Sweat dribbled down my back and I thought my heart was going to beat itself out of my body but I didn't faint or collapse. I didn't die.

If I can survive an experience like that then I can take my daughter by the hand and I can lead her down a street I don't remember. I can show her the sea for the very first time. If I can do this, then I can do anything.

We reach the bottom of Main Street within minutes. On the left are rocks, pitted with tiny pools of seawater and separated from a field by a high stone wall. On the right the beach stretches as far as the eye can see. Elise squeals with joy the second we set foot on the sand. She's bundled up in one of Ben's old winter coats. A grey beanie covers her head and she's wearing a pair of Transformer wellies. It's raining lightly and there's a strong wind, but it isn't the weather that takes my breath away. It's the look on my daughter's face. Her eyes are shining and her skin is flushed with excitement. It took every ounce of determination I have to step out of Mary's front door and walk down the street but I did it. I walked out of the door and I made it all the way to the beach. My lower back is clammy with sweat and I must have wiped the palms of my hands on my jeans countless times on the way here but it was worth it just for the look on Elise's face. Nothing bad is going to happen. I mentally repeat the mantra my CBT counsellor taught me. I am in a safe place. Although maybe I'll stop using the mantra. Nowhere is safe.

'Sea!' Elise tugs on my hand as she jumps up and down and points. 'Sea! Sea, Mummy!'

'I know, isn't it wonderful.'

I let my daughter lead me down the wet beach, past the large rocks to our left, slick with water or green with lichen or seaweed. As a child I spent hours clambering over the rocks and peering into rock pools with a bucket in one hand and a net in the other. Mum would keep one eye on me and another on the sea, to watch for high tide. One memory that hasn't faded with time is watching the sea come in with Mum. We were holding hands – I was wearing red woollen mittens and she was wearing soft brown leather gloves. We were up on the road where it was safe, watching as a storm brought the tide closer and closer. I can still see the waves now – swallowing the rocks whole and then smashing against the brick wall at the end of Mr Galway's garden, surf leaping and spraying over the top. I was mesmerised. I'd never seen anything so terrifying and beautiful in my life.

'Mummy, look!'

Elise tugs at my hand and gestures towards her

right welly as she stomps down into the wet sand. Seawater splashes up and brown sand splatters over her wellies, jeans and the bottom of her coat.

I glance back at the sign at the entrance to the beach warning that the rocks can become submerged, then check my watch – 9.30 a.m. Mary told us that high tide is around 12.40 p.m. We're safe for another few hours.

'I can do it too,' I say and stomp my trainered foot onto the beach. This time we both get splashed. Elise laughs loudly.

'Again, again!'

I glance to my right. The entire beach is empty. We have the place to ourselves.

'How about we run instead? All the way down to the sea?'

My daughter's smile widens.

'OK. Three, two, one . . . go!'

We sprint down the beach, Elise's little legs going nineteen to the dozen as I take long, loping strides to match her pace. As we reach the sea, pink-cheeked and gasping, I give a small tug on her hand to stop her from speeding straight into the waves.

'Let's jump them,' I say. 'Here it comes. Ready, steady, jump!'

My daughter's shining eyes don't leave mine as we jump and jump and jump. We're both laughing, both gulping down lungfuls of clean, icy-cold sea air. Drizzle still mists my face and the sky is grey. We both squeal as we mistime a leap and the sea crashes over our shoes and wellies, wetting our trouser legs, wrapping the material around our skin. My daughter looks up at me, her bottom lip wobbling, and I scoop her up and into my arms. She clings to my neck, knocking my hood off my head.

'Naughty sea.' I unzip my coat with one hand and wrap it around her damp legs. 'Shall we tell the sea off for splashing us?'

She frowns at me, her eyes glazed with tears, ready to spill.

'Shall we shout it?' I say. 'As loud as we can?'

Shouting isn't something that's normally encouraged, at home or at nursery, so my suggestion has the effect I was hoping for. A smile flickers at the edges of Elise's mouth.

'Naughty sea!' she says.

I kiss her on the cheek. 'Louder!'

She gazes down at the waves breaking a couple of feet away. 'NAUGHTY SEA!'

'That's it!'

'You say it, Mummy.'

'Only if you say it too.'

'NAUGHTY SEA!' we shout. 'NAUGHTY SEA!'

There is no horizon. No end to the sea, no start to the sky. They are the same shade of grey misted together by the weather. Three weeks ago I would have been terrified by how vast they are and how tiny I feel in comparison but, right now, I don't think I've ever seen anything more beautiful. My hair is clinging damply to my head, my fingers are almost numb beneath my thin, acrylic gloves and my legs are wet, but I feel alive. For the last three and a half years I felt like I was trapped at the bottom of a hole. I could see other people walking past above – laughing, loving and living their lives. Some would ignore me, others would glance down and then walk past. Some people stopped and shone a spotlight into the hole and shouted for me to get out.

I tried. I tried. I tried so many times to scramble out to join the rest of the world but the harder I climbed the deeper I fell. When Elise was born she reached a hand into the hole but instead of scaling the walls to join her I pulled her in too. I kept my daughter in the hole with me for two long years and I waited and I waited and I waited for someone to lower a ladder so I could climb out. I didn't realise there was an escape hatch in the side of the hole. I'd spent so long staring up that I didn't think to look around me.

I tip back my head, suck in a cold breath and whoop with joy.

'Mummy!' Elise presses her hands over her ears and screws her eyes tightly shut.

'Sorry.' I press my cold cheek against her. 'I'm sorry, sweetheart. Mummy's just really, really happy.'

Her grip on the back of my neck tightens and her body stiffens in my arms.

'Look, Mummy.' She raises one arm and points across the beach. I follow her line of sight, to the blue car slowly tracking its way across the sand towards us.

Chapter 44

Mary stands quietly in the hallway and listens. It's 7.15 p.m. and Helen and the child have been up in their room for half an hour and she can still hear the boy crying and whinging. He'd seemed so cheery over breakfast but he's been upset for the best part of the day. Mary had quite a shock when they'd burst back into the B&B that morning, less than an hour after they left for the beach. The woman looked even paler than normal and the boy was crying. From the way Helen was carrying him over her shoulder, Mary had immediately assumed an accident, or worse, and she'd rushed out of the kitchen, her hands wet with soapsuds and her heart thudding in her chest.

'No, no,' Helen had said, when Mary asked if she should call an ambulance. 'He's . . . he's fine.'

She sounded breathless, as though she'd run all the way back up from the beach. Her red hair was plastered to her head, her trainers were sodden and her coat was undone. The boy still had his hat on but his trousers were wet to above the knee.

'So he didn't fall on the rocks then?' Mary had to resist the urge to reach out and touch the child. 'He didn't hurt himself?'

'No.' Helen rubbed her hand back and forth on the child's back and shush, shush, shushed him but she seemed close to tears herself. She glanced back towards the closed front door. Mary could see the fear and indecision in her eyes when she looked back at her.

'You look scared,' she ventured. 'Did something happen?'

She crossed the hallway and reached for the door handle but Helen cried out before she could turn it.

'No!'

'What is it?'

'There was a car, on the beach, it was heading straight for us so I ran.'

Mary pressed a hand to the door to steady herself as fear flooded her heart. It was like what had happened to Niamh all over again, only her daughter was all alone when the car gunned up the road towards her. It was like history repeating itself, almost to the day.

'What . . . what colour was it?' she stuttered, praying that the car wasn't a white Ford Fiesta.

'Blue. Quite a small car. I couldn't tell what type it was.'

It wasn't the same car. How could it be?

'Jimmy.' Mary breathed. 'Jimmy McCall. His da's been giving him driving lessons.'

251

'On the beach?' Helen still looked like she might jump out of her skin if she heard a loud noise but the fear had faded from her eyes.

'Yes.' Mary let go of the wall and straightened up. She nearly let her defences slip then. And she doesn't let anyone see her vulnerable side. She really should close the B&B around the anniversary of Niamh's death because putting on a brave face is getting harder, not easier. She thought her grief would ease over time but it hasn't. It's not as raw as it was the day that Niamh died, but the passing of time brings with it its own pain. The years roll by without Niamh and every February Mary marks what might have happened – she would have started primary school, secondary school, gone to university, graduated, been in her first job. She might have married, had a baby. Grandchildren.

'Mary?' Helen's soft voice cut through her thoughts. 'Are you OK?'

'Yes, sorry. What was I saying? Driving on the beach has been banned. The council put up signs but everyone turns a blind eye in the winter. It's the safest way for the young ones to learn. Jimmy's been at it for a few weeks now.'

Helen didn't respond. She stood in the hallway, dripping water all over Mary's freshly cleaned tiles, with the strangest expression on her face as she hugged the sobbing child to her chest. Mary has had all sorts in her B&B over the years – couples who embarrassed her with their loud lovemaking, businessmen who never said a word other than to complain about the lack of Wi-Fi, hikers, the elderly, small family groups. All her guests had their little quirks and ways – some that made her smile, some that drove her spare – but she'd never met anyone like Helen. She was fearful and prickly at the same time. There wasn't an air of mystery around her, there was a wall.

'You might want to go and get changed,' Mary suggested. 'You'll both catch a chill if you stay in those wet clothes.'

Helen had jolted at the sound of her voice then nodded sharply and hurried off up the steps with the child still in her arms. Mary remained in the hallway for a couple of minutes, staring at the puddle on the tiles, thinking, then she snapped herself out of it and went into the kitchen to fetch a tea towel.

Mary glances down at the basket of toys at her feet. She knows that Ben has his own toys. He was clutching a fluffy grey elephant when they first arrived at the house and she could see an iPad poking out of the top of Helen's carrier bag. But children quickly grow tired of playing with the same thing day in, day out, and if she surprises the boy with some new playthings it might stop him crying. When Sean got in earlier he told her that the sound didn't bother him. It bothers her though. It cuts right to the bone.

She didn't deliberately set out to follow Helen and Ben at lunchtime. She'd tidied all the rooms, other than theirs, and was having a welcome cup of tea in the living room when she heard the front door click. She rushed to the window and saw them walking up the road, hand in hand. They'd both changed their trousers and the boy was wearing a different-coloured hat. Mary considered her options. The house was now empty and she was free to clean their room. On the other hand the rain had finally stopped and she needed to fetch some fresh bread from the baker's and a pad of invoice forms from the post office. It wouldn't take her more than a few minutes and she could still finish her cleaning before anyone got back.

I'm not spying on them, she told herself as she put on her coat, hat and boots. I'm simply making the most of a gap in the weather.

It didn't take long before she found them on Main Road. They'd stopped outside one of the little cottages. With their whitewashed walls, tiny, deep-set windows and thatched roofs, the cottages were always a draw for the tourists. The residents joked that if they charged a euro a photo they'd be rich enough to sell up and buy a big house in Drogheda. Only Helen didn't have a camera in her hand. She was staring at the house, as though in a trance. Mary hung back, hiding behind a large bush. If Helen looked round she wouldn't be able to see her, but Mary still had a perfect view from between the leafless branches. She opened her handbag and held it in front of her as though she was looking inside. If anyone she knew walked by she could make an excuse about searching for some stamps or a handkerchief.

Why was Helen staring at the house? Did she know the Kennedys? She'd spoken to Nora after Mass on Sunday and she hadn't mentioned that she was expecting any visitors. And all Helen had said was that she was visiting Ireland for a break. Or had she? She'd barely said a word since she'd arrived. That wasn't unusual in a guest; a lot of Mary's customers kept themselves to themselves and Mary never pried. But she couldn't shake the feeling that all was not right with Helen and her son. And that made her nervous.

She'd quizzed Sean about her new house guest over breakfast but he wasn't much help. Helen was Irish, not English, he told her. He didn't know much more than that. Mary hadn't been surprised by the revelation – she'd had plenty of American guests who claimed they were Irish when actually they were only distantly related – but she wanted to know more. She'd tried to engage Helen in conversation over breakfast but then the young woman had dropped the bombshell that she was widowed and Mary felt as though the carpet had been pulled from beneath her feet.

There was no point in speculating, she decided as she closed her handbag, straightened her coat and stepped out from behind the bush. If she wanted answers she needed to be forthright.

'Pretty, isn't it?' she commented as she approached Helen, still crouched on the pavement beside her son.

The woman jolted in surprise and looked up at her. 'I'm sorry?'

'The cottage.' She looked herself, noting that a new ornament – a figurine of a dancer – had appeared in the living-room window. 'Do you know the Kennedys?'

'No, no.' Helen shook her head, her dyed red hair fluttering on her shoulders. She stood up and reached for her son's hand. 'I don't suppose you know if there's anywhere round here that we could get some lunch?'

Inwardly Mary smiled. She knew a distraction technique if she saw one. 'There's the Little Strand restaurant but it doesn't open for lunch at this time of year. There's a pizzeria further up Main Road. If that's closed too there's always the takeaway.' She glanced at Ben who was tugging on his mother's hand and calling her name. 'They do good chips if he's hungry.'

'Thank you.' Helen smiled tightly. 'That's very helpful.'

'Sghetti,' the child said. 'I want sghetti, Mummy.'

'OK.' She glanced up the street and tugged on his hand, eager to be on her way.

'One . . . er . . . one second,' Mary said.

Helen stopped in her tracks and looked back. 'Yes?'

'What was it about the cottage that you found so interesting?'

'The . . . er . . . the cat.'

She started walking again.

'What cat?' the boy asked as he ran to keep up with his mother's quick strides. 'What cat, Mummy?'

What cat indeed, Mary thought as she turned to walk in the other direction. The Kennedys didn't have one. They didn't have any animals. The danders sparked Rory's asthma.

* * *

From outside Helen's room Mary can hear the low drone of the television, the high-pitched wail of the boy and, somewhere in between, Helen trying to console him. Mary knocks on the door – three sharp taps – and then waits. The television goes off, the boy continues to cry and she can distinctly hear Helen making a shushing sound.

She knocks again. This time she adds, 'It's just me.'

A couple of seconds later the door opens a crack and Helen eyes her warily. Her hair is tidied back in a messy ponytail and she's removed her glasses. There's a red ridge on the top of her nose and dark circles under her eyes.

'I'm so sorry,' Helen says. 'Is Lee's crying disturbing you? He's overtired and I'm struggling to get him to sleep. He's refusing to change into his pyjamas.'

'These are for him.' Mary thrusts the basket of toys forward.

'Oh.' Her mouth forms a perfect 'o' as her eyes flick over the wooden sorting box, Fisher Price clock, chunky jigsaws and the plastic zoo animals. She looks back up at Mary. 'That's so kind of you.'

She opens the door to reach for the basket. As she does so, Mary catches sight of the child, half naked, sitting on the edge of the double bed. He's stopped crying and is swinging his legs back and forth as he watches the exchange at the door.

'Mind that he doesn't break anything,' Mary says as Helen lifts the basket out of her hands.

'Yes, yes, of course. Thank you again. Really. That's so kind. Lee will be ever so . . .'

Helen is still expressing her gratitude as Mary turns to go. She takes the stairs one at a time, gripping the banister as she quickly returns to the ground floor. She hurries across the hallway, steps into her living room, shuts the door behind her and then grips the back of the armchair. She bends over it and sucks in air, gulping it into her lungs. She'd only caught a glimpse of the child, sitting on the edge of the bed in pink and white spotty knickers with bruising on his back and chest. But, in that brief moment, she could have sworn she was looking at Niamh.

Chapter 45

'Right, I'd better get changed.' Sean pushes back his chair from the breakfast table and stands up. I didn't expect to see him in the dining room this morning but he was sitting at the table by the window, sipping a coffee, when we walked in half an hour ago. He immediately invited us to join him and made Elise laugh by pretending that the salt and pepper pots were scared of her and running away along the table. When I asked him whether he had a day off he told me that he didn't have a client meeting until 10 a.m. so he'd gone for a run along the beach instead. His hair is smoothed back from his face, still damp from the shower, and he's dressed casually in jeans and a sweatshirt. 'You have a good day now, you hear.'

'And you, little man,' – he ruffles Elise's hair as he walks past her – 'you be good for your mammy.'

'My not a man,' Elise shouts after him. 'My a girl.'

I inhale sharply. Mary's not in the room with us

but that doesn't mean she's not listening. She drifts silently from room to room like a ghost in an apron, grey slippers and pearls. Unlike Sean, who stomps around the house, slams the front door and clomps around in the room next to ours, Mary appears as if from nowhere. Just like she did yesterday afternoon when I was standing outside Mum and Dad's old cottage, and yesterday evening when she knocked on my bedroom door.

'Course you are.' Sean pauses in the doorway and turns back. He winks at me and then smiles at Elise. 'And a very lovely girl you are too.'

Satisfied with his response she flashes him a winning smile.

'See you then!' He raises a hand in goodbye. A second later the front door clicks shut, a shadow passes by the window, and he's gone.

'So,' – I reach across the table and touch my daughter on the hand – 'I thought that, today, we could go back to the beach and explore the rock pools. But first we need to ring Granny.'

It's been days since I last spoke to Mum and I desperately need to talk to her and not just because I have no idea where to find my aunts Sinead and Celeste or Uncle Carey. The last time I spoke to her she said Dad wasn't great. I hate to think of her having to make decisions about his care with no one to turn to.

'Go Gan's old house?' Elise says.

'No.' I shake my head. 'We're not going back there today.'

I didn't think I'd recognise our old house, not after so many years and when the streets of Clogherhead are so unfamiliar, but the second we turned the corner by Lea Cottages onto Main Road my breath caught in my throat. Scissored snapshots of my childhood flashed through my mind – striped wallpaper, a dark-green paisley carpet, a tiled fireplace, a framed photo of Jesus in the hallway and *Wanderly Wagon* on the TV in the lounge. Smells too – my dad's aftershave and the booze on his breath after he returned from the football, the floral scent of the lavender Mum grew in the front garden and the warm yeasty scent of bread being baked in the kitchen. I heard the wind whistling under the front door when someone forgot to put the draught excluder back in place, and seagulls cawing outside my bedroom window. I felt the atmosphere of our home as though it was a soft, warm blanket. That blanket was whipped away the day Dad disappeared.

'He's a bad man and we're better off without him.' That was Mum's stock response whenever I asked where he was. As a child I eventually stopped asking about him but my desperation to find out what had happened to him returned when I hit my teens. I was a shy, overweight and desperately unhappy girl. I felt different from my bright, outgoing peers and I became convinced that if we'd stayed in Ireland, I'd have been happier. I tried to get Mum to tell me what had happened to Dad. I shouted, I cried, I called her names and I told her that I hated her for taking me away from Ireland and forcing me to live in a shithole

261

in north-east England instead. All I had to remember him by was a faded photograph I'd found shoved into the back of an album hidden under Mum's bed. It was of my parents on their wedding day. I hid it in my room, tucked behind a framed photo of me and a friend.

'What kind of mother steals her child away from her father?' I screamed at her.

'A mother that doesn't want her child to be judged for the sins of her father. A mother that wants to protect her child from finger-pointing and gossip. A mother that wants the best for her child.' She placed her hands on the kitchen table that separated us. 'You don't think I miss my old life? You don't think I'd go back in a heartbeat if I could? Everything I've ever done, Joanne, I've done for you.'

A tear shone in the corner of her eye then spilled onto her cheek. It was the first time I'd ever seen her cry and I felt so wretched that I silently swore that I'd never ask her about my dad again.

What kind of mother steals her child away from her father? The irony isn't lost on me.

'Are you finished?' I gesture at Elise's plate and she nods. 'OK then, let's get our coats on.'

She jiggles and wobbles on the spot as I wrestle her into her coat, hat, scarf and gloves, then I pull on my own coat and snatch my handbag up from the floor.

'OK then, let's go and ring Granny.' I open the front door then pause. Have I got enough euros for the phone? I open my handbag and root around for my purse. It's not there. It must have fallen out upstairs.

'Damn.' I give the door a shove to, then lift Elise onto the chair in the entrance of the hallway.

'Stay here. I'm just going to get my purse from our room. Don't move!' I cross the hallway before she can object and take the stairs two at a time. I fumble the key into the lock, push the door open and there it is, my purse, lying on top of the suitcase on the other side of the room. I snatch it up. As I do, a terrible wailing sound drifts up the stairs. It's so wretched it makes my blood run cold. I drop the purse and fly out of the room.

'Li!'

A hundred different possibilities flash through my mind as I speed across the landing – my daughter trapped beneath a heavy piece of furniture she pulled on top of her, or hurt and bleeding because she grabbed something sharp. Or worse – kicking and screaming as a stranger drags her from the house.

'Li! Mummy's coming! Mummy's coming, Li.'

My foot catches on the top step of the stairs. I reach for the banister to stop myself falling but I twist awkwardly and my shoulder wrenches in its socket as the base of my spine hits the step. The pain takes my breath away and Elise's anguished wail stops as suddenly as it started. Her silence is more terrifying than her scream.

'Li!' I scramble back to my feet, leap down the next three steps and round the staircase. There's only one person in the hallway below – Mary. She's sitting on the floor facing the door. Her back is curved, her arms are gripping her knees and her head is bowed. The hairs on my arms bristle as a chill wind gusts up the stairs towards me. The front door is wide open.

'Mary.' I run towards her. 'Mary, where's Li?'

When she doesn't reply I pull on her arm. That's when I spot Elise, squashed into my landlady's embrace, her head pressed against Mary's chest, her little blue wellies gripped by Mary's slippered feet. She twists to try and look at me but Mary's holding her so tightly she can't move.

'Mary.' She doesn't move when I touch her on the shoulder and she doesn't look up. Instead she begins to rock back and forth. 'Mary, what happened? You're scaring me. Please, Mary, tell me what's happened.'

Chapter 46

Max hurries out of the imposing glass-walled building clutching an envelope. Two days he's waited to get an appointment at Newport passport office. Two days when he could have been in Ireland, tracking down his wife and child. He could have paid for an emergency appointment the day before but he'd woken up in his hotel room with horrific stomach cramps that had sent him scurrying back and forth to the en suite all day. It was the bloody kebab he'd grabbed after he'd left the office. That or the beers he'd drunk. Either way, that was the last time he was going to let himself get in that kind of state. He needs to keep his wits about him now he's got a passport and the address of the church in Meara where he thinks Brigid married Jo's father. He's booked his ticket to Dublin for the next morning, bought a map of Ireland and paid for a hire car at the airport. In less than 48 hours he'll have his daughter in his arms again and it will all be over.

His phone rings as he unlocks his car. It'll be Fiona again. She's been ringing him since nine o'clock that morning. Why is she hounding him like this? She told him he could take time off if he needed it and he's sent her an email to tell her that he's going to Ireland to look for Jo and Elise. What else is there to talk about?

He steps into the car and fits the keys into the ignition. He doesn't start the engine. Instead he rests the back of his head against the headrest. For the last three weeks he's been surviving on caffeine, booze and adrenalin. He's barely slept or eaten. And the stomach bug and the drive to Newport have used up the last of his energy.

He should get back to Bristol. He needs to check out of his hotel room and tidy the house so it looks warm and inviting when Elise comes back. His girl, back where she belongs. If he sets off now there'd still be time to visit Cabot Circus and buy her some toys. He'd buy her everything in the whole shop if he could.

His eyelids grow heavy. He fights to keep them open but he's too exhausted. I'll just have a quick nap, he tells himself as he yawns and crosses his arms over his chest. He smiles as an image of Elise, laughing and running into his arms, flashes behind his closed eyes and then his phone rings again. Why can't she leave him alone? He just wants to be left alone.

He fumbles in his inside pocket for his mobile,

vaguely registers that the number is withheld, and then presses it to his ear.

'Hello?'

'Hello, Max.'

That sing-song tone. So cocky, so self-assured, so repulsive. His grip on the phone tightens but he doesn't say a word. He doesn't trust himself to respond.

'You know, you really should work on your conversational skills,' Paula says softly into his ear. 'I'd have expected better from a journalist. Was the message I sent you not clear enough? Don't tell me you need it repeated, Max. Because I could arrange that. You just say the word.'

Max grits his teeth.

Don't rise to it. Don't let her know she's got to you.

'Don't tell me I have to send a message to your wife, Max. Really? I know you're a thief. I didn't realise you were a gutless, heartless bastard too. Jesus, you really are a piece of work, aren't you, Max? You probably wouldn't even bat an eyelid if I sent a message to your lovely little daughter. I know I'm a bitch but you're a grade-A cun—'

'Fuck you!' All the anger, rage and frustration that have been building in Max over the last few weeks explode as he screams into his phone. 'You fucking bitch!'

Slam! He smacks the phone against the dashboard. 'Fuck you!' He slams it again. The glass screen shatters but he doesn't notice. 'Bitch!' Slam! 'Bitch!' Slam!

The phone crumples in his hand but he continues to pound it against the dashboard. Only when the muscles in his shoulders seize up and he can't lift his arm does he stop. Then he slumps over the steering wheel, rests his head on his hands and sobs.

Chapter 47

Mary's eyes widen with surprise as she searches the young woman's face. Who is she?

'Please,' the red-haired woman says. 'Please, Mary, tell me what happened.'

Mary stares at her blankly, then down at the child nestled in her arms. She touches a hand to the child's cheek. She's warm. She's moving. She's breathing. This isn't a dream. She did it. She got to the door before her daughter. She wrenched her back from the road. Niamh isn't dead. She saved her. Tears spill down her cheeks. She saved her.

'Mary!' The woman pulls on her arm. 'Mary, please let go of Li. You're holding him too tightly. He doesn't like it. He wants me. He wants his mummy.'

Mummy.

His mummy.

She's lying. Mary knows her own daughter. She knows the dark blonde hair that curls at the back of her neck, the bright, inquisitive green eyes that fill with love whenever she walks into her bedroom in the morning, and the sweetest rosebud lips she has ever kissed.

'Mary, please let go of Li. Please. I need to check he's OK.' She can hear the anguish in the other woman's voice, but she can't, she won't, let go of the child.

'Mummy!' the child screams, reaching for the red-haired woman.

Mummy. Not Mammy. The word is a rock, hurled against Mary's heart. It shatters like glass. Niamh is still dead. She didn't save her. She's still in the ground.

'The door,' she says as Helen plucks at her fingers, trying to loosen her grip on Lee. 'You must shut the door. You could have lost him. You could have lost him for ever.'

She tries to let go of the boy but she can't. Her mind and heart may have realised the truth but her body is still clinging to the delusion that it's Niamh in her arms, and Helen has to help her stand. She ushers her into the living room, with Lee still in her arms, and helps her into a chair. Helen says something about getting a glass of water but before she can leave the room her child starts to cry. And, just like that, Mary's locked limbs release him. Her body aches with loss as he scrambles away from her, then, as his mother lifts him up and into her arms, a wave of shame washes over her.

'What happened?' Helen perches in the chair next to her. 'Please, Mary. Please tell me what happened.'

'I was in the kitchen,' she says. She feels numb,

270

detached, as though someone else is speaking the words that are coming out of her mouth. 'And I felt a breeze. I realised that the front door must have been left open so I went into the hallway to close it. That's when I saw Lee, standing outside, all alone. He was about to step into the road.'

'Oh my God.' Helen covers her mouth with a hand. 'But I shut the door. I could have sworn I shut the d—'

'A car was coming,' Mary continues. 'I snatched him out the way.'

'Oh my God.' The other woman bursts into tears. 'Oh, thank you. I don't . . . I don't . . . if anything happened . . .'

Mary doesn't say a word as her guest continues to praise and thank her. Her chest is so tight she can't speak.

She was in the kitchen stacking the dishwasher when she felt the breeze. The radio was on and she was quietly singing along to Queen's 'We Will Rock You'. The song reminded her of Patrick. He'd been a huge fan of the band and played their CD in the car wherever they went. Mary used to needle him to play something else, The Beatles or The Beach Boys, maybe a little Daniel O'Donnell, but he'd insist, 'My car, my music.' Over the years she'd grown to like Queen as much as he did and she'd learned all the words without actively trying to. Singing along made her feel close to her late husband. It reminded her of happier times.

In the quiet bits of the song, the pauses between

notes, she heard snippets of the conversation going on in the dining room. She couldn't make out what Helen was saying but she could hear the child, Lee, saying something about his grandmother. When she'd served them breakfast she'd asked Helen what her plans were for the day. She'd been quite non-committal in her reply, something about continuing to explore the area. Mary didn't push the issue; she was too busy watching the child. At his age most children didn't look distinctly masculine or feminine – they all had soft, round faces and large eyes – so you had to look at the way they were dressed to decide their gender. Lee was dressed as a boy, Helen referred to him as a boy, and yet Mary had seen him sitting on the bed in girls' underwear. The image had confused her – Lee looked so much like a little girl that she'd thought immediately of Niamh. There were lots of reasons why a boy might wear a girl's underwear – he had a sister, Helen had run out of his normal underwear but had only been able to buy girls' under-wear in the shops, or even that he'd requested knickers rather than pants. But none of that was the issue. Lee was a little girl. Mary was 100 per cent sure of it. Now she could see past the short cropped hairstyle and the sweatshirt, jeans and trainers, she could see how delicate Lee's features were: how long her eyelashes were, how feminine her cupid's bow was, how tiny her hands were. Why would Helen dress her little girl as a boy? Mary had seen a programme on RTÉ about transgender children, but Lee must be, what, two years old, nearing three? She considered herself to be fairly open-minded about most things but that was too young to let a child decide that they wanted to be a different gender. Surely?

The Queen song ended as she arranged the last of the plates in the dishwasher and she became aware of footsteps on the stairs. She hadn't thought anything of it but then she'd shivered as a cool breeze drifted through the open kitchen door. Someone had left the front door open. She felt vaguely irritated as she walked out of the kitchen into the hallway to close it. And then she saw the child, standing at the open front door. And it was Niamh, in her red and white spotted summer dress, bouncing up and down on the balls of her feet, pointing outside at the blue summer sky shouting, 'Kite! Kite!' Mary watched, frozen to the spot, as her daughter, in her shiny patent red shoes, stepped out of the door and onto the pavement. A scream caught in Mary's throat. She tried to run but each step was heavy, laden and slow.

But she made it. She reached her daughter before the car did. She snatched her up and into her arms. She half stumbled, half fell into the hallway and she doubled over, wrapping herself around Niamh, and sobbed with relief. She'd dreamed of this moment a thousand times. The sliding-doors moment when, instead of talking to her friend in the kitchen, she glanced into the hall to see what her daughter was up to and she saved her. There was no squeal of brakes. No heart-stopping terror when she realised she'd disappeared. No searching. This time she'd saved her. She'd never have to go to her grave again.

Never wish what if. Never berate herself. Never hate herself. She had her Niamh back. She could continue to breathe, to live, to love.

And then Helen had appeared and pulled at her arm.

They sit in silence for five, maybe ten minutes, then Lee starts to grizzle about wanting to go to the beach. Mary can tell that Helen is conflicted. She wants to take her child outside but she's worried about leaving her on her own. She needs a push to make the right decision.

'Just go,' Mary snaps. 'I'm perfectly capable of looking after myself. It's your child you should be worrying about, not me.'

Helen reacts with a shocked 'Ooh!' but Mary's deliberate harshness does the job. She stands up, reaches for her child's hand, says, 'Thank you' again and heads out of the living room. Lee pulls on her hand, twisting round to look at Mary. She raises a hand, smiles and says, 'Bye! Bye!' in her soft, squeaky voice.

Mary turns her head to hide her tears.

Chapter 48

As Elise's eyelids flicker and then close I inch away from her and swing my legs over the edge of the double bed. I need to ring Mum. I couldn't face calling her earlier, after what happened with Mary. I should have double-checked that the front door was closed. Anything could have happened to Elise. She could have been hit by a car, got lost or been snatched. And it would have been my fault. Thank God Mary got to her first.

I knew Mum would be able to hear the anxiety in my voice if I called her so I went to the beach with Elise instead, hoping that a walk would calm me down. It was easier, leaving the house for the second time. My hands weren't nearly so clammy when we reached the beach. After years of fearing the unknown I actually felt calm. The sea, the rock pools and the excitement in Elise's voice whenever we discovered a shell, crab or tiny fish slowly melted away the tension in my body and the sick feeling in my stomach. It didn't return until we walked back into the B&B and I saw Mary, still sitting in the living room where we'd left her, with a haunted look on her face.

'Mary?' I say now as I hover in the doorway in the lounge. She's not a tall woman but her presence fills every room she enters. Not now though. She seems tiny, swallowed up by the large floral armchair she's sitting in. Her hair is ruffled, her cheeks wan and her eyes glassy and staring.

'Mrs Byrne.' I take a step towards her. 'Mary?'

Her gaze flickers towards me but there's no emotion in her eyes. She's obviously still traumatised by what happened this morning and it's all I can do not to throw my arms around her and give her a hug.

'Mary, are you OK?'

'I'm grand, thank you,' she says, her eyes still glassy. 'Did you enjoy your trip to the beach?'

'We did, thank you. Are there . . . um . . . any phone boxes nearby that work? I found one on our way back but it was out of order and Li was too tired to walk any more so we came back. He's napping now but I thought we could head out again this afternoon, after he wakes up.'

'You can use the phone here.' She points across the room to a black cordless phone on a pine side table. 'Are you ringing a number in Ireland?'

'No, the UK.'

'OK. Could I ask that you ask them to ring you back once you get through? The number is on the phone.'

'Yes, yes, of course. Thank you.'

'I'll leave you to it then.' She grips the arms of the chair and stands up. She crosses the room but turns back when she reaches the doorway. 'Could I ask you something, Helen?'

'Anything.'

'I'd be grateful if you didn't mention what happened this morning to anyone local. I'd rather people didn't talk.'

I'm not sure I understand why she's worried about people talking – she did something heroic in my eyes – and there's no one I could mention it to, other than Sean, but I say, 'Of course. Yes.'

Mary nods. 'Thank you, Helen.'

I snatch up the phone the second it rings. 'Hello, Mum?'

'Joanne! Oh, Joanne. I've been so worried about you. How are you? How's Elise?'

'She's fine. I'm fine. One second.' Mary left the door ajar when she left. I close it quietly, the phone still in my hand.

'You're all over the news,' Mum says when I press my phone to my ear again. 'I can't turn on the television without your face staring back at me. The newspapers say you're in Ireland. Is that right, is it?'

'We're in Clogherhead, in a B&B.'

There's a sharp intake of breath on the other end of the line.

'Mum?'

'What are you doing there?'

'I thought someone might be able to help me. One of our relatives.' I tell her, as quickly as I can, about the ferry crossing, the Gardaí at the B&B in Wexford, and Sean rescuing us when we broke down. Mum doesn't comment on any of it. Instead she snaps.

'Have you told anyone who you are?'

'No, I'm pretending I'm Helen. I dyed my hair red to look like her.' I don't mention that I cut off Elise's hair. It would break her heart if she knew.

'You mustn't tell anyone who you really are.'

'I know.' I'm startled by her tone. She sounds almost angry with me for coming here.

'And you mustn't go looking for Sinead or the others. You need to leave them out of this.'

'But . . . but the car's still in the garage and I need some money.'

'I'll give you the name of a friend in Cork who might be able to help you out with some money but you *cannot* stay there, Joanne. Do you hear me? You're in danger.'

'I know.'

'No, Joanne. You don't know. You've stepped out of the frying pan and into the fire. You need to leave as soon as possible.'

'But where? Who's your friend in Cork? I want to come home, Mum, but I'll be arrested the minute I set foot in a British airport.'

'Oh, Joanne.' I hear the quaver in my mum's voice then the sound of her blowing her nose. She never gets this upset. Ever.

'We miss you,' I say. 'We both miss you so much.'

Mum blows her nose noisily again and I hear her juddering breath as she tries to control her tears. I hate that I'm adding to her stress. I should be with her, helping her with Dad, not hundreds of miles away across the sea. I shouldn't have come to Ireland. I should have found somewhere closer to Chester to hide.

'How is he?' I ask. 'How's Dad?'

There's a pause and I wait for Mum to tell me that Dad's OK, that the carers have been in, that he's comfortable. But the pause stretches on. Outside the window an elderly woman in a heavy wool coat and clear plastic rain cap strolls past with her grey-muzzled dog.

'Mum?' My throat tightens. 'Mum?'

She stifles a sob. 'He's not good, Joanne. The doctors don't think he'll last the week.'

Chapter 49

'Yes?' Fiona jabs the *call answer* button on her speakerphone.

She's going to have to talk to HR about getting a new receptionist. Ever since Sally left she's been inundated with requests to take calls or greet visitors that really should be given short shrift. How the hell is she supposed to concentrate and get her job done when she's continually interrupted?

'There's a Paula Readman here to see you.'

'Who?'

'She said she needs to talk to you about Max Blackmore.'

Fiona sighs. 'Her and the rest of the world. Tell her I don't know where he is.'

It's true. She has no idea where her crime reporter is. Two days earlier he sent her an email telling her he was going to Ireland to find his wife and child. She immediately picked up the phone to talk to him but her call went to voicemail. So has every call since. He hasn't answered his work phone or replied to any of her emails either. Yesterday she rang the hotel he'd been staying at only to find out he'd checked out two days previously. There was no answer when she rang his doorbell, and his car wasn't in the street outside. He'd definitely gone, with no word when he might be back.

'Miss Readman says she has something you need to see,' the receptionist adds. 'She says it's proof that Max Blackmore has broken the law.'

She sighs. Another complaint about Max. What had he done this time? Got an OAP's name wrong? Taken their photo without permission? 'What law does she think he's broken?'

'She won't say and she's refusing to leave reception until you see her. Should I get security involved?'

Fiona sighs again. 'Give it five minutes and then show her up to my office.'

The blonde woman takes off her black Puffa jacket, sits down in the chair opposite Fiona and flashes her a warm smile.

Fiona returns the smile but tightly. Paula's made herself comfortable. This isn't going to be a quick chat, she's settling herself in for a long stay.

'I like your earrings,' Paula says.

'These?' Fiona touches the chandelier earrings that dangle from her lobes. Her husband Mike wouldn't notice if she went to work dressed in a bin bag, and everyone she works with is too scared of her to risk commenting on her appearance.

'The colour really brings out the amber tones in your eyes.'

'Oh . . . um . . . thank you.' For a woman who supposedly refused to leave reception, Paula seems very calm and self-assured. Pleasant, even.

'Expensive, were they?'

Ah. OK, time to revise her opinion of Paula. There was something deeply unpleasant about the way her eyes just glittered when she said the word 'expensive'.

'Not really, no.' Fiona frowns as Paula twists round in her chair to stare out of the large glass windows into the open-plan office.

'Would you rather I close the blinds?' she asks.

'If you like.'

Fiona closes the blinds then sits down again. 'OK, what exactly are you here to talk to me about?'

The blonde sits forward in her seat. She taps the edge of Fiona's desk with the sharpened tips of her nails. 'Where's Max?'

'He's off sick.'

'No, he's not.'

'Can we get to the point here?' Fiona fights to stay calm. She's tired; Mike forget to take his snoring medication and she was woken up every couple of hours, and letting this woman into her office was a mistake. 'You told the receptionist that you've got proof that one of my journalists has broken the law. That's a very serious allegation.'

'It is, isn't it?'

Stupid cow. She needs to stop playing games and

get to the point. 'Just tell me what it is that you think Max has done.'

'You can find out for yourself if I give you the footage.'

'What footage?'

'CCTV.'

Getting information out of this woman is about as easy as getting a drink from the Cornubia on a Friday after work. 'Of Max doing what exactly?'

Paula leans forwards and, before Fiona can stop her, grabs the silver-framed photo of her family from the desk. She flips it over and examines the photograph. 'I bet your eldest boy's a bit of a heartbreaker, isn't he? That's one nice-looking family you've got.'

'Thank you.' Fiona reaches for the frame but Paula snatches it away.

'You'd do anything for them, wouldn't you?'

'I'm sorry?'

'You wouldn't put their safety at risk because of something you'd done, would you?'

Fiona stares at the blonde-haired woman with the frozen forehead and the red glossy lips. What is she implying?

'Are you suggesting Max has put his family at risk because of something he's done?'

'I'm not *suggesting*,' – she stresses the word – 'anything. It's just a question, Fiona. Just a simple question. And you seem like an honest kind of woman,' – she smirks – 'for a journalist.'

Fiona doesn't bother to hide the look of disdain on her face. This woman is scum, pure and simple, but she's got something on Max and Fiona's not going to let her leave the office until she finds out what it is. 'No,' she says. 'I wouldn't put my family at risk.'

Paula nods. 'There we go, I was right. Honest. Exactly as I said. I imagine you'd respond to a request to return lost property too, wouldn't you? You wouldn't need repeat reminders. *Firm* reminders.'

There's something about the implied threat in the word *reminders* that makes Fiona shift further back in her seat. Who the hell is this woman and how did Max get involved with her?

'OK, Paula. OK.' She holds up her hands. 'Enough with the questions. Just tell me what it is that you want.'

'Ten thousand pounds.'

Fiona laughs but the other woman doesn't crack a smile. 'For what?'

'The CCTV footage I've got.'

'C'mon, Paula, you're going to have to give me that. CCTV footage of what? I'm not handing over ten grand just because you ask me to.'

The blonde tilts her head to one side and purses her lips as though she's considering the request.

'You do like Max's wife?' she asks after a lengthy pause.

'I've never met her.'

'I have. She's . . . fun. Reminds me of a horse. Quick to startle, big nose.' She laughs. 'You know she's run off to Ireland, don't you?'

'I do, yes. It's all over the news. What of it?'

'I can find out where. Consider the ten grand a finder's fee. And I'll throw in the CCTV footage for free. You'll have two stories for the price of one – the Runaway Wife and the Bent Hack. The truth is, Fi, I'm not getting any younger and I haven't got the energy to go charging over to Ireland to get my lost property back. I mean, I could send someone to get it back for me but, you know, overheads . . .'

Fiona doesn't buy the 'not getting any younger' line for one second. This is extortion, plain and simple. Paula has pretty much threatened to go after Max and Jo unless she pays her £10,000.

She rubs the index finger of her right hand over her lips as she considers her options. Morally she should take this straight to the police. If Paula's telling the truth about knowing where Jo is, they really need to know. And if Max has broken the law, she really shouldn't sit on that.

But she also can't ignore the twinge of curiosity she's felt ever since Paula opened her mouth. What exactly is it Max is supposed to have done?

'If you're not interested I'll take my story to one of the other papers,' Paula adds. 'One of your journalists up to no good – they'll have a field day.'

Fiona's heart rate quickens. The last thing she needs is for one of her journalists to be torn apart by the opposition. It would bring her paper into disrepute. 'You did the right thing, Paula,' she says quickly, 'coming to me.'

The blonde smiles victoriously. 'Great. I knew I liked you, Fiona.'

However,' Fiona adds quickly, 'I need proof that what you said is true.'

Paula's smile doesn't slip an inch. 'I thought you'd say that.' She reaches into her handbag and pulls out a piece of paper. She unfolds it and slides it across the desk but keeps hold of the edge.

'There!' She taps the centre of the grainy image. 'That's Max.'

Fiona nods. It's definitely Max and she can see exactly what he's doing but there's no way she's going to write Paula a cheque for £10,000 on the basis of a single black and white image. She needs to buy some time while she decides how to handle the situation.

'OK, Paula,' she says as the blonde tucks the image back into her handbag. 'I'll tell you what I'm going to do. I'm going to ring the accountants and I'm going to authorise a payment to be made to you. But it's going to take a few days. This isn't petty cash money we're talking about. I need you to do something for me while it's going through. I need you to promise me that you're not going to take this to any other paper.'

Paula smiles. She thinks she's got the upper hand. 'I'm not promising anything. They might offer me more.'

'True. And they might offer you nothing. News travels fast and if I find out that you've peddled this story to our competition you'll get nothing. Do we understand each other?'

'Yeah.' The other woman pushes back her chair and stands up. 'We do.'

'One thing before you go.' Fiona pushes a pen and

a blank piece of paper across the table. 'Give me your mobile number. That way I can ring you when the money's been authorised.'

Paula gives her a long look, as though she's trying to work out whether that's a good idea or not, then she picks up the pen.

'Anything?' Fiona hovers behind her IT manager's chair and rubs her arms. It's perpetually freezing in the office, thanks to the stack of servers that take up most of the room.

'Nothing on Max's computer from a Paula Readman. Is there another name you want me to search for?'

'No. Can you access his voicemails?'

Graham raises his bushy eyebrows. 'Mobile or office phone?'

'Both.'

Most of Fiona's staff would have asked her a dozen questions by now, but not Graham. He's been with the paper for nine years and, other than the fact that he's single with no kids, she doesn't know the first thing about him. He hasn't attended a single staff party or get-together in the whole time he's worked for the *Bristol News*. Ask him to do something and he does it, but if it's not in his contract then you may as well forget it, and that includes social occasions. At first Fiona found his automaton attitude to his work strange, but now she welcomes it. It's so much easier to get things done without constantly being asked to justify your request.

'I can't access his mobile phone voicemails, but

you could listen to the ones on his office phone,' Graham says.

'Great, do that. Let me know if there are any messages from a woman called Paula, or any woman who sounds like she's blackmailing, threatening or trying to extort money from him. Oh, and can you see if you can trace this number?' She hands him the piece of paper Paula wrote on. 'A home address would be ideal.'

Fiona follows Graham out of his arctic room and back into the open-plan office. It rumbles with the sound of voices and clacking keyboards. Several pairs of eyes follow her as she makes her way through the desks, then look away, uninterested – or possibly relieved – as she walks back into her office and closes the door. She ducks down under the desk and retrieves a piece of paper. All it took was a tap of the handbag to tip it onto its side as she questioned Paula's phone number, then a subtle slide of her foot. She looks at the printout of Max and smiles. Honest journalist? Paula Readman has no idea.

Chapter 50

'Mary?' I say.

My landlady, who is folding bed linen into neatly stacked piles that cover the dining-room tables, turns sharply at the sound of my voice. I sat alone in the living room for ten minutes after I said goodbye to Mum on the phone. It took me that long to stop myself crying so I could leave the room.

'Yes – oh.' The sheet she is folding drags on the carpet as she steps towards me. 'Whatever's the matter?' Her eyes search mine. 'It's not the little one, is it? Nothing's happened to—'

'No.' I take a deep, steadying breath. 'It's my Dad. He's . . . he's not been well for a while and my . . . my mum . . . she said he hasn't got,' – a sob steals my voice – 'long.'

'Oh, no. Oh, I'm so sorry.' Mary gently pats my shoulder. 'Is there anything I can do?'

I swipe at my eyes with the backs of my hands but

new tears swiftly replace the ones I wipe away. I try to talk but my chest judders with each breath and all I can manage is a shaky 'I . . . I . . . I . . .'

'It's OK. You've had some bad news. You take your time.' Mary guides me by the elbow to one of the chairs then stands silently beside me. 'Will you have some tea?' She leaves the room, not waiting for an answer.

When she returns with two hot mugs of tea in her hands I've managed to get my breathing back under control again.

'Thank you.' I pull down the sleeves of my jumper and wrap my hands around the mug. 'You're very kind.'

She takes the chair next to me. 'What will you do?'

Do? I don't know what to do, I think. If I go, I could lose Elise, and if I stay I'll never get to say goodbye to Dad. I won't get to tell him how much I love him or how grateful I am that he came into our lives when he did. I won't be able to thank him for making Mum happy or for being the best dad in the world to me. I'll spend the rest of my life thinking of all the things I never got to say to him. It's a risk, but I've still got Helen and Ben's passports. If the police haven't figured out that I'm pretending to be her I might be able to get back into the country. I might even make it to Dad's bedside before I'm arrested. That's *if* I am arrested. I might have luck on my side. I'm going to have to leave Clogherhead anyway and I haven't got the slightest clue where else I could go in Ireland.

'Fly back to the UK, I guess.'

'Can you change your tickets?' Mary asks. 'Bring the date forward?'

'I didn't fly. I bought a one-way ticket on the ferry and my car isn't back from the garage yet.'

'Oh. Well, I'm sure it can't be much longer. They've had it for a few days now, haven't they? But if you're desperate to leave now I'm sure Sean would run you to Dublin airport if you asked him. I would offer myself but—'

'No, no need.' I shake my head. 'But, perhaps, could I use your computer? So I can book some tickets?'

Mary pulls an apologetic face. 'I'm sorry. I don't have broadband at the moment. There's been a big mess-up with me switching providers and they can't come out to see me until next month. I've been taking my laptop over to my friend Carmel's house a couple of times a week to check for bookings and the like.' She pauses. 'I'm sure she wouldn't mind if you went over. Do you have a computer?'

'I've got an iPad.'

'That might work. Or you could use Carmel's computer, I'm sure. She'll be in now. Should I give her a ring for you?'

'That would be great, thank you so . . . oh!' I glance at my watch. Elise has only been asleep for half an hour. Normally she naps for two hours after lunch. 'I guess I should wake Li.'

'No. No. You let him sleep. I'll keep an eye on him. It won't take you long to print out a couple of tickets, will it?'

* * *

'C'mon, c'mon, c'mon.' I tap my nails against Carmel's white lacquered computer table and glance at my watch for the third time in as many minutes.

Carmel, a small, thin woman with brown, wavy hair down to her shoulders, tears her eyes away from the large flat-screen TV on the other side of the room. 'Taking a while, is it? The broadband can be awfully temperamental round here. It'll speed up again, you'll see.'

Her house is only a couple of streets away from Mary's but I still ran here. Instinct told me not to leave Elise's side for a second but what was the alternative? Wake her up and bring her with me – miserable and demanding attention. Or wait for her to wake up and bring her with me – excited and demanding attention. It's not as though I can't trust Mary. She saved Elise's life this morning. The thought of what could have happened still makes me feel sick.

'Come on.' As the circle in the centre of the Aer Lingus website continues to swirl around and around I open a new tab and type in the URL to access my work email. I haven't seen or spoken to my boss for well over a week. I imagine the police will have been in touch with her to ask if she knows where I've gone. She'll be worried sick.

My emails load and I quickly scroll through the messages I've received. Five emails from Max – I don't bother opening those – and one from Helen asking me to let her know if I'm OK. There are several emails from Diane, the last one saying that she saw me on the news and she wants me to get in touch. There are dozens and dozens of enquiries from academics and students. I don't open those either and instead continue to scroll down, past messages to all staff from HR, past announcements about visiting lecturers, past an email with the subject line 'See for yourself, Jo' that's been flagged with a spam warning, past a request to meet with the financial adviser. Past Naija Mattu.

Naija Mattu.

I stop scrolling. Naija has sent me four emails. That's strange. We don't have each other's mobile phone numbers and we only swapped email addresses so I could send her the details of a course.

I open the first email. It's dated almost three weeks ago.

Hi, Jo, how are you? Sorry to email you at work but I was surprised to see Max returning to your house at lunchtime. He said you had a burst pipe. Is everything OK? Should I be worried about our house?
Naija

Next email:

Hi, Jo, me again. I haven't seen you for a few days. Can you let me know if the burst pipe has been fixed as we're off to India tomorrow and I don't want to return to a flood! I don't want to add to your stress. Sorry!
Naija

Third email:

Hi, Jo, don't worry about the last email. I saw Max coming out of your house earlier. He said the burst pipe was sorted. I haven't seen you for a while. I hope everything is OK. See you when we get back.
Naija

Fourth email:

Hi, Jo, we're back from India and I just saw your photo on the news. They're saying you've run off with Elise and you need to return her for her own safety. I can't believe it. What happened? Are you OK? I haven't seen Max to talk to and I don't want to interfere but if you need someone to talk to then this is my mobile number . . .

I click the square box next to each of her emails and hover the mouse over the delete button. It's not unusual for Naija to freak out when something goes wrong with our house. She was the first one to complain when the roofers decided to throw the broken tiles off the roof and into the skip below rather than use a chute, and she was at our front door within minutes of the pest-control man pulling up outside to sort out our mouse problem. But . . .

I lift my finger from the mouse. Burst pipes? We've had all sorts go wrong with the house since we bought it – not least an ongoing damp problem – but nothing's ever gone wrong with the plumbing. The estate agent told us the last owner had had it all professionally replaced. And it can't be the boiler because it was serviced a couple of months ago.

Burst pipes?

I stare at the date of Naija's email. Thursday, 10 February. I was at work that day. I remember because I'd had to deal with a student complaint about a member of staff and I didn't have a spare second to go through my emails. Then I'd picked Elise up from nursery and returned home. There was no burst pipe. No flood. Not that day or the day before.

Oh my God. That was the day the police turned up, searched the house and arrested me for possession of drugs. I rang Max to pick me up from the station and he spent the night on the sofa. I asked him how his day had been and he said he hadn't left the office. But Naija said he'd come home to deal with a burst pipe.

I re-read the second email:

Hi, Jo, me again. I haven't seen you for a few days. Can you let me know if the burst pipe has been fixed as we're off to India tomorrow and I don't want to return to a flood! I don't want to add to your stress. Sorry!

She'd sent that when we were up in Chester seeing Mum and Dad. And the third one:

Hi, Jo, don't worry about the last email. I saw Max coming out of your house earlier. He said the burst pipe was sorted. I haven't seen you for a while. I hope everything is OK. See you when we get back.

That was . . . I count the days off on my hands. That was the day we drove back to Bristol to meet with Lorraine Hooper. He told me on the phone that he hadn't been in the house since the Thursday when I was arrested. That was a lie. He'd let himself into the house the morning after I told him that Lorraine would be visiting. He told Naija that he'd fixed the flood.

But there were never any burst pipes to fix.

He let himself into the house and he tipped rubbish all over it to make it look like I couldn't look after our daughter.

And the drugs. The reason I was meeting Lorraine Hooper in the first place. He'd planted those too.

Chapter 51

I burst into the B&B, clutching a printout of my tickets to Dublin, and take the stairs to the bedrooms two at a time. I'm sweating, and not just because I just ran across Clogherhead in my thick woollen coat and hat. It was Max. Every awful thing that's happened to me is down to Max. Paula threatened me in my car and in the street but he was responsible for everything else. Naija's emails prove that. There were no burst pipes. I would have known if there were. And why would Max lie to her unless he had something to hide? He must have taken the spare key, then he set me up with Social Services, convinced me that Paula was responsible.

I stop running and dry retch as I reach the top of the stairs. Was Max responsible for Elise's bruises too? Did he deliberately hurt our daughter to ensure the courts gave her to him? How could he claim to love her and do something so awful? He must have really hurt her to bruise her like that.

'Elise?' I fly through the open bedroom door then stop short. There's no bump under the duvet. No short, scruffy hair on the pillow.

'Elise?' I run to the other side of the bed but she hasn't fallen onto the carpet. She's not hiding behind the curtains. She's not in the wardrobe or the en suite.

'Elise?' I thunder back down the stairs and into the kitchen. 'Mary?' I shout as I leave the empty room and run into the dining room. 'Mary?'

The sheets and towels are still piled high on the tables but there's no sign of my landlady.

'Mary? Elise?' I run into the living room but that's empty too.

I take the stairs again, my heart racing in my chest as I push at every door on my floor. They're all locked.

'Mary?' I push back the curtain that covers the stairs to Mary's private quarters in the top of the house and speed up the steps.

But Mary's bedroom is empty. The curtains are pulled back, her double bed is neatly made, with a blanket tucked over the end of the duvet, and there's a book splayed open on the bedside table. There's no one in the en suite either.

I head towards the last remaining door on the second floor. They have to be in here.

A gasp catches in my throat as I push at the door.

A cot. A rocking horse. A nursing chair. Teddies. Dolls. Pink cot linen. Winnie the Pooh pictures. An ABC border. Pink and white spotted pyjamas folded neatly on the pillow. A tiny child's pushchair. An open chest of drawers with a girl's clothes spilling onto the floor.

It's a child's nursery. But Sean told me that Mary doesn't have any children or grandchildren. She told me she didn't have a cot. Across the room a silver photo frame glints in the weak February sunlight that streams through the open curtains. I walk towards it, slowly, as though in a dream.

It's a photograph of a little girl, not much older than two. A little girl wrapped up for the winter in a cream knitted bobble hat and a red woollen coat with gold buttons. A little girl who looks a lot like Elise.

'Mary! Mary Byrne! Elise!' I run down Main Road towards the beach but the tide is high and the seafront is deserted so I double back the way I came, my coat flapping in the wind. The streets are deserted. Televisions flicker and lights glow beyond the net curtains I pass. I stop when I reach Strand Street and double over, sucking in cold air. Mary's car was parked up outside the B&B so they have to be on foot. Unless somebody took them. No, no, I won't believe it. They're still here. I know they're still here. I straighten up and continue to run. My lungs burn and my cheeks sting as I run along the main road. I slow down as I reach the amusement arcade but, other than a man playing the slot machines, it's empty. An older man, walking his dog, passes me as I stare through the window. I call out to him, asking if he's seen an older woman and a little girl.

'A little boy?' I correct myself breathlessly. 'The child may have looked like a boy.'

The man shakes his head and yanks on his dog's lead.

As I continue to run down the road, a fresh wave of fear washes over me. Max. After everything he's done he wouldn't think twice about snatching Elise from the B&B. But what possible reason could he have for taking Mary too? He can't have found us. Elise and Mary have to be here but Clogherhead is a small place and I'm running out of possibilities. Think, Jo, think. There's the RNLI Lifeboat Station, further along the beach, but that's little more than a shed with a lifeboat in it. The doctors' then? Perhaps Elise woke up with a fever or fell out of bed? But where's the doctor's surgery? I have no idea. The woman in the post office might know.

It takes me less than two minutes to run to the post office but I'm gasping by the time I reach the door. A bell tinkles as I push it open.

Standing at the confectionery display, with her back to me, is a little girl in a cream knitted hat with a big bobble on the top and a red woollen coat with shiny gold buttons.

'Li-Li?' The word comes out as little more than a whisper but it's enough to make the little girl turn to see where the sound came from.

'Mummy!' Her face lights up and she charges towards me, arms outstretched.

'Oh my God.' I snatch her up and hold her close, pressing my face against hers. But she doesn't smell of my daughter. Instead of her fresh, warm scent she smells musty and sour. She's wearing clothes I didn't buy her. Clothes Helen didn't give me.

'Helen?' Mary appears from one of the aisles, a lolly in one hand, a loaf of bread in the other. She glances at the woman behind the counter who's staring at us over the top of her spectacles with ill-disguised curiosity.

'Helen,' Mary says again. 'Let's talk outside.'

I don't give her chance to speak. Instead I back out of the door, with Elise still in my arms, and set off at a run. Only she's too heavy to carry far and my run slows to a jog, then a fast walk. I can hear Mary behind me, her shoes tapping on the pavement as she hurries to catch up.

'Helen, wait!' she shouts.

'Leave us alone.' I try to speed up but my arms are aching and sweat is rolling down my face. Elise shifts in my arms and removes a hand from around my neck.

'Lolly!' she shouts.

She wriggles wildly, kicking her wellies into my thighs and arching her back. I haven't got the strength to fight her so I lower her to the ground and grip her mittened hand.

'Do you have any idea how scared I was?' I say as Mary draws close. 'You can't just take my child out of the house and not let me know where you're going. You can't do that, Mary!'

She stops abruptly. 'I only took her out for a lolly. When she woke from her nap she wouldn't stop crying. I tried everything to calm her – the TV, a biscuit, songs

'– but she kept calling for you and so I . . .' She opens her palm, revealing the plastic-wrapped lolly in her hand. 'I didn't want to disturb you. I saw how upset you were about your dad and—'

'I got back to the B&B and she was gone. I was terrified that something awful had happened.'

'But . . . but I left a note.'

'What note?'

'On the hallway table. I left you a note, telling you where we'd gone.'

'I didn't see any note.'

'Well, I . . .' Mary looks genuinely distraught. 'I definitely left one. Oh, Helen, I'm so sorry. I didn't mean to scare you but she's OK. I put her in some warm clothes because hers were still damp from your rock-pooling this morning. She hasn't come to any harm.'

Her. She. A cold shiver runs through me. This whole conversation Mary has been referring to Elise as 'her' and 'she' and I've only just realised. Mary dressed Elise in another child's clothes and she keeps referring to her as a girl. How long has she known? Since she dressed her in another girl's coat? Since we arrived? She hasn't asked me why I've been dressing my daughter as a boy or why I introduced her as my son. But she will. I can tell by the way her gaze keeps flickering back to Elise. I need to get out of here before she starts asking questions. Or, worse, before she talks to the police.

Chapter 52

'Hello, hello!' Sean saunters down the stairs in jogging bottoms, a long-sleeved running top and trainers as Elise, Mary and I step out of the cold and into the warm hallway. Conversation was stilted on the walk back to the B&B. Mary didn't mention the fact that my 'son' is actually a girl and I didn't mention the nursery I'd discovered on the second floor. We focused on Elise instead, asking her whether she'd enjoyed rockpooling that morning or if she could see the seagull perched on a lamp post. Out of the corner of my eye I could see Mary giving me strange sideways looks as we walked. I could almost feel her mind whirring. Was she, like me, playing along that everything was fine, while secretly planning to call the police the second we got back? I wanted to tell her the truth. I wanted to explain why I'd overreacted when I discovered that Elise wasn't in her bed. But how can I trust a total stranger when I can't trust my own husband?

'I've got good news for you, Helen,' Sean says now, holding out a hand for Elise to give him a high five. 'The garage rang earlier and your car's going to be ready to collect in the morning.'

'Oh, that's great.' I feel weak with relief. That gives me options. The flight to Manchester isn't until late tomorrow night. I can drive to Drogheda to get some money to pay Mary and then go. We can stay in Dublin overnight.

'I thought you'd be pleased. Hey, Mary,' – he turns to look at our landlady, who is crouched beside the hallway table – 'what's that you've found on the floor? Someone been sending you love letters?'

'No.' She hands the piece of paper to me then turns and walks into the kitchen.

'What's that then?' Sean asks as I unfold it. He laughs. 'Eviction notice?'

I shake my head.

Helen, gone to post office to buy the little one a lolly. Lee woke up upset and I didn't want to disturb you at Carmel's.
   Mary

Elise is asleep, curled up beside me on the double bed with her face buried in her elephant's soft grey fur. It's dark outside, beyond the closed curtains, and the only light in the bedroom is the silent flicker of the television in the corner of the room. It's 11 p.m. and I should be asleep too but I can't stop my mind whirring. I can't shake the feeling that I made a mistake deciding to stay here another night. The walls feel as though they're closing around me but, without the car, we can't run. We can't go anywhere.

The floorboards above my head creak as Mary moves about in her bedroom. She's not asleep either. I can't get the image out of my head of her shoulders sagging and the light in her eyes going out when she handed me the note. Or the face of the little girl in the photograph in the nursery. Who was she? Mary's daughter? Her granddaughter? Why else would she keep a room ready if they weren't related? But the décor looked so tired and the photo was so faded. Mary crumpled when I told her that I was widowed. And she was distraught when she stopped Elise from walking out into the road. Did something terrible happen to her daughter? I'm not the only person keeping secrets in this house.

I want to talk to Mary, to apologise to her. She saved Elise's life and she was so kind to me when I found out about Dad, and how did I repay her? I shouted at her when she took my daughter out for a lolly. I've turned into someone I don't recognise. The sort of person who avoids talking to strangers, who peers from behind curtains, who's suspicious when a kind man stops his car to help. Who runs and runs and runs.

I've done things over the last few days that would have provoked a full-blown panic attack a month ago. I've driven unfamiliar routes, been on a ferry and stayed in a caravan and two B&Bs. I never would have dreamed I could take such huge steps towards overcoming my agoraphobia but I'm not free from anxiety. I'm not free from fear. I've breathed sea air. I've run down the beach hand in hand with my daughter. I've laughed with her, I've played with her, I've explored with her, but I haven't done anything without looking over my shoulder. I'm not living. *We're* not living. How can I give Elise a happy childhood when I'm constantly checking for danger? When I'm too terrified to let someone get close in case they betray me?

Max. He's the reason I feel this way. But what evidence do I have? Even if I ask Naija to talk to my solicitor and the police, what does that prove – that Max let himself into the house that he co-owns? That he lied to our neighbour about having a burst pipe? He could claim he said that because she was being nosy or because he wanted to wind her up. I can't prove that he planted the drugs unless his fingerprints are on the packet. When I asked DS Merriott during my interview if he was going to take fingerprints, he said no, it was too small a quantity for them to bother. On his court application form Max listed my arrest as one of the reasons why I'm unfit to look after Elise. When I told Mr Harrison it wasn't true he raised an eyebrow and said, 'If he's lied to the court about anything on this form he could end up in the criminal court on a perjury charge.' I need to prove that he lied. But how? Maybe Naija knows more than she let on in her emails. I need to talk to her.

I rub my thumb over the blank screen of my mobile.

Do I dare turn it on and send her a text message? I have to take the risk.

I tap the button on the side of the phone, wait for the screen to swirl to life and then open my text messages. The phone bleeps and bleeps and bleeps as the screen fills with new, unread texts. I ignore them all and tap out a message.

Naija, please ring me as soon as you get this. It's URGENT. Jo. x

I place the phone on the bedside table and settle back against the cushions as Elise snuffles beside me, but not because I want to relax. There's something niggling at the back of my brain. Something I've seen or heard that was important but I ignored it. But what was it?

Chapter 53

I've made it, Jo. I'm in Ireland. Not long now until we're reunited. Well, I say 'we'. I actually mean Elise and me. I won't be taking you back to the UK with us. You can make your own way back. Or maybe I'll hasten the process by giving the Gardaí and Avon and Somerset constabulary a ring. They'll make sure someone keeps you company on the plane. I don't think you're going to like it in prison, sweetheart. For one, there's no way to escape. Then there's the other inmates. I don't think they'll take too kindly to a woman who hurt her child. I still feel sick when I think about the bruises. Lorraine Hooper told me how the doctor had described them – huge great welts all over Elise's body. Why would you do that to our little girl, Jo? Were you frustrated by the drugs arrest? That was meant to make you realise how vulnerable you were without me, Jo, not make you lash out at our baby. You were planning on taking

*our little girl to Chester but being arrested stopped
you in your tracks, didn't it? It made you realise
how much you needed me. Who was the first person
you rang? Me. Who did you ask to stay overnight?
Me. You needed me, Jo. All I did was try to prove
to you how much.*

Max parks the hire car in the street and, barely
glancing at the beautiful gable wall of the Church of
the Sacred Heart, walks through the black iron gates
and into the building. He finds himself in an unusual
oval-shaped room with white walls, deep inset
windows and row after row of heavy oak pews. At
the far end, beyond the altar, is a huge twelve-paned
window with a stunning view of the beach and the
Irish Sea. But it's not the view he's come to see, it's
the priest. There was no phone number on the website
he found so he drove straight up from Dublin. Only
there's no priest to be seen. The only other person in
the church is an elderly woman, placing candles in
their holders.

Max glances at his watch. It's 9.30 a.m. The website
said Mass would take place at 10.15 a.m. so the
priest can't be far away. He looks again at the elderly
woman. Perhaps she might know where he can find
the priest. As he walks towards her one of the doors
in the side of the main building opens and a man in
a black suit and white dog collar appears. Bingo!
Max hurries towards him, holding out his hand as
he gives him what he hopes is a winning smile.

'Max Blackmore, lovely to meet you.'

The other man grasps his hand and shakes it firmly. 'Father O'Shea. How can I help you?'

'I'd like to take a look at your marriage banns if that's possible. I'm tracing my Irish roots.'

'Ah.' The priest pulls a face, one that makes Max's heart sink. 'I hope you've not come far.'

'From Bristol.'

'Oh, that is a way. I'm afraid, Max, that we don't have the marriage banns. They were destroyed in a fire a couple of years back. It was a terrible thing, we lost a lot of priceless artefacts.'

'But . . . but they were on the site . . . the ancestry website I accessed.'

'Well, yes. They were photographed a long time ago and there are copies of the marriage certificates in the GRO in Roscommon. Does the website you accessed not have copies available? I was led to believe you could order them.'

'You can, yes. But . . . er . . . time's of the essence and I was hoping I could find out some information today.' Max passes a hand over his hair and tries not to show the irritation he's feeling. He knows the priest is trying to be helpful but he might as well be saying, *You're fucked, son.*

'Oh dear.' The priest runs a hand over his chin. 'I've been here for ten years. If the marriage was recent I might be able to help.'

'It was in the seventies.'

'Ah, I see. Long before my time, I'm afraid.'

'Yeah.' Max nods curtly. 'Anyway, thank you. I appreciate it.'

'God bless,' Father O'Shea calls after him as he walks out of the church.

God bless? I don't need God's help. I don't need the police's help either. I can find you all by myself, Jo. I'm good with people. I tell them what they want to hear – just like I told you that I'd reported the break-in. Just like I told your friends how worried I was about you when you didn't turn up to collect Elise from nursery when all along you were asleep on the sofa. Yes, Jo. I saw you through the window. When I knocked and you didn't wake up I took Elise to a hotel to try and shock some sense into you. Then, when you were arrested for possession of drugs, I told you I was helping the police with their enquiries. You believed me, didn't you, when I said I'd told DS Merriott about the people I'd investigated at work? I didn't even mention my work. I told them how mentally ill you were, and how you'd been self-medicating with illegal drugs to get through the day, just like I told Lorraine Hooper. And they bought it because people believe want they want to believe. There was no way I was going to mention Paula.

Oh yes, I know Paula. Of course I do. But I wasn't going to admit that to anyone. Least of all you.

Chapter 54

'Beebies,' Elise says, pointing at the television screen. When we returned to our room after breakfast she insisted on pulling off all her clothes and now she's sitting on the bed in her pants sipping a glass of milk, as happy as anything. Her cold has all but gone now and her bruises have faded but they're still there. I feel sick every time I see them.

'Elise, you'll get another cold.' She objects loudly as I wrestle a long-sleeved T-shirt over her head.

'Sssh,' I say. 'Mary will hear you.'

Our landlady hasn't forgiven me for what happened yesterday. When she entered the dining room she stared at a spot about six inches above my head and asked, in flat tones, what we wanted to eat. All the warmth, all the vulnerability, all the kindness she'd showed us over the last 48 hours had vanished. She was as cold and impenetrable as she was the day we arrived. I shifted my seat back and stood up, desperate to deliver the apology I'd spent all night rehearsing, but she shot me down before I could say a word.

'Two Irish breakfasts, one with no pudding. I'll be back shortly.'

And then she was gone. She didn't say a word when she returned with the coffee and milk. And she didn't so much as glance at Elise as she placed her food in front of her. I tried again after breakfast was over. I followed her into the kitchen and begged her to talk to me. I told her how very, very sorry I was. She looked at me coldly, told me she had work to be getting on with and then turned her back and opened the dishwasher. I had no choice but to return to my room.

'Beebies,' Elise says again now.

'There's no CBeebies but this looks like a nice programme. It's about numbers, you'll like it.' I reach for a dirty pair of pyjamas on the bedroom floor and stuff them into a plastic bag. Now that we're flying back to the UK rather than going by ferry I'm going to have to leave a lot of our stuff in the car in the airport car park. God knows when I'll be able to collect it, if ever. I'll have to find a way to get it shipped back to Helen.

'Want *Justin's House*,' my daughter says forlornly but she settles herself back against the pillows and tucks Effie Elephant under the duvet as a toddler on screen wobbles his way towards the number 1, made out of plastic balls. It may not be her favourite TV programme but it's bright and colourful and the background music is suitably chirpy.

A shrill noise makes me jump. My mobile is

juddering on the bedside table and Naija's name is flashing up at me from the screen.

'Naija?' I press the phone to my ear.

'Jo! Oh my God. We've been so worried about you. Where are you?'

It feels like a lifetime ago since I last spoke to her, standing outside our houses, asking her to hold Elise so I could run after Paula.

'I can't tell you,' I say. 'And I need to be quick. I don't know if this call is being traced.'

'Traced?' I can hear the shock in her voice. 'Oh my gosh, Jo. What's happened? Are you OK?'

'I'm fine. Elise is fine. Listen. I received your emails, the ones about Max and the burst pipe.' I reach for my daughter's pad of drawing paper and flick through the pages until I find the notes I wrote last night. 'Are you sure you saw Max go into the house on Thursday the tenth of February?'

She's silent for a second, then: 'Yes. Totally sure. I'd just got back from taking the twins to the zoo and Jayesh had been sick all over himself and the car seat. Shaan decided to throw his toy out of the window as I was trying to clean up his brother. That's when I saw Max walking up your path. I commented that I didn't normally see him during the day and he said he'd had to come home because you had a burst pipe.'

'Did you see a plumber turn up?'

'Well . . . I didn't spend the whole afternoon looking out of the living-room window but no, I don't think so. The boys normally run to the window when someone parks outside in case it's their dad, but they didn't do that.'

'Did you see anyone else go in or out the house?'

'No.'

'And you didn't hear Max talking to anyone? Or see anything unusual? No one in the garden or the alley at the back of the houses?'

'No, nothing. Nothing at all.'

'And the next time you saw Max was on Sunday the thirteenth of February?'

'That's right, yes. It was the day before we flew to India, just after lunch. Dad had arrived to collect the cat. I was saying goodbye to him at the front door when Max came out of your house. I was surprised because I hadn't seen either of your cars out the front for a few days. I didn't even realise Max was home. He didn't stop to say hello so I called after him and asked if the pipes had been fixed. He said yes and kept on walking.'

'How did he seem?'

'Unfriendly. What the hell's going on, Jo? When we got back from India last week you were all over the news. Aakarsh saw your picture on the TV and called me into the living room. I couldn't believe it.'

'It's a long story.' I glance across at Elise who has slipped off the bed and is rummaging around in the box of toys that Mary loaned us. 'Listen, Naija. I might need you to talk to the police.'

'I already have.'

'What?'

'They knocked on the door a couple of days ago,

shortly after I'd emailed you. They asked me if I knew where you were. I said I didn't know.'

'I'll need you to talk to them again, to tell them what you just told me about Max.'

'Of course but why?'

'Because he's the reason I'm on the run. He set me up to the police and Social Services to make me look like an unfit mother.'

'So come back. Tell them that. I'll go to the station with you.'

'I can't, not yet.'

'Why not? If you haven't done anything wrong then surely—'

'Elise, no!' I cry out, distracted by my daughter. She's lost interest in the box of toys and is reaching for Henry's box. I moved it from the wardrobe to the bottom of the bed before breakfast so I wouldn't forget it. As I lunge towards her she grasps the box with two hands and attempts to lift it up. I watch, horrified, as it tips forward, the lid opens and dozens of banknotes flutter to the floor.

Chapter 55

Come on Max, you can crack this. You can find her. You didn't travel all this way to give up now.

Max shifts uncomfortably in his car. He's moved the seat back as far as it goes but his legs are still horribly cramped. He's still parked up outside the Sacred Heart church, his new mobile phone in his hand, and he's squinting at the screen. According to the website he's found, the only records held in Roscommon are mostly births, deaths and marriages that took place before 1921, and if you want to get hold of them you have to fill out a form and send it in. He might as well have stayed in Bristol and waited for the ancestry website to send him a copy of the bloody marriage certificates.

But he's here, he's in Ireland, and so are Jo and Elise. It's a big country and they could be anywhere. If he was on the run he'd go somewhere completely random, a town or a city he had no connection with so he could lose himself in the crowds and the hubbub. But Jo's not like him. She's soft and sentimental, not to mention agoraphobic. He can't imagine her hiding away in a bedsit or a hotel room somewhere big and unknown like Dublin or Cork. No, she'd go somewhere she'd been before, somewhere she'd felt safe. She'd flee to the village on the east coast where she grew up. He feels sure of it.

He unfolds his map of Ireland, takes a pen out of his pocket and circles the villages on the east coast that are north of Dublin: Howth, Portmarnock, Malahide, Skerries, Balbriggan, Laytown, Bettystown, Termonfeckin, Clogherhead, Annagassan. He keeps circling the names of villages until he reaches the border with Northern Ireland then he stops and flips open his notebook.

Brigid Gallagher
Liam O'Brien
Joseph Kearney

One of those two men is Jo's father.

He takes his phone out of the inside pocket, unlocks it and cricks his neck to the left, then the right. It's going to take him a while to enter all the different combinations of names and villages into the Irish News Archive but, other than wait for a marriage certificate to be sent to him, it's the only lead he's got.

He taps on the text box, enters the words *Brigid Gallagher, Howth* and then presses the *Search Now* button. A pop-up appears on the screen:

'Searching Archives
Please wait . . .
Loading

Due to the large amount of data there may be a short wait.'

A short wait. I can wait. I know all about patience. It took me a long time to gain Ian White's trust. He wasn't about to give up his secrets to some bloke who'd walked in off the street and applied for a job as a loan collector. But I wheedled my way in. I kept my head down, I did what I was told and I didn't ask questions. I studied the other men. I watched how they interacted with each other and with Ian. I noted what made him laugh and what pissed him off. He grinned when one of the others described the way he'd terrorised a family with young kids. I grinned too, when I really wanted to smash my fist into his skull. I acted impressed when he told me how many shops he had around the country. How it was easier to intimidate people in the south-east than the north-west. I called women stupid slags. I flirted with Paula, being careful not to cross the line. Paula was seeing Ian. If you pissed her off you pissed him off. My first breakthrough was when Ian invited me into the back office to do a line of coke with him.

Coke. I didn't want that shit anywhere near me but I lowered my head to the desk and I snorted it back. Ian began to confide in me. He told me who he trusted and who he thought was a worthless twat.

He let me count the day's takings but he asked me to leave the room when he put it in the safe. One day he wasn't quite so careful. We'd been to the pub. He'd forgotten to get some money out of the safe to give to his dealer and asked me to go back to the office with him. He wanted a bit of muscle at his side in case he ran into any disgruntled clients who wanted to give him a kicking. Did I mention how paranoid he was? Paranoid and a coke addict. It's a dangerous combination. But he was pissed that night and he didn't bother sending me out the front when he opened the safe. I saw the combination and memorised it. I also saw how much money was inside.

By that point I had enough on him to write my story and pass the evidence I'd gathered to the police. All I had to do was make sure no one was in the office when the police arrested him. My contact tipped me off. They'd be arresting him at 3 a.m. on Sunday. That way he'd be in bed, unprepared. I went to the office at 3 a.m. I lifted the spare set of keys from the back office on the Friday. I knew the alarm code. I knew the combination on the safe. I took ten grand. It was for Elise. For three months I'd worked evenings and weekends. I'd missed out on vital time with my little girl. The money was my way of making it up to her. I didn't have a pot to piss in when I left school but she would. Her dad would make sure she never wanted for anything.

What I didn't know was that Ian had installed covert CCTV in the back office. But Paula did.

Chapter 56

'Sean?' I tap on his bedroom door, praying that he's in. He wasn't at breakfast and, with it being a Saturday, there's every chance he's driven back to Dublin to spend the weekend with his parents and sisters.

'Sean?' I tap again, twice this time and louder.

I hear a thump, a loud 'Feck!' then the door opens.

'Oh, it's you.' Sean, naked apart from a pair of navy boxer shorts, stares at me with bleary eyes then reaches down and rubs the big toe of his right foot. 'I banged it on the bloody skirting board. Skirting board, for God's sake. It's not like it wasn't there when I went to bed last night.' He straightens up and smiles. 'Sorry. How can I help you, Helen?'

'I'm so sorry to wake you up,' I say. 'But I . . . I need a favour. I wouldn't ask if it wasn't important.'

'No problem. I should be out running now but I overslept.' He shivers and crosses his arms over his bare chest. 'What is it you need?'

321

'I don't suppose you could take me to an Internet café in Drogheda, could you? I need to access my work email.'

'You can use my laptop if you'd like. Work gave me a dongle so I can connect to the Internet. Just give me a second to get some clothes on.'

'That would be great. Thanks so much, Sean.'

'No problem.'

As he closes the door I go back into my room and join Elise on the bed. We watch TV for a couple of minutes but, as soon the credits roll, she loses interest and slides onto the floor.

'Box! Mummy, box!'

She wanders up to the wardrobe, reaches up with both hands and makes a high-pitched whining sound.

'What's wrong with the little man?' Sean asks from the doorway, dressed in jeans and a T-shirt, his laptop in his hands.

'She's crying because I won't let her play with the box I put on top of the wardrobe.'

'She?' His confusion shows in his eyes. 'Lee's a girl?'

'She's always been a girl.' I gesture for him to enter the bedroom. 'Come in. I'll explain everything.'

'Jesus!' Sean glances at Elise who has finally stopped crying and is sitting on the carpet, gawping at the TV. 'Sorry.' He lowers his voice. 'Is your husband some kind of monster, Helen?'

'Jo.'

'Jo, of course.' He looks incredulous and I can't say I blame him after what I've just told him. I could have lied. I could have made up some stupid story about why I pretended that Elise was a boy, but I had to tell him the truth. I need to start trusting people. I can't do this alone any more.

'It makes sense now,' Sean says, 'why Elise kept saying her name was Lee, and the dolls and stuff.'

'I tried to get her to say her name was Ben but she wouldn't have it.'

'No.' He smiles. 'I don't imagine she would.' His gaze switches to the wardrobe and Henry's box and a plastic bag stuffed with money, perched on the top. 'How much do you reckon is in there?'

'Thousands and thousands.'

'Jesus.'

'I know.'

'How did it get in there?'

'I don't know. But I think there might be an email that explains it.'

See for yourself, Jo.

It came to me this morning, while I was getting Elise washed and dressed. The email in my work inbox that was marked as spam. It had an attachment. I didn't think anything of it at the time. But now I'm convinced it's something I need to open.

'OK, well, here you go.' Sean hands me his laptop. He waits as I log onto my work email and scroll down all the unread emails.

See for yourself, Jo.

The sender's name is Fiona Spelling. Max's boss. I double-click to open it. Please let it be important, please, please.

I scan the email then read it again.

Hello Jo

I don't know if you'll get this email but I felt I had to reach out to you. There's something you need to know. Max lied about knowing Paula Readman. He lied to you. And he lied to me. Paula Readman was an employee of Cash Creditors, the loan shark ring your husband investigated. Max took something Paula believes belongs to her. He stole a large amount of money from the safe. We've accessed the voicemail messages Paula left him on his work phone, making threats to harm you and your child. Max deleted them but my tech guy managed to retrieve them.

I'm attaching an image taken from the CCTV so you know I'm telling the truth. Paula tried to extort money from me for the footage but I won't be paying her a penny. I've passed everything on to the police. They're looking for Max and Paula as I type this.

I don't know why you decided to go on the run with your daughter and I can only imagine how scared you are, but I'm here if you need someone to talk to. You've already got my direct line.

Best wishes,
Fiona Spelling

'Oh my God. Read this.' I slide the laptop onto Sean's knees then slump forwards and rest my head in my

324

hands. I can't take it in. Not only did Max try and paint me as an unfit mother, he did this too. He lied to my face about knowing Paula after she threatened me. He swore on Elise's life. What kind of man steals thousands of pounds and knowingly puts his family at risk? He could have given it back to Paula. Instead he lied and lied and lied, and all the while the money was hidden in Henry's memory box. Just the thought of him shovelling dirty banknotes over precious memories of his son makes me feel sick.

'Have you seen this?' Sean jabs a finger at the laptop screen.

And there he is, my husband, scooping wads of banknotes out of a safe, staring right up into the CCTV camera with a smile on his face.

'You know what this means, don't you?' Sean says. 'You're safe. You don't have to keep running. Everything's going to be OK.'

Chapter 57

It was a victimless crime, Jo. That money was never going to be given back to the people Ian White ripped off. The government would have seized it. I just took a little bit off the top for my trouble, for Elise.

Nothing happened for a couple of weeks after I took it. I thought I'd got away with it but then my story was published in the newspaper and Paula realised who I was. That's when she started ringing me. She left message after message on my work voicemail telling me that if I didn't return the money she'd go after my family. I didn't believe her. She's a mouthy bitch but she's not a thug. There's no way she'd risk breaking a nail by attacking someone. Her muscle was gone – Ian and his cohorts were in jail – she was alone. I freaked out when I got your voicemail telling me you thought Elise had been taken. Until I ran through the front door I really believed that Paula had gone through with her threat. But she hadn't been anywhere near Elise. The stunt she pulled, getting in the car with you and giving you Elise's glove, that was bullshit, a weak attempt to unsettle me. She unsettled you though, didn't she? Any sane mother would have attacked a stranger who threatened their kid. Or at the very least rung the police. Not you though, Jo. You scurried off and you let her think she had the upper hand. If you'd nipped it in the bud there and then Paula might have fucked off. But no. She upped her game. She turned up outside my work and told me about the CCTV. Not that I was worried. What was she going to do with it – show the police? My boss? She wouldn't get her money if she did either of those things.

And then she turned up on our street and you pushed her. I almost had respect for you then, Jo. Almost.

I tried to help you. I did everything I could to support you after Henry died even thought I felt as if someone had ripped out my heart. I gave you space. I let you cry. I waited for your grief to subside so we could rebuild our lives. But nothing I said, nothing I did, made any difference. Do you have any idea how frustrating that was? To watch someone you love shrivel into themselves? I tried reasoning with you, encouraging you, cajoling you. I begged you to get help and, when you refused, I told you I'd leave you if you didn't see a doctor. You hated me for saying that but that threat was a last resort. It was all I had left.

You seemed to get better after you started your medication and your CBT classes. You were less anxious, more hopeful about the future. You even let me touch you again, but the first time we had sex you got pregnant with Elise and it all went to shit again. You barely slept. You wouldn't let her out of your sight and there was no way you were going to let her leave the house, even if she was with me. Do you have any idea how emasculating that felt? Your own wife not trusting you to look after your daughter? I felt as though I was suffocating but still I didn't leave you. I let you decide what Elise could and couldn't do and I threw myself into my work because it was the one area of my life where I still felt in control.

How fucking naïve was I to think that you might be grateful? That you appreciated the sacrifices I'd made? That you loved me? Really fucking naïve as it turns out because all along you were secretly planning on leaving me. And you were going to take our daughter with you. AFTER EVERYTHING I DID FOR YOU. You KNEW how fucked up I was when my dad left me and how I swore I'd never do the same thing to my kids. And yet you still planned to take Elise away from me. You stupid, selfish, cold-hearted bitch.

I was so pleased when you told me you'd hit Paula. It meant you couldn't report her to the police and they wouldn't find out about the money. It also meant I could plant the drugs, safe in the knowledge you'd blame it on her. I wouldn't be the bad guy any more. You'd turn to me for help and support. You'd tell me that you needed me to protect you and Elise. And you did feel like that, didn't you, after you were

328

arrested? But only for a night because the next day you fucked off back to your mum and dad's. You used me, Jo. AGAIN. That's when I realised I'd had enough of giving you second chances. Why not let Social Services see what an unfit mother you really were? All I had to do was make the house look like a shithole before Lorraine Hooper showed up. It was almost too easy.

And now I've tracked you down. It's taken me the best part of two hours to go through all the different permutations of names and villages. The newspaper archive website was stupidly slow and my signal kept dropping out every couple of minutes, but that wasn't going to stop me. All I had to do was drive around until I found a stronger signal and start again. It's called perseverance, Jo. I never give up until I get what I'm after. You should know that by now.

And I've found him. I've found your daddy. Liam O'Brien – address: Ard na Mara, Main Road, Clogherhead. Husband to Brigid. Father to you.

Clogherhead. So that's where you headed. I've looked it up on the Internet. A fishing village in County Louth with a population of 3,026. Three pubs, three restaurants and a takeaway. Even if you've holed yourself away in one of the holiday chalets you'll have to leave at some point to get food.

Are you wondering how I found your old address, Jo? Guess what? Your daddy was in the paper. Brigid was right. Your daddy was a bad man. He was a very bad man. I understand why she didn't tell you why he disappeared.

But I will.

And I'll enjoy seeing the look on your face when I tell you. You won't want to stay in Clogherhead after I've left with Elise. And I'm pretty sure the locals won't want you to either.

Chapter 58

Mary slips out of the front door of the B&B. She doesn't pull the door shut behind her. Instead she leans forward ever so slightly, so her body remains hidden, and glances up and down the road. Helen is already halfway up Strand Street, pushing the little girl in her buggy. Mary was in the back room, putting a load into the tumble dryer, when she heard the front door slam. She'd hurried into the dining room and pulled back the net curtains to see who'd left but the street outside was empty. All morning she'd heard footsteps clomping around upstairs and doors opening and shutting. At first she'd thought it was the little one, playing, but when she hovered at the bottom of the stairs, pretending to polish the banister, she heard voices. Sean said, 'I've found it,' to which Helen replied, 'Brilliant'. A couple of seconds later a door closed and the house fell silent again. Mary waited a couple of minutes then climbed the stairs.

The only sound from Helen's room was the jangling noise of children's television. Sean's door was ajar. A quick peek revealed that he wasn't inside.

Mary ran a finger over the pearls at her neck. Normally their weight on her collarbone gave her comfort but now they felt too tight, almost as though they were strangling her. It wasn't that she didn't like her guests striking up friendships. She'd seen some great relationships grow and develop over the years, especially from some of the older regulars who wore their loneliness like overcoats, but there was something about the frantic activity on the first floor that made her feel uncomfortable. Sean hadn't come down to breakfast that morning and he never missed a meal. Helen and her daughter had shown up though. Mary had walked into the dining room to find them sitting at the table by the window; Helen with a glass of orange juice and the little girl with Niamh's pull-along wooden dog that had a spring for a tail. It made Mary's heart hurt to see them sitting there, looking so contented when she'd barely had a wink of sleep. Everything she'd done for little Lee she'd done out of the kindness of her heart. And how had she been rewarded? By Helen storming into the post office and glaring at her like she was some kind of child abductor. There'd been a moment when Mary had felt drawn to Helen's vulnerability and fearfulness but she was no different from the school-run mums who'd smile tightly as they walked past Mary's window, whilst simultaneously placing a protective hand on their child's shoulder. She could almost read their thoughts:

I mustn't let my child leave my sight or what happened to Mary could happen to me. Poor Mary. Opening her home to strangers because she has no family of her own to care for. It's a lesson to us all.

Helen tried to apologise. Mary lost count of the number of times she said sorry over breakfast, and afterwards. She knew that the right thing to do would be to forgive the younger woman and tell her that it wasn't a problem – but it was a problem, wasn't it? She was angry. More angry than she'd been for a long time. Angry with Helen, angry with Sean for avoiding her, angry with the world. She was a good mother. She cared for Niamh. She washed her, dressed her, played with her. All she did was turn her back for a couple of seconds and her daughter was taken from her. One . . . two . . . gone. But Helen still has her daughter. She dresses him in boy's clothes and calls him by a boy's name. A boy's name that changed from Ben to Lee in a heartbeat. Helen says she's a widow but the patch of pale skin on the third finger of her left hand suggests she only recently removed her wedding ring. When she arrived, her dyed red hair was tightly curled and she was wearing glasses. But she never wears the spectacles to breakfast, only when she leaves the house, and if her hair isn't as curly as normal she pulls on a hat over it. The look of fear in her eyes is constant though. That never changes. What is she so afraid of?

Mary waves at little Aoife Flannigan, scooting down the street on her balance bike, then she steps into her car and starts the engine. Helen is hiding something and she intends to find out what.

Chapter 59

Mary followed me to the post office. I'm almost certain it was her in the silver car that parked up on the opposite side of the street when I went in, then swiftly drove off when I came out. I noticed a silver Ford Fiesta parked up outside the B&B when we arrived and it hasn't moved since. If it was Mary she must have quickly circled Clogherhead and returned to the B&B because I can hear her clattering around upstairs.

'Mary?' I unstrap Elise from her buggy and carry her up the stairs. 'Mary, are you up there?'

The door to my room is ajar. My suitcase is still open and there are piles of clothes on the floor from when I had to abandon my packing and sorting when Elise upturned Henry's memory box.

'Mary?' I step into the room. 'Are you in here?'

'Yes.' She steps out of the en suite, bathroom cleaner in one hand and a cloth in the other. She's wearing

334

her apron and slippers but the pearls have disappeared from around her neck. She looks from me to my daughter but her eyes remain blank and glassy. It's the same look she had on her face after Elise ran out of the door.

'I was . . . I was going to finish packing,' I say.

'No need. I can clean around the mess.'

'But wouldn't it be quicker if—'

'It would be quicker if you just let me get on. Your flight isn't until this evening. Am I right?'

'That's right, but—'

She turns her back on me and flicks her cloth over the television. 'The sooner I get on, the sooner I'm finished.'

'Mary, I'm so sorry about what happened yesterday. Honestly, I was up half the night thinking about—'

She walks back into the bathroom without saying a word and drowns me out by running the taps. I know I should just leave but I hate the thought of Mary having to pick through all my things as she cleans.

'Why don't you go to the beach?' She reappears in the doorway to the en suite as my fingertips graze an abandoned pair of Elise's socks.

'I . . .' I want to tell her that I don't want to go to the beach. I want to get my stuff, get my car and go. But I don't want to upset her more than I already have.

'OK,' I say. 'We'll be back in an hour.'

Chapter 60

You know what, Jo? I really didn't expect Paula to send someone to beat the shit out of me. I thought she'd get bored or give up. But I wasn't scared as I picked myself up off the ground, my eye split and my body pounding. I was fucking angry. Who the hell did she think she was? The money wasn't hers. She hadn't worked her arse off for it. She'd sucked Ian's dick and filled her nose with coke. She'd laughed when one of Ian's goons told her how he'd intimidated a single mum with a baby in her arms. I'd exposed that shit. I'd risked everything to expose the evil bastards. I wasn't going to let her intimidate me and my family. But I wasn't going to put them at risk either. When I say 'family', I mean Elise. You were a lost cause, Jo. You'd become so unpredictable, so devious, so wrapped up in your own head you'd completely abandoned your grip on reality. If you weren't knocking yourself out with drugs you were screaming down the phone or lashing out. It wasn't just Paula I needed to protect Elise from. You were so unstable you'd become a danger to her too. Screw the court order. I knew the courts would award me a residence order but it would take too long. I needed Elise with me. Now.

As I approached the house I saw two cars parked outside. I didn't recognise one of them and felt sick with fear. What if the man who'd beaten me up was in the house? What if you'd changed the locks and I couldn't get in? But no, you're not that smart, are you, Jo? If you were you'd have realised that I'd taken the spare key from inside the front door when I planted the drugs, but you never once mentioned it.

I was still drunk when I let myself in. My plan was to snatch Elise and then get Henry's box from the living room. I'd moved the money there when I ransacked the place. I didn't feel safe keeping it in my sports bag in the hotel room, not after Paula showed up outside work. But I knocked against the shoe rack as I weaved my way down the hall. One of my work shoes tumbled onto the floor. The sound seemed to reverberate around the house and I nearly walked right back out the back door. But nothing happened. The house fell silent again and I crept up the stairs. It didn't wake Helen, who I discovered lying flat on her back in the spare room. It woke Elise though. She was halfway out of her cot. And you know the rest.

When I woke up the next day, sober and in pain, I realised what a fucking idiot I'd been the night

337

*before – pumped up with hurt pride, booze and
bravado. Screw the money. I'd give it back to Paula.
I'd shove it in her smug face. What mattered most
was keeping my Elise safe. But when I turned up at
the house to get her I discovered that you'd gone –
taking Elise and the box full of money with you.*

Max stands outside the cottage, hands in pockets, as
he takes in its whitewashed walls, small, deeply set
windows, thatched roof and bright-red door. Ard na
Mara, Main Street. According to the newspaper report
it's the house Liam O'Brien was living in with Brigid
and Jo when he was arrested. It's where Jo grew up.
He's never seen a photo of the house – Jo's always
bemoaned the lack of photos of her childhood in
Ireland, but it makes sense. It's small, homely and he
can imagine Brigid inside, bustling about in the kitchen,
wiping down surfaces and rearranging the cutlery
drawer. And Jo, in the living room, sitting cross-legged
on a rug in front of the TV. Would her dad have been
in there with her, slouched in an armchair with a
newspaper spread over his lap, or was he more of an
absent dad, like Max's? Never there when you needed
him and everywhere when you didn't.

He reaches into his back pocket as he approaches
the door. His fingers close over the glossy photo of
Jo and Elise, taken six months ago at Elise's birthday
party. Not that it was much of a party – just him,
Elise and Jo. Brigid couldn't come down from Chester
and Jo didn't want to invite anyone from nursery.
When they'd discussed it she'd said the thought of

people she didn't know in the house made her feel panicky.

She's smiling at Elise in the photo. Elise is staring wide-eyed at the two candles on the cake Jo is balancing on one hand. His daughter won't have any more quiet birthdays, not once he's got her back. He'll invite the world and its mother round for her third birthday. No, screw that. He'll rent a hall. He'll pay for a magician and a caterer and someone to decorate the place with balloons and streamers and banners with his daughter's name on. He'll do whatever it takes to give her the best damned birthday she could ever wish for.

He clenches his right hand and knocks on the red door. There's a car parked up outside and he's pretty certain someone's in but he's not pinning his hopes on Jo being inside. The chances are the house has been sold on several times since Brigid upped and left but the current owners might know Brigid's relatives. Or, even better, have seen Jo and Elise.

'Hello?' The door opens and a tall woman with short dark hair looks out at him. 'Can I help you?'

'I hope so.' Max shows her the photo. 'I'm looking for this woman and this child. Have you seen them?'

The woman peers at the photo then reaches for it. 'I haven't got my glasses. Do you mind?'

'Of course not.'

He waits as the woman extends her arm and narrows her eyes as she tries to focus on the image of his wife and child.

'Police, are you?' she asks, looking at him.

'No. I work for Heir Hunters. You might have heard of us. We reunite people with money they've inherited from distant relatives' wills.'

'Ooh, is that so.' The woman glances down the street. 'No TV cameras with you?'

Max shakes his head. 'No. This isn't for a TV programme. It's a private firm.'

'Oh.' The look of excitement on the woman's face fades.

'Have you seen them?'

'No, I'm sorry.' She shakes her head. 'They live here, do they? I know a lot of people in Clogherhead but they don't look familiar.'

'They're visiting. But they're from the area originally. Do you know of a Liam O'Brien or a Brigid O'Brien? Her maiden name was Gallagher.'

The woman shakes her head again. 'There are a lot of O'Briens and Gallaghers about but I don't know those names. I've only lived here a couple of years. You could ask at the post office. Clodagh's lived here her whole life. If anyone will be able to help you she will.'

Max flashes the woman a smile then tucks the photo back into his pocket. 'Thank you, you've been very helpful.'

'Nora Kennedy,' she calls after him as he turns and walks back down the path. 'Let me know if there's any money coming my way, won't you!'

Money. Another cheap bitch obsessed with money. Just like Paula. I thought she was the main threat to

Elise, but it was always you, wasn't it, Jo? You trapped her within the walls of our house, you neglected her, you forgot about her and then you abused her. I will never forgive you for hurting our little girl, for covering her little body in bruises and, when I get her back, I will ensure that she hates you as much as I do.

Chapter 61

Mary stands slowly and presses a hand to her lower back as she surveys the tiny but sparkling clean en suite bathroom. For fifteen minutes she's been spraying, scrubbing and wiping. Her forehead is damp with perspiration, her arms ache and her back is spasming, but the anger that was building all morning has subsided. She didn't discover anything when she followed Helen earlier, just that she popped into the post office. Mary had parked up outside, hoping to see something, but the weak February sun was glinting off the window, making it impossible to see inside. She'd quickly returned to the B&B, hoping Sean would shed some light on the conversation she'd partially overheard after breakfast, but there was a space outside where his car had been and no answer when she knocked on his door. So that was that. In a couple of hours Helen would collect her car, pack up, pay and leave – taking her daughter with her, the little girl who so resembled Niamh it made her heart ache just to look at her. In that split second, when she'd seen the child sitting on the edge of her bed in her pants, Mary was convinced that her daughter had come back to her. But then she'd blinked, and she'd vanished. She tried to explain it away as a trick of the light, the reflection of the television on Lee's face or sheer wishful thinking, but no amount of logical thought would remove the image of Niamh's small heart-shaped face from her mind. Her child had been dead for over thirty years and she'd never once appeared to her. Why had she appeared in Helen's room? Was Niamh trying to warn her about something? Or was her own subconscious warning her that another child was in danger?

Mary steps out of the en suite and into the small bedroom. Helen had her handbag with her, strapped across her body, under the child, when she came in earlier but all the rest of her belongings are in the room. Mary moves towards the open suitcase then stops. She's never gone through a guest's things. Never. But this isn't about curiosity. She'd invited Helen into her home in good faith. She'd given toys to the little one, she'd offered her phone when Helen needed to call the UK and she'd taken the girl out for a lolly when she was distressed. And what had she received in return for her kindness? Abuse, mistrust and lies. Helen had told a barefaced lie the moment she'd walked through the door – letting her believe that the child was a boy. What kind of woman would do that? You wouldn't lie about something as big as that for no reason. No little girl would willingly agree to wear boys' clothes and have her hair hacked off. Helen must have forced her to change her appearance. It makes Mary sick just thinking about it.

She reaches for her neck, touching the space where her necklace should lie, as a horrifying thought occurs to her. What if Helen isn't the child's mother at all? That would explain why she'd gone to so much trouble to disguise the girl's appearance. It would explain everything. If only she had broadband she could check the news to see if there were any reports of snatched or missing children. Mary doesn't read or watch the news because she finds it too depressing. But there's no time to buy a newspaper now. She has to discover the truth before Helen returns and packs up her things.

She crouches down by the suitcase, glances behind her to check that the bedroom door is still closed, and roots around in the pile of clothes and toiletries. She doesn't find anything of interest so stands up again and casts her eye around the small room. There are various toys on the floor, a plastic bag on the bed, half stuffed with clothes, and another plastic bag on the top of the wardrobe next to a wooden box. She reaches for the box, then sits down on the bed and rests it on her lap.

HENRY

She traces a finger over the engraved name on the top, then carefully lifts the lid. Her heart thuds in her chest as she lifts out a tiny knitted hat. She glances at the door again, certain she heard a sound on the landing. She gets up to lock the bedroom door then returns to the bed and picks up the hat again. It's so small it fits in the palm of her hand. Instinctively she lifts it to her nose and sniffs at it but it doesn't smell of anything. It's too small to be a baby's hat and it wouldn't fit a dolly. Mary takes another knitted item out of the box. It's a blanket, but a very small one, maybe twice the size of her hand. There's a teddy too, with pale-brown fur and a blue ribbon around its neck. And a scan picture. Mary never had one for Niamh; they weren't available in the 70s. She didn't even know what gender her child was until she was born. She traces a finger over the black and white image. It's clear it's a baby. She can even make out the umbilical cord, twisting its way out of the baby's abdomen, but what's this?

There's a name at the top of the scan. Mrs Joanne Blackmore and a date, four years earlier. Joanne Blackmore? So that's Helen's real name then.

She carefully places the items back in the box, returns it to the top of the wardrobe and reaches for the plastic bag. It's set quite far back and she has to stand on tiptoes to grab the handle. She sees the contents before she's even pulled it off the wardrobe. It's stuffed with money. She yanks it towards her and rifles through it. There must be thousands of pounds in here.

She drops onto the bed as her legs give way. No one carries that amount of money with them in cash. It has to be stolen. Unless Joanne Blackmore is on the run? Mary stands up again and replaces the bag of money on top of the wardrobe. Her heart thuds heavily in her chest as she gazes around the room. What else is Joanne hiding?

She lifts up the pillows and the duvets but there's nothing beneath them so she turns her attention to the mattress, sliding her hands underneath, feeling for anything unusual. When she doesn't find anything she tips the mattress up. The pillows, the duvet and plastic bag full of clothes slip to the floor. Nothing. There's nothing under the mattress. Under the bed then? She drops to her knees and looks underneath. Nothing there either, apart from a couple of socks and the pink and white knickers she'd seen the girl wearing.

Where else? Where else? She returns to the suitcase and searches through it again, looking for zipped compartments and hidden pockets, but doesn't find anything unusual. The only place left to look is in the drawer of the bedside table. It's one of the first places she looks when a guest checks out. They're forever leaving their glasses, medication and books behind. Out of sight, out of mind, when they're hidden away.

She yanks the drawer open but there's nothing unusual inside. Just a couple of blister packs of medication, some Sudocrem, some wet wipes and what looks like a slim photo album. She reaches for it and opens the first page. The first photograph is of Joanne, but with long blonde hair. She's lying in a hospital bed with a baby, wrapped in a white blanket, in her arms. Mary turns the page. There's another photo

346

taken in hospital. This time of Jo and a man with fair hair with the baby cradled between them. There's a wedding ring on the third finger of the man's left hand. And one on Jo's finger too. Her husband then, the one she said died. Mary continues to turn the pages. As she does, the child grows – from newborn to smiling baby to crawling to standing. Some of the photos feature Joanne, some feature the man, some are just of the child. Mary's confusion grows as she reaches the penultimate photo in the book. There's no doubt that the child in the book is little Lee. She's got long fair curly hair in the images but her face – her wide blue eyes and rosebud lips – is exactly the same. It doesn't make sense. If Lee is Joanne's child why cut off all her hair and dress her as a boy? Why keep thousands of pounds in a plastic bag?

Mary turns the final page. The last photograph is of the girl standing by a bed with an older woman. In the bed is a gaunt-cheeked man. He's looking at the camera but, unlike the child and the woman, he's not smiling. He looks unwell. Mary's gaze flicks towards the face of the older woman. There's something very familiar about her. Her smile has sparked an uneasy sensation in the pit of Mary's stomach. She runs a finger over the clear film covering the photograph. It feels unusually thick so she peels back the plastic edging and reaches a finger behind the photograph. She touches something and carefully pulls it out. It's another photograph but this one is folded in two.

She unfolds it, takes one look at the two people

in the black and white image, and then hurls it away from her.

It floats down to the carpet and lies still. A man and a woman gaze up at her. They are both smiling. The woman is Mary's childhood best friend Brigid Gallagher on her wedding day. She's standing outside the Church of the Sacred Heart dressed in a simple white dress with a veil in her hair. Beside her is a man in a cheap dark suit.

Liam O'Brien.

The man who killed Niamh.

Chapter 62

I've found you, Jo.

This is it – Seamount B&B – where you've been hiding with my daughter. The woman in the post office didn't immediately recognise you from the photo but, when I suggested that you might look different, she'd told me that she'd served a tourist that looked a little like the woman in my photograph. Only she had red hair. I covered your hair with my fingers and asked her to take another look. Could the woman with the red hair be the woman in the photo? Yes, she said, nodding, you could be sisters, but the woman she'd served was definitely with a boy. A fine-featured boy admittedly, but definitely a boy. I was about to leave. I was going to ask at the caravan instead but then the shop owner called me back.

'Lee!' she said. 'The boy's name is Lee. I distinctly remember his mother calling him that when he was trying to snatch some sweets off the shelves.'

Lee. Li-Li. So that's what you've been doing, Jo. You've been trying to pass our daughter off as a boy.

The shop owner was very forthcoming when I asked her if she knew where you might be staying. She gave me the address of Mary's B&B and told me that I should hurry if I wanted to catch you because your landlady had told her that you had a flight to catch in Dublin this evening. That was nice of her, wasn't it, Jo? Very helpful.

'Hello?' There's no answer when he knocks on the door so Max knocks on the window. A net curtain is hung behind it but he can make out chairs and tables and a dresser at the back of the room.

He returns to the front door and is about to knock again when it opens. An ashen-faced woman in her sixties stares out at him. The door is only open a crack so he can only see her face.

'Yes?'

Max reaches into the back pocket of his jeans then changes his mind. There's something strange about the way the B&B owner is looking at him. She looks fraught and fearful. Has Jo told her about him, is that why she's hiding behind the door?

'I . . . er . . .' He clears his throat. 'I was wondering if you have any rooms available.'

'No.' She shakes her head.

'But there's a sign in the window saying you have vacancies.'

'I don't. I need to change the sign. Goodbye.'

'Wait!' He pushes against the door before she can close it. 'Please, I need to talk to you.'

'Take your hand off my door or I'll call the police. I told you, I don't have any rooms.'

'I know and . . . I'm sorry . . . I know I'm intruding but I'm desperate.' He bites down on the inside of his lip so hard he tastes blood in his mouth and his eyes water.

His 'tears' have the desired effect. Mary stops pushing back against the door and her face softens.

'Desperate for what?'

'To find my wife and daughter.' He keeps one hand on the door and reaches into the back pocket of his jeans with his free hand. He pulls out the photo and shows it to her. 'Have you seen them?'

He watches Mary closely as she looks at the photo. You don't spend nineteen years as a journalist without learning how to read body language. Sure enough, her eyes widen, ever so slightly. Recognition.

'I'm sorry.' She pushes the photo back towards him. 'I've never seen them before.'

Interesting. Everyone else he's shown the photo to has pumped him for more information. Why are his wife and daughter missing? Where is he from? How long have they been gone for? But not Mary Byrne. She looks like she can't get rid of him fast enough.

'The woman at the post office told me that they're staying here.'

'She's mistaken.' Mary looks pointedly at his hand. 'I have things to do.'

'She's a drug addict. Did you know that, Mrs Byrne?' The older woman flinches as he says her name but he hasn't got time to explain why he knows it. 'The police arrested her for keeping drugs in our home. And she's mentally unstable. She's ill and incapable of looking after our daughter. I've got a court order that has awarded me custody of Elise. Would you like to see it?' He reaches into the inside pocket of his jacket but Mary waves him away.

'There's no need. As I told you, I don't recognise the woman and the child in the photo. Good day to you.'

'Please! Jo's a very manipulative woman.' He pauses, gauging the older woman's expression. He definitely saw her lips tighten when he said the name *Jo*. 'She's given you a different name, hasn't she? You see! That's the kind of woman we're dealing with. She's manipulative and she's a liar. What's she said to you? That she had to go on the run with our daughter to protect her? But Jo's the one that's putting Elise in danger.'

He waits for Mary to say something. He can see the indecision in her face. He's been in this situation hundreds of times before – witnesses to crimes who are unsure whether to talk to him. They want to share what they saw, they're dying to talk about it to someone who might understand, but a journalist? Everyone knows that journalists twist your words. And what if there was some kind of repercussion from the criminal or their family? He can tell when they're wavering. When they need one more push to spill their guts. That's the stage he's at now with Mary. He's going to have to show his hand.

'I know who you are,' he says, softening his voice and adopting the most sympathetic, heartfelt expression in his repertoire. 'I know the tragedy you've been through and I'm so very, very sorry for your loss. I can't begin to imagine how much you've suffered. I was sickened when I discovered that Jo's staying with you. Of all the places she could have chosen to stay . . .' He shakes his head. 'She's more unwell than I thought. Unless,' – he pauses for dramatic effect – 'unless she deliberately sought you out, Mary. In which case she's as dangerous as her father. And now another child is in danger, my child, and you're the only one who can stop something terrible happening to her. You could save her life.'

He cringes, inwardly, as he says the last sentence. It's a horribly cheesy line, the sort of thing television adverts for abandoned dogs or overworked donkey charities close with. Every single word of those adverts is meticulously crafted to tug at your heartstrings and make you put your hand in your wallet.

He drops his chin, wrings his hands together and swallows hard, as though he's fighting back tears. And he waits. His words will be sinking in. Mary will be wrestling with her conscience. She might even have tears in her eyes. Five, four, three, two . . .

The door slams shut.

What the fuck?

'Mary!' Max hammers on the door then crouches down and shouts through the letter box. 'Mary Byrne.

Please! You need to help me. I know they're living here. Please, Mary. You need to do the right thing or you'll be an accessory to child abduction.'

He waits, but Mary doesn't appear in the hallway. The only sound he hears is his own desperate heartbeat, thundering in his ears.

He slips one of his business cards through the letter box. 'Here's my number, Mrs Byrne. Think about what I said and give me a ring. You couldn't save Niamh but you could save Elise. Do the right thing, Mary. I know you're a good person.'

The letter box clatters shut as he stands up and looks around. There are two cars parked outside the house. One is his hire car, the other is a silver Ford Fiesta. He peers through the windows, looking for any indication that it's Jo's car, but there are no CDs scattered on the passenger seat, no Diet Coke bottles, no car seat, no crisp crumbs on the back seat, or toys, books and games. Jo had to have hired a car to get here from Rosslare. But did she make the journey with Elise alone or with someone else? What if they're already on their way to Dublin to catch a flight?

He slams the top of the car with the palm of his hand. What now? He looks from the Ford Fiesta to the B&B and then back to his own car. He could wait outside the B&B to see if Jo comes back or he could drive to Dublin airport and hang around Arrivals. Or . . .

No!

He hurries back to the B&B, opens the letter box

and peers inside. There's a silver buggy parked up in the hallway, just like Elise's.

Max smiles.

So, you haven't left then, Jo. You're still here, either hiding in the B&B or somewhere in the town.

Either way I'll find you. I'm going nowhere until I do.

Chapter 63

Mary watches from behind the net curtains, her heart twisting with indecision, as Max gets into his red Vauxhall Astra. She'd been so startled when she'd opened the front door to him. It was as though the photograph album had come to life. One minute he was frozen in time, smiling out of the photograph, and the next he was on her doorstep, pleading with her to help save his child's life. What was going on? First the revelation that red-haired Helen was actually a blonde-haired woman called Joanne, then the discovery of the photograph of Brigid and Liam, and now Max, threatening her, telling her she was an accomplice to child abduction. When he'd mentioned that Jo was Liam's daughter she'd felt as though the foundations of her home were rumbling under her feet and the walls were shaking. Every bone in her body told her to slam the door shut in Max's face and hide away until the devastation was over.

But she didn't. She stood in the doorway, guarding her home from the man with tears in his eyes and devastation in his voice. He spoke so quickly she couldn't take it all in. Jo was a mentally unstable drug addict. She was manipulative and a liar. She was putting Elise's life in danger. She was Liam O'Brien's daughter and she was dangerous. It was as though he was speaking Mary's fears aloud and she was so close, so close to telling him that Jo and Elise were on the beach. But then he'd mentioned Niamh – he'd intimated that she should save his child because she'd failed to save her own – and her heart and the door had slammed shut simultaneously.

How dare he use that against her to try and manipulate her! What did he know about what had happened? What did he care? He didn't see her as a person. He saw her as a means to an end.

Brigid Gallagher had known the real Mary. They'd met on the first day of primary school. Mary had admired Brigid's long black plaits. Brigid had admired the red bow in Mary's hair. It was their very first conversation and one that had started a friendship that stretched throughout childhood, adolescence and into their early twenties. They shared their worries and their fears with each other, the details of their first kisses, their hopes and dreams for their future. They'd talked about soulmates, baby names and careers. They went on holiday together. And when Mary met Patrick at a dance in Drogheda and decided that he was the man she wanted to marry, Brigid was the first person she told. That was the first time their relationship hit a rocky point. Mary spent a lot of time with Patrick in those first heady months and rarely saw her best friend. Brigid accused Mary of abandoning her. She said she was glad that she'd found love but she was in danger of losing her friendship.

'I'd never do that to you,' she said. 'Not for a man. Not for anything. We made a pact when we were little, remember? To be friends for ever.'

That night Mary couldn't sleep for crying. She was madly in love with Patrick but Brigid was right, she had been a bad friend. The next day she organised to go to tea with Brigid. She also rang Pat to ask if he had any nice friends that he could introduce to Brigid. But before she was introduced to any of them Brigid met Liam when she was walking the family dog on the beach. Mary didn't like him at first. She thought he was a bit of a gadabout, a drifter, five years older, who moved from town to town in search of work, but he was nice to Brigid. He treated her well and made her laugh.

And then Liam went off to England for a building job and Brigid found out that she was pregnant.

She cried like her heart was breaking. They both did. It was the worst possible shame to befall an unmarried mother in Ireland in the 70s. Brigid's mother suggested she go to Cork, stay with a second cousin and have the baby away from prying eyes. She said she should give it up for adoption if she wanted any kind of respectable life for herself. Brigid did go to Cork to have the baby but she didn't give it up for adoption. She returned to Clogherhead shortly after the birth with a tiny pink bundle in her arms and she told her parents that if they didn't accept little Joanne she'd move so far away they'd never see either of them again. Brigid's da was furious. He raged at her, shouting that no one threatened him, particularly not his own daughter. But Brigid's mam wore him down. If her daughter could walk through the streets of Clogherhead with her head held high then so would she. And woe betide anyone who judged them.

They did, of course. There were whispers and sly glances and raised eyebrows. Some of the older people in the village crossed the street when they saw Brigid walking towards them, pushing her pram. Mary knew that inside she was burning with shame and anger but she never showed it. Not once. Instead she would raise her chin and wish them a very good morning.

No one thought Liam O'Brien would come back, least of all Mary, but Brigid was insistent. She said that, when he read the letter she'd sent him about the baby, he'd come back and he'd marry her. And he did. Against all expectations he returned to Clogherhead. The local priest wouldn't marry them so they were forced to go to a different parish, and in the Church of the Sacred Heart he put a ring on her finger. Mary didn't attend the wedding. No one did. Brigid said she understood why her parents hadn't attended but Mary could see past the stoic look on her best friend's face. She was bitterly, bitterly hurt.

Niamh was born six years after Joanne. Brigid was bridesmaid at Mary and Patrick's wedding. She'd whispered in Mary's ear, after the ceremony, that tonight would be the night she'd conceive her child, but it had taken longer than that. A lot longer. Every night for five years Mary prayed to God to bring her a child. And then, finally, her prayers came true.

She was a mother for two glorious years. They were the happiest years of her life. And then Liam O'Brien stole them away.

Mary stands up so quickly all the blood rushes from her head and black spots swim in front of her eyes. She grips the windowsill and waits for them to disappear then hurries to the front door. She wrenches it open and looks up and down the street but Max and the red car have disappeared. The wind whistles into the house and, out of the corner of her eye, Mary notices something small and white fluttering along the hallway floor. She ducks down and picks it up. It's a business card.

Max Blackmore, it says on the front.

Crime Reporter

Bristol News

There's a mobile telephone number and an email address in the corner of the piece of paper.

The more she stares at it the more her head swims. What should she do?

Chapter 64

The wind whips my hair around my face. Red tendrils wrap themselves over my cheeks, nose and throat. I brush them back with both hands, only for them to attack me again a split second later. Elise prods the rock pool with her net and says something I can't hear because it's carried away by the wind. I wipe my damp palms on my jeans but they're wet too. I twist round, expecting to see several large rocks and a large expanse of beach behind us. But it's gone. The sea, which was at least a hundred metres away the last time I looked, has travelled so far up the beach that waves are crashing against the rocks we're playing on. When we arrived it was flat, almost serene, with the sun glinting off the water, but grey clouds have gathered in the sky, and the sea – striped with the crest of huge waves – has turned black.

Smack! Another wave hits the rocks – suddenly, ferociously. It's all I can do to grab Elise under the armpits and whip her up and into my arms before white surf leaps into the air and curves towards us. It misses, just, and smashes against limestone less than a metre away from us. There's another wave right behind it, taller and darker. We have to move. Now.

I glance at my watch as I hurry across the damp rocks, towards the mainland and safety. The tide doesn't come in until midday and it was only ten o'clock the last time I looked and—

Ten o'clock.

How can it still be ten o'clock?

I tap the glass face.

The second hand doesn't move.

I glance back at the sea as a wave hits the rocks, with more force than the last one, and this time we're sprayed with seawater. Elise screams and tightens her grip around my neck. As she does, her net slips out of her hand.

'Net!' she screams in my ear and she tries to twist out of my grip. 'Net, Mummy!'

I don't reach for the net but I do stop running, my heart thundering in my chest. Where do we go now? I reached the end of the rock face but a high stone wall separates the beach from the safety of a grassy verge. Sharp, jagged pieces of stone are embedded in the top. There's no way I could get over it. The only way off the beach is to scramble across the rocks until I reach the small patch of beach at the end of Main Road. Once we're on the road we'll be safe.

Elise continues to shout for her abandoned net as I take off again. Her screams cut through the wind, deafening me as I carefully pick my way across the rocks. The sea spray has made them damp and slippery, and my daughter lurches in my arms as my left foot slides away from me. I fight to keep my balance but, violently twisting to one side, I wrench my right knee and it nearly gives way. I wince as I take another step.

'Mummy!' Elise shouts in my ear. 'I'm scared!'

I pull her even closer, locking her against my body. The sea is raging and thrashing now. Huge grey waves roll towards us, leaping and crashing, gathering speed and height the closer they get. I feel like we're standing near the jaws of an enormous dark monster that wants to swallow us whole. 'It's OK. I've got you. We're nearly—' I sense someone watching us and turn to look.

Mary is standing on the beach at the edge of the rocks, her navy woollen coat buttoned up to her neck, her paisley scarf twisted around her throat and her grey knitted hat pulled down over her ears. Her gloved hands twist together as she stares at us. She's come down to warn us about the tide.

'Mary!' I jump down off the last rock and land heavily on the sand. My landlady doesn't reach out a hand to steady my fall. She doesn't move an inch, not even when the wind snatches the scarf from her neck and lifts it up in the air. Elise watches it as it twirls and dances above our heads before the wind whips it further down the beach.

'Mary?' I shift Elise onto my hip. 'What's wrong? What is it?'

She blinks, but her eyes are glassy and blank, staring right through me.

'Mary, come on.' I touch her elbow. 'We have to get going. The tide's coming in. We need to—'

She whips her arm away from my touch and grabs my wrist in one lightning-fast move.

'Mary?' I try to pull my hand away but she's surprisingly strong and, with my other arm around Elise, there's no way I can break her hold without dropping my child. 'Mary, you're hurting me. Let go, please.'

'Who are you?'

'You know who I am.'

'I know who you pretended to be.' The glassy look in her eyes vanishes as she spits the words at me.

'Mary!' I pull away but she still has a tight grip on my wrist and a jolt of pain shoots through my shoulders as she yanks me back towards her. Her eyes are steely behind her rain-misted glasses.

'I know all about you, Joanne Blackmore. I know that you have a husband called Max. I know you snatched Elise from him. I know you have drug and mental health problems—'

'That's not true.'

'No? You've got enough medication in your bedside drawer to knock out a horse.'

'That's for my agoraphobia and anxiety.'

'Do agoraphobics spend a lot of time on the beach?'

'Please,' I beg. The sea is creeping nearer and nearer. There's only a thin strip of rocks left that aren't submerged and a tiny stretch of beach ahead of us. 'Let's go back to the B&B. I'll explain everything. I promise.'

'Why'd you come here, Joanne? Why'd you come to my house?'

'Because Sean gave me a lift and said you had rooms available.'

'Are you lying again, Joanne? I heard you were good at that.'

'Mary, I don't know what you've heard or what you've read in the papers but you've got it wrong. I'm not a bad person, I promise. I—'

'Curiosity, was it? Was that what brought you here? You wanted to see for yourself how much damage your daddy did?'

I start at the mention of my father. What's she talking about? I was sweating under my thick winter coat with Elise pressed up against me, but now I can't stop shivering.

'Forgotten, have you, Joanne? Blocked it out of your head?'

'I don't know what you mean. Please, Mary,' – I drop my voice – 'you're scaring me. And I need to get Elise to safety.'

Mary's eyes don't soften. My plea was snatched away by the wind. Either that or she deliberately ignores it.

'You were in the car. Remember? Your daddy's white Ford Escort. You'd been to the football with him. He made you sit outside in the car with a book, a can of pop and some Tayto crisps while he went in to watch the match. He had a few beers. A lot of beers. Don't you remember, Joanne? Don't you remember how strongly his breath smelled when he finally got back into the car?'

'No.' I shake my head but it's a lie. I can remember. I remember countless occasions when I'd wait in the car while my dad hung out with his friends. I remember how bored I was. How I'd wander into the club to ask him whether it was time to go, only to be told, 'I'll be out shortly.' But shortly seemed to last for ever and, when I finished my book, I fell asleep on the back seat. I remember being surprised, when I woke up, that it wasn't dark outside and that my dad was sitting in the driving seat, starting the engine. He was smoking a John Player Special cigarette and it stank.

'Do you remember him going fast, Joanne? Putting his foot down and swinging around corners. Remember that?'

I nod, dumbly, too terrified to speak.

'He was going to take you down to the beach to meet your mother and some of her friends, wasn't he? But he was late and he put his foot down. He must have been going fifty miles an hour down Strand Street.'

'No, Mary.' My eyes fill with tears. 'No, Mary, please.'

'Did you feel a little bump, did you? As your da was driving down Main Road? Did he tell you it was a cat?'

I don't want to hear this. I can't. All my life I've been told that my dad was a bad man and I never believed it. I couldn't. How could the man who gave me rides on his shoulders, who made me laugh with his stupid jokes, who gave me bags of sweets when Mum wasn't looking, be a bad man? Bad men had scars on their faces and strange, uneven teeth. They didn't have bright-blue eyes and thick pale hair. OK, so he stank of booze and fags sometimes, he didn't take me down the park and he wouldn't talk to me when he was watching the telly, but wasn't everyone's dad like that? When I hit my teens I thought maybe he'd cheated on my mum. He left her to be with another woman. Or, worse, had a baby with another woman, and it was such a scandal that she had to leave Clogherhead. But not this. I know what Mary's about to say. There's only one thing she can say.

'That was my little girl, Joanne,' Mary says. 'That was my baby your daddy killed, not a cat.'

Tears stream down my cheeks as I place my hand on top of Elise's head, feeling the dampness of her woollen bobble hat as I press her warm face into my neck. I close my eyes but I can still see her – the little girl smiling up from the photo. I can still smell the musty red coat. My dad killed her. He killed a child. She wasn't much more than a baby. She was almost as old as Elise. I fight to control the pain that's ripping through my chest but I can't do it – I can't bear the anguish in Mary's voice – and a strangled sob escapes from my lips.

'My best friend's husband killed my baby, Joanne. He dropped you at the beach, then he drove home and he opened a beer like nothing had happened. And all the while Niamh was lying broken and bleeding in the road.'

'Oh God, Mary. I didn't know. I swear I didn't know.' My landlady has loosened her grip on my wrist but I can't bring myself to pull away. The big, empty house, the shrine in the nursery, the loneliness and sadness that follow Mary round like a cloud – my dad caused that. He ran over her child and he didn't stop. What kind of man does that? What kind of monster?

'Mummy?' Elise looks at me curiously. 'Mummy cry?'

She dabs at my cheeks with her mittened hand then looks at Mary. 'Mary cry.'

She reaches a hand towards Mary's face but the older woman jumps away as though burned. She touches a hand to her throat, as though feeling for her scarf, and looks surprised to find it isn't there.

'Mary,' I say, 'I swear I didn't know. I never would have stayed with you if I had. I wouldn't have come back to Clogherhead. I'm so, so sorry. Honestly, I—'

'But your mammy knew, didn't she, Joanne? He was her husband. How could she not know something like that?'

'She didn't. She can't have. She hates Liam. I saw it in her eyes whenever I tried to talk about him. She told me he was a bad man. She told me never to talk about him in her house.'

The light in Mary's eyes changes. The hatred dims, ever so slightly. She wants to believe me.

'Mary,' I say as the surf breaks over my shoes. 'Mary, we need to go!'

But my landlady doesn't react. Instead she stares at Elise, a strange, fixed smile on her face, and reaches out her hands.

368

'Give the child to me.'

'No.' I take a step backwards but there's nowhere to run to. Mary's trapped me between the rocks and the road. I'll have to swerve around her or push her out of the way to get past her.

'Give her to me,' she says again. 'You nearly fooled me, Joanne – with the tears and the apology and the talk of Brigid. You're as clever as your husband said.'

Fear courses through me. 'Max? When did you speak to Max?'

'You can't steal a child.' She lurches forward and grips Elise by one arm. 'You can't take her away from a parent who loves her. I won't let it happen again.'

'No, Mary.' I try to twist away but Mary doesn't let go and Elise screams. 'Whatever Max told you is a lie. He's the liar. He's the one that forced me to run. I had to do it to protect my daughter.'

'You're not well,' Mary says softly. 'That's a trait you share with your father. How could you hurt a child and pretend it didn't happen unless there's something wrong with your brain—'

She breaks off, startled by the sound of a car speeding along the beach towards us. The tide is so high now there's barely space for it to travel along the sand. As the tyres splash through the surf the left indicator light flashes. It wants to turn left onto Main Road and we're in the way. I react instinctively, grabbing Mary's forearm, yanking her out of the way of the car, and onto the rocks. The car flashes past us, missing us by a couple of inches as it turns into the road.

Mary stares at me, wide-eyed and panting. As the

369

surf rains down on us, Elise screams and sharp rocks press into my back. He could have hit us. That idiot could have killed us al—

The sound of brakes squealing cuts through the roar of the sea and the howl of the wind. Red tail lights flash. The car hasn't disappeared up Main Road. It's parked up sideways, cutting off access to the street, trapping us on the beach.

The driver's door opens and a man steps out.

It's Max.

Chapter 65

'Hello, Jo.' My husband stands beside the car and crosses his arms over his chest. He's wearing a grey quilted jacket and smart brown shoes but his jaw is stubbly and there are dark circles under his eyes.

He smiles. After everything he's done to me. To our family. To Elise.

He smiles.

And I am paralysed with shock and fear. All this time I thought I was running from the police and Paula when all along it was Max I should have feared. Max who lied, stole and deceived. Max who put our daughter in danger and then convinced the world that her biggest threat was me.

'Come on, sweetheart.' Before I have a chance to react, Mary yanks Elise out of my arms and heads straight for Max and the car. His smile widens as she draws closer and he opens his arms wide, his eyes fixed on Elise.

'No! Mary, no!'

I take off after her, pumping my arms as I lean into the wind. Each icy breath stings my lungs, each step through the heavy, sodden sand is slow and laboured. It's as though I'm running through treacle.

I'm nearly thirty years younger than Mary but she had the element of surprise on her side and she reaches Max before I do. He holds out his hands for her to give Elise to him. His fingertips graze the front of Elise's coat. It's as though I'm watching a horror film in slow motion. Or I'm in a nightmare where, no matter how fast I run, I don't leave the same spot. I have to stop him taking my daughter but I can't move fast enough. Max's hands curl as he slips them around Elise's waist and Mary shifts her up and towards him.

'No!' I scream. 'No!'

This time the wind doesn't steal my voice and Elise, startled, twists towards me.

Three metres away.

Max's hands fall away from Elise's waist as he snaps round to look at me.

Two metres away.

He shoves Mary's shoulder, pushing her and Elise away from him and to the side.

One metre away.

His hands twitch at his sides and he raises his arms but he's too slow to defend himself and I smash straight into him, hitting him full force in the chest with both hands. He stumbles backwards and smacks against the closed passenger door. Before he can recover I run towards Mary, who's standing near the boot of the car trying and failing to console a wailing Elise.

'Give her to me!' I snatch at my daughter but, before I can touch her, Max grabs a handful of my coat, right between my shoulder blades. It tightens over my chest as he yanks me away from Elise.

'Get off me!' I twist to my right and try and elbow him in the side but he steps away. I kick out at him and feel my boot make contact with his knee or shin but he doesn't so much as flinch. Instead he wraps his arms around my shoulders, pulling my back against his chest, locking me into his body.

'No!' I jerk my head backwards but I'm too close and there's no power behind the blow to his chest. When I try and kick him again he hooks his ankles around my feet and leans back against the car. I'm trapped. My body is completely encased by his.

'Jo,' Max hisses in my ear. 'You need to calm down. Elise just saw all that and she's crying. You're scaring her.'

'*I'm* scaring her?' I can just about twist my neck to stare up at him. 'I'm her mum, Max. She loves me and you . . . you—'

'I did what was right, to protect her. You're not well, Jo. You've been ill for a long time. I was only ever trying to help you.'

'By taking my daughter away from me? By . . .' I swallow the rest of my sentence. He doesn't realise that I've discovered what he did. He thinks I still believe that Paula was behind everything. I can't let him know yet. It's the only weapon I have.

We both stiffen as we hear the noise at the same time. Elise is howling with frustration.

'It's OK, sweetheart,' Max says. 'Daddy's here.'

I arch my back, just enough to be able to turn my head to the side. Mary, still by the boot of the car, is desperately wrestling to keep Elise in her arms. My daughter's face is red and blotchy and her hair plastered to her skull.

'Mummy!' She holds out both hands, clawing the air to reach for me.

'She needs me, Max,' I say. 'Look at her face. You have to let me go. Please.'

'It's OK, Li-Li,' he says softly. 'Everything's all right. Mummy and Daddy are just having a little hug. Aren't we, Mummy?' He squeezes me so tightly I can barely breathe but I force a smile for my daughter.

Mary catches my eye.

'Help me,' I mouth, but she glances away.

'OK,' Max says. 'Enough with the chat. Mary, could you put Elise in the car seat in the back of the car, please?'

'No.' I bend my knees to try and slip out of Max's arms but he tightens his grip around my shoulders.

Mary gently touches a mittened hand to Elise's cheek. My daughter snaps her head away angrily and continues to scream for me.

'The car seat, please, Mary,' Max says again.

Mary's gaze flicks from Elise's face to Max's and then to the car. She doesn't look at me.

'Mary, don't do it! Please.'

Max laughs tightly. 'Remember what I told you

about Jo? About how manipulative she is? How everything that comes out of her mouth is a lie? She hurt Elise. That's why the police are after her.'

'That's not true! You know I wouldn't hurt Elise, Mary. You've seen her with me. You know how much she loves me. None of this is my fault. Just like what happened to Niamh wasn't your fault. I know you blame yourself for leaving the door open but you mustn't. You couldn't have known what would happen. There's no way you could have. What Liam did was unforgiveable. And I hate him for what he's done. And you hate me. I understand that, but please, please, Elise hasn't done anything wrong. She's innocent.'

Mary doesn't move a muscle.

'She's an innocent little girl,' I shout. 'Just like Niamh. If you let her go with Max she'll get hurt. He's dangerous! Please, Mary. Please. You can stop this. Please!'

'Come on now, Mary,' Max says. 'Just put Elise in the back of the car.'

Still Mary doesn't move. Her coat is clinging to her body and her blonde hair is flattened to her head. There's only a couple of feet between us and the waves. Why isn't Mary saying anything? Why isn't she helping me? Surely she can't believe what Max is telling her.

'Mary,' Max says. 'Jo's not like you. She's not a good mother. Look what she's done to Elise's hair. She's hacked it off. What kind of mother could do that? You wouldn't, would you? You'd never do anything as awful as that.

'Jo was right about one thing,' Max continues. I

can tell he wants to scream at Mary to put Elise in the car but he's holding back. He expected her to comply, not freeze, and now he's worried about her doing something stupid. 'Elise is innocent. She's an innocent little girl who doesn't deserve a life like this where she's dressed as a boy and she's doesn't know where she'll be living from one day to the next. She needs her home. Security. Safety. I can offer her that, Mary. I can look after her. I can give her everything she needs.'

As he continues to talk, I slowly, slowly bend my right arm and reach my hand into my pocket and wrap my gloved fingers around my phone. I lift it out of my pocket as carefully and as subtly as I can. I rub my thumb over the screen and down over the buttons. 1 . . . 2 . . . 3 . . .

I move my thumb down. 6.

And again. 9.

999. That's emergency services in the UK but I've got no idea if it's the same in Ireland. I could chance it. I could press the button three times and scream that there's an emergency on Clogherhead beach but Max would hear me. He'd snatch Elise and drive off before they get here. And that'll be it. He'll take her back to the UK. If I go after them I'll be charged with child abduction. I'll be lucky if I ever see her again.

'Mary,' I say. 'Mary, you need to listen to me. Everything Max is telling you is a lie. I'm not a bad mother. My husband set me up to make me look like one. He planted drugs in our house and he rang the police to say they were mine. I was arrested and Social Services were informed. Max trashed the house before their visit, to make it look like I couldn't look after Elise. Then he . . . he broke in one night and stashed some money he'd stolen in my baby's memory box. Henry. The baby I carried before Elise. He died when I was four months pregnant. That box contained priceless, precious memories of our little boy but Max doesn't care about that. He defiled Max's memory when he shovelled his dirty money on top of the only things I have to remember—'

'It was for Elise,' Max hisses, his lips pulled back tightly over his teeth.

'You stole it! That's why Paula came after me. That's why she threatened me. You put both our lives at risk for what? Ten thousand pounds that you stole from a loan shark. And you call yourself a good father?'

'I want her to have a good life.'

'She had a good life!'

'Really? You really believe that, Jo? You think keeping her locked inside day and night is a good life? You think getting off your head on pain meds and leaving her at nursery, pissing herself and crying, is a good life?'

'I was trying to get better. If you'd just have been a bit more patient with me—'

'What? What would have happened? I'd have watched you swan off to Chester with my daughter, that's what would have happened. You threatened that I'd never see her again!' Spittle sprays out of his mouth and dampens my skin as he shouts in my face.

It's just like the argument in the living room all over again. Elise is wailing, my heart's beating so hard in my chest I feel sick and I'm shaking all over, but I can't stop now. I can't back down. I can't. I won't let him intimidate me.

'That's why you planted the drugs, isn't it? To stop me from moving to Chester. To teach me a lesson. That's it, isn't it? You wanted control back. Didn't you? Didn't you, Max?'

'Yes,' he snaps. 'Yes, I fucking did. And it worked, didn't it? Because who did you call? Me? Who did you beg to sleep on the sofa so you felt safe? Me. You were a wreck, Jo. You *are* a wreck. You're weak, you're flaky and you're unstable. When I wasn't around, you had to ask your best friend to stay over.'

'Because I was scared after *you* ransacked the house and tipped rubbish everywhere before the Social Services visit. And it was a good job I asked Helen to stay over, because you broke into the house and hurt Elise.'

'I didn't hurt her! I grabbed her because she was climbing out of the cot.'

'She had bruises all over her body, Max.'

He shakes his head. 'You can't blame that on me, Jo. I barely touched her. We both know that you're the one who hurt her. Why else would you run off instead of taking her to the safeguarding team at the hospital?'

'I'm calling the guards.' Mary rounds the boot of the car, hand in hand with Elise. The car's blocking

378

access to Main Road. She'll have to lift Elise over the boot to get her to safety and then clamber over herself. 'They can decide who the child should be with.'

'No!' Max hurls me away from him with such force that I sprawl onto the sand. A wave crashes over me as I scramble desperately to my feet.

'Stop!' Max grabs Mary by her shoulder.

She turns to face him, tucking Elise behind her. 'Get your hands off me.'

'Mrs Byrne.' He shakes his head. 'I just want my daughter. That's all I want.'

'Well, you can't have her. If you've any sense you'll get in your car and you'll go.'

'I'm not going anywhere without Elise.' I can hear the warning sound in his voice as I creep up behind him, stepping lightly so I don't attract his attention.

Mary's gaze flicks towards me, subtly signalling with her eyes that I shouldn't move, then she reaches into the left pocket of her coat and pulls out her mobile phone. With her right hand she pushes Elise out from behind her and to one side.

'Hello, is that the—'

'Give me the phone,' Max says.

'Please! Come quickly. We're at Clogher—'

There is flash of grey as Max's arm swings through the air. Mary lurches backwards. She twists away so the phone's out of Max's reach but, as she turns, the heel of her shoe catches on a small rock and she tumbles onto the sand. Max dives for her outstretched arm and the phone and there's a flurry of movement as she tries to fight him off. I rush forwards and grab hold of the back of his jacket but, before I can pull him off her, Mary shouts, 'Jo! Take Elise! Take her and run!'

Chapter 66

'Hold on!' I scream. 'Elise, hold on and don't let go!'

My daughter wails in terror as she squeezes her thighs around my waist and digs her nails into the back of my neck. I'm holding her in front of me like a monkey carries its young, supporting her weight with one hand so I can use the other to grip the rock. There's less than a metre of exposed rock between the stone wall and the sea. I've minutes, if that, to reach the low section of wall before the water does and scrabble over it and into the field. The alternative would have been to run along the beach or scramble over the car bonnet to get to the road but Max was already getting to his feet when I lifted Elise off the sand and into my arms.

I can hear him behind me now, breathing heavily, swearing each time he slips and falls. He's faster than me, much faster, but my trainers give me a better grip on the slick, wet rocks than his smart office shoes.

I've been over them with Elise several times before – I know where to place my feet to stay upright, and when I need to jump because the crevice between the rocks is too deep.

'Mummy!' Elise screams as a wave crashes against the rocks, showering us with seawater. The shock of the icy-cold water momentarily takes my breath away but I don't stop running. The surf is so close now, one huge wave is all it would take to whip us off the rocks and pull us out to sea.

I shift my daughter in my arms and reach my left hand out to touch the wall that separates the beach from the land. It's over six feet high and the stones are damp. My trainers would slip if I tried to scale it and there's no way I could safely lift Elise over the jagged stones on the top. Further down the beach, about fifty metres away, the wall dips – it's only about five foot high. If I can make it I should be able to throw Elise over. There's a grass verge on the other side that should break her fall. I don't care what happens to me. I just want my daughter to be safe.

'Jo!' Max shouts. 'Jo, stop!'

His voice cuts through the howl of the wind and the roar of the sea. I glance over my shoulder to see how far away he is.

Shit.

He's gained on us.

He's pulled off his shoes and socks and he's running in bare feet, his eyes trained on the ground as he leaps from rock to rock. He senses me watching him and pauses, poised to jump, and looks up.

The coldness in his eyes makes me catch my breath. He's never going to give up. If I get over that wall he'll come after me. If I fly back to England he'll follow me. Wherever he goes he'll spread lies about me and turn people against me. Even if I do find somewhere to hide with Elise I'll spend the rest of my life looking over my shoulder, wondering how much time I've got until Max finds us.

I turn to continue running but, as I do, another wave crashes against the rocks. It rises up, up, up, curving over us like a rainbow, almost in slow motion. There is no time to run or shout. No time to pray or scream because, as quickly as time slowed down, it speeds up again. There is silence, just for a second, then my feet are swept from beneath me as the wave crashes over our heads.

The sea doesn't roar when you're underwater. It hums, a deep bass-baritone sound that envelopes you and pounds at your body, your head, your eardrums. I am suspended, weightless and, for a split second – less than a heartbeat – a strange feeling of calm washes over me. It's over. I've lost. I'm going to die and there's nothing I can do about it. Then my lungs start to ache and I feel something twist in my arms. Elise! I open my eyes and see . . . nothing . . . just the thick, murky, brown fog of the sea. I can feel the current pulling at Elise, trying to wrench her out of my arms. I tighten my grip but I can feel her slipping out of my grasp. I kick again, frantically. My lungs are burning. I need to breathe. I need to get to the surface. But which way is up? I can't see anything.

Still the dark, swirling water surrounds me. The compulsion to open my mouth and suck it into my lungs is too strong. We're going to drown.

I can't do it. I can't keep holding my breath. I can't keep fighting. I'm sorry, Elise. I'm so sorry. I said I'd keep you safe and I failed. I'm so sorry. I have to take a breath. I have to—

Bam! As quickly as the wave snatched us up, it drops us back down, smashing us against the rocks before it retreats back into the sea.

A violent, dagger-like pain rips through my left shoulder. But it's not the pain that makes me cry out in terror. My daughter is lying limply against my chest. Her eyes are closed. Her lips are blue.

'Elise!' I shake her. 'ELISE!'

She doesn't move. She doesn't respond in any way.

'Elise!' I shake her again. Her skin is grey and feels deathly cold. 'Elise! Open your eyes!'

Still she doesn't move.

'Elise.' I can barely move but, somehow, I manage to twist her onto her side and hit her, hard, on the back. She can't die. She can't.

'Elise!' I hit her again.

She coughs. It's the tiniest of sounds but it's there. 'Elise!'

She coughs again and thrashes from side to side, her arms whirling and jerking like a puppet. Her right hand smashes against a rock and she screams in pain. There's no time to comfort her. Another wave is approaching, bigger, more powerful than the last. There's no way we could survive if it crashes over us. I have a choice to make – die with Elise or give her to Max and pray he doesn't hurt her again. I can't do that to her. I can't let her suffer like that. But what's the alternative? If I do nothing I'm sentencing her to death. I touch a hand to my coat but the mobile phone in my pocket is long gone, swallowed by the sea. I close my eyes. Please, I pray silently, please let the call have connected on the beach. When I open my eyes again I scream my husband's name.

'Take Elise! Quickly! Quickly, Max.'

Suddenly he is beside us, sopping wet and grey-faced. He reaches down for our daughter and I use what little strength I have left to grip her around the sides and push her up and away from my body and into his arms. I just want her to be safe. I've only ever wanted her to be safe.

Max cradles her to his chest. Fear fills his eyes as he looks out to sea.

'It's coming,' he shouts as he takes off, his bare feet skidding and slipping over the rocks. 'I'll get her over the wall and then I'll come back for you. I promise.'

I try to sit up but my left arm is floppy and useless and I can't move it. Pain ricochets through my body as I twist to my left, grip the rock with my right hand and haul myself into a sitting position. Max has reached the wall with Elise. He's lifting her up and over the spiky stones that stud the wall. I don't hear her cry out as she lands. I can't hear anything other than the roar of the sea and the sound of my own heartbeat thudding in my ears. I shift onto my knees and crawl forwards, my left arm hanging loosely at my side. I have to get to the wall before the wave hits.

'Max!' I scream as he grips the spiky stones with both hands and jumps so one foot is flat against the wall. 'Max! Help me!'

He glances back.

'Max!' I reach out with my right hand. 'Help me!'

His face seems to soften, just for an instant. He's going to come back and get me. He promised. He wants Elise with him but he won't leave me here to die.

'Max!' I shout again. 'Please! Elise needs me.'

The softness in my husband's face vanishes and he turns away. A split second later and he's gone, up and over the wall.

He's gone to check on Elise, I tell myself as I twist round to see how far away the next wave is. He could still come back for me. But the wave is already towering above me like a great grey scythe. I close my eyes and wait for it to fall.

Chapter 67

Max jolts in his seat as the plane touches down but it's not relief he feels as he flashes a reassuring smile at his two-year-old daughter sitting beside him, it's fear. Nearly 48 hours have elapsed since he snatched his daughter to safety but he can't wipe the image of Jo's face from his mind. After he'd dropped Elise over the wall he'd looked back, expecting to see Jo scrambling after him. He hadn't expected to see her sprawled on the rocks, staring at him with a look of desperation on her face and fear in her eyes. He was torn. Elise was lying on the grass on the other side of the wall, wailing with shock. She was safe. Jo wasn't. A great grey wave was thundering towards her, growing taller and taller with every frantic beat of his heart. He could make a dash for it. He could slip and slide his way across the wet rocks to pull her to safety. But if he was too slow the sea would claim them both. Elise would lose both of her parents, orphaned six months before her third birthday.

When Jo screamed at him to help her all the hairs went up on the back of his neck. She thought she was going to die. He could see it in her eyes.

'Help me!' she'd screamed as she'd reached out a hand. 'Help me, Max!'

But it was too late. In the time he'd taken to reach a decision the wave had risen like a wall above her. He didn't have time to promise that he'd take good care of Elise. He only had time to jump.

As soon as his feet hit the ground he was up again, with his daughter in his arms, and he was running. Running along the wall, back to the car. He half expected to see Mary Byrne still lying on the sand where he'd left her but she was gone. The sea was lapping at the wheels of his car so he'd jumped in, fumbled Elise into the passenger seat and fastened the belt over her lap, then he was off. He heard police sirens wailing as he sped up Main Road and out of Clogherhead but there were no blue lights behind him and no roadblocks sealing his exit. He drove all the way to Dublin without stopping and checked himself and Elise into the first hotel he found.

He hadn't expected to be able to board a flight the next morning. His forehead was damp with sweat and his shirt was clinging to his back as he approached border control in Dublin airport. He felt sure that his passport, or the replacement he'd ordered for Elise, would spark some kind of alert and he'd feel a heavy hand on the back of his jacket. But none came. The border control officer gave him a long look, transferred his gaze to Elise and then nodded them through.

And now here he is, walking through Bristol airport with his daughter in his arms. There's just a few hundred metres between him and freedom. It's a shame he isn't going home with the ten grand as well as his daughter. God knows what will happen to that. But at least Elise is safe. That's the most important thing. And he'll find a way to get Paula off his back. Maybe he'll sell the house and move up north. He could buy a place in Tynemouth or Whitley Bay and work in Newcastle. Elise would enjoy living beside the sea.

An image of Jo's anguished face as the wave closed over her flashes through his mind but he blocks it out. Just like he's blocking out the conversation he'll have to have with Elise about where she's gone.

Jo was ill, he tells himself, as he walks through the green 'nothing to declare' doorway. And she was getting worse. Even if she hadn't died the chances are the court would have ruled that she shouldn't have any contact with Elise. She'd gone on the run instead of taking their daughter to the paediatric unit at the hospital. That was an admission of guilt as far as he was concerned. And to think she'd blamed him for that! Her level of self-deceit was astonishing, even at the end.

He's nearly through the 'nothing to declare' hallway now. There are two uniformed customs officers, standing by a table to his right. Should he acknowledge them or ignore them? he wonders. Ignore them, he decides. His arms are growing tired after carrying Elise all the way through the concourse but he doesn't shift her into a more comfortable position. He doesn't want to attract any attention. He just wants to get out of there, find his car and get home. He can already imagine the expression on his daughter's face when he shows her all the wonderful new toys he's bought her and—

'Mr Maxwell Blackmore?' Two uniformed officers and a blonde-haired woman in a suit step in front of him, blocking his exit from the hall.

He freezes, fighting to keep his breath steady. They've come to tell him that Jo is dead. That's all it is. No need to panic. No need to run.

'Mr Maxwell Blackmore?' the woman says again.

This time he nods and one of the police officers places a firm hand on his arm.

Chapter 68

'Elise!' I come to with a start, arms flailing, snatching at the air, trying and failing to grip my daughter's red winter coat as she floats away from me. My chest is burning, my ears are ringing and my hands, as they pass in front of my face, are pale and blurry. I can't hold my breath for much longer. The instinct to inhale is too strong.

'Breathe, Jo, breathe.' A woman with dark hair and a strong Polish accent appears beside me. She tentatively touches me on the shoulder. I twist to knock her away but, as I do, a searing pain shoots through my side.

'Jo, you're in hospital. Remember? You have cracked ribs and severe bruising. If you are in pain I can give you some drugs.'

'My daughter!' I try to struggle up to a sitting position but the pain is more than I can bear. 'Where's my daughter!'

'Jo. It's OK.'

'No, it's not.' I grab hold of her wrist. 'It's not OK. I need to know where my daughter is. My husband took her! We were on the beach in Clogherhead and—'

The nurse twists her wrist from my grasp. 'I'll get someone who can help. Don't move. You need to stay still.'

As she pulls back the curtain that surrounds my bed I ease myself onto my back and stare up at the whitewashed ceiling. Tears run down either side of my face and drip onto my neck as I clench the sides of the bed. My chest, beneath my cracked ribs, feels hollowed out. When the wave closed over me I thought I would die. I closed my eyes, I curled myself up into a ball, took a long deep breath and prayed that it would be over quickly. When I was younger I feared death. The unknown terrified me. Would I, as Mum drummed into me, go to heaven and be reunited with Jesus? Or, as someone in the playground told me, would it be more like a light switch – a darkness that lasted for eternity? But as I waited for the sea to crush the last breath out of my lungs it wasn't my fate I worried about, it was my daughter's. I couldn't bear it, the thought of her small face crumpling with a grief she didn't understand. The tears. The confusion. The dawning realisation that, no matter how many times she called for Mummy, Mummy wouldn't come.

And so I fought. As the sea lifted me up and crashed me down against the rocks I told myself not to panic.

If I panicked, I'd run out of air. I'd gulp seawater. I'd drown. But it was hard not to panic as the rocks slashed at my arms, my legs, my face and my skull, and my lungs burned and every fibre of my being urged me to unstop my throat and breathe. I waited and I waited and I waited for my head to break the surface of the waves and, when it did, I sucked in the cold, cold sea air, only to be pulled back down again. Down, down, tossing and turning and tumbling. And then another gulp. And back down. It felt like for ever, that torturous cycle, and I felt myself grow weak as the cold seeped through my skin and into my bones. And then there was a tug on the back of my jacket. I thought it was a riptide and I lashed out with my arms and my legs and I battled, but then I was lifted up, up, up and my eyes stung and my breath rasped in my throat as my body, my soaking wet, lead-weight body was dropped onto the floor of the lifeboat, slipping and sliding like a landed fish. I saw a man's face, peering into mine, telling me to breathe. And then everything went black.

'Jo?'

There is concern in the Polish nurse's voice and I don't turn my head at the sound of the curtain being pulled back. I already know that it's not my daughter stepping silently through the gap. She's not in this hospital. She's not even in Ireland. She's gone.

'Jo? It's Mary.'

I slowly turn my head to the left as my landlady tugs the chair out from beside my bed. She winces as she sits down, but it's not the sound that makes my heart constrict, it's the lump on her forehead like a large, flat mushroom, swollen and puffy, and the violent black and purple bruising above her closed right eye.

'Mary?' A fresh tear runs down the side of my face. 'Mary, I'm so sorry.'

'No, no.' She presses a hand over mine and squeezes it. I don't resist her touch. There is no fight left in me.

'He hit you.'

'No.' She shakes her head, then grimaces. 'I hit the side of my head on a rock when Max tried to grab the phone.'

'I shouldn't have run . . . I should have made sure that you were—'

'No.' She tightens her grip on my hand. 'You did the right thing, Joanne. You tried to protect your girl.'

'But I left you. I left you on the beach. You could . . .' My throat tightens and the words dry up. Mary could have drowned. So could Elise. I risked everyone's lives because I couldn't bear to be parted from my daughter. I never should have left Bristol. I should have taken Elise to the hospital. I should have fought Max in the courts. I told myself that Elise would be safe in Clogherhead but it wasn't my daughter who would feel safe there, it was *me*. I didn't do what was best for her. I did what was best for me.

'Why did you help me?' I whisper. 'I thought you were going to give Elise back to Max.'

'I was going to,' she says softly. 'I wanted to believe all those awful things he told me about you. I wanted to believe that Liam O'Brien's daughter was as evil as he was. It felt like retribution, you know, for what had happened to Niamh. He'd taken my child so I'd punish his. As I walked across the sand with Elise in my arms I didn't care about what was right or wrong, forgiveness or the Church. I wanted you to hurt as much as I was hurting. I wanted you to know how violent the pain is when your child is snatched away. I wanted you to suffer for the rest of your life, just as I'd suffered.

'I'm not proud . . .' Her face crumples as she lowers her head, unable to meet my eyes. 'I'm not proud of the woman I was in that moment but the anger I was carrying in my heart . . . the pain I'd felt when I found the photograph in your room . . . it was so powerful. It consumed me. When you ran up and tried to snatch Elise back I felt certain that I'd done the right thing but then Max took hold of you and you pleaded with me. You appealed to me, one mother to another, and I could see the fear and desperation in your eyes. And little Elise, she wanted you, Jo. She was fighting to get out of my arms so she could be reunited with you. And then you and Max started fighting about who had hurt her and I didn't know which of you to believe. I'd never forgive myself if I made the wrong decision. That's when I decided to call the guards and Max attacked me. I knew then who'd hurt the child.'

'Oh, Mary.' I search her face, looking for anger and resentment, but all I can see is sorrow. A deep, deep sorrow that makes my heart twist in my chest.

'I'm so sorry you got dragged into all this. I swear I didn't know about Niamh or what Liam did. I promise you, Mary. There's no way I would have come back to Clogherhead if I had.'

'I know. Brigid told me.'

'You've spoken to my mum?' I can't hide the shock in her voice.

'Yes.' Mary nods.

'But I thought . . . I thought you hated her.'

'I never hated her, Jo. I said some people thought she knew more than she was letting on. I never did, not in my heart, not after a lifetime of friendship. But Brigid never once rang me or set foot in my door after Liam was arrested and I was hurt. I was so, so hurt. I thought she was a coward, for slipping away in the middle of the night like she did. She left me when I needed her most and I could never forgive her for that.'

'But you've spoken to her – recently?'

'I got her number from your Auntie Sinead.'

Sinead? So Mum hadn't just sent birthday and Christmas cards to her relatives. They'd been ringing each other too. What else has she kept from me?

'I thought they'd lost touch too,' Mary says, reading the expression on my face. 'Not that I ever asked. I only know Sinead to say hello to at Mass. We keep our distance otherwise. But I went round to her house, yesterday, after the doctors said you still hadn't woken up, and I asked if she had Brigid's number. I had to let her know what had happened to you, Jo.'

'Was it OK, the phone call?'

'We talked for a very long time. About you, about the past. She told me about Andy.'

'What about him?' I can't tear my eyes away from Mary's face. Is that why she looks so sorrowful? Has Dad died? 'Please, Mary. Please tell me. I need to know.'

She gently touches my hands. 'He's sick, Jo, but he's hanging on. Brigid thinks he's hanging on to say goodbye to you.'

'Oh God.' Fresh tears fill my eyes. Poor Dad. Poor Mum.

'Did Mum . . . did she mention . . .' I am desperate to ask Mary if she's heard anything about Elise. I wanted to ask her the second she appeared from behind the curtain but I'm too terrified to ask the question. I don't know how I'll cope if she tells me that Max and Elise have disappeared.

'Max was arrested at Bristol airport,' Mary says. 'His editor gave the police some files. Voicemail messages or something, Brigid said.'

It worked. Oh, thank God, it worked. When we were on the beach, standing beside the car, I didn't know if 999 would connect to the police so I made a split-second decision and tapped 5 on my phone instead. As I goaded Max into telling me the truth about what he'd done I prayed that the call would go through to Fiona's voicemail. If I escaped it would give me the evidence I needed to prove that I wasn't an unfit mother and that Max had staged the whole thing.

'And Elise?' I ask. 'Where's Elise?'

'She's in the hospital but your mammy's seen her. She's not sick, she's just being observed.'

'Oh my God.' I turn my head away as tears stream down my cheeks. The relief I feel is unbearable. She's safe. Elise is safe. And my dad's still alive. I try to push myself up and into a sitting position. I should be with them. I need to get out of the hospital and onto the first flight back to the UK.

'No, no.' Mary applies gentle pressure to my shoulder. I'm so weak I immediately slump back onto the pillow. 'You need to get your strength up, Joanne. You're no good to anyone like this.'

'Why are you doing this?' I look up into her soft, lined face. 'Why are you helping me? Why are you being so kind when my family are the reason you lost your little girl? You should hate me.'

Mary looks at me for the longest time then she reaches into the pocket of her cardigan and pulls out a white handkerchief. She touches it to my cheek and softly dabs at my tears.

'How could I hate you?' she says softly. 'You were just a little girl when it happened. I wasn't the only one who lost everything that day. You did too.'

Chapter 69

Mary walks slowly along Clogherhead beach, her sandals in one hand, a picnic basket in the other. She curls her bare feet as she walks, relishing the sensation of the warm sand between her toes, the sunshine on her face and the warm breeze in her hair. The sea, so wild and angry just four months earlier, is still and serene – a sparkling grey-blue sheet that stretches as far as the eye can see. The glorious June weather has lured the tourists out of their holiday chalets and the locals out of their homes and the beach is alive with the sound of laughter and chatter.

Jo and Elise, several feet ahead, are hand in hand. They dawdle rather than walk, distracted by the pretty shells and stripy stones that catch their attention. Elise breaks contact with her mother, dips down and snatches up a shell then drops it into the blue bucket she's filled with seawater. Her tinkling laughter drifts towards Mary. No one is in a rush to lay a blanket on the sand and tuck into the lunch that she prepared that morning. Least of all her.

Mary turns her head to look at the dark-haired woman walking alongside her. Brigid's face is more lined than it was thirty years ago. Her hair is finer, her waist is thicker and there's a looseness to her jawline that matches Mary's own sagging jowls, but she's still the same Bee. Her blue eyes still sparkle when she becomes animated, her lips still thin into a tight, straight line when she disapproves of something, and her laugh is still horribly, wonderfully raucous.

'How are you?' Mary asks. It's their second day together and the awkwardness that accompanied their reunion, in the hallway of Mary's B&B, has long since vanished. Mary barely slept the night before Brigid arrived on a plane from Manchester. She oscillated between fear and excitement. Jo had reassured her on the telephone that Brigid was desperate to see her, but what if the reality didn't match the expectation? What if they were cold with each other? What if thirty years had changed them beyond recognition? What if too much damage had been done? They'd stared at each other in her hallway for one minute, two, three, neither of them saying a word, not even when Jo announced that she was taking Elise down to the beach to give them a moment. But the second the front door slammed behind her Brigid blurted out, 'Forgive me, Mary. Please.' And then there were tears and hugs and tea, lots and lots of tea, as they both talked themselves hoarse.

Now, Brigid gathers her thin cardigan around herself. 'I was just thinking how much Andy would have loved this.'

Mary nods. 'Patrick too.'

'He was a good man.'

'The best. I just wish I'd met Andy. He sounds like a good man, from everything you and Jo have said.'

They share a look, loaded with meaning. Both single, both married and now both widowed. Neither of them mentions Liam. They did talk about him, on the first night that they were reunited. They talked about everything that had happened and then, with neither of them actually saying the words, they decided to leave the past where it belonged.

'I'm glad Jo got to see Andy before he passed,' Brigid says softly. 'A week. That's what the doctors gave him, but he held on for nearly three times that.'

'He wanted to say goodbye.'

'Yes. I think he did. And he was at home when he passed. That was important to him.'

'I'm so sorry, Brigid.'

'Thank you.' She nods and the two women fall into a companionable silence as they watch Jo trying to teach Elise how to skip a stone across the sea.

'They look so happy,' Mary says.

'They are. But there was a horrible couple of weeks when we weren't sure if Jo was going to get her back.'

'I didn't know that.'

'No, Jo doesn't like to talk about it but, after Max was arrested and Elise was taken to the hospital, Social Services stepped in. Jo wasn't allowed to see her. Not until the hospital could be sure what had caused Elise's bruises.'

Mary's hand flies to her chest. 'Bruises?'

'They found them all over her little body when they checked her over. Jo told them Elise must have got them when they fell onto the rock but, for a while, the doctors were convinced that someone had hurt her.' Brigid closes her eyes for a split second, as though she can't bear to relive the memory. 'It was a horrible time, particularly for Jo, but then blood tests showed that Elise had a virus. Comes on sometimes after a cold or what have you and it makes little ones bruise more easily. I can't remember the name. Idiopathic thrombo–something.'

'So no one hurt her?'

'They don't think so, no. Jo's friend Helen gave the police the photos of the bruises on Elise's body after someone broke into the house, and Max admitted that he was there that night. He said he wanted to make sure that she was safe after he was attacked and he had to grab her to stop her from falling when she tried to climb out of her cot. The doctors can't say for sure but they think the bruises were caused by the same virus. Jo said that Elise was sick before they left Bristol, a temperature and snotty nose and so on.'

'Poor little thing. She's OK now though?'

Brigid smiles as her granddaughter stoops to pick up a stone. 'She's grand.'

'So Max admitted everything, did he?'

'No, not intially. But he admitted it to Jo on Fiona's

voicemail recording and they found his DNA on the bag when they finally decided to test it, so . . .' She shrugs. 'Jo had to wait for the police to close their investigation, then she had to go through the courts to get Elise back. It was stressful but her solicitor was very good.'

'Thank goodness. Maybe she can get on with her life again now.'

'Eventually. She wants answers from Max first. I know that much. And she wants Elise to see him too. Whether that's a good idea or not I don't know.' Brigid tightens her grip on her cardi. Mary tries to read the look on her friend's face but she can't decipher it. Is it guilt because she didn't take Jo to see her father in prison? Or regret because she hid the truth from her for so many years? When Jo returned to the UK Brigid told her everything, including the fact that Liam O'Brien was dead. He was stabbed in the stomach during a fight in a cell, a year after he was sentenced. He died in the ambulance on the way to the hospital. The guards visited Mary at home the next day but the news didn't lessen her grief. Instead she felt angry. Her torment would last a lifetime whilst his was over.

She shivers, despite her thick coat. She doesn't want to think about Liam O'Brien any more.

'Does Elise ask after Max?' Mary asks Brigid.

'She did. Not so much now. She's OK. She's a resilient little girl.'

'And Jo?'

'Ah.' Brigid pulls a face. 'Still wobbly if the truth

be told. It's going to take her a while to get over what happened. But she's better than she was. Not as jumpy and she laughs more often.'

'So maybe I shouldn't invite Sean over to dinner tonight?'

'Your man from the B&B?'

'He has a house now, on the other side of the village. He often asks about Jo and Elise.'

Brigid smiles. 'I think she'd like to see him, but maybe not tonight. Give her – give all of us – a little time to find our feet first. It's strange, being back. There are good memories but bad ones too.'

Mary's heart aches as she gazes at the woman who used to be her best friend. It feels right, walking along the beach with Brigid and her daughter and grand-daughter. For so many years there was a hole in Mary's life she thought could never be filled. But last night she slept soundly and, when she awoke, the empty sensation in her chest had faded and she felt at peace.

Brigid has told her that she feels sad and stifled in Chester without Andy, and Jo doesn't want to live in Bristol. She's said that they need to find somewhere else to live. So why can't Mary speak? Why can't she bring herself to ask Brigid one simple question?

Because she's scared, she realises as Elise lets go of Jo's hand and charges along the sand towards them. If Brigid says no the sun will go out and the world will grow dark again. I'm not brave enough to go through that again, she tells herself as Elise grabs her left hand and Brigid's right hand. If I don't ask the question I'll still have hope. Without hope, I have nothing.

'Granny?' Elise says, gazing up into Brigid's face. 'Mummy says we can live here. Can we? Can we, Granny?'

Mary glances away at Jo, paddling in the sea with a smile on her face and her skirt hitched up above her knees. She senses Mary watching and turns to look at her. Her smile widens and she raises her arm and waves. She's going to be OK, Mary thinks. She's stronger than she thinks. Maybe I am too.

'Can we, Granny?' Elise asks again. 'Can we live here?'

'What do you think, Mary?' Brigid says softly. 'Do you think we should live here? Because we'd like to. If you'd have us back.'

Mary doesn't reply. Her throat is so thick with tears she can't speak. Everyone is looking at her. Jo, Brigid, Elise. They're all looking at her and they're smiling. They're waiting for an answer.

She clears her throat, steadies herself and looks Brigid in the eye.

'I'd like that,' she says.

EPILOGUE

'You got the VO then?' Paula says as I take the seat opposite her. A white Formica table separates us. To our left a young woman in her twenties, her brown hair pulled back in a ponytail, is chatting, across an identical table, to an older woman in a brown padded coat with a fake fur collar. To our right a woman about my age, with a neat black bob, is talking to a bald-headed man in a white Nike T-shirt with a tattoo on his neck. We are surrounded by people sitting around tables. Chatter, laughter and the occasional sob merge to create a loud hum that fills the room. This could be a canteen or a church hall if it weren't for the presence of uniformed guards passing between the tables in their short-sleeved white shirts and black trousers.

'Yes,' I say. 'I got the Visiting Order. I wasn't sure if you'd reply to my letter.'

Paula smirks. I'd expected her to be make-up-free and dishevelled but her eyes are ringed with black kohl and her eyelashes are crusty with mascara. 'You like writing to me, don't you, Jo? It's because you find me fascinating, isn't it?'

'Yes,' I play along. 'That's exactly why I'm here.'

It's not the first time I've been in a prison visiting room. Last month I went to see Max. Unlike Paula, who's barely changed, physically or in terms of her extraordinary bravado, Max was almost unrecognisable. His skin was grey. He had bags under his eyes and there were wiry white hairs in his beard. As I approached his table he sank down in his seat, his hands hanging loosely at his sides, his fingertips almost brushing the floor. I knew why, without having to ask. I didn't have Elise with me. There was no way I was bringing her along on the first visit. Not when there was so much I needed to say.

Max didn't say a word as I sat down. He didn't reply when I asked him how he was so I told him that I was OK, that I was building a new life for myself in Clogherhead. I told him that Mum had sold her house in Chester and we'd bought a place together but he couldn't even bring himself to look at me. So then I told him how he'd made me feel. How alone I'd felt, how terrified I was, when he convinced the world that I was a danger to my own daughter. I asked him what I'd done that was so bad it merited taking Elise away from me. I asked him if he genuinely believed that I was a bad mother. He didn't reply. I got everything off my chest. I said everything I needed to say but Max didn't utter a word to me the whole visit. When the buzzer sounded I got up to go. I said goodbye and told him that I'd give Elise a kiss from him. He didn't look up. He didn't say a word. But when he blinked, a single tear rolled out of his right eye and dribbled onto his cheek.

'So go on then,' Paula says now, crossing one leg over the other. She looks short and stumpy in her blue sweatshirt, grey jogging bottoms and trainers. It's going to be a while before she gets to wear skinny jeans and heels again. 'What is it that's so important? This thing you want to give me?'

'I've got a question for you first.'

'Yeah.' She tucks a strand of blonde hair behind her ear and frowns. She can do that now the Botox has worn off. 'Go on then.'

'Why me, Paula? Why go after me instead of Max?'

She shrugs nonchalantly. 'Like I told you, you were more fun.'

I shake my head. 'I don't believe you. I think there was more to it than that. I think there's something you aren't telling me.'

'OK then.' She crosses her arms and rests them on the table. 'Let's just say you were easier. Weaker. Softer. I knew Max from work, remember, when he called himself Martin. I knew exactly what kind of man he was.'

'What kind of man was he?'

She smiles, revealing her tar-stained teeth. 'Evil.'

'Go on.'

'All that stuff he put in the paper, about Ian and the other guys beating up old men and threatening single mums with babies in their arms. Do you think

Max just sat back and watched that? You think he just filmed it? Do you really think Ian would have kept him on as a collector if he was Mr Nicey Nicey?'

'You tell me.'

She shakes her head. 'Why'd you think I had to set someone on him when he was drunk? You've got no idea what that husband of yours is capable of, Jo.'

I do, I think. I really do.

'That's why I came after you, sweetheart. I thought that if I put enough pressure on you he'd eventually cave and give me the money. Only he didn't give two shits about you, did he, Jo?'

Inside I jolt, but I don't let Paula know that.

'No,' I say, 'he didn't.'

'I wouldn't be fussed either, Jo. Men are ten a penny. I was only with Ian for his money. Talking of which, what kind of fucking idiot are you, burning the money?' She drops her voice as a prison guard walks past. 'I got it, your little parcel you sent from Ireland with all the torn-up tenners. My daughter opened it after I was arrested. Think that was funny, did you?'

It didn't take long to find Paula's home address after Fiona gave me her full name in her email. It took me and Sean a while to go through all the Paula Readmans living in Bristol but we found her eventually. Her Facebook page wasn't secure and we could see who her friends and relatives were and what part of Bristol she lived in from the pubs she'd tagged in her selfies. After that all we had to do was look her up on the electoral register, pay a few pounds and we had her address.

'I didn't believe your note by the way,' Paula says. 'Claiming you'd burned the rest of the money. Not even you'd be that stupid.'

'It was dirty money. I didn't want it anywhere near me.'

'Liar.' She sits back in her chair, her arms crossed over her chest. 'I know you've kept it, Jo. What've you done? Used it as a deposit on a nice little place in Ireland, have you? Treated yourself to a designer handbag?'

'You're right,' I say. 'I didn't burn the money. I gave it back to the police, minus the handful of notes I tore up and sent to you.'

'You're a stupid bitch.' She jolts forward, anger flaring in her blue eyes. 'A stupid, weak victim. You deserved everything that happened to you.'

'Goodbye, Paula,' I say as the bell sounds to signify the end of the visit and I stand up. 'Oh, one more thing before I go. The reason I wanted to see you today.'

I reach into my coat pocket and place a silver necklace with a big glittery S pendant on the table in front of her. It took me a while to find one that exactly matched the necklace Paula's 21-year-old daughter Sadie was wearing in her birthday selfie. 'You should keep an eye on your daughter's things.

'And your daughter,' I add as I turn to leave.

ACKNOWLEDGEMENTS

Huge thanks to my amazing editor Helen Huthwaite. Not only is she an absolute joy to work with, she's also bloody good at her job. Her insight, suggestions and eye for detail helped transform *The Escape* from a book with potential to a book I am hugely proud of. Helen, you are a star. I can't thank you enough. Thanks also go to the rest of the team at Avon, particularly Oli Malcolm, Helena Sheffield, Hannah Welsh, Victoria Gilder and everyone in the sales, digital and design teams. For a small imprint you pack a lot of punch and it's because you all work so damned hard. I'm very lucky to be working with you all.

Love and thanks also go to Madeleine Milburn, Thérèse Cohen and Hayley Steed. The Madeleine Milburn agency is a powerhouse and it's all down to the hard work, commitment and drive of those three women. Thank you for supporting, encouraging and cheering for me every step of the way. Maddy, you're the best agent I could ever ask for.

The Escape was the most heavily researched of all my books. It took me three months to gather all the information I needed before I could write a word and that's down to these fantastic people: Joe Rotherham, for driving me around Ireland so I could research locations and experience Irish B&Bs (sorry we didn't get to stay in fancy hotels with spas!). Ex DCI Stuart Gibbon, for answering all my police procedural questions (www.gibconsultancy.co.uk). Clare Hewitson, for answering my questions about social services and child protection procedure. Dr Charlotte McCreadie, for answering my questions about injured children, safeguarding and diseases that can cause bruising. My childhood friend Emma Shotton for putting me in touch with her colleague John Randle who endured an exhaustive telephone conversation about family law whilst he was on holiday! Mark Murray for talking to me about phone systems, IT and servers. Claire Allen for answering my questions about journalism and newspapers. Niamh O'Connor for clarifying a few things about the Gardaí and police procedure in Ireland. Celeste Ní Raois for answering questions about Irish culture. Margaret Bonass Madden for filling me in about Ireland in the 1970s and 80s and giving me snapshots of family life, and also for reading through an early draft of *The Escape* to make sure I hadn't made any terrible clangers.

I'd also like to thank my wonderful family. Reg and Jenny Taylor, you're the best parents anyone could hope for. Thank you for all you do and all the love and support you show me. Bec and Dave Taylor, you're the only brother and sister I've got so you'll do. Seriously, thank you for bombarding your Facebook pages with my book stuff and for keeping me entertained on WhatsApp. Sophie and Rose, you're the sweetest nieces an auntie could ask for. Love you. Love also to Great Nan, Steve, Guin, Ana, James, Angela and Nick. Thank you to all my friends, particularly Rowan, Julie, Tamsyn, Miranda and Kate for cheering and comforting me every step (through life and this book), and to all the authors I regularly chat with on Facebook when I should be writing (I particularly blame the crime writers for the fact that I don't write more than two books a year).

And finally, my own little family. Thank you to Chris for everything you do. I genuinely couldn't do this without your love, support and the occasional plate of chicken when I'm too busy to cook! And Seth. My son. My heart. My everything. This book is for you.

A huge thank you to the blogging community for being such a support. I really do appreciate the time you take reading and reviewing my books and the fact you so generously share your love of them with the world. And finally, my readers. Thank you for buying my books and for letting me know how much you enjoy them. I treasure each and every email and message you send me. They lift me when I'm feeling low and they convince me that, no matter how hard writing a book can feel at times, I wouldn't want to do anything else.

If you've enjoyed *The Escape* please do get in touch. If you sign up to join the FREE C.L. Taylor Book Club you'll receive an exclusive short story, access to my book news, cover reveals, giveaways and reviews of the books that I think will be the 'next big thing':

http://www.callytaylor.co.uk/cltaylorbookclub.html

Or contact me on social media:
www.facebook.com/CallyTaylorAuthor
www.twitter.com/CallyTaylor
www.instagram.com/CLTaylorAuthor
www.cltaylorauthor.com

P.S. To my son's old nursery, I did use the same layout as your building but none of the characters are based on the staff at Courthouse. You're all lovely and I was never once told off for being late or forgetting to bring a family photo!

BOOK CLUB QUESTIONS

1. Jo offered Paula a lift despite feeling very uncomfortable about it. Have there been any occasions when you've done something you really didn't want to do because it was the socially acceptable way to behave?

2. Jo and Max both had absent fathers. What impact do you think their childhoods had on their relationship? Was there any point in the story that you felt their marriage could have been saved?

3. How much sympathy did you feel towards Max in the first half of the book? How much sympathy did you feel towards him in the second half?

4. Jo's reaction to stress and fear was to run. At what point(s) in the story could Jo have changed her fate by confronting her fears rather than running from them?

5. At what point in the story did you realise that Max was responsible for some of the awful things that Jo experienced?

6. Brigid, Mary, Helen and Jo – discuss the roles of friendship and motherhood in the book.

7. Did Brigid do the right thing by protecting her child from the crime her father had committed? If you were Jo, would you have taken Elise to visit Max in prison?

8. How do you think Jo changed over the course of the book? What would you have done in her situation?

9. What did you think of the ending? Would you have liked it to end differently?

10. What do you think the future holds for Jo and the other characters?

Keeping this secret was killing her . . .

Get the *Sunday Times* and eBook bestseller now.

She trusted her friends with her life . . .

Get the *Sunday Times* and number one eBook bestseller now.

You love your family. They make you feel safe. You trust them.

Or do you . . .?